Marsh

Marsh

and Stories From After

A Post-Self anthology

Edited by

Madison Rye Progress

ISBN: 978-1-948743-41-9

Marsh

Cover © 2025, Iris Jay — irisjay.net

First Edition, 2025. All rights reserved.

This book uses the fonts Gentium Book Basic, Gotu and Linux Biolinum O and was typeset with X∄L∆T∃X.

Post-Self books

The Post-Self Cycle
by Madison Rye Progress (as Madison Scott-Clary)

I. *Qoheleth*
II. *Toledot*
III. *Nevi'im*
IV. *Mitzvot*

§

Stories of Reconciliation

Marsh
by Madison Rye Progress *et al.*

Idumea
by Madison Rye Progress, with Samantha Yule Fireheart
& Krzysztof "Tomash" Drewniak

Kaddish
by Madison Rye Progress

§

Clade — A Post-Self Anthology
Various authors

Unintended Tendencies
by JL Conway

Motes Played
by Madison Rye Progress & Samantha Yule Fireheart

Ask. — An Odist Q&A
Various authors

Learn more at *post-self.ink*

Marsh

Stories From After

Marsh

Madison Rye Progress

Fourmillante cité, cité pleine de rêves,
Où le spectre en plein jour raccroche le passant.

Unreal city, city full of dreams,
Where ghosts in broad daylight cling to passsers-by.

— Charles Baudelaire, via T.S. Eliot

Reed — 2399

"If you had to boil down this year into a sales pitch, what would it be?"

I laughed and bumped my shoulder against Hanne's. "A sales pitch?"

"Yeah," she said, leaning briefly against me as we walked. "I'm in the market for a new year. Sell me the 2399 model. I've got a wide variety to choose from, so tell me why you decided to live through this one."

"You're a nerd. You realize that, right?"

"Tell me why I should be a nerd in the year 275. Next year we can decide on systime 276."

I scuffed my heel against the pavement of the street. New Year's Eve, and everyone was still inside. Bars: full. Restaurants: packed. There were a few scattered couples or groups around, but they were all walking with purpose. Champagne called. Canapes. Crudités.

And there we were, Reed and Hanne, arm in arm, strolling leisurely down the street, heedless of the passersby, to celebrate the last day of 2399, systime 275+365. Many, lingering on the calendar still used phys-side, were doubtlessly partying extra-hard to celebrate the turn of a century.

"If you're looking for the utmost in luxury, then it's really hard to go wrong with 2399. The ride was just about as smooth as could be."

"How about comfort?"

"Oh, very comfortable. Cushy, even," I said, poking her gently in the belly.

Hanne laughed, covering her stomach with her hand. "Cute. How about the exterior?"

"No clue. It's been a long, long time since I've had any reason to pay attention to the world outside. I imagine it looks just as confusing as it always has."

"Well, okay, fair enough. You've been here longer than I have."

"I keep forgetting you're younger than me."

She nodded. "Robbing the cradle, you are."

"You're 83."

"Barely legal."

It was my turn to laugh. "Whatever."

"How about, uh... Features? Amenities?"

"Well, it's got us in it, doesn't it?"

She snorted and shoved me away from her. "Now who's the nerd? Gross."

I stumbled to the side, laughing. Our own champagne from earlier added a pleasant freedom of movement I only ever notice at two drinks. Any more and I become too loose and have a hard time staying upright. Any less and I don't notice that any freedom had been lacking.

"Is that so bad?" I asked. "Alternatively: am I not allowed to be a bit maudlin? It's fucking New Year's, Hanne."

"'Maudlin'? Is that even the right word?"

"What? Uh..." I hunted down a dictionary on the exchange, prowled through it. "Oh. Mawkish, that's the one. Or saccharine, maybe? I don't know. Maudlin still kind of works, doesn't it?"

She tilted her head at me.

"'Extremely sentimental', it says. Pretty sure that fits."

Hanne rolled her eyes, grinning. "Okay, yeah, that fits you to a tee."

We walked in silence for a few minutes. I tallied the occupants of the various restaurants along the way, making note of the busiest to check out on some less-busy night. Good date spots, perhaps.

"What was it like when you uploaded?"

"You mean phys-side?"

Hanne nodded. "What was Earth like? What was your life like?"

I shrugged. "Fine, I guess. The Western Fed was swinging conservative again, it was hot as hell all the time, some places were arguing about upload subsidies leading to a rising birthrate. I guess that makes it sound terrible, and maybe it would have gotten worse, but I wasn't around to see it. We were doing alright, so maybe I was kind of sheltered."

"I hear you on the hot as hell part. We couldn't afford moving south when it got too bad, so we moved up into the mountains. It helped a little bit, at least."

"When was that?"

"2320 something. I don't remember. I think I was under ten, at least."

I nodded. "I guess that's what I mean by sheltered. We were already up in Newfoundland. Summers sucked, winters sucked, but it was alright between them. It was worse when I lived in New York."

"Autumn or spring?"

"Huh?"

"Pick one, dummy," she said, laughing.

"Oh, autumn, for sure. Autumn bitch all the way."

"I knew it."

I rolled my eyes. "I'm nothing if not myself."

"So why'd you upload?"

"You know that already."

Hanne shook her head. "You said to transition, sure, but didn't you already do that back phys-side?"

I stayed silent, picking apart my thoughts on the matter. "I– Marsh got sick of being trans. They wanted to just be a man, not a trans man."

"*You're* a trans man, though."

"Sure, but that's not what they wanted at the time. They started to miss it by the time they forked."

"Why?"

I laughed. "So many questions tonight."

She grinned, shrugged.

"Well, I think half of it was that there was just too much pressure at the time. Like I said, the WF was swinging conservative, so there was this push to assimilate, and we internalized that pretty hard. We felt pushed to just shut up and be a man, just disappear—that or become a woman, have kids, let the first upload for the payout—and always felt that we fell short despite all we did to try, but on Lagrange, we could do that right off the bat."

"So they went back to being trans–"

I shook my head, cutting her off. "They've given up on gender. I became the way they experienced that again."

"Sorry, Reed."

"No, it's okay," I said, feeling a rush of warmth to my cheeks. "Didn't mean to get too pushy. It's still a little tender, I guess."

The shadow of her shoulders relaxed again in the dark of the night. "Even after so long?"

"Yeah. Like I said, we internalized it pretty hard, even as they tried to diversify later on. I headed back trans, Lily headed back feminine, and Cress embodies the negation."

"Is that why you forked, too?"

I grinned. "I forked for fun. Even if it's still a tender spot, I think I'm still way more relaxed than Marsh is, though it's been a while since we talked. There may be a bit of that in Tule, I guess. He's still pretty happy being a guy—he's the only one out of all of us, come to think of it. Rush is as ve is of vis own choice, though, and Sedge is pretty much us pre-transition."

Hanne looped her arm through mine. "Well, I still like you as you are."

"What, trans?"

"No, a huge nerd."

"Of course." I bumped my shoulder to hers. "Why'd you upload, then?"

"The weather. The money. All the same stuff the government told us. Same as most people, I think. I internalized that as much as Marsh did the whole gender thing."

"Was the WF still on its conservative swing?"

"The Republic of Argentina wasn't part of the Western Federation."

"Oh, right. I guess I knew that."

She shrugged. "Sure. But either way, they were somewhere in the middle, maybe. There was this big push from the liberal side on the climate, and this big push by the conservatives on the financial side. They said they could cut costs on services if there were fewer of us. Dad was with them, mom was with the libs. It was one of the few things they could agree on. They said they'd miss me, but they weren't exactly sad when I went the Ansible."

"'Went the Ansible'? Is that what you called it?"

"'Uploading' sounds so sterile," she said, nodding. "'Went the Ansible' just made it sound like moving away from home."

"Well, I'm glad you went the Ansible, then."

"Sap."

I laughed. "Got it in one."

§

Champagne tinted evenings faded, as they do, into brandy-colored nights. Amber nights and fireplaces for the hell of it, me and Hanne settling in for a little bit of warmth for that last hour, not quite decadence and a ways off from opulence, but still a plush couch and a fire and snifters slightly too full of liquor. We tucked ourselves in under a whole-house cone of silence, one tuned to block incoming sensorium messages so that our New Year's Eve was ours alone.

We shared our warmth, sitting side by side on the couch, and we continued to talk, talking of the year past, of years past beyond that, and of however many we decided were ahead. A hundred years? Two hundred? Only five? I made an impassioned argument for five more years of life, then laughed, changed my mind, and said I'd never die. Hanne said she'd live for precisely two hundred, give up, and disappear from Lagrange. She'd fork at a century and never speak to that version of her again, and should that instance decide to live on past two centuries, so be it, but she'd decided her expiration.

I scoffed. "What? And leave me behind?"

"Of course. Can you imagine six score years with someone? Absolutely miserable." She rested her head on my shoulder and shrugged. "We're a ways off from that, I think I still like you now."

"You think?" I draped my arm around her shoulders. "Still not sure?"

"I'm sure that I think I like you."

I laughed. "Yeah? Well, what can I do to cement your opinion of me? What can I do to make you sure that you like me?"

"There's a whole laundry list," she said, sipping her brandy.

"Pop one. I could use a goal for 276."

Hanne held up her glass appraisingly. "Well, we could work on your taste in liquor."

I snorted. "What would you rather I drink?"

"Scotch."

"That always struck me as so manly, though."

"Sounds fake."

"Oh, I'm pretty sure it is, but we're beholden to stereotypes."

She poked me in the side, grinning. "You must be drunk if you're using words like 'mawkish' and 'beholden'. Let's see. You could introduce me to Marsh, maybe."

I shook my head. "That's not on me, you know that. We have a one-way relationship."

"But they're your down-tree instance! You're patterned after them. You talk every year *at least* once, right? You'll talk to them later tonight, right? You have for the last hundred."

"No, probably not. If I hear from them directly, anything more than just a ping, I'll know something's gone horribly wrong." I leaned back—carefully, what with her head resting on my shoulder. "Like I say, it's a one-way relationship. All I do is live my own life, right? I stay in touch with the rest of the clade to greater or lesser extent, but Marsh has their own life."

"They have several."

"Right. We all fork, we all merge back down to whoever our down-tree instance is, and since I was forked from them, I merge down directly. They get all our lives, one year at a time, but we don't really get anything in return."

I could hear the frown in her voice. "How miserable."

"What, our relationship?"

"Just...them. How miserable they have to be, right? They live their life doing whatever, spending their whole year remembering the previous year from, what, five instances?"

"Six. Me, Lily, Cress, Rush, Sedge, and Tule."

"That's another thing you could do: be a little less weird."

I chuckled, kissed atop her head. "Uh huh. Love you too."

"But I was saying they have to be just miserable. They chill out in their house and spend their days remembering yours, you and your cocladists, and just living vicariously through you all."

"That's not all they do. They sing. They have Vos and Pierre, right? They spend time with their partners. They go to Vos's plays. They have friends over. They sing a *lot*. They cook–"

"Are they as bad a cook as you?"

"Oh, worse, according to Tule's girlfriend. Truly terrible."

She laughed.

"They have a full and fulfilling life, is what I'm saying. They're happy, it's just that their happiness doesn't include communication with their up-tree instances."

"Why not?"

I yawned, slouched down further on the couch along with

her. "They very specifically want us to live our own lives. They don't want us to just be other versions of them. They can make all of those they want for their little tasks. They specifically want us to be something other than what they are so that they can experience that on their own terms."

"Don't see how that's any different," she mumbled. Sleep threatened, even with some time left before midnight. "You all merging down like that is just doing the same thing in reverse, You're making them a version of you all, even if you're not just a version of them."

I turned that thought over in my head, held it at arms length, let the light of the fire shine through the fog of champagne and brandy onto it to admire just how strangely it was shaped. "Well, huh."

"See? You're so weird."

"I guess we are," I said, smiling and nudging Hanne upright once more. "No dozing off, now. Not yet."

She grumbled and rubbed at her face. "Sorry if that came off as rude. I guess it's just outside my understanding."

I scooted up onto the couch, myself, sitting cross-legged to face her. "It's okay. It's not wrong, even, I just don't think it's wholly right, either. It's a matter of intent. Our intent is to live our own lives to the fullest, and it's their intent to let us do so and yet still be able to experience that at one layer of remove. We've been doing it for a century, and it's worked out well enough since then. If all this–" I waved around the room, feeling the gentle spin of drunkenness follow the movement, "–is just a dream, if we're all doing our best to dream in unison with each other, then I think intent may be all that we have, right? However many billion or trillion people have uploaded are all trying to dream the same dream together, all mixed up and poured into the same System, we have to form what meanings we may on our own."

"I think we broke two trillion instances a while back. I don't know how may uploads, but I don't think it's hit a trillion yet. Probably only forty billion or so."

"Right. Sorry, guess I'm kinda rambly when I'm drunk."

Leaning forward, she gave me a light kiss. "It's okay, I like it when you ramble. Just don't lose track of the time."

23:46.

I started to nod, then stiffened as I felt first one, then another set of memories crash down onto me. "*Fuck.* One of these...days I'll convince...them to give me some warning...sec..."

Hanne laughed and shook her head, standing from the couch to go get herself a glass of water.

With a rush of intent, I forked, bringing into being beside me a new instance of myself. Exactly the same. *Precisely.* Had such a thing any meaning to an upload, we would be the same down to the atomic level, to the subatomic. All of the memories, all of the personality, all of the history.

For a fraction of a second, at least. From that point on, we began to diverge, each remembering things differently. The Reed that still sat on the couch heard Hanne in the kitchen from *this* angle, yet the one that stood beside the couch heard her from *that*. The one that sat on the couch felt the fire on his cheek, the one standing felt it on his back. I watched this other Reed—a new instance of me without these demanding memories, one who would not have the shared memories of my up-tree cocladists— wander off to the bedroom to presumably stay out of the way while I processed.

I closed my eyes to turn down one of my senses, setting the sweet-smelling glass of brandy aside to rid myself of another as best I could. I sat and spent a moment processing, savoring the memories. Rush had merged down first; ve had split off a new copy of verself, and then the original had quit. On doing so, all the memories ve'd formed over the last however long fell down onto me, ready to be remembered like some forgotten word on the tip of my tongue: all I needed to do is actually remember. Clearly, Tule had already forked and merged back down into Sedge, as their combined memories piled yet more weight on me. Three sets of memories—two from my direct up-tree in-stances and one from a second-degree up-tree instance—rested on my mind, ready for integration.

There'd be time for Marsh to do their full perusal and re-membering later. It was rapidly approaching midnight, and I needed to get the memories sorted into my own, interleaved and zippered together into as cohesive a whole as best I could man-age, all conflicts addressed—though with as separate as their lives had been until then, there was thankfully quite little in the way of conflicting memories—so that, shortly before midnight, I could quit and let all those memories—those of Rush, Sedge, Tule, and myself—fall to Marsh to process, savor, and treasure for themself, while that new copy of me, off making the bed or simply taking some quiet, lived out the next year with Hanne, with all their joys and sorrows.

After so many New Years Eves, this had all become routine. Some years, I kept the memories, some not. It had been a nearly a decade since I'd bothered, and there didn't seem to be any rea-son to do different this year.

I heard Hanne return, heard her climb back onto the couch beside me, felt her press a cold glass of water into my hand.

Five minutes left.

Three.

23:58, and I opened my eyes and smiled. "Well, seems like it's been a pleasant enough year for everyone involved, though Marsh will deal with all the rest of that later."

"It continues to amaze just how good you are at that."

"What, merging?"

She nodded.

"It feels pretty straight forward for me," I said. "I just...remember it all, and when memories or outlooks on life don't line up, I choose mine."

She laughed. "Still, far better than I am at it."

23:59.

"Practice, maybe," I said. "But hey, happy New Year."

"Is it time, then?" she asked.

I nodded, willed away the drunkenness, took a sip of water. "Alright. I love you, Hanne Marie. I'll miss you."

She rolled her eyes. "Tell Marshl [illegible]"

Reed — 2401

"See? You're so weird."

"I guess we are," I said, smiling and nudging Hanne upright once more from where she'd slumped against me. A flash of *déjà vu* struck me squarely in the right temple, a headache amid the buzz of alcohol. "Hey now, no falling asleep on me."

"Right, sorry. Still, uh...still fifteen minutes." She grumbled and rubbed at her face. "Sorry if that came off as rude. I guess it's just outside my understanding."

I scooted up onto the couch, myself, sitting cross-legged to face her. "It's okay. It's not wrong, come to think of it, I just don't think it's wholly right, either, you know? It's more a matter of intent. Our intent is to live our own lives doing as we will rather than as they would, and it's their intent to let us do so—and by not interfering, even with communication, *force* us to do so—and yet still be able to experience that almost like a dream. They forked us off a century ago, me, Lily, and Cress, and we've been doing it ever since, and it's worked out well enough since then. They're more than just Marsh, now. They're Marsh and all of us. If all this–" I waved around the room, feeling the gentle spin of drunkenness follow the movement, "–is just a dream, if we're all doing our best to dream in unison with each other, then I think intent may be all that we have, right? However many billion or trillion people have uploaded are all trying to dream the same dream together, all mixed up and poured into the same System, we have to form what meanings we may on our own."

"I think we broke two trillion instances a while back. I don't know how may uploads, but I don't think it's hit a trillion yet."

"Right. Sorry, guess I'm kinda rambly when I'm drunk."

Leaning forward, she gave me a light kiss. "You know I like it when you ramble. Just don't lose track of the time." She stood up straight again and squinted out towards nothing. "Weird. *Déjà vu.*"

23:46.

I started to nod, willed away the drunkenness, then stiffened as I felt first one, then another set of memories crash down onto me. "*Fuck.* One of these...days I'll convince...them to give me some warning...sec..."

Hanne laughed and shook her head, stepping away from the couch to go get herself a glass of water.

With a press of will, I forked, bringing into being beside the couch a new instance of myself. Exactly the same. *Exactly.* Had such a thing any meaning to the uploaded consciousness, we would have been the same down to the atomic level, to the sub-atomic. All of the memories, all of the personality, all of the love and hate and past that made us *us.*

For a fraction of a second, at least. From there, we began to diverge, each remembering things differently. The Reed that still sat on the couch heard Hanne rummaging in the kitchen from *this* angle, and yet the one that stood beside the couch heard her from that. The one that sat on the couch felt the fire on his cheek, the one standing felt it on his back.

I closed my eyes to turn down one of my senses, taking one more sip of the sweet-smelling brandy before setting it aside to rid myself of another two as best I could. I sat and spent a moment processing, savoring the memories. Rush had merged down first; ve had split off a new copy of verself then the original had quit. On doing so, all the memories ve'd formed over the last year fell down onto me, ready to be remembered like some forgotten word on the tip of my tongue: all I needed to do was actually remember. Clearly, Tule had already forked and merged back down into Sedge, as their combined memories piled yet more weight on me. Three sets of memories—two from my direct up-tree instances and one from a second-degree up-tree instance—rested on my mind, ready for integration.

There would be time for full perusal and remembering later. It was rapidly approaching midnight, and I needed to get the memories sorted into my own, interleaved and zippered together into as cohesive a whole as I could manage, all—or, at least, almost all—conflicts addressed (though with as separate as their lives had been until then, there was thankfully quite little in the way of conflicting memories), so that, shortly before midnight, I could quit, myself, letting that new copy of myself live out the next year with Hanne, with all their joys and sorrows, while my original instance quit and let all those memories—those of Rush, Sedge, Tule, and myself—fall to Marsh to process, savor, and treasure for themself.

After so many New Years Eves, it had all become routine. Some years, I kept the memories, some not. It had been a nearly a decade since I'd bothered—I always checked with Rush, Sedge, and Tule before keeping their memories—and there didn't seem to be any reason to do different this year.

I heard Hanne return, heard her climb back onto the couch before me, felt her press a cold glass of water into my hand.

Five minutes left.

Two.

23:59, and I opened my eyes. "Well, seems like it's been a pleasant enough year. Marsh can deal with all the rest of that later."

"It continues to amaze just how good you are at that."

"What, merging that much at once?"

She nodded.

"It feels pretty straight forward for me," I said. "I just...remember, and when memories or outlooks on life don't line up, I choose mine."

She laughed. "Still, far better than I am at it."

"We've been at this for ages," my up-tree fork said. "That's a lot of practice. But hey, happy New Year."

"Is it time, then?" she asked.

I nodded, took a few long gulps of water.

"Alright. I love you, Miss Hanne Marie. I'll think of you often."

She rolled her eyes. "No you won't. Tell Marsh I said hi."

I laughed and, as the clock struck midnight, willed myself to quit.

Then frowned.

"Something wrong?"

I held up a finger and closed my eyes. Once more, I thought to myself, *I'm ready to quit*, then then willed that to be reality.

Rather than the sudden nothingness—or sudden oneness for Marsh—that should have followed, I felt the System balk. Resist. I felt an elastic sensation that I'd never felt before. There was a barrier between me and the ability to quit. I felt it, tested it, probed and explored. It was undeniably present, and though I sensed that I could probably have pressed through it if I desired, it was as though Lagrange desperately did not want me to quit. It didn't want the Reed of now to leave the System.

"I can't."

My lingering fork took a step back, looking disconcerted.

"You can't?" Hanne tilted her head, then leaned forward to take one of my hands in her own. "I mean, it's okay if you don't want to. I don't think Marsh will mind if you're a few minutes late. Hell, you can even send them a message saying you don't want to this year. I think they'll–"

"No, Hanne," I said, carefully slipping my hand free so that I could stand. I needed to pace. "I mean I can't. I'm not able to. It's impossible. Or possible, but– wait, hold on."

It had been more than a decade since I'd done so, but if ever there was a time, this was it. There were very few reasons that the System would try to stop an instance from quitting and one of them...well, no– It'd been more than a decade since I had broken the communication embargo we had agreed on, but I sent Marsh a gentle ping.

Or *tried* to, at least.

All the ping was was a gentle nudge against the recipient's sensorium, a sense that someone was looking for them, was seeking them out, was just checking if they were free, if they were even there. From the sender's side, it felt like a gentle touch, a brush of some more metaphorical finger against the symbolic shoulder of the recipient, a reassurance that they were indeed there.

But there was nothing. I felt nothing. No sense of Marsh. Attempting to send a sensorium ping to someone that doesn't exist just felt like daydreaming. It felt like a silly, pointless imagining, as though one was imagining that they could touch God on the shoulder or shake hands with the devil.

I frowned, pinged Hanne.

"What?" she said, her frown deepening.

"Hold on, one more sec." I nodded to my new fork, who quit; I declined the merge. This would just have to be a year where I kept the memories. I wanted to keep the feeling of being unable to merge down, to know it viscerally. Something was wrong. I could work it out with my up-trees later.

00:02.

I thought across the clade, thought of one of Marsh's other forks. Pinged Lily, who was almost certainly out camping.

The response was immediate, words flowing into my consciousness through some sense that wasn't quite hearing. *"What's happening? I can't–"*

Pinged Cress, the other fork. Asked, *"Cress? Can you–"*

"What the fuck is happening?" came the panicked response.

"My place," I sent back, followed by my address. I repeated the message to Lily and, on a whim, my own up-tree instances, Rush, Sedge, and Tule.

00:04.

Cress arrived almost immediately along with Tule—they

shared a partner, so it made sense they'd be together for the evening—leading Hanne to start back on the couch. "Reed," she said, voice low. "What is–"

Lily arrived next, dusty and dishevelled from her day in some mountainous sim, already rushing forward to grab my shoulder. "You can't either?" she said, voice full of panic.

Before I could answer, Sedge and Rush arrived. The living room became quite crowded, all five of the other instances of the Marsh clade clamoring over each other to talk to me, the first long-lived fork from Marsh.

"Reed!" Hanne shouted, standing and stamping her foot. She spoke carefully, and I could hear anger just beneath that tone. "What happened?"

The rest of the clade looked to me as well, and I quailed under so many gazes. "I can't quit. I can't merge down. I can't reach Marsh. They–" my voice gave out and I had to take a shaky sip of water. "They're not on Lagrange, as far as I can tell."

00:07.

Silence fell thick across the room. The clade—Marsh's clade—stared, wide-eyed. Their expressions ranged from unsure to terrified. I couldn't even begin to imagine what expression showed on my face.

"Okay, no, hold on," Hanne said, shaking her head and waving her hand. She appeared to have willed drunkenness away, much as I had, as her voice was clear, holding more frustration than the panic I felt. "Did they quit? They couldn't have, right? You just pinged them earlier today."

I nodded.

"And they said nothing about quitting?"

"Nothing."

Hanne glanced around the room, singling out Marsh's other two immediate up-tree instances, Cress and Lily. Both shook their heads.

"I was just talking to them about an hour ago, actually." Lily admitted. "They and Vos were wrapping up the first part of the night's celebration and they were going to–"

"Vos!" I shouted. "Shit, sorry Lily."

It took a moment for Vos to respond to my ping. *"Reed? It's been a bit. What's up?"*

"Is Marsh there?" I sent back.

"I don't know. I figured they were in the study waiting on you, so I just made us drinks. Is something wrong?"

"Can you ping them?"

There was a short pause, followed by a sensorium glimpse of a familiar room, that study from so long ago, every flat surface that wasn't the floor covered in stacks of unread books. Empty.

"What's happening?" Vos sent. There was an edge of caution to her voice, the sound of a thin barrier keeping anxiety at bay.

"Pierre?"

"One second." Another pause, and then, quickly, *"Wait, can we just come over? What's your address?"*

I messaged over the address, and a few seconds later, Fenne Vos and Pierre LaFontaine arrived holding hands, leading to another yelp from Hanne.

"You must be Vos! Hi," she said, preempting any of Marsh's up-tree instances. "Do you know where Marsh is?"

Some small part of me looked on in admiration. Hanne had kept much of the panic that was coursing through me and my cocladists out of her voice. I could feel a shout building within me and I knew from past experiences with Vos and Pierre that that would only make things worse.

Vos had been Marsh's partner for decades now, nearly half a century. With so much time at one's disposal, such relationships felt natural enough, and taking a break of a few months or years was well within reach of at least us.

She was a strikingly tall black woman with close-cropped hair and a penchant for styles that would leave anyone with a passing interest in haute couture impressed. She was prone to laughter and smirks and grins.

She was not grinning now.

"We didn't see them around," Vos answered, that barrier between caution and worry seemed to be giving way. "Why? If you're all here, I'm guessing something happened."

"Have you been able to ping them?"

Both Vos and Pierre shook their heads.

The sight of Cress and Tule bowing their heads to whisper to each other caught my eye, and a moment later their partner, a short, stocky woman with curly black hair, appeared between them, looking as though she'd come straight from a party, herself. I felt a muffled pang of affection for her, lingering emotions from my up-tree instance's memories.

"Stop!" Hanne said, then laughed nervously at the silence that followed. She gestured absentmindedly, pressing the bounds of the sim outward to expand the room. It had started getting actively crowded. "You're doing it again, Reed."

"What?" I tamped down indignation. "Sorry, Hanne, there's a lot going on."

"Right, I get that, but can you start at the beginning for those of us outside your head? What did you mean, you don't think they're on Lagrange?"

At this, both Vos and Pierre took a half-step back, looking startled.

00:11

I spent a moment composing myself. I stood up straighter, brushing my hands down over my shirt, and nodded. "Right. I'm sorry, hon. When midnight hit, I forked and tried to quit as usual. I couldn't, though. The System wouldn't let me."

Cress and Tule's partner, I Remember The Rattle Of Dry Grass of the Ode clade, stood up stock straight, all grogginess—or perhaps drunkenness—from the party fleeing her features.

"That's only supposed to happen when quitting would mean the loss of too much memory, though. The root instance can barely quit at all in the older clades–" Dry Grass winced. I did my best to ignore it and continued. "–because the System really doesn't like losing a life if it won't be merged down into a down-tree instance."

"So, you couldn't quit because…" Hanne said, urging me on.

"Well, I imagine the same is true for anyone with lots of memory inside them. I had my new fork, but the intent was to merge down, and I guess the system picked up on that. If there's no one to merge down into, it just looks like…like…"

"Like death," Dry Grass said darkly. "It looks like death. You could not quit because, to the System, you and all of your memories would die, and the System is not built for death. That is what it felt like, is it not? It felt like you could not possibly quit without pushing the weight of the world uphill?"

I frowned. "Perhaps not all that, but it certainly felt like I was trying to push against something really hard. It didn't feel like it was impossible like anything else the System would prohibit, it just felt like I was being forced away from that option."

"Like death," she muttered again. Pierre began to cry. "Marsh is not on the System, then, no."

"So are they…is Marsh dead?" Pierre whispered, his voice clouded by tears. Vos towered over him—over all of us, really—and had always seemed as though she could weather a storm better than any stone, but even she looked suddenly frail now, fragile in the face of the loss they were all only talking around.

"They are not on the System," Dry Grass and I echoed in unison.

"How can you be sure, though?" Hanne asked. "You can't merge down, sure, and you can't ping, but could they just be in some locked down sim or a privacy cone or something? Can those even block merges?"

Lily shook her head. "Not that I know of, no. I don't think anything blocks a merge."

"Nothing blocks merges, correct," Dry Grass said. "That would leave potentially much in the way of memory lingering with nowhere to go, and the System does not work that way."

Slowly, all within the room began to face her rather than me, at which I breathed a silent sigh of relief. That I was the oldest fork of Marsh's didn't necessarily give me any more of the information that they all so desperately craved. Dry Grass was more than a century older than I was, however, and if anyone might have answers...

"How do you know, love?" Tule asked.

"I worked as a sys-side System technician."

Cress laughed. It sounded forced. "And you never thought to tell us?"

"This was before you were born, my dear. Before Marsh's parents were born, even. It was a long time ago, and I have since moved on."

"Well, is there a way to find out what happened?"

She frowned down to her feet as she thought. "It used to be that there were rotated audit logs for events like forking and quitting. I do not know if those are kept any longer, though, given how large they would get in a very short amount of time. Perhaps?"

"Well, how do we check those?" Rush said, speaking up for the first time since that initial clamor of voices.

Dry Grass spread her hands helplessly. "I do not know. Again, it has been almost two centuries since I worked as a systech. The technology has changed much. I would need access. I would need time to remember. Time to research."

"Do we even *have* time?" Lily growled at her, frustration apparently winning out over panic. Cress and Tule both gave her a sharp glance.

00:15

"I do not know. I am sorry," Dry Grass said, bowing. "I will fork and read up as fast as I can, and contact In The Wind. I may even be able to get my systech bit back. May I remain here?"

"Please," Cress and Tule said in unison. Sedge, Rush, and I, along with Marsh's partners, all nodded. Lily did not. Hanne only frowned.

Dry Grass bowed once more, forked, and the fork stepped from the sim to, I suppose, go lose herself in the perisystem architecture, hunting down what information she could. They could only hope that she still had the connections to find what she needed.

"Hey, uh," Sedge said into the uncomfortable silence that fell once more. "Has anyone checked the time?"

Everyone looked up almost in unison. It was more a habit than anything, hardly a required motion—the time certainly wasn't written on the ceiling—but the habit that Marsh had formed so many years ago had stuck with all of the Marshans throughout their own lives.

Systime 277+41 00:17.

"Wait, what–"

"277? But–"

"It says 2401, too!"

Everyone talking at once quickly grew overwhelming. I shook my head, covered my ears with my hands, then, remembering that I was standing in the middle of a small crowd, tried to mask the movement by turning it into running my fingers through my hair.

"Okay, one at a time," I said, having to speak up to drown out further exclamations. "I'm seeing 277+41. Everyone else seeing the same thing?"

Nods around.

"Any, uh..." I swallowed drily, looked around, and grabbed the glass of water that still sat, neglected, on the table beside the couch. After a careful sip, I tried again. "Any ideas as to what might have happened?"

Silence.

"Well, has anything like this happened before?"

We all turned to look at Dry Grass, who shrugged helplessly. "Not that I can remember. The closest would be periods of downtime. It has happened several times over the centuries. There was a few weeks of downtime while Lagrange was being set up during Secession, a few hours here and there."

"But not, what...thirteen months?" Cress asked.

"I have never seen that amount of time lapse, no."

Sedge piped up, saying, "Nothing on the perisystem about anything like this happening before, but holy shit are the feeds going off."

"Really?" I asked, then laughed. "Sorry, stupid question. Of course they are."

"And?" Rush said, impatient. "What are they saying?"

"It's pretty much this conversation repeated a million times over. I think a lot of people doing the same sort of thing we are. A lot of talking about the jump in time, about missing instances, about trying to quit and..."

Vos frowned. "And what?"

"Well, I mean," Sedge stammered. "Same thing, I guess. Nothing."

Dry Grass tilted her head, then nodded. "Another fork is keeping a tally. Missing instances are now numbering in the thousands."

Vos took another half-step back. "Wait, *thousands?*"

"It is proving difficult to keep up with the feeds," she said, speaking slowly. Perhaps still receiving updates? "One of me is just reading the feeds and marking a tally every time a missing instance is mentioned."

"Thousands, Jesus," Hanne whispered. "I should check in on Jess. And probably–"

She started as Pierre sagged briefly against Vos, then either quit or left the sim. "He...I mean..." Vos began, shook her head, and then followed suit.

"Do you two need anything?" I sent to Vos. *"Or just space and quiet?"*

"The latter," she replied after a few long seconds. The sensorium message was so clearly sent between sobs that I had to swallow down the same sensation rising in my throat.

"Give them some space," I mumbled against that awkward pressure in my chest. "So, okay. What's the whole story again? Midnight hit and suddenly it's thirteen months–"

"Thirteen months and ten days, almost exactly," Sedge corrected.

I sighed, nodded. "Right. Midnight hit and the date jumped forward and now there are thousands of–"

"Tens of thousands," Dry Grass said, then averted her gaze. "Apologies."

"It's alright. Tens of thousands of people missing. The feeds are going nuts. What about phys-side? Anything from them?"

"I have not been looking. I am uncomfortable with phys-side. There is a reason I am no longer a tech."

"I'll take a look," Sedge said. She forked quickly, the new instance almost immediately disappearing as she stepped from the sim. "Though I'm not as fast at it as you are."

"Anything from Castor or Pollux? Or Artemis? It's only a few months round trip, definitely less than thirteen. We don't really talk. I don't have anything from any of the Marshans on the LVs."

"Shit," Dry Grass whispered, expression falling. "Yes, there is."

When she didn't continue, Lily stamped her foot, growling, "And? You can't just leave that hanging there! I don't fucking get you Odists, you're always–"

"Lily!" Tule and Cress said as one.

She made a show of regaining her composure, movements overly liquid as she straightened up and brushed a lock of dirty blond hair out of her face. "Sorry."

An awkward silence lingered, overstaying its welcome. Eventually, Dry Grass's shoulders slumped. "You do not need to apologize. The messages will only affirm your feelings about my clade. The eighth stanza continues to manage the flow of information in–" She cut herself off and dug her hands into her pockets, an oddly bashful gesture. "I should not be telling you this, understand. I am not even supposed to be in contact with them, Hammered Silver would have my head if she knew, but Need An Answer has been in contact. Please do not share any of this."

"'Eighth stanza?'," Hanne asked.

"Yes. One hundred of us, each named after a line in a poem broken into ten stanzas," she said. "The eighth is–"

"True Name," Lily said through gritted teeth.

"Sasha," Dry grass corrected, then shook her head. "Apologies. Yes, that is the stanza focused on...politics and information control."

Lily pointedly looked away.

"They continue to manage the situation, I mean, and, from the sounds of it, they are describing it as an issue with the Deep Space Network and the Lagrange *station*. There are few mentions of the Lagrange *System* itself. I can read between the lines as well as any of them, though, and I do not think this is true. At least, not wholly."

"Wait," Cress said. "So they're saying that there's a problem with the DSN and the station? How do you mean?"

"There are few—surprisingly few—messages from over the last thirteen months, but they are queued up as though they have been held until now. There has been no contact between the LVs or Artemis and Lagrange." There was a pause as Dry Grass's gaze drifted, clearly scanning more of those messages. "Most messages have been locked in a way I cannot access...only a few from the Guiding Council on Pollux plus the Council of Ten on Castor...have been let through...outgoing messages are gated..."

"There's a bit about that in news from phys-side, actually," Sedge said, looking thoughtful. "Communications failure on the Lagrange station. Something about aging technology. The DSN was also having problems so a few new repeaters were launched. Some from the station, even."

"But nothing about the System?"

Both Sedge and Dry Grass shook their heads. "There isn't actually all that much news from phys-side," Sedge admitted. "Like, less than a week's worth."

"What did you mean about reading between the lines, though, love?" Tule asked.

"The messages are very stilted. There is panic beneath the surface. That they mention so little about Lagrange is as telling as if they were to say they did not know. They *do* know, they are just refusing to talk about it over messages." She paused. "Or the messages that are being let through, at least."

"Why?" Lily asked. While there was still an edge to her voice, genuine concern covered it well.

"'Information security and hygiene'. At least, that is what they would say were I to ask. Even if the messages were to fall into the wrong hands, sys- or phys-side, they would not show anything else having happened. I am of them, however. I can read some of the words that were not written."

"But Sedge said that news from phys-side says the same thing," Rush said.

She shrugged, another sheepish motion, and looked away. "Do you really expect that we are receiving unfiltered information from phys-side?"

I stole a glance at Lily. She looked to be spending every joule of energy on keeping her mouth shut.

There had been an enormous row within the clade when first Cress, then Tule, had gotten in a relationship with a member of the Ode clade. Most of the Marshans had largely written off the stories of the Ode clade's political meddling as overly fantastic schlock, yet more myths to keep the functionally immortal entertained. Even if they had their basis in truth, they remained only stories.

Lily, however, had had an immediate and dramatic reaction, cutting contact with the rest of the clade—including Marsh—for more than a year. She had even refused to merge down for years until tempers had settled.

Hanne spoke up. "Listen, can we maybe give this a bit to play out? I need to sleep, and if Reed doesn't take a break, he's going to explode."

The others laughed.

I felt a twinge of resentment. Shouldn't we be dumping all

of our energy into this? Shouldn't we all fork several times over and throwing ourselves at the problem? Still, it was true enough, and if we stood around the living room spinning our wheels any longer, tempers would continue to flare.

"Yeah," I said. "Give me at least a few hours. I'll do a little digging and maybe grab some sleep, then we can meet up somewhere else and talk through what we've learned."

"I'll keep digging at the feeds," Sedge said. "Want to help, Rush?"

Ve nodded.

Tule and Cress nodded as well. "We'll help out Dry Grass," Cress said.

"Lily?"

"I'm just going to get some sleep," she said stiffly. "Sorry for yelling."

Cress shook its head, leans over, and hugged her. "Take the time you need."

"Right. Let's meet at a park or something in the morning. Hanne will kill me if you all pile in here again," I said, at which Hanne nodded eagerly. "And I imagine things are going to be really weird out there, so I don't want to pile into a bar or whatever."

"Really, really weird," Sedge muttered.

As one, the other Marshans stepped away from my and Hanne's sim, leaving just the two of us, the fire crackling, the weight of the evening hanging over, between us. We stood in silence for a few long moments before I stumbled back over to the couch and fell heavily into the cushions. I buried my face in my hands and only then let the grief take me.

Hanne sat beside me, arm around my back. She rested her head on my shoulder as the wave of emotion overtook me. At first, she asked if I was alright, then she whispered a few "I'm sure it'll work out"s and "it's going to be okay"s before eventually just sitting with me in silence.

"This is really fucking weird," I said once I was able to speak again. The sound of speech echoed strangely in my head, muffled in that post-cry mess. "I don't even know who I'm crying for. It's not like they're a parent. I came from them, but they aren't me, either."

"A bit of both, maybe?"

I shrugged. "Maybe."

"Do you really think they're gone?"

I shrugged again, stayed silent.

Hanne nudged me gently with her shoulder. "Come on, Reed. Let's get you to bed."

"I don't think I'll be able to sleep. Not after all that."

"Still," she said, leaning over to kiss my cheek. It felt too hot, too intense a sensation, but calmness radiated from that spot all the same. "If nothing else, you can lay down in the dark and give your poor eyes a break. Plus, *I* need to sleep, at least."

How could I stand, knowing as I did that the clade had become unmoored? How could I think of sleep when there might be some remnant of Marsh somewhere in the wires? Some ghost of them in the machine that was the System? If this System was a dream, as Dry Grass and the rest of her clade had promised the world, then oughtn't there be some wisp of them, some memory from deeper archives which could be dredged? Even a Marsh from decades ago would still be a Marsh worth bringing back.

I sighed, nodded dully, and let her pull me to my feet.

I swayed for a moment, feeling reality shift unsteadily beneath me. Once I straightened up, I followed Hanne off to our bedroom. We'd spent the previous night, as we often did, sleeping in two separate beds—I always got too warm sleeping next to someone—but any grounding force feels welcome now, so, with a gesture, the two beds slid together, merging seamlessly into one.

A hollow feeling bubbled up within me. The two beds merging into one was an image of something now well beyond the Marsh clade. I was thankful I'd already cried myself dry.

The lights dimmed to near darkness and the temperature

dropped a few degrees as Hanne and I stripped and settled beneath the covers, her arms snug around me.

"I love you, Reed," she mumbled against the back of my neck. "I'm sorry I got so stressed before, but I love you. You know that, right?"

I leaned back against her. "I know. I love you too."

§

As expected, sleep did not come. Exhaustion pulled at me, exerting its own gravity, but too many emotions crowded it out. Too many emotions and too many thoughts. I spent a few minutes chiding myself—shouldn't I sleep, if only to be more refreshed for the next day?—before giving in and letting my mind circle around each of those emotions, each of those thoughts. I have no idea how long I cycled.

There was the faintest brush against my sensorium. Vos.

"How're you two holding up?" I sent.

"Not well."

"I imagine not." After a moment, I added, *"Do you have any more information?"*

The faintest sense of a shake of the head before Vos said, *"Nothing. They were here, then they weren't. There's no trace. It's almost as thought they never existed. Pierre fell asleep a bit ago. I think he wore himself out trying to reach them."*

"It's pretty late."

"Or early," Vos mused. *"No sleep for you, either?"*

"I gave it a go, but have just been laying in the dark."

"Have you heard from any of the others?"

"Nothing yet," I sent. *"I need a bit of a break from them, anyway."*

"How come?"

"We wind up in feedback loops a little too easily." I stifled a snort of laughter. Hanne mumbled something incoherent against my neck in her sleep. *"It drives Hanne nuts. That's why she was yelling about me doing it again."*

"Oh, trust me, Marsh winds up in-" The message stopped abruptly, and I found myself holding my breath, checking the time several times in a row, wary of further jumps. A few seconds later, Vos continued, voice shaky. *"They, uh...they wound up in their own feedback loops."*

I buried my face against the pillow, take long, slow breaths, willing myself to make as little noise as possible so as not to wake Hanne. How could I lay there, knowing as I did that Marsh was gone? How could I speak to Vos, knowing that I should be doing something, not crying in bed, accepting a fate that made no sense? Was it just some hopeless part of me that had accepted Marsh's absence? Oughtn't I be striving even now to find some way to get them back?

No answers, only questions.

"I'm really struggling," I replied, realizing after that it's been nearly ten minutes of silence since Vos messaged last. *"I'm laying here in the dark like a fucking idiot instead of doing literally anything to figure this out."*

Her reply was gentle. *"So are we, Reed. Just laying in bed, staring at nothing. I don't know how to make that...okay in my head, but it's all I've got."*

"How's Pierre doing, then?"

"Not well."

"He seemed like it hit him really hard, yeah."

A pause, and then she sent, quieter than before, *"I don't want to say this is hitting any one of us harder than the other, but...well, we care for him. That was our dynamic, I mean. He's young and full of emotions, so we occasionally fall into that guardian role. It hit him hard, and so he needs care, but..."*

"But it's also hitting you hard?"

"Yeah."

"Pass on my love, will you?" I send.

The sense of a sniffle from the other end of the message. The sense of a nod.

The message stopped.

I lay in bed, then, thinking about Marsh. Thinking about all that I knew of what they'd become since I was last them, however long ago that was. We'd seen each other a handful of times at this event or that gathering, and we'd talked a few times over messages, but they were always distant, always held at arm's length.

It was both our arms, too, I know that. They kept their life separate from mine, just as I kept mine separate from theirs. It was ever our arrangement that all of their forks would live out their own individual lives, merging down as the year ticked over.

They'd laugh whenever it came up, saying, "So I'm greedy. Sue me."

We'd all laugh, too. It wasn't really greed, that desire for our memories in a way that we could never get in return. It was just the dynamic that we held to ever since I'd been forked. Of course it was mutual: I *was* them when I'd been forked. An exact copy that only slowly diverged over the years. It had been my idea as much as theirs. That Lily had been talking to them some hours ago was an aberration, a new thing.

I thought of Marsh, their laugh, their words, their open expression, the way their tousled, brown hair always fell in front of their eyes, the way the loose and soft clothing they wore hung off their frame, the bright colors of silk and cotton.

Hanne rolled away from me and I took that as my chance to at least no longer be laying down. I forked a new instance standing beside the bed and then quit, just in case the motion of me getting out of bed might wake her.

I needed out of the house. Nowhere public—I didn't want to see what others in the System were dealing with right then. There would be time for that later, but for now I needed out and away from everyone.

The sim I wound up in was simple and bucolic. There was a pagoda. There was a field, grass cut—or eaten, I suppose, given the sheep in the distance—short, stretching from stone wall to stone wall. It was day—it didn't even seem like the owners included a day/night cycle—and foggy. Cool but not cold. Damp but not wet.

There was a bench in the pagoda, at least, so I made my way there, trudging tiredly up the whitewashed wood of the steps to sit on the well-worn seats. Whoever made this place seemed to have put more effort into the pagoda than the field. Fog like that was usually the sign of a border of a sim of limited size, so it was clearly just this single paddock, the grass and sheep and stone walls likely purchases from the exchange.

It was a public sim, but the listing had shown zero occupants. I was lucky it was empty, I guess.

A pang tugged at my chest. Empty of people because they were simply not here? Empty of people because everyone was dealing with the same problem that we were? Or empty of people because those people were gone, too?

The seat of the bench had been worn smooth by who knows how many butts over the years, but I picked at the velvety wood all the same. *You're not alone, Reed,* I reminded myself. *Hanne's at home. The rest of the clade is there. Dry Grass is there. Vos and Pierre are there.*

I sighed and slouched against the back of the bench. Exhaustion was warring against the drive to do *something*, and both of those were striving against the need to be alone and away from this whole spectacle. All of those "how can I" questions were clattering up against equal-sized armies of "too tired"s and "it doesn't need to happen now"s.

I spent an hour out there, all told. I picked at the bench. I called out to the sheep. I walked circles around the pagoda in the gray day. I bent down, plucked a blade of grass with the intent to...I don't know, chew on it like I've seen in films, but it smelled so strongly of sheep manure that I dropped it instead and headed home to finally lay down beside Hanne and sleep.

§

I woke, exhausted, to a cup of coffee steaming on the bedside table.

At some point while I'd slept, Hanne had once more split the bed into two separate mattresses and very gently instructed the sim to slide them a few feet away from each other. Perhaps I'd been tossing and turning, or maybe I'd been snoring. I promised myself I'd ask later, then promptly forgot about it in favor of the coffee mug waiting for me.

Coffee and chicory, nearly a third oatmilk by volume. Perfect.

I was two sips in when the weight of what happened hit me once again. I didn't quite know how it was that they had escaped me in those minutes after waking, but a pile of 'how could I' questions started to hem me in again—how could I possibly forget, when this is the biggest thing that has happened to our clade ever? Never mind sys-side or phys-side; ever.

I forced myself to sit up in bed and drink my coffee. I set myself the goal of sipping until it was finished. I stared out the window for a bit. I cried for a bit. I drank about half my coffee before the wait became unbearable.

Five minutes. Hah.

I couldn't quite interact face-to-face yet. Not with Hanne, not with the occasional bout of sniffles still striking me. Instead, I sent the gentlest ping I could manage to Vos, received no answer.

I tried various members of the clade next. Lily flatly rebuffed me. There weren't any words, just a prickly sensation of solitude and the physical signs of anger. Rush didn't respond, but ve always did sleep better than all of us. Sedge begged another hour's rest, and I acquiesced. Tule and Cress were both asleep.

Well, that was the first layer of contacts. None of us were single, but of all the partners I knew, the only ones I'd talked to in any depth were Vos and Pierre. Beyond them, there was...

I reached out mentally to send a sensorium ping to Dry Grass, only for the perisystem architecture to present me with a series of options, numbering well above a dozen. She'd been busy, apparently, forking as needed throughout the night and– yep, two of those available instances disappeared as they quit, followed shortly by one more new one being added. She was certainly still awake.

"Good morning, Reed," her root instance murmured through a message. *"More well rested, now?"*

"Best I can be, at least," I sent back. *"I, uh…sorry for interrupting. The rest of the clade's asleep and I don't want to pester Hanne any more than I need to, not after last night."*

There was mirth on the other end, some barely-sensed laughter that didn't quite rise to the level of coming through the message. Another tug at my emotions, more leftovers from Tule's merge. *"It was rather stressful, was it not? You do not need to apologize. How are you feeling?"*

"Honestly?"

"Please. I want to hear."

"I'm feeling like shit." I laughed, shaking my head. *"I mean, of course I am. I'm some awful mix of mourning Marsh, hopeful that there's some solution, kicking myself for mourning them maybe preemptively, kicking myself for not doing more, and just plain confused."*

The Odists were an old clade—far older than any of us, having been born decades before the advent of the System—so it was no wonder that Dry Grass was far more adept at sensorium messages than anyone else I'd met. It wasn't that I saw her lean back in her chair, nor that I felt the act of leaning back myself, but the overwhelming sensation that I got from that moment of silence was of her sighing, leaning back, crossing her arms over her front. I had no clue how she managed to pull that off. *"There is little that I can say to fix any one of those, and anything else would ring hollow. All I can do is validate that, damn, Reed, that is a shitload of emotions. There is a lot going on, and I do not blame you for feeling confused."*

"Thanks," I responded, feeling no small amount of relief that she hadn't tried to dig into any one of those feelings, nor even all

of them as a whole. *"How are Tule and Cress holding up? Hell, how're you holding up?"*

"They are asleep," she sent. I could hear the fondness in her voice. *"One of me is keeping an eye on them, pretending to sleep."*

"And the rest of you?"

"Working."

I finished my coffee in two coarse swallows, winced at the uncomfortable sensation that followed. I took another moment to stand up and start making the bed again. As I did, I asked, *"What on? I saw a ton of forks."*

The sense of a nod, and then, *"Several things. One of me is still keeping tallies on how many are missing based on reports, which appears to be some few million so far. Another of me is collating the varied types of posts on the feeds—wild supposition, unchecked grief, confusion, and so on. Another is speaking to a member of the eighth stanza, even though–"*

"This 'Need An Answer' you mentioned?"

"Yes. The Only Time I Dream Is When I Need An Answer. She is the one who has focused on interpersonal connections, which is only relevant in that she is the one in the stanza who will still pass information on to the portions of the clade that cut them off, about twenty of us."

I snorted. *"Minus you, I guess."*

"Well, yes. Nominally twenty of us," she sent, and I could sense that almost-laughter again. *"Though it is far more complicated than that."*

"Sure seems complicated. Any news from Castor or Pollux?"

"Yes, in a way," she replied, then hesitated. *"Though would you be willing to go for a walk to discuss what I have heard?"*

"I guess. Why?"

"So I can get out of the house. So you can get out of the house. So we can actually talk instead of me sitting in a war room populated by too many of me and you making your bed or whatever it is you are doing now."

I hesitated, halfway through smoothing out the sheets. *"Oh, uh...alright. Let me say good morning to Hanne. Do you have a place to meet?"*

She sent the address of a public sim, to which I sent a ping of acknowledgement and a suggestion of five minutes' time.

Hanne sat at the dining room table, coffee in her hands, staring out at nothing, a sure sign that she was digging through something on the perisystem architecture. Probably poking her way through the feeds, looking for news. She had her own friends, after all, her own circle of co-hobbyists, those construct artists—oneirotects—who shared her interest in creating various objects and interactive constructs. She had her own people to care about that weren't just me, weren't just the Marshans.

I chose to make us another pot of coffee instead, letting a cone of silence linger above me so that I didn't disturb her, even though her eyes did flick up toward me once or twice, joined by a weak smile.

"Want some space?" I asked once the pot sat in the center of the table.

"Kind of, yeah," she said, voice dull. "Jess isn't responding. She's *there,* but not responding. Shu is gone though. Just..." A sniffle. "Completely gone. It's like she was never even there in the first place."

I felt my expression fall. It was bound to happen, I figured; we knew enough people that if, as Dry Grass had said, millions had already been reported missing, Marsh wouldn't be the only one.

I reached forward to pat the back of her hand, which she tolerated for a moment before lifting it out of the way.

"I'm sorry, Hanne," I said. "I know you liked them."

She nodded.

"Any word on Warmth In Fire? I'm going to head out in a moment to see Dry Grass, and I'm wondering how bad the Odists got hit."

Hanne shrugged. "Ey's there. I haven't talked to em yet, though." She snorted, adding with a smirk, "Though even if a chunk of their instances got taken out, I doubt any whole...lines, or whatever they call them, any cladists, were completely destroyed. They fork like mad."

I laughed. "Yeah, when I pinged Dry Grass earlier, she had something like eighteen instances."

"Doubtless you'll be meeting up with number nineteen, then."

"Probably."

"Did she have anything new to say?"

I looked down into my coffee, considering how much to pass on. "It sounds like a lot of people are gone. 'A few million', though doubtless that's getting bigger as more people report in. Everything sounds pretty chaotic."

Hanne furrowed her brow. "A few *million?* Jesus. Any word from phys-side?"

"Not that she mentioned, no."

"Great. Of course not."

I nodded, covering my anxiety with a sip of coffee.

"Well, hey," she said, leaning over to kiss me on the cheek. "Go on and go talk with Dry Grass. Could be she's learned more, could be they've said something and we just haven't gotten it yet. If she's as plugged in as she says she is, then doubtless she knows more than she's telling."

"Right." I laughed. "Of all of us, she would."

§

We met in front of a small coffee shop. A bucolic small town main street lined with gas lamps and paved with cobblestones.

"Coffee and chicory, yes?" Dry Grass said, offering me a paper cup.

I nodded as I accepted. I had left my second cup of coffee back at home, half-finished. "Cress and Tule still drink that?"

A small smile tugged at the corner of her mouth. "Much to my chagrin, yes."

"Not a fan?"

She shook her head. "Too bitter for my tastes. Mocha, extra chocolate, extra whipped cream," she said, lifting her own cup. "Apparently a sweet tooth can last more than three centuries. Who knew?"

"Yeah, that sounds way too sweet for me," I said, chuckling.

Grinning to me, she gestured down the street in an invitation to walk, and we fell in step beside each other, saying nothing.

The sim was, indeed, beautiful, though it did bear some trademarks of early sim design, with the cobblestones perhaps a little too perfectly fit together, a little too flat, and the hexagonal lamp posts bearing corners that were perhaps a little too sharp. Still, for a morning walk with coffee (my third of the day; I'd have to turn off the caffeine sensitivity later), it was ideal. The sim was quiet and calm, with the sun blessing the street with long shadows and cool air that felt on the path to warming.

"It's so quiet," I observed. The act of speaking out loud into the still air was enough to knock me back into the context of what had happened. "Oh."

Dry Grass readily picked up on the meaning behind that syllable, nodding to me. "I do not imagine that it is so quiet because so many are missing, but I do think that many are staying home, hunting for lovers and friends, trawling the feeds. Heading out to public sims is, perhaps, not at the tops of their minds."

Looking around did indeed provide a better sense of the mood. Those who *were* out and about looked somber, distracted, walking with heads down or talking in hushed tones two-by-two.

So were we, I realized.

I made an effort to straighten up and look out into the clear morning. "Is the toll still climbing?" I asked.

"It is currently–" She tilted her head for a moment before continuing. "–just over two hundred million. I have also been able to get in contact with a phys-side engineer who has been...well, she has been cagey, but she is at least confirming some of my estimates and guesses as I pass them on."

"Oh?"

She nodded. "Günay is quite nice, if perhaps a bit breezier than one might expect on hearing that millions of individuals have disappeared from the System. I do get the sense that she is a fairly cheerful person overall, at least."

"Did she have anything to say about what might have happened?"

"No, not particularly. When I say that she has confirmed guesses, what she has done is invite me to talk and simply agreed when something I have said is right, perhaps expanding on it by small amounts." Her expression soured. "I get the impression that she would *like* to share more with me, but that she is simply not allowed to."

I frowned. "You mean someone's keeping her from doing so?"

"It is a hunch. Perhaps her implants limit her by NDA. Perhaps our communications are being monitored, and she is being instructed to limit the topics or to act in this way. While talking with Need An Answer, she suggested that this is also what the eighth stanza is used to doing, but they are the political ones."

I dredged up what history of the System I had learned, all of those sensationalist stories about the few old clades steering the direction of the lives of however many billions of uploaded minds and their instances—certainly well over two trillion, if one counted the two launch vehicles, Castor and Pollux that had been sent zooming out of the Solar System at incredible speed seventy five years prior. More, if what Hanne said was right.

"And they'd be sneaky like this, too?" I asked.

A snort of laughter and she nodded. "Sneaky is one way to put it, yes. They shape interactions by second nature, for which a portion of the clade has distanced themselves from them. We—Hammered Silver's up-tree instances—are not supposed to be speaking to any of them, but there are a few that I like plenty, and given our current status, I have begun interacting more openly with Need An Answer."

Wary of letting the topic drift too far, I said, "Have they gotten anything else from phys-side, then?"

She shrugged. "There has been little enough interaction with phys-side over the years, and even less of late, now that the climate has started to level out back on Earth. The rate of uploads has even leveled off from its slow increase over time. We rarely hear much except what comes through the newly uploaded." She sipped her mocha, seeming to take that time to sort out her thoughts. "Our political relationship with phys-side is cordial. It is one borne of necessity. Our social relationship is more complicated. Many have expectations of a long peace for themselves once they join us, and many more have loved ones who have joined us."

"Right, I still talk to a bunch of friends I knew phys-side who uploaded later. Or Marsh does." I winced, amending that statement. "Did."

Dry Grass rested a hand lightly on my arm. "I am sorry, Reed."

Memories of Tule's relationship with her had me reaching for her hand without thinking, though I at least manage to simply pat at the back of it rather than anything more intimate. This must've shown on my face, as she smiled kindly, gave my arm a squeeze, and reclaimed her hand, saying, "Memories are complicated, I am guessing."

I nodded, doing my best to ignore the heat rising to my cheeks. "A bit."

"I am sure we will discuss it soon," she said. "But for now, let us return to the topic at hand. Tule and Cress are awake and have expressed interest in discussing this in person, as well. Would you be amenable to them joining us? Sedge, Rush, and Hanne are welcome, though they have requested some space from Lily, and Vos and Pierre have requested their own privacy."

Shaking the confusing, conflicting memories of Dry Grass from my head, I sighed, letting my shoulders slump. "Lily really should be here, as well," I grumbled. "But I get it. She's...well, she's Lily."

She bowed stiffly. "Yes. It is okay, my dear. We are used to it, even this many years later."

"Sorry all the same."

She made a setting aside gesture, dismissing the topic easily. "Another topic to discuss another time. Cress and Tule are grabbing coffee now, and will meet us in a few minutes."

We stood in silence, then, saying nothing and letting the sun warm the backs of our necks. A few people poked their heads out of various shops, looked around sullenly, and then disappeared. Everyone who passed us did so in a cone of silence, and most of those opaqued from the outside, hard-edged cones of darkened and blurred background gliding down the sidewalk, hiding faces and silencing words.

"Why do you think they're out?" I asked, nodding towards one such cone.

Dry Grass clutched her coffee to her chest, both hands wrapped around it to draw warmth through the paper cup. "Why are *we* out, Reed?"

I blinked, then shrugged. "You asked to meet up in person, didn't you?"

"Of course, yes. And you agreed, did you not?"

"Well, yes." I hastened to add, preempting her point, "I guess there is a lot to get out of interacting in person."

She nodded.

"So why here, then?" I asked.

"Good coffee," she said, lifting her cup. "Good weather. Good memories. Some of them really good. This place is comforting to me. It is comforting to a good many people. I suspect that those who are out are doing much as we are. They are talking about the difficult things in a place that at least makes them feel a little better."

"I suppose it's nicer than moping at home."

"It is, is it not?"

"Is she talking your ear off, Reed?" came a familiar voice from behind us.

"Oh, absolutely," Dry Grass replied, turning and leaning over to give Cress a kiss on its cheek. "How are you feeling, loves?"

"Terrible," Tule said cheerfully. They had apparently collected Rush and Sedge before arriving, as all four stood in almost identical postures, each holding their coffees in their right hand—just, I realized, as I was doing. "All my emotions are wrong. I'm jittery and tired and I want to get another few hours of sleep but feel guilty every time I lay down."

I laughed. "Yeah, that sounds about right. I keep feeling like I'm having the wrong sort of reaction to all of this."

"When was the last true trauma that befell the Marshans?" Dry Grass asked, smiling gently. "I imagine it was before you uploaded, yes?"

A moment of silence followed.

"We as people have fallen out of the habit of dealing with crises," she continued when we all averted our gazes. "Do not be hard on yourselves. We—the Ode clade—have more experience with crises than the vast, vast majority of the System, and even we are reeling. We are struggling to internalize something this big."

"Have you lost any?" Cress asked, and I thanked it silently for getting to the question before I worked up the courage to do so myself.

Hesitating, Dry Grass's confident mien fell. Eventually, she reached out to take both of her partners' hands in one of her own, then nodded to me. "Come. Let us walk, yes? We will talk as we hop sims. I have more places full of comforting memories to show you."

While I mulled over her focus on comfort and memory, we linked by touch, Tule and Cress with their partner, and Cress, Rush, and Sedge with me.

We stepped from the quaint, small town sim and directly into warmth and sunlight, into the salt-tang of sea air and the low rush of waves against a beach. We stood atop a stone walkway of sorts, which seemed to run along the edge of a town. On further inspection, it appeared to be a retaining wall, holding up the town that meandered up the hill to keep it from sliding inexorably down into a bay.

Between the wall and the water was a sandy beach, partially obscured by intricate and crazed markings in the sand. It took some time of peering at them for me to make out just what they were: it seemed as though, throughout the tail end of New Year's Eve, dozens or hundreds of people had been drawing in the sand using, I assumed, the sticks that were leaned against the wall.

All of the designs seemed to feature the New Year, now that I was able to pick them apart. Visions of fireworks, scratched over mentions of the year, scrawled names of, I guessed, couples who had met up on the beach.

I turned away with a hollow feeling in my chest, wondering just how many of those couples were still couples.

The town, while no less visually chaotic than the beach, was at least more heartening to look at. Everything—*everything*; the walls of buildings, the roofs, doors and window shutters, even the roads—was covered with a blindingly colorful mosaic of tiles.

"*To Limáni Ton Khromáton* is nearly two centuries old," Dry Grass explained as we started trudging up one of those streets. "When you enter, you are given a single tile—if you check your pockets, it should be in there."

Sure enough, when I dug my hand into my pocket, I found a cerulean tile, a little square of porcelain about three centimeters on a side. The rest of the Marshans dug in their pockets and pulled out tiles of their own, all one shade or another of blue.

"Unless you hold a color in your mind when you enter, you are provided with your favorite," Dry Grass explained. She pulled a golden yellow tile out of her own pocket and flipped it up in the air like a coin. "All of this—all of the mosaic—has been placed by visitors.

"Set No Stones told me about this place." She smiled wryly.

"Because of course she did. We are consummate pros at living up to our names. You may place your tile wherever you like, and so long as it is touching the edge of another, it will stick. You will not be able to remove it after, so make sure to place it carefully."

Rush laughed. "Holy shit. This place is amazing."

"It's a bit hard to look at in some places," Sedge added, nodding towards a few buildings whose walls were covered in a rainbow static of tiles. "But yeah, this is wild."

"It really is, yes," Dry Grass said, grinning. "Used to be, you would get one tile per day to place, but as the popularity grew, that was slowly reduced to one tile every six weeks. Still, whole fandoms have sprung up around this place among a certain type of individual. Set No Stones started organizing groups of fifty to a hundred cladists to plan out images. They would meet up once a week to go build their pictures. That is where we are going now."

The street was steep, but, despite the glossy look of the tiles that paved the road, none of us slipped.

We walked past buildings that depicted animals, some that depicted people, some that had words set in porcelain. There were scenes of nature and of cities. Even one that Cress spotted which appeared to be a building in the process of being covered by tiles exactly the same color as the stucco beneath it. The slow shift into square tiles led to a sense of the structure dissolving into pixels, or perhaps voxels.

If the small town sim had been relatively quiet, this one felt all but abandoned. Perhaps all such sims with a singular purpose would be like this today: if your friends are missing, if other versions of you were missing, then an attraction would doubtless lose some of its draw. We passed only a few tilers tramping up the hill with determination, ready to place their colors for the day.

Finally, Dry Grass led us down an alleyway, dim and cool, and gestured to a wall. The scene was of two figures sitting at a bar. Given the scale, it was impossible to make out any detail on the figures, though they seemed to be furries of some sort—one tan and one black and white. Each had a drink, and before them, a wall of bottles stood, still in the process of being built. Dry Grass stood up on her tiptoes and touched her tile to the edge of a bottle, adding a bright glow to a fledgling bottle of whiskey.

"Here," she said, gesturing us to grab a crate that had been stacked nearby. "All of these are just props to help people reach higher. You can probably add your blues to the edge of the lamp. They are not quite the right color for green lamps, but I do not care."

One by one, we took our turns standing on that box and setting our tiles into place. I reached up as high as I could to flesh out the glowing rim of the green glass-shaded lamp. As soon as my tile touched the edge of the tile Tule had placed, it snapped into place with a satisfying click. It was completely immobile after that. No amount of nudging could get it to slide more perfectly into alignment.

As she helped Cress, the smallest of us, up onto the crate to place her tile, Dry Grass said, "Thank you for coming with me on this little jaunt. If I spent any more time at my desk, I was sure that I would lose my mind. That I still have forks doing so is unavoidable, but at least I can get out of the house, yes?"

Tule nodded, kissed her on the cheek. "For which I'm glad. I've never met anyone more prone to overworking themselves than you."

She laughed. "Yes, yes. The whole of the clade is like this, I can promise you that."

"Are you ready to talk about what you've learned?" I asked. "If you need a bit more time, that's fine, of course."

"I am ready. Thank you for giving me a bit of space." Once Cress had finished setting its tile and hopped back down to the ground, we all walked back out into the street, back out where the sun shone down on us. "We have passed one billion reported missing instances." She held her hand up to forestall the comments that were already coming. "That is all instances, to be clear, not differentiated individuals, not cladists, and certainly not clades. Many of those who were reported missing were ephemeral: they were one-offs created here and there. We do not yet know about cladists or clades. The number is high, but I did want to provide that qualification; there are three totals to consider, and we are learning only one of them."

"Hanne said that one of her friends, Shu, was missing entirely," I said, once the words had sunk in. "Similar to Marsh, I mean. It wasn't just that she wasn't responding, it's like she was just never there, like the System didn't know about her."

"Too many names have passed beneath my fingers for me to say one way or another if I have come across her, but one of my instances will do a search to confirm and get in touch with Hanne directly, if she would like."

I shrugged. "It might be worth asking, at least."

She nodded and gestured us back down to the beach. "I will." She took a deep breath before continuing. "Now, the current population in terms of *instances* is something like 2.3 trillion. A billion is a very small fraction of the System in terms of numbers, but it is what we are working with. A billion instances appear to have been...ah, lost, along with thirteen months, ten days, seventeen minutes, and some seconds. On speaking with Günay, this downtime was observed phys-side, though she was not able to tell me much about it besides that. I have the sense that there is more that she *could* have said, but that she was not able to for whatever reason."

This had apparently been the first that Rush and Sedge had heard about this, so a few minutes were spent bringing them up to speed as we walked down the hill to the shore once more. I took the opportunity to focus at something far off, something further ahead of me than my own two feet. The horizon, the dark ocean breaking against the shore in a rush of white out where the arms of the bay projected into the water.

We passed only one more person. They were rushing up the hill, breathing coming in quick puffs, a white tile clutched in their hand, tears streaming down their face.

We said nothing until after they had passed.

"Reed?"

I startled back to awareness, smiling sheepishly at Sedge, accepting the hand that she held out for me. "Sorry, lost in thought."

"It is okay," Dry Grass said, smiling gently to me. "The next sim that we are headed to does not have a very large entry point, so please huddle in closer. It will also be quite warm, so, fair warning."

The entry point—a platform of wood slats set upon stilts above stagnant water—was far smaller than I had anticipated, and my foot rocked against an uneven plank set along the rim of the platform, forcing me to lean against Sedge. One edge of the platform led into a narrow, somewhat rickety wooden walk-way that headed out over the water in a straight line until it came upon a tall patch of grass, where it turned a few degrees to the right to make its way to another. It appeared to mean-der in this way from island of vegetation to island of vegetation in an uneven zigzag toward a copse of trees—the word 'banyan' floated to mind, though I wasn't sure if that was actually the case—where it disappeared into shadow.

That shade looked delightfully appealing as the humid heat pressed in around us.

"What the hell is this place?" Tule asked, wrinkling his nose at the scent of rotting vegetation in the air.

"A swamp," Dry Grass said simply, a lopsided smile tugging at the corner of her mouth. "A marsh, perhaps."

If it had been intended to be a joke, it fell flat. We remained in silence for a few awkward moments.

She sighed. "My apologies. It is still important to me, how-ever. It is- Ah, there she is." She raised an arm and waved to a figure crouched at the edge of the walkway just before the next platform. With the heat-haze and mugginess, their form was somewhat indistinct. They wore a frowzy white dress, along with some sort of hat—or perhaps a rather tall hairstyle. As we walked toward them in single file, she explained, "This sim was designed by Serene; Sustained And Sustaining, whom you shall meet in a moment. She is my cocladist from the ninth stanza, and one of my favorite people in the world. I asked her to meet us here."

As we got closer, the strange hairstyle that I had noticed on the figure resolved into a pair of tall canid ears, and what I had assumed was a mask of some sort turned out to be a short, pointed muzzle. Serene stood up and stretched, smiling wanly to us before bowing in greeting.

"Serene, this is Tule and Cress, my partners, as well as a few more of their clade: Reed, Rush, and Sedge."

The fox—a hunch confirmed by a quick check of the perisystem—nodded. "Of the Marsh clade? How droll," she said, that smile veering perilously close to a smirk. "Welcome to my own little marsh."

"What *is* this place?" Rush asked, a note of wonder in vis voice. "Other than a swamp, I mean."

"It is mostly just a swamp," the other Odist said. "But it is one of my favorites. I make a lot of sims, you must understand, but this is one of the least popular that I have made to date, and for that I love it all the more. There, see?" She pointed to a patch of coarse grass at the edge of the 'island'. "Rushes!"

At this, we all *did* laugh.

"I have asked to meet with her and several others to ensure that we could get a view of what is going on from someone else," Dry Grass said, "because this is getting a bit out of hand for even me."

Serene nodded and started strolling down the path toward the next patch of grass, claws clicking dully against the wood. We fell in step behind her as she asked, "And what was it that you wanted to hear from me, my dear?"

"I would like to hear what you are seeing."

The fox—a fennec, the System told me—nodded slowly. "I am

seeing quiet chaos. I am seeing most of my sims emptying out. Few are out for walks or adventures. I sent forks to each of them when I noticed my own missing instances to ensure that they all still existed, as well. Thankfully, sims seem to be unaffected.

"The ones that are not empty, however, remain dreadfully quiet. Most of those who are out and about have set up over themselves cones of silence." She hesitated, took a deep breath, and then continued. "Those who have not, though, are decidedly not quiet. More than one silence has been broken by weeping and wailing."

I nodded. A few sniffles passed through the Marshans as the reality of what had happened once more struck us.

"I have also checked in with several of my students. Very few have been totally unaffected by this sudden loss, and more than one has disappeared from the System completely"

"More than one?" Sedge asked. "I suppose at least someone is bound to be unlucky enough to have been completely disappeared."

Serene nodded. "I have had many, many students, you must understand. It would not be surprising to me that at least one of them was that unlucky soul. However, I have come across three such cases so far."

"Out of how many?"

"Hundreds. However, I am still not done checking yet."

We walked in silence, then, digesting this, passing through the island of grass and turning left at nearly a right angle to head to the next. One more until we hit the patch of shade.

"Did you lose any instances?" I asked.

She nodded. "One, yes. She was working on a sim of her own, a wild park of sorts. She had not yet merged down, however, and her plans are now lost with her. The sim remains incomplete. Posts of gray sprout from the forest floor where the trees were intended to appear, but I do not yet know what trees she intended to place. There is no leaf litter to indicate what she was planning, nor is there yet a sun in the sky to indicate latitude."

The fox turned her head to smile back to us, expression once more wan. "I am thinking that I will turn it into a memorial of sorts."

Rush said, "I'd love to see it some day."

She simply nodded.

"The feeds seem to be more chaotic," Dry Grass said after a few moments, dragging us back on topic. "The world has taken to the perisystem to talk about what has happened. There, it is loud. It is filled with grief, yes, and increasingly more anger."

"And you said there hasn't been any word from phys-side except through Günay?" I asked.

She shook her head. "Not really. Not that I know about, at least, but that is not to say that a sense of that sentiment is not evident. Günay sounded excited."

Sedge snorted. "Excited?"

"Yes. You must understand, though, that more than a year has passed for them, as well, and this is perhaps the first that they have heard from us since then. I do not know."

"Oh, so, excited that whatever they did worked?"

Dry Grass nodded. "Yes, that was my guess. She is disappointed, of course, that so many of us are missing, but she is excited that so many of us still remain. As I have said, her words have been careful and measured, but I can still tell that she was excited to be able to talk to us."

"So, sims are empty," I said, ticking off items on my fingers. "The feeds are nuts. Phys-side is excited to see us. Has there been any indication on any of those fronts as to what actually happened?"

"Not as yet, no. We are missing key bits of information."

Serene added, "It is perhaps not yet time to be asking that particular question."

I tamped down the urge to bridle, waited for her to continue.

The fox gestured out toward the copse of trees before us. "Before we can ask what each of the trees is named, we have to observe that there are trees. Before we can ask what actually happened, we have to observe the things that have happened."

I glanced to Dry Grass, who gave a wry smile and half shrug.

"I am perhaps a little off-kilter," Serene admitted, smirking back to us over her shoulder. "But what I mean to say is that by figuring out the state of the world, we will be able to better ask how it got to be that way. That is the current objective. We are in the information-gathering stage of addressing this particular problem."

"Good thing Lily isn't here," Cress sent over a sensorium message. *"She'd lose her fucking mind."*

I stifled a snort of laughter.

"Okay," Sedge said. "So we're seeing some billion or so people lost, sims and objects are apparently unaffected, and there was a skip in time. People are sad and angry, and phys-side is largely unresponsive."

Serene nodded. "These are the things we require to start asking the correct question. Or questions, perhaps. What happened to the lost instances? What happened during the thirteen months' downtime? Last, and this may be a question for after those first two are addressed, why is phys-side being so careful in talking with us?"

We walked on in silence for a few minutes. I was disappointed to find that the shade beneath the trees was nearly the same temperature as out in the open. The heat clung to us, and the sweat dripping down my face provided no relief.

The next platform was at the base of one of those thick tree trunks, a few of the dozen or so roots plunging into the water providing the posts that held it in place. We circled there to all face each other.

"I have one more sim to take us to, where I aim hoping to meet up with representatives from all ten stanzas. I have asked them to congregate and discuss how many of their up-tree instances are missing," Dry Grass said.

Serene crossed her arms over her chest and slouched back against one of the Banyan tree's roots. "How did you manage *that,* my dear?"

"I yelled at Hammered Silver until she agreed, then convinced her to yell at In Dreams until *she* agreed," she said, smirking. "I do not think that either of them will be there themselves, but I will, and I am hoping that In All Ways will be there in In Dreams's stead, as perhaps there has been news from new uploads. You are welcome to join, of course, though I have already heard from Praiseworthy."

A second instance of the fennec blipped into being beside the first on the already crowded platform. "I will go," she said, taking one of her cocladist's hands in her paw. "Now?"

Dry Grass nodded and once more took Tule's hand in her own. Once we had all linked hands we stepped away, out of the heat and humidity. The last thing I saw was the remaining instance of Serene crouching down on the edge of the platform, once more poking a claw sullenly into the water.

While this new sim felt far brighter than the sunnier portions of the last, the air was also far cooler and far drier. It still had a feeling of morning to it, as though the day itself had yet to wake up completely. A check of the time showed that it was not yet 7, a fact obscured by the noonday sun of the previous sim.

The sun here shone low in a cloudless blue sky, lighting a rolling field of grass with the dawn. 'Lawn' may have been a more apt word, as the grass itself seemed to have been cut at some point: it was cool and prickly, all of uniform height and color. All, that is, except for the fact that it was dotted liberally with golden yellow flowers, each perfectly round as it stood shyly above a spray of wide-toothed leaves.

The air was thick with a sweet scent, and the sound of bees making their way from flower to flower hung just below the level of perception unless we all stayed completely silent.

We stood alone on the empty field for only a few moments before the other Odists started to arrive in ones and twos.

They seemed to come in two general categories. There were those who looked largely like Dry Grass: short, stocky women with curly black hair. There was some variation, to be sure, as one might expect from a clade almost three hundred years old. One, introduced as Time Is A Finger Pointing At Itself, was quite a bit taller and slimmer than the others, looking chic in a form-fitting outfit of all black. Another, Hold My Name Beneath Your Tongue And Know, was taller still and visibly transfeminine.

The other category seemed to be made mostly of furries of some sort. These, at least, I knew to be skunks. The stories surrounding them, the very same that had driven Lily away, were numerous and dramatic, so I was surprised to see just how...well, normal they looked. A Finger Pointing arrived holding the paw of a skunk, introduced as Beholden To The Heat Of The Lamps, shaped almost exactly like Dry Grass. Hold My Name also appeared hand-in-paw with a skunk, Which Offers Heat And Warmth In Fire. Warmth In Fire was much slimmer, however, almost wiry, and far shorter. They launched emself immediately at Serene and wrapped its arms around her before catching my eye. "Reed, yes? Hanne said you would be here."

I nodded and started to reply before cutting myself off as a few more Odists showed up in quick succession. Another skunk, looking far more prim and proper than the others, arrived and shot Dry Grass a quick glance. I couldn't quite read her expression, but she certainly didn't look happy. If she was this Then I Must In All Ways Be Earnest, it perhaps made sense, as the next Odist to arrive was a human introduced as The Only Time I Dream Is When I Need An Answer.

From what I gathered both from my knowledge of the history of the System that I'd picked up over my years on Lagrange as well as the memories of Tule's relationship with Dry Grass, there had been a schism within the Ode clade some fifty years back surrounding the political elements of the clade—of which Need An Answer was one—and those who disagreed. This included the stanzas to which both Dry Grass and In All Ways belonged. Beyond those such as Lily who held resentment, even some Odists mistrusted—or hated—some of their own.

I just hoped they'd be able to set that aside for now.

Need An Answer was the first to speak, calling aloud to the twenty or so people on the field, "Thank you all for coming, and thank you as well to those who have set aside differences enough that we may meet."

Scattered mumbling.

"Dry Grass, you have been taking point. Would you like to begin?"

"Yes," she said, stepping out in front of the loose crowd that had gathered. All turned to face her. "At midnight on January first, 2400—that is, systime 276+1, but some are speculating that the phys-side date is related for reasons that I will get to—a disruption in the software underlying the System occurred. This led to a discontinuity of approximately one year, one month, and ten days."

More muttering—darkly, this time.

"There have been more than two hundred thousand instances of downtime throughout the history of Lagrange. Most amount to a few seconds or minutes, with the longest being approximately three weeks, which took place during the Lagrange station's insertion into the L5 orbit in which it currently resides. We usually do not notice any downtime unless we are specifically paying attention to systime. However, in this instance, when the System returned to functionality, several instances were missing–"

"Several!" one of the Odists said, snorting.

"–several instances were missing. At current count, the missing instances number about one and a half billion, though that number continues to climb.

"I have re-acquired my systech credentials through an expedited process, which has led to me talking to a phys-side tech on the Lagrange station named Günay Sadık. While she appears to be somewhat restrained in what she is willing—or able—to tell me, she was at least able to confirm or deny guesses as I made them. She has confirmed that the missing instances are due to corrupted data, that Lagrange experienced full downtime, and that phys-side engineers were finally able to get it running at full capacity just last night."

Dry Grass paused, taking a deep breath. "Here are the things she was not able to confirm, but which I do not believe were outright denials. She was not able to confirm the reason for the downtime and did not respond to any of my guesses. However, as this discussion took place over AVEC, I was able to see her as she spoke. I asked if there was any physical damage to the System hardware: no change. I asked if there was any permanent damage to the System internals: no change. I asked if there was any trouble phys-side that led to the downtime: she looked down to her hands on the desk. Finally, I asked if this downtime might have been intentional, whether there might have been malice behind it: she looked off-screen, her expression appearing tense, perhaps frightened. I suspect an NDA block on her implants. I have heard these are uncomfortable at best."

At this, the muttering grew darker still.

"We have called you here to the field for a reason," Need An Answer said, picking up smoothly. "We would like you to tally up the amount of up-tree instances that you have. *All* up-tree instances, whether or not they are public. Please provide that tally to me, including only the instances you are positive about. If you would like to obfuscate that number and only respond via sensorium message, that is acceptable."

There followed nearly half an hour of silence. Most of the Odists looked distant or distracted, some of them sitting on the ground or pacing. I imagined them getting in touch with their up-tree instances, having them go through the same procedure.

By the end, many of them were in tears.

"Alright," Need An Answer said. "The amount provided to me is 748. Combined with those who are not here who have responded, there are 1,338 Odists. Please now provide tallies of how many of these instances are missing."

"Why?" In All Ways asked. Her expression had shifted from upset to unnerved.

"The goal is to use us as a synecdoche for the System. By tallying the percentage of missing instances within our extended clade, we may have a guess as to how many on the System might be missing. We are working with other clades who are doing the same thing, and by averaging, perhaps we will wind up with an approximate number for Lagrange as a whole."

Another, longer silence followed. By now, more of them were sitting in the grass. There were more tears, more open crying.

"The number..." Need An Answer began hoarsely, then cleared her throat. "The number of missing instances for those here is eleven. For the total respondents in the clade as a whole, there are twenty-eight missing instances."

"With a population of 2.3 trillion instances, we are looking at a loss of approximately 48.1 billion souls," Dry Grass said. Her voice sounded as sure as it had all morning, but her expression was aghast.

Silence fell for a third time. Silence except for sniffles.

My own were included, as were Sedge's and Tule's. The number was unimaginable. 48 billion! Yes, many of those instances were ephemeral, merely those sent out on errands or to enjoy multiple parties to ring in the new year. How many did not matter, though. Even if only one percent of those who were lost were long-lived instances, that was still 480 million dead.

The loss of Marsh suddenly felt insignificant, and with that feeling of insignificance came an anger, a despair.

"Are other clades seeing the same?" Rush asked. "We are seven and have lost one. We've lost fourteen percent, you've lost two percent. Are you expecting that you'll really be representative?"

Dry Grass shook her head. "The threads on the feeds focused on similar tallies show that many clades have experienced zero losses, while others have been all but destroyed. A branch of the CERES clade has reported a loss of more than 99.9%, while another experienced almost no losses."

"How big was that branch?" I asked, taken aback.

"Approximately 70,000," Dry Grass said. "Of which only twelve remain."

"Jesus fucking Christ," Rush said, laughing nervously.

"Jesus fucking Christ indeed," she said, then turned to Need An Answer. "Have any lines been lost, my dear?"

The other Odist's shoulders sagged. "Two."

"Who?" Beholden asked, sounding impatient.

"Should We Forget and–"

"*What?!*" Warmth In Fire said, clutching tightly at Serene's paw in one of hers, the other grasping for Hold My Name's hand once more. "No. No no no..."

"I am sorry, Which Offers Heat And Warmth In Fire. I know that you two were close."

The skunk didn't reply other than to continue whispering 'no' quietly.

"The other lost line is No Longer Myself. She no longer associated with the clade, but still maintained her identity as one of the lines of the first stanza. Of the others I know who have rescinded their clade membership, Sasha, E.W., and May Then My Name all remain in some capacity."

A Finger Pointing spoke up, casting a careful sidelong glance at her partner, Beholden. "We have spoken of the Ode, yes, of the two lines, but we should not omit those long-lived instances that were lost. I have lost one of my own up-trees. I have lost A Finger Curled."

At this, Beholden let out a cry and burst suddenly into tears, eventually rolling to the side to slip out of the sim. A Finger Pointing quickly forked to follow while the other instance remained.

"You are right. I apologize, my dear," Need An Answer said, bowing. "Of the 28 missing, five are long-lived instances that are not named lines, including A Finger Curled. My condolences to you, to Beholden, and to her up-tree instance."

"Do we have enough information to ask about whether or not they'll be recoverable?" Cress asked. "Serene said we'd need some questions answered first."

Dry Grass tilted her head thoughtfully. "None of my forks have reported any success along that front. Most, however, are still processing. When I asked Günay, she simply shrugged and said, "I do not know. Perhaps there is something that can be done with more hands sys-side, but best efforts were made in recovering lost data.""

"Are any of your forks working on that, love?"

"Working on recovery? I have an instance working on collating information on that topic, but the data itself is inaccessible to me, if it exists at all. Need An Answer?"

She nodded. "Several of us are working on that, yes, and from across the stanzas."

One of the gathered, From Whence Do I Call Out, began to pray. "*Barukh atah Adonai Eloheinu, melekh ha'olam, dayan ha'emet.*"

Dry Grass lowered her head as several of the other Odists joined. After a moment, she forked and gathered the Marshans around her, setting up a cone of silence above us.

"I believe we are done with pertinent business for now, and we are going to circle inwards and discuss those who have been lost," she said. "I would like to suggest that we give them space. Would you mind stepping away?"

"Will you come with?" Cress asked, alarmed.

"Not yet, my love. I will rejoin before long. One of the lost long-lived instances was one of my own, and this will give me a chance to step back and grieve, myself–" Her voice trailed off into a hoarseness that spoke of tears to come.

Cress's expression fell, and it wrapped its arms around her. "I'm sorry, I didn't know..."

"I did not say," Dry Grass said, shrugging. Whatever confidence she had been leaning on before was gone. She looked to be struggling to hold herself together. "We will talk later. More of me remain at home, too."

We all took turns, ensuring that she got a hug from each of us, then stepped away, this time to the pagoda that I had discovered earlier that day before sleeping.

As we stepped into that foggy morning on the close-shorn grass, the sound of a clanking bell or two from the direction of the sheep, we all let out a pent-up breath together. I wasn't quite sure what the breath represented for each of us. Even in myself, I couldn't tell if it was a sigh of resignation, of exhaustion, or of the simple sensation of being just by ourselves again, just those of our clade.

Oh. Well, there was an idea.

"Hey Lily? Want to meet up and talk with the rest of us?"

There was a long silence, followed by a sigh of her own. *"Just us?"*

"Yeah," I sent. I tried to keep any disappointment out of my voice. It wasn't hard with how tired I was.

Another long pause, and then a sense of a nod.

A few moments after I sent her the address of the sim, she popped into being beside me, looking freshly showered. Her expression was flat and motions stiff as she walked with me to join the rest of the clade in the pagoda. Even as the rest of the Marshans greeted her, she simply nodded, saying nothing.

If I'd been expecting us all to jump into conversation, I was disappointed. However, there was still relief when we fell back into silence, each thinking our thoughts, looking out over the pasture at the fog and the shadows of sheep. The only sounds were those of the sim—a hint of rain further out on the grass, another tinkle or two of a bell—and my own breathing.

Once more, questions bubbled up within me. What could I possibly do in the face of such enormity? How could 48 billion people just disappear? What was phys-side doing about all of this other than hiding the details they doubtless had? More 'how could I's dogging my heels—how could I be sitting here in silence? How could I have stepped away from Dry Grass, the one person I knew who was working hardest on this? How could I not have looped Lily into this whole conversation?

"So," Lily said. "What's up?"

Cress laughed nervously, brushing its hand up through its hair. "Uh...everything."

"The folks we went to talk to–" I set aside the fact that I felt compelled to leave out just who those folks were; I was sure Lily could guess. "–were doing some looking around and tallying up losses within their clade and others. It sounds like, if they're representative of losses across the System, there might be almost fifty billion people missing."

"Dead," Lily corrected, face darkening. "Fifty billion dead."

"Right," I said all but under my breath. "And phys-side has said relatively little. They confirmed there was downtime and data loss, and I guess maybe hinted at the fact that...this whole thing may have been deliberate."

She sat up straighter, brow furrowed. "Deliberate? Like a bomb or something? I was thinking maybe a solar flare took us out."

"Exactly at midnight on New Year's Eve at the turn of the century?" Tule asked. I was pleased to hear only tiredness in his voice, rather than any ire. "How small are the chances for that?"

She shrugged. "Not none, I'm sure."

"What would an attack on the System even look like?" Rush asked. "I don't know that a bomb sounds right. That would have taken out a lot more data. It would have taken out some sims, at least, some objects."

"Ye-e-es," I allowed. "So maybe it was a virus or something. CPV that affects everyone doesn't exist, does it?"

Silence and headshakes around the pagoda. The contraproprioceptive virus—the one sure way to kill anyone on the System—only seemed to work when tailored specifically to an individual's sensorium, disrupting their sense of proprioception until they either dissipated and crashed or quit out of agony. Not only that, but, from what I'd learned from the stories that came out surrounding it a few decades back, it had to somehow pierce the skin, to breach that sense of physical integrity, before it could do it's awful job of unwinding a person entirely.

"Well, if this...attack or whatever was deliberate and we don't know anything about *how* it was done, do we know anything about who might have done it?"

Sedge leaned forward, resting her elbows on her knees. "There's always been a bunch of people who hate uploading. Sometimes it's because they feel like we've abandoned Earth, sometimes it's because everyone makes Lagrange out like some sort of heaven while Earth is still kind of hellish. Even after all the work they've gotten done in the last fifty years, even with a lot of the climate shit either halted or actively starting to improve, Earth has hardly gone back to what it was like before the industrial revolution or whatever."

"Yeah, but hate it enough to destroy it? Kill billions and billions of people?"

"I'm not sure they think of us as people."

Lily snorted. "'Not as people'," she sneered. "Sorry, Sedge, I know it's not on you. You're probably right. I'm just feeling like shit now."

Rush smiled faintly. "I think we all are."

"And you said no sims have been hit?" she asked. "You're the one of us who's at all interested in that."

Ve nodded. "Yeah. Ser... Well, some of the people we'd been talking to were sim designers, and they said they hadn't seen any of their sims messed up or disappeared or anything."

She nodded slowly. "Odists, then? Dry Grass and her clade?"

Ve hesitated, looked to me.

"Yeah, Dry Grass met with us because she's back to working as a systech."

"Alright," Lily said, shoulders sagging. "I'm sorry I'm having a hard time letting go of that, but I'm not exactly disappointed that you're all close with someone who knows about all of this."

"Thanks," Tule and Cress mumbled in unison. Cress continued, "You don't have to like her or anything. Not everyone needs to like everyone else. She just also has information, too."

"I get that. Did she have anything else to say about Marsh? Like...that's why we're all coming together, isn't it?"

"Just that phys-side said they weren't able to recover anyone beyond whocver's still alive now, and that there might be something to try now that we're back, but she didn't exactly sound hopeful."

"Hopeful," she mused.

"Not much of that to go around," I said, feeling exhaustion pulling at my cheeks, pressing at my temples. "But I guess it's all we have to go on for the time being."

Interlude

<u>Feeds</u>
Various Authors

Lagrange Central Feed — 2401

Instances Spontaneously Quitting?

by İpek Aydin of the Sevgili clade

Mavi was over for the celebration with some of os Riãos, and she and Bay suddenly quit. I pinged Mavi and I got her down-tree? But she hadn't received a merge request, and Bay's co-cladists couldn't reach em at all; Louie didn't have a merge request either.

Mavi is okay, I think, although she lost track of the party which is a little sore. We'll just have to throw her another anniversary I suppose. But Bay is gone. One sentence ey was there, fine, gossiping gladly and drinking champagne with us. We look away, we look back, and ey is nowhere to be found. It doesn't make sense for em to quit like that, so suddenly, without warning.

Do you think this is like the virus Ioan Bălan wrote about in *Individuation & Reconciliation?* But that was described as a breaking up of oneself, and there was no such distress. Bay and Mavi just disappeared as if they had simply quit. Nobody touched them, but we are all staying in quarantine until we figure out what happened, just in case it's contagious.

I've been keeping a spare fork in another sim, too, but they probably have the same thing I do if it is contagious. We're all so worried. If anyone has any information from the engineers, please let me know.

§

What the Fuck Happened and What We Can Do About It

by Sedge of the Marsh clade and I Remember The Rattle Of Dry Grass of the Ode clade

Judging by the feeds, everyone and their dog knows that things are a little bit messed up right now. On New Year's Eve 275, Lagrange went down and stayed down for one year, one month, and ten days. When it came back up, we didn't immediately notice anything changed in the fabric of our existence here. Sims are here, bodies work as planned, forking and merging work, sensoria work, cones of silence and the perisystem architecture work, the reputation market works.

What *didn't* come back, however, were a bunch of our instances. How many are missing is still up in the air. Dry Grass has counted more than two billion based on what everyone is saying on the feeds, but she's still going and obviously isn't going to catch those who won't be posted about.

She's spoken with a phys-side System engineer, and answers are pretty slim. They've confirmed all that we're seeing, and say that they've done their best efforts for recovering everyone. They're unable to say just what happened or how many people were affected.

So, what happened? We don't know. If phys-side knows, they aren't telling anyone we've spoken to, and The System Consortium isn't talking to anyone but systechs. AVEC is unavailable, and phys-side news feeds are blocked.

That means that, at least for the moment, those of us who aren't techs are on our own when it comes to hunting down information. Thankfully, Dry Grass is a systech! Still, information from *everyone* is useful. To that end, I propose that we start pooling our resources. Here are the things we'd love to know, but if you have anything else to share, please do let us know.

How many of your clade are missing? Stick with just your clade, and just the ones you know are missing. You can check by trying to ping them; it'll feel impossible to reach them if they no longer exist. If you don't know everyone in your clade, have everyone you do know do the same.

What percentage of your clade is missing? Total up the instances that are missing, then divide that by the total number of people in your clade that you know of from before Lagrange went down and multiply it by 100. Once we start collecting enough of these percentages, we'll be able to average them out and get a rough estimate of how many on Lagrange are gone. The more we get, the more accurate that estimate will be.

List any friends you're missing. Please give their full signifiers—name and tag both as they appear in the clade listing—so that we can weed out duplicates. These will be added to the list of missing, which will help others search for friends and family.

Do you remember anything out of the ordinary? If you remember anything that seems weird, write it up in as much detail as you can. Maybe some people will wind up remembering something from before the end, as all of our memories stop just before midnight. Many of us mentioned a sense of déjà vu, though that may be a side effect of the System coming back online.

Any news that might help? Have you heard any rumblings, either sys- or phys-side, leading up to this that might help explain what happened? Maybe you're still in touch with relatives back on Earth, or maybe you have archives of some feeds that we're still hunting for. The more concrete the data, the better!

To everyone who helps add information to this pool, *thank you!* The more we have, the better, and the better our information, the better we can communicate with phys-side about what happened. To anyone who wants to help, *double thank you!* Get in touch with me or Dry Grass. We need folks tallying losses and coding responses. Fresh eyes are better.

Keep going and stay safe!

— Sedge and Dry Grass

§

THE END THE END THE END THE END!

by Diana Serene Moon of the Moon-Bright clade

THIS HAS TO BE IT! THIS HAS TO BE THE END!!! May God have mercy on our souls! Come to Lagrange Life Church#88295aac for 24/7 SERVICES to OFFER OUR PENANCE!!!

— Rev. Jared Moon

§

TO ALL OWNERS OF ACM-CLASS SYNTHETIC CANID COMPANIONS, THIS IS A MESSAGE FROM 9IN INDUSTRIES

by Andréa C Mason#Foundry, of the CERES clade

This is a call for help.

More than likely, your robot canid friend is gone. We are sorry. I am sorry. Words are not enough for the loss you are experiencing. Yes, even you.

Answers to some questions you may be having:

- No, we have not been able to restore any models.
- No, we do not keep backups.
- No, at this time we are not Issuing new models or contracts.
- No, we have no idea what the fuck happened either.

As you were informed in your contract, your companion was a direct fork of a core Andréa model, and was a cladist, not a construct. Each of you had an individual copy of us. The Andréa you had was custom forked for you, and took the time to get to know you and your needs.

They are gone. I am so fucking sorry, but even if a version of them merged down into me I cannot sort your Andréa from the rest. Or from myself.

Until further notice, High Falls Millworks#46b147c4 is closed to all visitors, and 91N INDUSTRIES is shuttering. I cannot begin to describe what I am going through.

In the event you still have your beloved Synth companion, please instruct her/them/it to fork and merge down as soon as possible. If you know of an ACM companion in the wild or out of the reach of the feeds, please Contact Andréa Mason#Central.

Of the nearly 64,000 active duty Companion instances and 6000 91N INDUSTRIES staff instances, we have managed to confirm that only ten besides me and #Central are still alive.

We send our condolences, and know for fucking sure we are grieving with you.

§

Four-Winds Bar and Grill Shut Down

by Simon Knight, Tarot clade

Hey folks.

So I'm not going to beat around the bush here; the Bar on Parkway Vale#b1306638 is going to be closed for business until further notice, given recent events (or *apparently* recent as the case may be). The Flynn Clade, the owners and proprietors of the establishment, are currently in mourning, having lost one of their cocladists and a not-insignificant number of friends and loved ones.

We ask of you all to be patient and to take your time with this. Give Casey and their clade the space they need; they are particularly fragile, even if they don't always show it. There will be a time when the Four-Winds open up again, yes, but it is not today, it is not tomorrow, and it is probably not any day this week. I know we can't guarantee when things will be back underway, and I know things may never return to the way they were, but I ask of you all to hold on, and hold together. We who remain are all we have left. Ping those you haven't spoken to in a while, those you regret having broken away from, and be there for your fellow instances in this troubled and uncertain time.

Stay safe, please. And take care of each other, for Gods' sake.

§

Help Locating Dawn/Horae Clade

By Liber/a ex anima labyrintho clade

We had a fight and she stormed out and then everything blinked out. I can't reach her. I know she's still mad at me, but I just need to know that she's okay. Please, if anyone's seen her, please let me know, or have her sent me a ping or something? She doesn't have to talk to me, I know I said some nasty things, but I have to know that she's okay. I just need to know she still exists. Even if she never forgives me, I have to know. Please.

Dawn, if you're reading this, please let me know. It doesn't even have to be direct. You can message Prayer or First Light and they can let Ops know and I'll even talk to Ops if it means I know that you're okay. That's all I want. No contact, I promise. I won't even try to message you if you'll just tell me, or not even me, but just get me a message. Please.

I can't ping her. I think she blocked me? Can you do that? And her name's not on the clade directory. Can she hide it? I don't want to bother her, honest, I don't care if she hates me forever, I just have to know that she's still somewhere.

It can't be that the last things we said to each other were full of venom. That's not fair. She has to still be here.

I have to say I'm sorry. She has to know that I don't hate her. Please don't let her have died thinking I hate her.

Please.

§

We are here to help.

We still do not know the fullest extent, but suffice to say this is the greatest loss the System has ever endured. We may not know the weight or size of the damage for much time yet to come, but the damage of the now is undeniable and unending. No one of us has gone untouched. Each of us feels how heavy emptiness and how loud silence both can be.

You do not need to struggle alone.

Some of us will lapse. Some of us will take our first drink. Some of us will struggle in a way we haven't in centuries. Some of us just want to help others.

We pass no judgment.

There is pain in losing. There is pain in surviving. There is pain in being unaffected. There is pain in waking up alone. We do not see it as weakness if you falter, just as we ourselves may falter.

There is work to be done.

You can tell us your life story. You can tell us nothing. You can set up every chair in the meeting hall. You can just come and drink our coffee. You can come alone. You can come with however many you need. We do not ask anything of you, but will not turn down any hand or paw or appendage offered.

There is work to be done.

We are here to help.

We pass No Judgment.

You do not need to struggle alone.

We are the Secular Recovery Sys-side Support Network, or SRS2N, for short. We hold meetings across the System. You can

ping any of us for a directory, or come to our main meetings on
tuesday nights in Golden Grass Community Center#89b75c1.
   With patience and open arms,

- That I May Find The Middle Path, of the Ode clade
- William Hauer, of the Luthier clade
- Ed Riviera, of the Hannan clade
- Genevieve Gancarz of the Pelech clade
- Magenta Solarhooves of the Sunshine clade
- Aeran, of no clade

Reed — 2401

The rest of the day was largely spent hunting for friends and tallying losses. The Marshans and a few of their assorted partners—minus Dry Grass—set up camp in Marsh's study, widened slightly by Pierre, who also held ownership permissions over the sim.

It raised a question that dogged me for a few minutes, cropping up now and again as I got in touch with more of our friends. What happened to objects and sims owned by individuals who had disappeared? If what Serene had said about her up-tree instance held true, the sim that she'd been working on remained. "When an instance quits, all of their items disappear," she explained. "But should an instance crash, that is not considered quitting. They remain in a core dump somewhere. That the sim remains indicates that she did not quit, but the ownership record is now invalid. I will need to file to have it revert to me."

It was sheer luck, then, that Marsh had shared ownership privileges with their partner.

This new study was expanded to include a few more desks and tables. Hanne and I worked at a table, for instance, compiling a list of friends, both mutual and individual. We rolled down over the list friend by friend, getting in touch with them and having small conversations where we were able, trusting in the cone of silence to keep from disturbing others.

For each person we managed to contact, we asked them a set of questions that Sedge and Dry Grass had come up with. Finding out how many of their cocladists had gone missing, as well as any friends or loved ones that were now unreachable. We collected some of that information for ourselves, building a better picture of how our friends group had been impacted, but all were directed to the official survey that had been set up by the Odists.

Truly official, as well. Dry Grass had had her systech privileges restored—as was evidenced by a floppy, felt witch hat she would occasionally summon, a physical token of her official capacity—but she had also taken on a leadership role in this project beyond simply being a tech. She had pulled some strings to leave their post pinned to the top of several of the largest central feeds. Responses were already pouring in as more and more people woke to the realization that missing friends and family. While Dry Grass assured us that such had been done in the past, none of us had ever seen such a thing before.

"It is a part of the long peace that your lives are so boring," she had said with a sigh. "Or at least were."

While our data gathering was productive when it came to learning about our own circle of friends, it was a drop in the bucket compared to what the others were accomplishing. Sedge and Dry Grass in particular seemed to be on a roll of information gathering. They had set up their own little side room of other instances just collating data, running them through various perisystem tools, and just generally trying to get a better picture of what had happened.

The picture, as it began to take shape, was grim.

While our 14% loss rate was far too high, the fact that the System was on track for a loss rate of 1% was still an enormous amount. On the surface, the number felt quite small, but on a System with 2.3 trillion instances, that meant 23 billion people suddenly wiped from existence. 23 billion people with friends and lovers, or down-tree instances waiting for updates. 23 billion regardless of how early or late they had uploaded.

"23 billion *souls*," Dry Grass corrected firmly after I kept speaking only of instances. "They are souls, Reed. I do not care as to your belief of the existence of a soul or not, they are souls. They are people who lived. They are people who died."

"Uh, sorry," I said, shying away from her.

Her shoulders slumped as she wilted. After a moment spent mastering her emotions, she reached out and squeezed my upper arm. "I am sorry, my dear. In The Wind is gone. A Finger Curled is gone. No Longer Myself and Should We Forget are gone, two lines from the Ode itself wiped out entirely. It is difficult for me to not see them missing as anything other than a death."

"Right, I guess I'm just struggling to square that with Marsh being, uh..."

"Gone?"

I nodded.

"I make no assumptions as to them, but for me, if I do not start internalizing the losses within my clade as deaths, I will run the risk of minimizing this loss across the System. Perhaps Marsh is not dead, but if I do not think of In The Wind as dead, then I will be hiding from myself a potential truth."

I winced at the import of her words. I couldn't help it. They bore too much weight, too much force coming from her mouth, from the one who was working the hardest out of all of us.

"Again, I am sorry."

"It's okay. Maybe I'll get there one day. I don't know."

She nodded, squeezed my arm once more, and then backed away. "I am going to return to counting. Anything to keep my mind busy."

And so our lives became a world of numbers for a few short hours. Hanne and I fell back into tallying up the losses in our circle of friends, counting lost forks and (thankfully very few) lost clades. Shu was indeed gone, as was one of my friends from way back in those heady days right after I'd been forked from Marsh. Benjamin had been unfailingly polite so long as he was sober. One drink, though, and he picked up a wickedly funny streak, and could string together far more curses than I had imagined possible.

Hanne and I weren't quite as adept at forking as Sedge and Dry Grass, though, or perhaps since they were working on tallying up the losses on all of Lagrange rather than just those within their own group of close friends, they were inured to the intimate reality of all of those losses. What was the loss of a hundred thousand nameless souls to them in the face of one of Hanne's closest friends?

We wound up stepping away from Marsh's sim before long. Even just being there in that emotionally charged room felt like too much.

"I'm sorry, Reed," Hanne said once we returned home. Her voice was raw. It hurt to hear the pain within it. "I just…"

I nodded and roped her into a hug, letting her rest her head on my shoulder as I did the same on hers. "I know. I'm going through the same with Marsh. Or similar, at least. Hearing the way Dry Grass talked about it, it's hard not to just assume that they're just gone. 'Dead', she said, and as much as I hate it, she was right that not assuming that will just lead to more pain."

I felt her hands tighten against my back, clutching at the fabric there. "Warmth In Fire said similar, both of Shu and Should We Forget," she mumbled hoarsely. "Ey's having a harder time than I am, but in a different way."

"How do you mean?"

I felt her shrug slightly against my cheek as she spoke. "I guess ey was particularly close Should We Forget, one of the Odists that disappeared. It said that she'd never forked, that she was from a part of the clade that struggled with mental health and something about trouble holding one shape. They're particularly upset at how hard Should We Forget worked to overcome all of those problems, and said how proud ey was that she had overcome a ton of losses and then disappeared without ceremony."

I nodded, quiet.

"Anyway, I don't know. I don't know that I've ever seen it that emotional before. Ey was just…crushed." She sighed. "And I am too, I guess, but maybe I'm just not old enough to have gotten that close to Shu. I guess I can't say much more other than it hurt to listen to them talk like that."

"Well, alright," I said after a moment's silence, gently disentangling myself from the embrace. "Let's at least focus on something else for a bit. What sorts of things can we take care of from start to finish that have nothing to do with...all this?"

She laughed. "'All this' is a hell of a way to put it." She shook her head as though to dislodge the thought. "But you're right. Uh...well, I've had too much coffee, I think. It's a bit early, but maybe we can make a drink or something? I also wouldn't mind inviting some others over just for some noise, otherwise I'm going to sit and stew up in my head."

"What, am I not enough to distract you from that?"

She snorted. "No. I love you, but you'll just wind up reminding me of it. Any friends you want to bring over? Or cocladists, I'm starting to remember that I love all of your clade, not just you."

"Good to hear," I said, smiling. "After last night, I was afraid you were about to write us all off."

"I may yet," she said, grinning tiredly. "But yeah, sure, feel free to invite them, too. I'll ask around, as well."

We both spent a few minutes puttering about, getting ourselves some water and poking through the exchange for a bottle of wine to have ready for when others arrived.

If others arrived, it turned out. There were a few maybes, with Sedge saying that she wanted to focus just on the work and not split her attention any. Both Pierre and Vos declined, saying they would rather stay together and focus on their own problems—certainly understandable. Few of my friends sounded appealing to have over, which also held true for Hanne, who wound up only pinging Jess and Warmth In Fire out of her circle of construct artistry friends. Both gave a definite maybe.

Of those I pinged who surprised me by saying yes, Lily was at the top of the list.

"I'm struggling with all of this, and starting to feel kind of lonely or...I don't know, left out, maybe," she said over a sensorium message. "I don't like it, Reed. I don't like having to just process all of this on my own."

"I mean, you're more than welcome over, of course," I replied. "Though I'd be surprised if Cress and Tule didn't also bring along an instance of Dry Grass."

There was a long pause, followed by the sense of a sigh. "Okay. I'll probably still come along. Maybe I'll find some way to get over my shit, at least enough to be around her."

"Well, okay. I trust you, but still, hopefully no snippiness, okay? I think we're all frazzled, but the goal is just to not deal with difficult stuff for a bit," I said. "At least, as best we can."

I could hear the smirk in her voice. "Right. I'll keep my mouth shut if I start to feel like biting her head off."

So it was that we cycled the weather outside to a comfortable springtime evening, set up a table with various small foods and a few different bottles of wine, and waited for everyone to trickle in.

Cress and Tule were the first to arrive, Dry Grass appearing between them a few seconds later, still wearing her witch's hat, which she quickly waved away. All three of them looked exhausted, but brightened visibly at the spread laid out for all to snack on, quickly loading up plates of bruschetta and glasses of icy rosé.

The next to arrive were Warmth In Fire and Jess, both of whom launched themselves at Hanne to wrap her up in a hug. Hold My Name, Warmth In Fire's partner, arrived a few seconds later.

I'd met Jess a few times before at dinner parties or the like, and she definitely shared Hanne and I's fondness for snarky banter, and was just as prone to falling into witty repartee as we were.

For some reason, though, I'd yet to actually meet Warmth In Fire beyond the brief introduction we'd had in the field. Despite

Dry Grass's average height and soft build, Warmth In Fire was quite short and wiry. Where Dry Grass was comfortable to move through life at a steady pace with measured speech, the skunk was spunky and energetic, speaking quickly and smiling readily, quick to hug—I received my own after Hanne—and quicker still to fork to accomplish such affection. They seemed to live in a pleasant sort of transgression, from the constantly shifting pronouns to the almost childlike nature that nonetheless seemed to be performed with a wink and a nudge, as though ey knew just how subversive such kid-like vibes could be.

Hold My Name, in contrast, stood tall and confident. She leaned more on Dry Grass's steady nature, though seemed perfectly content to keep up with Warmth In Fire's speedy intensity, at one point scruffing an instance of the skunk—who was nearly a meter shorter than her—to pull it into a bearhug. She was also visibly and effortlessly transfeminine in a way that I attempted to live into in my own trans identity. I liked her immediately.

Last of all, nearly an hour after we started, most of us a few drinks in, Lily stepped out onto the patio. She moved stiffly, awkwardly, and only nodded a greeting, wordlessly picking out a few of the *hors d'oeuvres* and pouring herself an over-full glass of a sweet wine.

Her silence put a damper on the rest of the conversations, all of us speaking quieter, eventually falling into silence as she sat down at the table.

A few seconds passed before she smirked and shook her head. "Well? Come on, entertain me."

I breathed a pent-up sigh of relief at the chuckles from around the table.

"I will tell you a joke as a way to break the ice," Dry Grass said.

Lily laughed, though it sounded somewhat forced. "Alright. I want to hear what counts as a joke to your clade."

Dry Grass bowed. "I assure you, it is appropriately atrocious. It comes straight from Waking World, who has set himself up as a father figure, complete with dad jokes."

Lily rolled her eyes, nodded.

"Alright. A horse walks into a bar, flumps down onto a stool, says to the bartender, "Whiskey and a beer.""

"A bar joke? Really, love?" Cress asked.

"I told you it was awful," she said, laughing. "Anyway, the bartender sighs, pours a shot, and sets that and a shitty beer down in front of the horse.

""Might as well leave the bottle," the horse says.

"The bartender reluctantly sets the bottle down as well, saying, "Hey man, you are in here every day. Every day you mow through a few beers and a few shots. You alright?"

""Of course I am fucking alright," the horse grumbles, downing his shot and chasing it with a glug of beer.

""I dunno, man. You think you might be an alcoholic?"

"The horse says, "I do not think I am," and then disappears with a *poof!*"

There was a pause, during which a few of us smiled, vaguely confused at the apparent punchline.

"You know, because "I think therefore I am"? And he did not think he...oh, never mind."

At this, there were a few dry chuckles. "You're right, that is atrocious," Lily said.

"Well," Dry Grass countered primly, "I would have said that last bit first, but I did not want to put Descartes before the horse."

At that delayed payoff, the rest of us laughed in earnest. Warmth In Fire, halfway through a sip of wine, snorted into its drink and started to cough, which set Hold My Name to laughing all the harder as she rubbed the skunk's back.

"Okay, okay, I'll give you that one," Lily said, still grinning. "That was pretty good. Still atrocious, but at least the good kind of atrocious. I'm sorry for the other night."

"That was only last night, my dear. We do seem to be living at a high skew, do we not?" Dry Grass bowed to her. "I appreciate it, Lily. I cannot and will not apologize for my clade, but I will all the same do my best to live as a counterexample to these stories you have heard that rankle so much."

"Yeah, thanks," Lily said, more down to her glass of wine than to Dry Grass. "I was thinking, actually, and part of the reason I wanted to come over and see you on...uh, neutral ground, I guess, is that I had a question about your clade."

Dry Grass nodded for her to continue.

"What was it like to get used to being a clade without a root instance?"

All three of the Odists present stiffened, sitting up straighter.

"Well," Dry Grass said after receiving subtle nods from both Warmth In Fire and Hold My Name. "It was different for all of us, I think. Michelle Hadje quit nearly a century ago, now, and at first, I was crushed. My whole stanza was crushed, and although we had long since diverged, many of us going our separate ways, we moved back into the old set of townhouses that we used to inhabit as a stanza for nearly a year. Some of us brought partners, some not, but we needed that company, that familiar association with *us*, with that commonality that came from her.

"Memory Is A Mirror Of Hammered Silver, the first line of the stanza, was hit perhaps hardest of all of us. She was the closest to Michelle, after all. Michelle struggled so much over the years, and lived largely in solitude but for a few close friends, many of whom were among the first lines. Hammered Silver was a sort of mother to her, and so to her, it was akin to losing a child. While the rest of us, her up-tree instances, were also saddened to varying degrees, she was a fucking mess, lashing out and then retreating, lashing out and retreating, over and over again."

She sighed, taking a sip of wine before continuing. "I had given up being a systech by then, and I spent nearly a month in my house, most of that either baking or in my room, constantly kicking myself for not doing more to help Michelle. She was...she was so broken, those last few years, and a good chunk of that was based on her engagement with the System itself, so it was difficult for me to hold both that fact and my role in working with the System together in my mind. I kept falling back to those how-could-I questions, to all of those suppositions that I ought to be doing something with all my knowledge and tools."

I tightened my grip on my fork, leaving it stabbed into a pile of salad. "I've been dealing with a lot of that," I said, voice cracking. "I keep thinking there has to be something more I can do, or wondering how I can do something like this." I gestured at the table with a forkful of greens. "Having a dinner party while Marsh is gone."

Dry Grass nodded. "Precisely that, yes."

"I got super angry," Hold My Name said, her comfortable alto dipping back into a tenor, as though the mood demanded less of her transfemininity. "Like, *really* angry. I had to move back into my own place for a while after, I was so mad. How could she do that? We—the rest of the second stanza—were already unmoored by Qoheleth's assassination only a year before, and now Michelle had quit, too. It stranded all the stanzas, leaving behind ten brand new clades."

The Marshans winced, suddenly understanding the same of ourselves.

She shrugged, turning her glass of water between fingers. "I slowly calmed down, but that anger hit again after I learned about all of the shit the eighth stanza did, all of that controlling. There were even hints that Michelle had been nudged to quit by True Name, who I had already suspected of being behind Qoheleth's assassination. Now I had a target for that anger."

I glanced surreptitiously at Lily, who was keeping herself still, tightly under control.

Another glance at Dry Grass showed her watching Lily warily in turn.

The moment of tension passed uneasily, as Warmth In Fire spoke up next. "I will say as I always do, my dear: your anger is based around a memory that does not fit the reality of the situation. I have met Sasha through my friendship with the fifth stanza, who ever stood up for her, even when she was True Name. I have eaten dinner with her. I have watched the way she smiles. I have watched the distance at which she holds herself from time to time. I have seen the flashes of regret-tinted understanding when topics of the past crop up. She is not who she was, but neither was she who you say she must have been. There was no wickedness in her, and I cannot even linger in discomfort around her."

Hold My Name sighed, tired gaze level on her partner. This carried the cadence of an old argument, one had dozens or hundreds of times before.

Lily only gripped her glass tighter.

"She is no murderer. Not of Qoheleth, and certainly not of Michelle," Warmth In Fire continued confidently, the gravity of their words held in tension with the ineffably childlike openness of her expression. "Yes, you may hate her, and yet I cannot. Yes, my up-tree, Dear, loathes her, and yet I do not. Yes, my down-tree, Rye, has had her complicated thoughts in the past, but on one thing she and I agree: she is no longer who she was, and even who she was is obscured by careful fictions. We are both suckers for character development. I am Dear. I am Rye. I am Praiseworthy, and Michelle too, but I am also my own person."

"I know, Bean," Hold My Name said, voice as tired as her gaze—and, perhaps, the argument. "You have said this countless times before, and I appreciate the balance that brings, but I am also my own person separate from you. I mistrust her, you do not. We are allowed to not be alike."

The skunk nodded, waiting for her cocladist and partner to continue.

"I did not even like Qoheleth all that much. I thought he was a putz who had lost his marbles," she said, smirking. "But Michelle–"

Warmth In Fire waved its paw jerkily, a flash of despair washing over eir features. "Michelle was murdered, yes, but the act of violence took place at the root of her trauma. Of *our* trauma,

My." The skunk was crying, quietly and bitterly. "The act of violence that led to us being so fucked up—beautifully, wonderfully fucked up—and which led to the creation of the System also destroyed someone centuries later because she was never given help. It was her right to quit as she did, leaving us ten clades and not one, but her murderers were all of us who did not help, not some wicked machinations of only one of us."

At the sudden force of their words, Hold My Name's expression shifted to one of alarm, and she reached out to take up one of her partner's paws. Dry Grass did much the same.

After a few moments of sniffling, ey shook its head, smiling faintly to the rest of the table. "I guess that goes to show that it still has not yet been fully processed."

"Not even close," Hold My Name agreed.

"I know that it is quite soon, and that there may yet be some solution as you have said," Dry Grass said gently, nodding to Lily. "But on that note, what are your feelings on potentially being without a root instance?"

Lily shrugged awkwardly. "I don't know yet. I'm still dealing with the stress of everything. That's a big part of why I wanted to come here in the first place. I was feeling left out and lonely."

We all nodded, and I reached out to pat the back of her hand.

She smiled gratefully at me before continuing. "Actually, I was starting to get paranoid that maybe this wasn't over. I guess there's no guarantee that it is. Who knows, maybe more people will start disappearing. I was getting worried that more of the clade would go missing, or that I'd just disappear without a trace, too."

Sniffling, Cress nodded. "I've been worried about the same. All of my friends, Dry Grass, all of you...I don't know, I was worried that maybe there was some ongoing problem with the System or that whatever phys-side was hinting at wasn't done."

"That's a big part of what I was thinking about," Tule said. "That this was some sort of fight or something. I've never lived through a war."

"Few have," Dry Grass said. "We almost did, back before the founding of the System, but the whole Lost saga interrupted that."

Jess, who had been fairly quiet up until that point, asked, " 'Lost saga'? Like, all that stuff about people being disappeared by the government? Didn't they all die?"

"Oh, heavens no," she said, chuckling. "We were among the Lost. *Michelle* was Lost. That is the trauma Warmth In Fire spoke about. That is part of why she was so fucked up."

At this ey looked quite proud.

"And, like it said, why we are so fucking weird," Hold My Name said. "*You* certainly are," she added ruffling Warmth In Fire's perpetually mussed up mane.

It snapped eir teeth at her, grinning wickedly. I was pleased to see their mood improved.

Hold My Name barely flinched, instead rolling her eyes. "You see the shit I put up with?"

"Yes, yes," Warmth In Fire said. "You are *so* put upon. We never hear the end of it."

Laughter around the table.

"But no," Dry Grass said, picking up the conversational thread once more. "Of the Lost who did not kill themselves, they all uploaded. There are several still alive today."

"Jesus," Jess said, shaking her head. "How old *are* you?"

"Three hundred fourteen years," Hold My Name said.

"Fifteen," Dry Grass corrected. "The date jumped, remember?"

Her cocladist frowned, but nodded all the same.

"Either way, I do not believe there shall be any more major losses. Phys-side seemed fairly confident of that. They have even promised that they will be ungating news and AVEC transmission back to Earth. We shall learn more before long."

"I hope so," I said. "I'm getting pretty tired of being in the dark."

§

The day that followed that wine-soaked afternoon and evening of half-obscured emotions was...well, I couldn't say it was calm, *per se,* as we were all still coming to terms with the reality of what had happened, but it was certainly more level. The mood was subdued and Hanne and I were both laid low by crying jags at one point or another, but we doggedly stuck to our pre-catastrophe routine in an attempt to keep some semblance calm. It felt like we had few alternatives. We both felt powerless.

Hanne holed up in her office for a while, working on some of her latest constructs. While the house had been littered with little *objets d'art* from her explorations, I'd requested that she stick to her office for working on this current trend of oneiro-impressionism. Something about the in-progress constructs hurt my eyes, and a few had led to migraines, even for her. Objects that brought the dream basis of the System into stark reality presented their own challenges.

Meanwhile, I spent some time catching up on reading. I'd fallen into the hobby of literary analysis and critique some decades back, and it had become a habit of mine to post on the feeds. Over the years, I had picked up my own audience.

I tried not to think about how much of that audience was missing.

The only break from the norm, other than those few spates of emotional overwhelm, were the occasional updates from Sedge and Dry Grass. Many of these boiled down to simple numbers. The more the responses flowed in, the better the picture we got as to the extent of the damage to Lagrange.

The news remained grim, as the total percentage of lost instances leveled out at one percent and varied little.

Twenty-three billion dead.

"Billion. With a 'B'," they wrote.

The numbers boggled the mind. The percentage of my friends that had disappeared overnight remained well below:

of the more than two hundred I checked in with, Benjamin was the only one missing. Even if I counted Marsh, the total number was less than that. Hanne tallied up similar results: Shu and one other, To Aquifer dos Riãos, could not be reached. They, like so many others, were unavailable to ping and listed as 'no longer extant' on the perisystem directory.

The directory was a deliberately vague bit of software. It couldn't provide a listing of all instances, couldn't run aggregates on all of the data, wouldn't provide a running tally on the number of instances living within Lagrange. One even needed permission to see more than a name, and that only if they were in the same sim.

"It is both a technological and a social problem," Dry Grass explained when asked. "The technology to provide that list would not be insignificant to implement, given some of the core mechanics of the System. We do not live in a database that can be queried so broadly. The social aspect is that we decided early on that we simply did not want that to be the case. We did not want that one would be able to discover random individuals, to hunt for old enmities on which to act. Privacy concerns here are of a different breed, and we leaned hard into more, rather than less, privacy early on."

Unsatisfying, but at least understandable.

So we sat and did what we had done nearly every day for years and years now. Hanne tooled around with impossible shapes and colors that appeared different for every person, objects that couldn't be discussed, while I read trashy novels and took notes in an exocortex.

It wasn't until well into the evening, dinner now simply crumbs on plates, that I decided to reengage with the overwhelming topic at hand. One half of me felt bad for having so thoroughly disengaged, while the rest felt blessedly refreshed, so maybe it hadn't been in vain.

While Hanne headed out for drinks, I stepped once more into Marsh's study.

The scene was much as I had left it previously, expanded and cleaned with desks, each inhabited by one or more instances of Dry Grass, Sedge, Rush, Pierre, or Vos. A new doorway on the far wall opened up onto a yet larger space with hundreds more instances at work, many of whom I didn't recognize. There were several other Odists, both skunks and otherwise, several mustelids of some sort dressed in all black, a few sandy-haired men in suits, and a few more tall black men in long, white thawbs that brushed the floor as they walked. For some reason, my down-tree instance's house had been linked up with some sort of headquarters for this particular purpose, likely due to the role that Sedge had played.

"Ah, Reed!" an instance of her said brightly as I entered. "Welcome to the madhouse. We're having fun!"

"'Fun'?"

She smiled all the wider, an expression lacking earnestness. "Isn't this fun for you? Billions dead and us having to make up answers on the fly?"

I shook my head.

Her shoulders sagged and her expression flattened to one of sheer exhaustion. "Alright, yeah, I can't keep the act up. How're you?"

"Alright, I guess. Not like there's much going on back at home, and Hanne went out to a bar to get plastered or something."

"Sounds nice."

I chuckled. "It kind of does, but I've had my fill of drinking these last few days. How goes the number crunching?"

"It goes," she said, shrugging. "The picture hasn't changed much, which means we're probably zeroing in on a final percentage. We'll keep digging of course, compiling that list of names so that we can post it somewhere, but I'm starting to lose steam."

"You look exhausted."

She nodded. "I am, but also I'm starting to feel numbed by all of this data, and it's getting to me that that's all I'm feeling.

You and Dry Grass have talked about"Oh, I should be feeling X or doing Y!" and I'm starting to get that. I *am* doing Y, and it's making me unable to feel X, if X is...I don't know. Grief? Fear?"

I frowned.

"It's not a bad thing," she hastened to add. "So long as the goal is escapism, that is. I'm sure it'll catch up to me. Probably pretty soon."

Hunting for an open chair to flop down into, I sighed. "Yeah, I get that. I think that's what I wound up with. Just kind of alternating between feeling awful and then trying to do something other than feeling awful."

"Fair enough, yeah. What brings you around?"

"I wanted to help, I guess."

She nodded, pointing back over her shoulder with a thumb. "Well, the politicians have taken over much of what's going on. I hear they even roped in some of the old ones who retired. I'm starting to feel like I'll get pushed out of the endeavor before long." She smiled wryly. "Or at least nudged into a data-entry role."

"Think you'll stick around for that?"

"I don't know if I'll have much of a choice.

I furrowed my brow.

"Not like I'm being forced," she said, smiling faintly. "I'm just not going to let myself stop until I have a better idea of what's going on."

"And do you think you'll ever have a good enough idea to let go?" I asked gently. "I know how we are when it comes to hyperfixations like this."

She waved her hand to bring her own chair into existence, falling back into it heavily. "Feeling seen, here, Reed. Feeling *perceived*."

I laughed. "Sorry, Sedge."

"No, no. It's good. I'll keep an eye on it." She pushed at the arms of the chair to sit up straighter. "Say, want in on this phys-side meeting? Dry Grass is pulling strings to get me in, and I think it'd be fine if you came, too."

"Meeting with phys-side? What for? Do they have more information for us?"

"We're hoping so. There's been a few meetings so far, but they've been dragging their heels, supposedly to let us organize this Emergency Council or whatever they're calling it. They don't like the whole sys-side anarchy thing very much."

I shrugged. "I'll send a fork, sure. Don't want to leave Hanne in a lurch if she drinks too much and comes home a mess."

Sedge laughed. "Fair enough. You have good timing, though. It starts in...uh, five minutes, actually. Come on."

I stood up and forked, my root instance stepping back to the house while my new fork followed along after Sedge—or at least one instance, her down-tree remaining in the chair, kneading her palms against her eyes.

The headquarters room beyond the boundaries of Marsh's study proved to be much larger than anticipated, stretching out to either side, where it was ringed with glass-walled conference rooms, many already populated with 'politicians', as Sedge had called them.

"They've got a bunch of people working on different aspects of this. Jonas, of course, and a lot of the Odists—don't tell Lily, but I'm starting to really like them—plus some folks from way back. The black guy is Yared Zerezghi, who wrote the secession amendment. The weasel is Debarre, who was on the Council of Eight. The blond woman–" She nodded over towards a huddle people matching that description. "–is Selena something-or-another. I never did catch her clade name. She seems neat, though. Ex-System Consortium. Well connected."

"So are you, seems like," I said, grinning.

"Well, sure," she hedged. "I *did* start that survey with Dry Grass, though, so I guess that gives me some sort of in with all these heavy hitters."

"Right." I hurried to catch up with her as she skirted around a surfeit of cinnamon-colored skunks. "So where's this meeting happening?"

"Through here, I've been told," she said, gesturing to a set of double doors.

These opened out into a wide space, all white walls and pinewood flooring, black slabs that must have been tables scattered around the area, surrounded by chairs and low stools of various sorts.

As we hunted down our own table, dozens of those politicians and technicians started to stream in through the doors or blip into existence from other sims. The room filled quickly and efficiently. Chatter was minimal, and everyone took their seats without fuss.

Sure enough, as the clock ticked over to 18:00, an AVEC setup sparkled into existence with a pleasant animation, set in an open space in the center of the room. As the lights dimmed and sound picked up, we were greeted by a low murmur of voices from various phys-side techs filing into their own seats in an auditorium of some sort, projected in from the L5 station. The transmission was set to be semi-translucent, a helpful affordance for us to see who was phys-side and who was sys-side.

After a minute or two of the last of the attendees figuring out their seats, a dour gentleman dressed in a station-issue jumpsuit stood and bowed towards the front of the auditorium, the AVEC projectors ensuring that it looked as though he was bowing towards the last standing person in the room, an instance of Need An Answer.

"The Only Time I Dream Is When I Need An Answer of the Ode clade, she/her," he said in a flat monotone. "Thank you for setting up this meeting."

The Odist returned the bow and replied in kind, "Jakub Strzepek, he/him, thank you for agreeing to set up this meeting. We have specifically asked for the attendance of phys-side systech III Günay Sadık, she/her. Is she present?"

Jakub's expression grew even more sour, but he bowed once more and gestured toward the front row. A young-ish woman with short-cropped black hair stood, hesitated, and bowed. After an awkward moment and a gesture from Jakub, she stepped up to the front of the auditorium as well, holding a tablet to her chest.

"Need An Answer, yeah?" she said, bowing once more. "Pleasure to see you. Dry Grass told me a lot about you."

"And she has told us much about you," Need An Answer said, smiling. "Thank you for agreeing to join us. Those of us working on this project sys-side have requested that you be our primary point of contact moving forward. We have–"

"*Me?*" Günay said, a look of panic washing over her face.

"Yes, you," Need An Answer said, voice calm. "You will be our primary point of contact among the phys-side systechs."

"But my boss–"

"We do not want to speak with your boss on these matters," she said, voice maintaining that eerie calm. "We wish to speak with you. Jakub Strzepek and the other members of the admin team have agreed after some...discussion. Thank you for joining us. We have a few questions that we would like to ask you directly. Your colleagues are there to provide guidance, and the representatives of the admin team are there to sate their curiosity."

"Uh," Günay said, voice hoarse. "Well, okay. I wasn't exactly expecting that, but sure, I'll do what I can."

"Lovely. It is my role to organize, not to ask questions. Picking up responsibility sys-side will be I Remember The Rattle Of Dry Grass of the Ode clade, she/her, Jonas Fa of the Jonas clade, he/him, Debarre of his own clade, he/him, and Selena of her own clade, she/her."

The four sys-side representatives stood up and bowed. Debarre, I noted, was quite curt in his bow. While my read on weasel expressions was less than perfect, he seemed to be giving Jakub a run for his money on the dourness levels.

"I will ask the first question," Dry Grass said, remaining standing while the others took their seats. "Based on an internal survey, we are estimating losses of about one percent. Do you have visibility on the number of lost or corrupted instances on your end?"

Günay opened her mouth, hesitated, and looked towards Jakub.

"Günay," Need An Answer said. "I will remind you that we are asking you, not your superiors. You may answer honestly without fear of reprisal. We are running this show, now."

There was a rustle of noise from the AVEC stage. Low murmurs and shuffling in seats, quickly quelled.

"This is intended to be a collaborative effort, Need–" Jakub began.

Need An Answer interrupted, and there was danger beneath the calm in her voice. "Have you lost 23 billion souls, my dear?"

There was no response for several seconds. The tension, even across the AVEC feed, was palpable. Eventually, he bowed. There was a moment of fiddling with something we could not see before he said, "Günay, you may carry on."

The systech nodded slowly, looked off into space for a moment—consulting something on her HUD, I imagined, after some NDA or another had been lifted—before sighing. "We only have an estimate, but yeah, our estimate is 0.977% of the total instances on Lagrange were lost or corrupted."

A low mutter filled the room, this time from those sys-side.

"And do you have a better sense of what caused this massive loss of life? What led to the one year, one month, and ten days of downtime?"

Another pause, longer this time, before Günay spoke. "We aren't sure, yet."

"I do not believe that," Dry Grass said, smiling and bowing toward the stage. "And I mean that in all kindness, Günay. The phys-side news feeds are being slowly ungated, and the tone is not one of questions with no answers."

The tech wilted under the cold kindness. "Well, okay. There is some suspicion of malicious actors, yeah. I say 'suspicion' in earnestness, I promise." She winced as a wave of discomfort washed over her face. "A lot of what you see—or will see, I guess—on those feeds is gonna be speculation, and I can promise that that's all I can— that's all I've got, too."

Jakub, apparently unable to restrain himself any further, stepped back to the center of the stage and bowed curtly. "Dry Grass, if I may."

The Odist nodded, a touch of haughtiness in her movements.

"We have been ensuring a certain amount of...information security and hygiene, at least until we were sure that Lagrange was back up and running at full capacity. It–"

"It isn't at full capacity," Debarre growled.

"If I may," Jakub said, glossing over the comment and continuing all the same. "It was determined that, with the conclusions produced by the investigative teams that dug into the root cause, certain data were to be protected by NDA and withheld from sys-side and phys-side *both*."

Jonas Fa smiled cloyingly. "I have to say, that doesn't exactly leave much in the way of doubt in our minds as to what might've happened. You either fucked up royally or we were attacked."

Jakub stiffened, bowed, muttered, "Unavoidable."

One of the other Odists at our table, To Know God, snorted. "Treating information theory like a game gets you shit on every time."

After an uncomfortable pause, Günay asked meekly, "Is that okay for now? Maybe once the NDAs are lifted or whatever, we can talk more about that."

Dry Grass smiled again, more warmly this time. "Of course, my dear. Perhaps instead you can tell us what happened to the unrecoverable instances."

At this she brightened. "Oh! Yeah, for those, we just had the System remove the core dumps from the sims where they'd been dropped and instead placed them in one single sim where they wouldn't be seen."

"You hid them from us, you're saying," Selena said.

"I...well, sure, we didn't want them just laying around wherever."

Dry Grass raised a hand to cue Selena to remain quiet. "We ask because, without that visual signifier that anything had happened, we were left with the sudden, inexplicable absence of loved ones and friends, our up-tree and down-tree selves. We would have been left with our grief either way, yes? But without the core dumps, we did not have the hope that there might be something recoverable from them. We were left without hope at all."

When Dry Grass dropped her hand, Selena picked up once more. "This was the only communication we received from you for hours. You didn't talk to us directly, didn't tell us what happened, but you *did* hide those core dumps. You *did* gate the feeds. You *did* turn off AVEC. These are acts of communication in themselves, and that's why we're left with a sour taste in our mouths."

As Günay wilted on the stage, Dry Grass shook her head. "Tensions remain high, my dear. We are not placing blame on you. Part of why we asked to speak to a systech rather than a manager or admin is because we would not be blaming anyone, just passing information back and forth. It is regrettable when it winds up with you in the middle, but for the most part, we just want to know what happened."

"Alright," she said, still looking meek. "So what more can I tell you?"

"There was no damage to the physical components of the System, correct?"

Günay nodded. "Right. No damage physically, nor even any damage to the firmware or corrupted software. The damage seems to be relegated to just the data. Just the...uh, well, you."

"Just the us, yes," Dry Grass said, grinning. "We have noticed the damage seems to have only affected instances. Sims and objects remain."

She nodded.

"This includes objects owned by missing instances. You have

confirmed that, given the core dumps, this is due to the instances crashing rather than quitting or being coerced to quit, as that would lead to those objects disappearing and the sims being marked as abandoned."

"Right, yeah. It was a mass crashing incident."

"But not a crash of the System itself?" Jonas asked.

"No, it doesn't seem to have been a full on crash, just the instances."

Debarre sneered. "23 billion instances just crashed? Just like that?"

"Uh, well, no," Günay said. "All of you crashed."

The silence that filled the room sys-side was profound. It was so pure that I suspected that everyone within the room had suddenly set up cones of silence above themselves, and I had to check to make sure that I hadn't done just that.

"Wait. Wait wait wait. No, that can't be it," Debarre said. The growl was gone from his voice. He looked panicked, rather than angry. "That's 2.3 trillion instances at best guess, right? Trillion, with a 'T', right? Everyone keeps saying that."

Günay nodded. "2.301 trillion instances crashed. 100% of the System was affected."

There was no silence at this. The room burst into scattered conversations. Dry Grass nodded to Need An Answer, who waved a hand toward the AVEC stage, which was suddenly overlaid with a muted microphone symbol.

"We all crashed?" Sedge asked an instance of Dry Grass who remained at the table. "All of us?"

Dry Grass frowned down at the table in silent thought. "We only have their word to go on, but yes, I suppose so," she said after a moment.

"But nothing happened," I said. "It was just...midnight and then Marsh wasn't there."

"Yes. I was home with Cress and Tule, and then I was called over to your place. I do not remember anything resembling a crash."

"*Would* we have remembered it?" Sedge asked.

"That is what I have been thinking about," she said. "I was trying to remember if it was possible to wipe memories."

"And?"

"There was some experimenting on that front from a therapeutic standpoint, but they were never able to remove a singular memory, only to wipe back from the present moment to a certain point in the past."

I prodded at the slab of table, unmoored from the floor as it was. It was immobile. "Are you thinking they did that for everyone?"

"Everyone who survived, perhaps," Dry Grass said, shrugging. She looked tired, as though the exhaustion were catching up with her. "Did you notice anything leading up to midnight?"

I thought for a moment, just pressing gently against the table. *I just wish it had some give,* I thought. *If it's going to be floating in air, it should have some give.*

Aloud, I said, "I remember mentioning some *déjà vu,* and then Hanne mentioned similar."

"I remember getting almost punched in the face with that, too," Sedge said, frowning. "That's why we asked about it in the survey."

Dry Grass sat still, looking down at the table as though tallying up these experiences. "We did notice some of that in our experiments, yes; memories whose tails were left dangling trying their best to dovetail into the new ones being formed," she said slowly. "But come, they are unmuting. We should be quiet. We should listen."

Sure enough, the mute symbol had begun to pulse, and a few seconds later, it disappeared and the small noises of rustling began to come through from phys-side once more.

"Thank you for clarifying," Dry Grass said, offering a hint of a bow to the gathered System techs and administrators. "We would like to ask if there has been a general memory modification that would have removed time leading up to midnight.

Nearly everyone within the room has reported a sense of *déjà vu*, which is a common side effect of such."

"Oh! Y– I...I can't talk–" Günay began, but the feed was once more muted, this time with an angry swipe of the hand from Jakub.

"I suppose that answers that," Jonas Fa said, laughing from up at the front of the room. "They're really terrible at this."

Need An Answer swiped up a keyboard and started typing rapidly. A few seconds later, a message appeared superimposed on the AVEC projection, reading: "Please unmute. Remember that we are communicating with Günay Sadık."

Another minute passed, and then the mute was lifted once more.

"Apologies, Need An Answer," Jakub said, sounding as though he spoke through gritted teeth. "I will let you question Günay as you've suggested."

"This is not an interrogation," she replied calmly. "Though perhaps I ought to say that it need not be."

The administrator bowed once more, more stiffly this time, and backed toward the rest of the techs sitting in the background.

"Apologies, my dear," Dry Grass said, smiling to Günay. "Please do continue. I believe we were talking about a potential memory trim."

Her expression far more subdued, the systech nodded. "Yeah, we trimmed about fifteen minutes of memory from everyone we were able to recover. I...was under an NDA."

"Why fifteen minutes?"

"A guess, mostly. We tried trimming it closer and there were some effects of the...of the crash that stuck around in everyone's memories." She hesitated, adding, "It didn't seem pleasant. Everyone affected was in agony, and they all quit within seconds, minutes at most."

Selena lifted a hand and, when Dry Grass nodded to her, said, "We seem to be talking around what *actually* happened. Jonas said we're talking about either an attack or gross incompetence. I'd really love it if you'd tell us what actually happened."

Günay looked nervously back to the audience of administration and technicians behind her—many of whom I suspected outranked her—and stammered, "Uh...well, I mean..."

"Günay, please," Dry Grass said, her voice quiet, earnest.

"Alright," she said after a moment of silence, during which none of the administration moved to stop her. She looked to Jakub, who swiped at his tablet and nodded. She continued, "What we think happened is that a broad-spectrum contraproprioceptive virus was released into the System environment, either destroying or inciting a crash in every instance it came into contact with. Since it propagated through the perisystem architecture, this was every instance on Lagrange."

Towards the end of her statement, she had to raise her voice to speak over the upwelling of murmurings and gasps that showed through sys-side. Holding myself separate from the whispered exclamations being shot around the table at which I was sitting, I watched as the representatives up near the AVEC stage scanned the audience.

"'Was released' implies a deliberate action," Selena said once the room had quieted enough. "Do you have any confirmation on that?"

"Uh..." Günay clutched her tablet in her hands. "Even if I knew anything—and I'm not on that team, promise—I'm *really* not qualified to talk about this. Mr. Strzepek only just lifted the inhibitor."

Jonas Fa raised a hand to silence any further questions. "No, you're right. Much as I hate to say, it's probably not the best time to talk about this."

Angry muttering from around the room.

"If it was a deliberate action, especially if phys-side played any role in it at all, then we're talking about a breach of the Articles of Secession," he continued, more to the sys-side room than to the AVEC stage. "We'd need set up a working group to get in touch with phys-side leadership as soon as we have more information. Thanks, Günay, you're off the hook for this one. Mr. Strzepek, no need to send details, but please send me a side-channel message as to whether or not I should be setting up that WG. No–" He held up a hand as Jakub started to rise. "–I don't need any details beyond a yes or no. Do it from your HUD right now."

Jakub looked as though he was about to explode, so thoroughly had he lost track of his planned meeting. "Now, hold on–"

"Jakub, shut up," Jonas Fa said, sounding chummy, almost fond of the man. "You're so fucking far out of your element I'm surprised they haven't filed a missing persons report. You're talking to an emergency council of a nation 2.28 trillion strong, a nation that you have already been reminded just lost 23 *billion* citizens. Three of the original Council of Eight are here, meaning you've got people more than three centuries old standing in front of you. People who *signed* the Articles of Secession. Hell, Yared here *wrote* them. Fuck you, fuck your meeting, send the message."

The rooms on both sides of the AVEC connection were silent. For all I'd read about Jonas as some massively manipulative political player on the System, out-manipulating even the famously manipulative Odists, seeing him bear down on an individual, sitting just shy of actively upset, was enough to leave me holding my breath. This man, this mover-and-shaker of politics both sys-side and, prior to uploading in the early days of the System, phys-side, was a figure out of myth, a character from the grand stories told in histories and novels. That I had even been allowed to sit in the same room as him suddenly felt wrong. Sure, Cress and Tule had their relationship with Dry Grass, and Marsh had known a few of the Odists through their singing and Vos working with some of the theatricians among them, but certainly none of the political ones.

Jakub wilted under the weight of the realization of the magnitude of the situation. He appeared to see, all at once, just how out of his depth he was.

After a pause, Need An Answer spoke up once more. "The final item that we would like to speak about before we end this meeting in order to discuss our next steps is the ongoing communications embargo."

Günay blinked. "That's not my area of expertise at all."

"But do you at least know the current status?" Debarre asked.

"Well, sure," she said slowly, as though hedging her words. "Communications to Earth are limited and censored at the moment, and communications between Lagrange and the two LVs are being slowly ungated. I don't know if those are being censored or not."

"Why weren't they just ungated immediately?"

"I don't know the political reasons, but there was also a worry about DSN capacity..."

"Is there an actual concern about the DSN?" Selena asked.

"I'm even less of a space nerd than I am an information theorist," Günay said, smiling wryly.

Dry Grass asked, "I would assume that you are gating communications from the LVs under a similar embargo. After all, to their eyes, we disappeared quite suddenly, yes?"

She shrugged. "Your guess is as good as mine, but I'd be surprised if that wasn't the case."

Dry Grass laughed, not unkindly. "Yes, fair enough."

"Are you able to ungate communications to a limited subset of clades?" Jonas asked.

Günay looked thoughtful, lips moving faintly and fingers twitching as she queried something in her HUD. "That should be possible, sure. You want your four clades ungated?"

Dry Grass nodded. "The Ode clade, the Jonas clade, Debarre's clade, Selena's clade, Yared's clade..." She trailed off, thinking. "And the Marsh clade, yes. We'll get a list to you later with more."

I frowned, shooting a glance over at Sedge who only shrugged.

"What would that get us?" I asked over a sensorium message.

"We could hear from those on the LVs, I guess."

My frown deepened. *"So we could hear from Marsh, then?"*

She sighed. *"I guess. I don't know what that buys us. I'm not exactly about to tell her to stop, though. I'm scared enough of these guys as it is."*

I snorted, nodded, turned my attention back to the front of the room.

"–will have a separate meeting regarding the ungating of transmissions," Need An Answer was saying. "That falls under the realm of politics, yes? It is hardly something you need worry yourself about, Günay."

"Thank God," she said, laughing nervously.

"Have you received the appropriate message from Mr. Strzepek, Jonas?"

"Yep, got it."

"Thank you," Need An Answer said, bowing. "Thank you for all of your hard work, everyone phys-side. Despite the terse tone of some of our questions, please do know that we are grateful for all that you have done in your efforts to bring us back online. Trillions of lives may continue, even if not unchanged."

Everyone on both sides of the AVEC link stood and bowed. Some, I noted, more curtly than others. Jakub and Debarre both seemed ready to start hollering at a moment's notice.

When the transmission ended, the noise in the room rose to a low murmur, and then a quiet chatter. Several instances quit or stepped out of the sim entirely while many more streamed back out into the ballroom-sized workspace. A few lingered, though, little knots of conversation in a still-dim room.

"I am fucking exhausted," Dry Grass—or at least the instance that lingered with us—said, slouching down in her seat. "Less than an hour, and I am fucking exhausted."

"Weren't you exhausted before the meeting even started?" Sedge asked.

"Well, yes," she said, voice muffled as her head drooped toward her chest. "But now I am tired on a much more existential level. I am tired in a way that feels like social burnout, like I have been around too many people for too long."

"Which I suppose you have," Sedge added, stretching her back before rubbing her hands over her face.

We stayed in silence for a few minutes. It was hard to dispute Dry Grass's words, too. Even for me, who had only been here for a bit over an hour, everything that had happened in that time, the sheer amount of information, had me feeling full to bursting. Still, I couldn't seem to think of anything else.

"What was with all the cageyness?" I asked. "That Jakub guy, sure, but it seemed like a more...I don't know, systemic thing."

"Oh, it very much is," Dry Grass said. "Jakub is a putz, but an innocent one. He is doing what he was hired to do, and he was hired by the System Consortium, which works with the world governments. There are several layers above him, and all of them are trained to act cagey."

"So it's just politics?"

She nodded. "I would say so, yes. It is more nuanced, but that is not my area of expertise. He is withholding the information he was told to withhold. The NDAs quite literally prohibit speaking about the things they cover. They are locking down communications for whatever reasons they have, which I am sure are good. It is our job, then, to press at that, to find all of the weak and sore spots and try to divine why all of this is being done."

Sedge's expression soured. "We can't just ask?"

"Of course not. There is a protocol to follow." Dry Grass laughed. "And that includes all of the little jabs Need An Answer and Jonas shot at phys-side. It was less that we were making a demand for that information as it was letting them know that we knew that they knew more than they were letting on and that we were not happy with it."

"Why promote Günay, then? She looked really uncomfortable getting stuck in the middle of that."

She shrugged. "I am guessing, here, but I think that that was intended to say to phys-side, "What is most important to us right now is the 'what', rather than the 'why', except inasmuch as the 'why' might help illuminate the 'what'." It is a way of saying, "We will have talks on whether you fucked up or we were attacked soon, but not until we know the full status of the System.""

I shook my head. "None of this makes any sense, but neither did all of the politics stuff in the *History*, so I guess that's par for the course. You certainly seem to know plenty, even if it's not your area of expertise."

"Unfortunately," she grumbled. "Regrettably. Unwittingly."

"At least you can translate for us poor peons," Sedge said, grinning.

Dry Grass smirked. "Yes, yes. But come, let us get back to Marsh's. This place has its uses, but I need cozy more than anything. Maybe we can gather the others for dinner."

§

We sat around the table, saying nothing, each doubtless lost in our own thoughts. The decision to pare down our dinner hadn't been made all in one go, but in fits and starts.

We arrived back in Marsh's study quickly enough, finding it far more full than when we had left. The initial offer of dinner was well received, but the longer we talked about it, the more that seemed to cool.

Lily, of course, refused almost immediately. Although she appeared to have made the decision to reconcile with Dry Grass, that didn't mean that it'd be easy for her. She still had her anger, her resentment for what she felt that the Odists had done in their shaping of the System and its history, their role in Marsh uploading in the first place, and for that, I could hardly fault her. I'd had my own share of feelings over the years that had lingered, that I had bathed in helplessly, struggling to escape the odd comforts of depression or angst or anger. I could hardly expect her to climb free immediately.

"I do not blame her, either," Dry Grass had said when I voiced these thoughts. "It is not comfortable, to be clear. I do not like that she hates me. My role—the role of my whole stanza—is to revel in feelings of motherhood. I saw myself as mother to the System on a very real, very mechanical level, back when I was working as a systech. To have a citizen of the very System I love hate me is perilously close to having a child hate me. Everyone wants to be liked."

Sedge had was the next to turn down the invitation.

"I'm feeling stretched really thin, all of that research over the last few days. I love it, don't get me wrong, I just can't think anymore," she'd said, shoulders slumping. "My brain has turned to mush and I just kinda want to find a really dark sim and stare at nothing."

Rush, initially quite interested in a communal meal, bailed not long after, saying that ve was too sleepy, that the night was coming on too quickly, ve felt, with so much new information coming at ver too quickly.

And finally, Hanne refused. She sent me a sensorium message saying that she was still out with her friends, with Warmth In Fire leading a drunken memorial for Shu. That was more important than dinner, and the prospect of forking of engaging with the mechanics of our world felt fraught to her.

So it was that Cress, Tule, Dry Grass, and I sat around a table, hotpot bubbling away in the center, in a nearly deserted restaurant. We said nothing, each doubtless lost in our own thoughts, as we dredged veggies and tofu, thin strips of fish and surimi, and thinly sliced lamb through the spicy broth, carefully fishing them back out after the scant few seconds it took for them to cook so that we could eat them atop bowls of rice.

It was Tule who broke the silence. "This is all incredibly fucked, but at least the food is good."

We all bust out laughing. Cress, most of all seemed caught

up in the humor, laughing uncontrollably until tears streamed down its face. That laughter briefly veered into hysterical sobs as it hunched over in its seat. We had long since set up a cone of silence, and I think we were all glad for that now, as it made the space feel more intimate, more comforting as Tule and Dry Grass bookended Cress and rubbed their hands over its back.

"Sorry," it said once it was able to sit back up. Its voice was round, stuffed up. "I don't even know why it hit me like that."

"Too many emotions at once?" I suggested.

It shrugged. "Maybe. I mean, that's definitely true, but I don't know if that's why I fell apart."

"You do not need to know why, love," Dry Grass said gently. "You are allowed to be a confused mess in this confusing mess of a life."

I nodded, dredging a skewer of fish through the bubbling hotpot and waiting for it to cool enough to eat. "I have no clue how to feel, myself. I keep alternating between tired and down on myself for not doing enough, and working frantically on what feels like a good idea until another comes up."

Dry Grass tilted her head, a curious gesture I'd noticed in her cocladists as well. "Are you still feeling conflicting emotions from your merge?"

I stiffened in my seat.

"Only if you are comfortable discussing it, of course," she continued, voice soft. "I just imagine that there is no more appropriate crowd than this."

Both my cocladists had a blank look on their face before Tule fell once more into laughter. "Oh my *god,* Reed."

"What?" Cress asked.

"I merged down before New Year's."

"Yeah? And? I don't–" it began, then flushed red in its cheeks. It started to laugh as well, "Oh no, Reed. You kept the memories?"

"Yeah. It was a confusing night, you merged down before I'd forked my new instance, then my spare instance quit," I said. I slouched down in my seat, feeling the heat rise to my cheeks as I watched both of my cocladists laugh while Dry Grass sat, smiling earnestly at me. I knew that smile well, knew it from nights and nights together, from Sunday brunches and afternoons lounging in the sun. I shook my head to clear it. "You really want to talk about this now?"

She nodded. "I would like to talk about anything—*literally* anything—other than what we have been talking about for days, and I will never turn down the chance to talk about feelings."

"It's not a bad idea, Reed," Cress said, still grinning. "If you want to, I mean. I imagine it's gotta be weird as hell."

"Oh, it is!" I said. "I certainly wasn't thinking I'd wind up with a bunch of feelings for someone I've only met a handful of times. I have six or seven years of memories of you two together, seeing each other every day, even you falling in love, and those have always gone to the instance that merged down with Marsh."

"Wait, so...everything?"

I shrugged. "My up-tree quit and I was left with a whole merge just sitting there so I merged the rest anyway to have less weighing on me, you know?"

Dry Grass nodded. "Pending memories get uncomfortable after a while, yes."

"Right, and I know we usually talk before I keep any of those, but there was so much going on and I really didn't know what to do or think about what else to do in that moment."

"Why, then, did you not choose to quit in favor of your up-tree? To let those memories go?"

I looked down at my plate, nudging my skewers into a neat row. "I don't know. Stress? All of that stuff started happening with Marsh and it felt more important to focus on that. I was the one who tried pinging them, right? It was very in my face, very immediate."

"So now you're left with our feelings," Cress said. The laughter had left its features, but so had the embarrassment. "You're left with our relationship."

I nodded.

"You're left with our hyperfixation, more like it," Tule followed on, laughing. "God, we were both just head over heels for you, love."

Dry Grass scoffed, hand to her chest in mock effrontery. "Are you not still?"

"Nah."

"Nope, not at all."

She snorted, shook her head. "Do you see the guff I must put up with, my dear?" she asked me, a look of long-suffering pain on her face. "I build a relationship with sweat and blood, and am repaid in snark and tired humor."

"Don't listen to her," Tule said. "She's just being a dramagogue."

I laughed. "I remember that, too," I said. "And I guess that's sort of the problem. I remember what it is about you that drew Cress and Tule—or, at least what attracted Tule—and I'm as much a Marshan as they are, so here I am, feeling awkward about being around you because I remember those months of hyperfixation, and then the comfortable normal that you settled into afterwards."

All three of them smiled, all three looked a bit bashful.

"You're all really cute together, is what I'm saying."

Dry Grass gave a hint of a bow. "We do try, I believe." She reached forward to the box of empty skewers and tapped it against the edge of the box, cycling through options until she wound up with another set of sliced lamb to drop into the bubbling broth before her. "Are these memories of us, of Tule's relationship, clashing with your lived experience to date? And how about those of Sedge and Rush?"

More food sounded good, if only for something for me to do, so I tapped through options until I came up with a skewer of fish cakes—Dry Grass having requested we skip my usual choices of thin-sliced pork or shrimp for her own dietary restrictions—which I let slip into the bubbling pot. "Since Sedge's merge-down fork incorporated Tule's memories whole-sale, they weren't exactly tainted. And besides, they mostly tallied with what Sedge, Rush, and I know of you already."

"That does not quite answer my question," she said gently, lifting her skewer and nudging the slivers of meat onto a bit of rice in her bowl. "I am pleased to hear that there was no great clash up against what you know of us. What I would like to know, however, is how memories of being in a relationship with some-one you already know are fitting in with your lived experience of *not* being in one with them. We have met, yes? Attended the same dinner parties? We have seen each other here and there, chatted now and then. Throughout all of that, I have just been that weird old woman that lives with Cress, and then with Tule, and now some part of you remembers, I suppose, loving me."

Following her lead, I pulled my own skewers and rested them on my bowl of rice. It was a good distraction, a moment for me to think as I nudged the fish cakes off of the skewer onto a bite of rice.

Or, well, I had hoped that I would have a chance to think.

Instead, I found my mind hopelessly empty. I found my thoughts focused on trying to get the chili-stained fish to stay atop that morsel of rice, on trying to get as much of that as pos-sible held in the precarious grip of my chopsticks, on trying to fit it all in my mouth without looking like a complete idiot.

The rice was too dry or too sticky, the fish cakes too chewy or too spicy, the bite too big and yet over with far too soon for me to make anything that could be considered headway on the topic at hand.

What a dumbass, I thought to myself.

"I don't know," I said aloud. "I guess that's not all that elo-quent, but it's only been a few days now, and...well, yeah, you're right. There's a part of me that remembers being in a relation-ship with you and all that goes with that. I–"

Tule looked aghast. Cress, laughing, shook its head. "Oh my *god*, Reed."

"Hush, my dear," Dry Grass said. "Had he not brought it up, I would have asked after the memories of sex next."

"*Love!*" Tule said, burying his face in his hands.

"*Love!*" she echoed, laughing and leaning over to kiss his cheek. "This is the future we have found ourselves in, and it is a future entire, not some clean story stripped of references to gross anatomy and base desires. Reed, please continue."

The exchange had led to a flush of embarrassment of my own. I had been talking about emotions when I said "all that goes with that", but I suspected that Dry Grass was right to bring the topic of sex up sooner rather than later. That she had done so so adroitly, with humor and not a shred of bashfulness about her, certainly helped to ease the humiliation that I felt brush past me. I was able to master it for the time being—or at least ignore the burning in my cheeks—in order to continue on.

"There's a part of me that remembers everything, but it still feels just like that: memories," I said. "I could dredge up any one conversation, but none in particular stick out to me in the same way as a conversation that I'd experienced directly would. The memories are there, and I'll be reminded of them, but they're not at the forefront unless something happens to bring them up."

Both Cress and Tule visibly relaxed. "So it's not exactly something you're thinking about, then?" Cress asked.

"Well..." I started, then stalled out.

"I suspect he might not be," Dry Grass said, speaking slowly with her curious gaze lingering on me, as though prepared to stop at the first sign of me jumping in. "Except for the fact that we have been working together quite closely these last few days, yes? That is part of why we are here now, is it not?"

I nodded. "I guess so. If things were...uh, more normal, then I guess there might be a strange moment or two at dinner parties, I would've missed you for a while, but we've been together more often than not the last few days, so it's...I don't know. It's weird."

"I bet," Tule mumbled. He still looked flushed from the previous rush of embarrassment. "I can't imagine what that must be like."

"Surreal," I said, laughing. "It's really highlighted just how parallel our lives are, because I'll be reminded of all of these things when you speak, Dry Grass, or by the way you look or move, and it'll mean two different things to me."

"Is that unpleasant?" she asked.

I shook my head vehemently. "Not at all, no. I can even mostly ignore it. It's like a dream that sticks with you through the day, you know? Except that it's a decade of memories that have been sticking with me for a few days, now."

"Do you *want* to ignore it?"

"How do you mean?"

She sat back in her chair, folding her hands over her stomach. "Well, you could continue on as you are, ignoring these concurrences as they arise, or you could act on this new life that you have been given. You could request that we not work so closely together for a while, for instance. This is a perfectly cromulent thing to ask of someone, yes? You have an issue to work through; the issue is spurred by someone's presence; them not being around would alleviate that stress; hey presto. There is your solution.

"You could talk about it *more,* much as we are doing now. That is just as valid an act. If you would like to engage with these memories actively, then there is nothing stopping you from doing so, least of all me." Her faint smile slipped into a smirk as she added, "Hell, you could decide to ask me on a date, if you wanted, since you already have memories of that working out quite well."

"God, love," Cress said, giggling. "Are you aiming to net the whole clade?"

She smiled primly. "Would that be so bad? Though I believe I shall pass on Lily."

The three of us Marshans laughed.

"Jokes aside," she said once we had calmed down, "what I am asking is if ignoring these memories is comfortable for you. I suspect not entirely, or we would not be having this conversation."

Put like that, I really did have to sit and think for a moment. I poured myself a cup of tea and watched as the other three settled back into a more mundane conversation. I watched as Dry Grass ladled broth from the hot pot over her bowl of rice to eat it like a soup, watched the way that she talked with her partners, my cocladists, one of whose memories rode shotgun alongside my own.

I had lived two lives in parallel, Tule's and mine, and so I let that parallel continue into the future in my own imaginings. One Reed slipped almost effortlessly into a relationship alongside his cocladists, one woman acting as the pivot for our three lives. That Reed sat Hanne down to dredge up the topic of polyamory, untouched these last few years, to discuss this new relationship. That Reed forked to share time where it was required. That Reed grew ever closer to Cress and Tule in this shared orbit around Dry Grass, fell in step with however many others had found themselves mingling with the Ode clade over the more than three centuries they had been alive. However many had had conversations in their heads exactly like this.

And the other Reed made the explicit decision to step back. It would have to be explicit, to; I wasn't sure I could ever keep such a thing from Dry Grass if I wanted, her whole personality seemed to be built around openness. That Reed simply...slipped back into life as it had been. There would be a few awkward meetings here and there. Some part of me would still love her, but then those memories would fade into comfortable normalcy, as might any dream that sticks with one. Life with Hanne would continue as it was. Life with the clade would be as it had always been. And what would that matter to Dry Grass? She didn't have these memories, this internal strife.

Dry Grass had truly left me two forks in the road of equal value. There was no 'winning' or 'losing', no better or worse. The only path that felt unequal was to continue trying to ignore these feelings. Not just unequal, it felt inaccessible to me. She'd forced the topic out into the open, for better or worse.

Better, I suspect. She knew the clade well enough to read those signs of discomfort in my words—no great feat; "I can even mostly ignore it" sounded like an equivocation even to me—that she had nudged me toward some more complete understanding by talking it out. She did so before anyone got hurt, too.

I—that me who had his own memories and not Tule's—could certainly see what had drawn my cocladists to her.

Setting down my tea and reaching forward to snag the ladle in the broth alerted the others to my return to the present. I focused on the task at hand, filling my half-full rice bowl with broth before sitting back once more. "Thanks for talking this through with me," I said. "I think you're right, that it'd just be uncomfortable for me to keep trying to ignore it."

"Wonderful," she said, smiling.

"I don't have an answer beyond no, I'm not comfortable ignoring all of this, I'm sorry to say."

She shook her head. "Nor should you. It has been five minutes and change, Reed."

I laughed.

"Yeah," Cress said, leaning forward on its elbows. "There's certainly more than enough going on besides, right? Not like you need to solve *every* problem."

"Ah!" Tule said, sitting up straight and shaking his head. "This is too good a break to be wandering back into talk of whatever it is that we've been working on. Let's stick with making fun of Reed instead, alright?"

It laughed, holding up its hands. "Alright, I wasn't going to say anything else, but fair enough." It turned to me, grinning. "Just enjoy dinner with us, is all I'm saying."

"I am," I replied. "It's been too long since I've had hotpot."

§

I was left that night with a sense of having taken a step forward. It wasn't completion by any stretch, I hadn't made any dramatic decisions, hadn't changed anything, really, except getting dinner with a polycule and talked about feelings.

I *had* made that small decision, though: the decision to continue to think about these feelings on Dry Grass lingering after the merge.

The immediate outcome of this was a hug and a conversation. The hug came from Dry Grass after dinner. She asked, I said yes, it was a mix of awkward and pleasant. The conversation came when I got home and spoke to Hanne.

"Wait, you kept the *whole merge?*" she said, laughing. "I mean, I guess I can't blame you with all that was happening, but still, why didn't you just discard it?"

I shrugged. "That was going to be my up-tree's role, remember? He discarded everything, I kept everything."

"Why didn't you quit, then?"

"I'm not totally sure. I don't remember that night very well. Not that I forgot, I mean, just that everything happened so quickly and was so scattered that all the memories are, too. I think part of me was worried that maybe I'd disappear, too, or that Tule would, or Sedge or Rush."

Hanne's expression fell, replaced by something far more serious. "Okay, *that* much I can definitely understand. Is this the only real fallout of the whole merge?"

"I guess. There's a bit of fussing about intraclade relationships in there, which, okay, another thing to consider, but I love all my cocladists at least as family, so it doesn't feel too bad to me. I definitely love all my up-trees."

"There's quite a jump between loving like family and loving like a partner, though."

I nodded. "Not denying that, just that I think Tule had...well, it's not that he didn't love the rest of us, he just didn't think of the rest of us all that often. Not as often as I do."

"Except for Cress?"

"Yeah, except for Cress. He thinks of it all the time. He really loves it. I'm old enough to remember the taboo around intra-clade relationships, but it's also been a few decades since that fell apart—I think close to six now—and a few years since Cress, Tule, and Dry Grass formally made it a triad, so I'm used to it by now."

"Well, fair enough. Everything else was just boring, then?"

"Pretty much. Good food, dates with Dry Grass and Cress, playing around with music."

"And what's the practical fallout for you?" she asked.

"You mean in terms of Dry Grass?"

She nodded.

"I don't know yet. I'm still kind of split on my feelings. Having memories of her as an acquaintance clashing with memories of her as a partner is still too stark a difference." I snorted. "Not to mention this all feeling like a distraction from all of the other problems at hand. Worrying about what she means to me feels like energy not being spent on trying to figure out what happened."

"You're all such workaholics."

"Guilty."

She grinned, reached over to take up my hand and kiss the backs of my fingers, one by one. "Well, whatever. I trust you'll overthink things and then come to a conclusion after a lot of bitching, and we'll keep talking about it."

"Right," I said, laughing. "Of course we will."

I spent the rest of the evening at home, lounging on the couch while Hanne slouched over my lap and asked me to play with her hair. While I did so, we both focused on our own thoughts or internal work. I spent much of that time in idle sensorium conversations, trying to get a better picture of the state of things.

Sedge had gone to sleep for a bit, but as she woke up, she

caught me up on news from when she'd been dozing. The politicians had drafted a letter explaining what had happened on a technological level to post on the largest of the perisystem feeds. Much of it was information that we'd gained from the AVEC session with the phys-side techs, explaining that nearly 1% of the System had been wiped out and deemed unrecoverable, that there had been a mass crashing event, that the world was assumed stable and the issue had been patched.

Conspicuously missing was any mention of CPV, any mention that everyone—all 2.3 trillion of us—had crashed, or that messages were being gated and censored. Sedge explained that the last had included some gentle untruths. Rather than this being a political effort, this had been phrased as "slowly bringing Lagrange up to full capacity". It wasn't wrong, *per se,* they really were working on bringing the feeds up to full capacity; it's just that the problem was political rather than technical.

Dry Grass, in our own conversations, explained that there were already rumors flying about, and that these were being subtly steered by Odists, Jonases, Selena, and, to a lesser extent, what she called 'the opposition party', a group of clades led by Debarre who had settled into an uneasy truce with the others some decades back. Rumors were being nudged away from "an attack by the Artemisians" and towards "solar flares or a power failure".

Rush, meanwhile, had latched onto Serene and talked her into letting ver follow along as she took a tally of all of her sims and those of her friends, seeing what remained and what had been marked as abandoned. While ve had always been one for exploring, seeing ver lock onto an interest this hard was new. Ve admitted quite quickly that it was something of a coping mechanism, something to do that wasn't fret about what had happened to our world.

The longest conversation I had that night was with Lily. I had initially been surprised by how chatty she was, but the surprise mellowed as she went on.

"I just want to make sure that all of my grouchiness isn't getting in the way of me keeping up to date," she said. *"Dry Grass has...well, it's actually been really cool, all that she's doing, so I definitely respect her."*

"You just don't want to be around her?" I asked.

There was a shrug, felt rather than seen. *"I guess not. It's just hard for me to let go of, even if I'm committed to at least trying to do so."* She sighed. *"But yeah, I don't want me hiding away to mean I'm not kept in the loop."*

"Well, Sedge–"

"I don't mean the logistics, Reed." I could hear the smirk in her words. *"Or not just the logistics—Sedge has been keeping me up to date, yeah—but just keeping up with the rest of you. Cress and Tule are glued to her side, which, fair enough. Sedge has found her in with the rest of the politicians through her. You've been hanging out with her through Sedge. Rush is off gallivanting with some other Odist..."*

I sighed, steeled myself. *"Well, yeah, fair enough. I've also been spending time with her because I got pulled into being a bit of management for everyone else, and because I kept Tule's merge."*

"You did? God, now you're going to wind up glued to her side, too," she replied after a moment of parsing out the ramifications. She laughed, though I couldn't judge just how earnest it was. *"But hey, it is what it is, right? This is why I want to keep up with you all. I'm out here trying to check in on friends, too, I don't want to wind up losing sight of the clade."*

"Yeah, I get that. I really appreciate it, too."

We chatted for a while longer before I noticed that Hanne had started to doze off, and I nudged us both to bed for the night.

My dreams were scattered, disorganized. In some of these scattered images, everyone who had gone missing suddenly returned, but changed. Sometimes they were mute. Sometimes they never smiled. Sometimes they were completely normal, but missing some integral memory, something that made them *them.*

Other images throughout the night veered away from fear

and into grief. Marsh was gone. They were *gone.* There was a hole in the world that would never be patched, and my dreams lingered on that lack. In my dreams, there was a literal hole in the world, a half-sensed maelstrom, and we could do nothing to avoid it. It was in the way of wherever we most needed to go.

The morning greeted me with a rising sun, another mug of coffee, and a queue of messages to work through.

These last fell into three camps. Several were messages from friends that were well-wishes for the work at hand, offers of condolences for the loss of Marsh, suggestions for things to try. These were all shelved for later. At some point, I'd have the spoons to respond to them, but certainly not now.

The second camp were ones surrounding the grief and loss of others. These were messages from friends that relayed stories of their own losses. Partners disappearing mid-conversation. Friends no longer sitting across from them at the bar. Games interrupted, now, apparently, never to be completed. These I mostly passed on to Sedge. My emotional bandwidth was running thin. Too many dreams. Too many strange floods of stranger emotions over the last few days.

The final camp I eventually tagged 'work'. These were a handful of messages, mostly from Sedge and Dry Grass, that pertained to plans for the rest of the day, items on various checklists that they wanted help ticking off.

I read these more slowly. Where there were questions, I answered as I could or, if not, delegated to the rest of the clade or other friends. Where my own attention was requested, I gave my opinions as I had them.

I'd apparently been tapped as one of the organizers, a sort of liaison between those involved, one who, as one of the messages hinted, had his shit together in a way that the rest of the clade did not. I counted myself flattered, though it also rankled that that had become my defining feature while I felt like I was only flailing, trying to pin down emotions while kicking myself for not doing more to directly address the clade's own problems.

How could I be a manager when I couldn't even figure out my own problems?

I put a halt to that line of thinking by repeatedly telling myself that my problems were now almost universal, that the feelings around Marsh being missing were now feelings that were being felt by millions, if not billions, of people all over Lagrange.

After finishing my message triage, my coffee, and the making of the bed, I stepped out of the bedroom, only to find the rest of the house empty. A note on the table from Hanne explained that she was meeting up with yet more friends from her construct artistry group.

I sighed.

No distractions, no reason to stick around, nowhere I wanted to visit. Might as well head back to Marsh's study, one part of the *de facto* headquarters for much of the response to this mass crashing event, and catch up with those who had taken charge.

"Reed," Dry Grass said, bowing informally and immediately leading me gently by the elbow out of the room, explaining as she went. "We are preparing for a meeting coming up in about half an hour. Messages are being sent from the study. I would not wish to distract the senders. Please step to Workroom#22a239ec in the future."

"Oh? This representative sample meeting?"

She nodded. "Yes. I am pleased you are here; I would like the Marshans well represented, as well."

"Sure, if you say so," I said, shrugging. "I'm still not really clear on what exactly it is."

"It is intended to be a sample of clades from across the System that have been hit in various ways. You are here, with your root instance gone. We are here, to represent the founders who have been hit to a lesser extent, yet who have experience being without a root instance. Andréa C. Mason#Central of the CERES clade will be there. They lost nearly seventy thousand instances."

"Jesus," I murmured. "I remember you mentioning that on the first day, and I still can't quite get over that number."

"Neither can I," she said, gaze drifting down and to the side. "This corruptive event hit everyone differently, and with such numbers as we have here on Lagrange, some clades were bound to get hit far harder than others. Debarre will be there as well, both as a political figure as well as a member of a clade of about one hundred that lost zero instances."

"So it's just a bunch of clades getting together to talk about what happened?"

She shrugged. "What happened. What to do. What to ask for."

I frowned. "'Ask for'?"

Dry Grass guided the two of us through the workroom, picking up more instances as we went with a gentle tap to the shoulder. "I do not mean to speak of reparations, though that may at some point come into play. What we might ask for are reassurances. We might want fixes. We may want greater visibility into the day-to-day running of the System. Harvey from SERG may request–"

"SERG?"

"System Emergency Response Group, one of the many, *many* groups of systechs. He may request greater access to the lower levels of the System's functionalities." She smiled faintly, tapping one last person—Debarre, as it turned out—on the shoulder. "I am having to ramp up on all of this quite quickly. I stepped away from my role as systech a long, *long* time ago, with a long-lived up-tree taking over my role."

"They can't merge down?"

"They no longer exist, Reed."

"Oh," I said dumbly, averting my gaze.

She rested a hand on my shoulder. "It is okay," she said, smiling reassuringly. "Or, well, it is not okay, but I understand. You did not know. I am dealing with the loss by burying myself in work. On that note, let us join the others, yes? I have ACLs enough to set up the room better."

I watched as Dry Grass got the room ready for this smaller conference. Without so many Odists, Jonases, Selenas, Debarres, Marshans, and however many others, there was no need for the presentation setup, and so those tables that had been set up before the stage were instead joined together. Dry Grass released them from their stolidly stationary positions and pushed them together. Merging like drops of mercury, the dozen or so smaller tables became one large circle. This was then corralled with gentle tugs of her hands to a much smaller shape, remaining a perfect circle. Chairs trailed after the edge of the table like eager puppies, merging together in similar fashion whenever crowding grew too great.

The next change was to the square platform of the AVEC stage. The light-gray material that made it up was similarly shrunk down with nudges from her foot. The table was given a gentle push so that it settled just over the edge of the stage.

I'd had little to do with sim manipulation beyond simply expanding or reducing bounds, and almost nothing to do with object manipulation beyond pulling items off the exchange. That had always been Hanne's game, and while I'd watched her work plenty, it had never been so casually exhausted as Dry Grass's manipulation here. She worked with such surety, such tiredness on her face, that her age seemed all the more evident. Of course someone more than three centuries old, someone who had spent nearly all of that time here on the System, would be able to move through this world with such ease.

"Alright," she said, flumping down into one of the chairs across from the AVEC stage. "I think we are all here. While I would obviously prefer you stay, it is not a requirement. If you need to duck out, feel free to do so. We are just waiting on Günay and we can get going."

About twenty people had shown up. It didn't seem to be twenty clades—there were two Odists, after all, with Dry Grass and another from the eighth stanza, Why Ask Questions When

The Answers Will Not Help—but the audience remained diverse. Only about half appeared to be human of some sort, with the Marshans, Odists, and Jonases accounting for most of those. I suppose it made sense, given the Odists' social circle, but that didn't quite tally with what I knew of Jonas's role in the leadership of the System. He didn't strike me as a furry.

When asked over a sensorium message, Dry Grass replied, *"The eighth stanza has been slowly tamping down on Jonas's role over the years. He has not been nearly as grounded as he once was. Prime quit in grand fashion some years back, and the rest have long since recognized that."* She cast a slight smile in my direction, adding, *"Too singularly focused, perhaps. All work and no play makes Jonas lose his fucking marbles."*

I stifled a laugh. It probably shouldn't have been funny, but the absurdity of the comment clashed just right with the mirrored absurdity of the situation. Probably best not to laugh in front of everyone.

Just in time, too, as there was a polite chime from the AVEC stage, and Günay faded into being. She was clearly sitting at her own table far different from ours, but some trick of the AVEC software quickly scaled her to the point where it looked as though she was sitting there with us. The opacity was even turned all the way up so that she was just as present as the rest of the attendees.

"Hey friends," she said, waving. "Wasn't expecting an invitation for just me."

Answers Will Not Help gave a hint of a bow without standing. Her voice seemed to sit just shy of laughter, though whether that laughter was teasing or convivial was difficult to say. "What can we say? We like you." She waved around the table. "We have a group of representatives from a variety of clades. I think you met a good chunk of us yesterday, yes?"

Günay nodded. "Yep. At least, I remember Dry Grass and Jonas and Debarre and Selena." Her eyes darted around those seated at the table, likely reading through name tags. "Answers

Will Not Help...I've heard your name, at least."

"Right, I bet you have," Answers Will Not Help said with a smirk. "We are a notorious group, yes? For those you have not met, we have selected a group of clades among friends who we believe to be both good people and representative of the various ways we have been affected."

The systech nodded again. "Alright."

"Reed, he/him, and Sedge, she/her, of the Marsh clade lost their root instance, a loss of 14%. We Odists have lost 2% of our number, including two lines of the Ode and a few long-lived up-tree instances. The Jonas clade has lost approximately 3% of their number. Andréa C. Mason, she/her, and Harvey, he/him, of the CERES clade have been hit particularly hard," she said, gesturing to an anthropomorphic coyote and goat across the table, "with Andréa's subclade losing 99.983% of their number, totalling about 70,000 instances destroyed."

There was a long moment of silence before Günay whispered, "What the fuck."

Answers Will Not Help continued smoothly. "Debarre, on the other hand, lost zero instances for a total of 0%. Obvious, yes, but I believe that will do well to illustrate the apparent random nature of this event from our end, yes?"

Günay nodded, expression lingering in shock even as the Odist continued around the table with introductions and percentages lost.

"Günay," Jonas Fa said once this had wrapped up. "Jakub and I had a pleasant little chat and, if you'll cheek, you'll see that NDAs have been lifted."

She frowned, blinked a few times, then said cautiously, "Okay."

"He also confirmed that this was an intentional attack on Lagrange. Some sort of deliberate widespread CPV event."

Silence fell around the table. Each of us processed this in our own way, whether that was the shock from the clades who had just been roped into the meeting to the exhaustion on Dry

Grass's face, the wariness on Günay's features to the almost smug satisfaction in Jonas's. He looked to be almost purring, as though springing this information on everyone present was a joy in its own right.

"So, now that NDAs are out of the picture and we've torn Mr. Strzepek a new one," he continued after a moment. "Can you tell us what happened?"

"Uh...hold on. I'm catching up too," Günay said hoarsely. She reached out of view of the AVEC recorder to grab a bottle of water, taking a long drink. She seemed to be buying time, organizing her thoughts, consulting her HUD. "Promise you won't tear *me* a new one?"

I was caught off guard by the humor, but many of the others around the table chuckled.

"I will promise no such thing," Answers Will Not Help said, giggling.

Dry Grass elbowed her in the side. "Do not listen to her, she is a snot. You are fine, my dear. No tearing, promise."

The systech chuckled nervously, nodding. "Well, alright. Then yeah, Jonas has it. As far as we can tell, there was a sort of CPV bomb set off right at midnight on New Year's Eve, 2399 which caused a full crash of all instances in less than a minute. With the crash, there was a spike in resource usage and then a precipitous drop."

"I'm still confused about that," Debarre said. "I thought CPV had to be tailored to a single instance or any of their forks that hadn't individuated much. How is it someone was able to blast the whole System?"

"We didn't understand it either. Hell, we didn't really understand how CPV worked up until recently. It *shouldn't* work. It shouldn't even be possible in the first place." Günay made a few gestures, doubtless reorganizing some notes in her HUD. "But whatever. Someone figured it out well enough to generalize it and took out everyone on Lagrange."

"And who is this 'someone'?" Selena asked. "The phys-side

feeds are being ungated, but it's a firehose of information to sort through to try and find anything of use."

"Yeah, I think they—the System Consortium—clamped down pretty tight. I'm just learning about this myself, since I just got access to the files a few hours ago and news from Earth's been censored. Let's see..." She frowned, continued in the tone of someone reading aloud, "Okay. The Our Brightest Lights Collective claimed responsibility for the attack exactly thirty seconds *before* it occurred via a message to every executive on the System Consortium board, as well as several major feeds, all of which were censored before being made public. The OBLC named the mechanism, provided a detailed timeline of events, and offered a list of names of individuals—or"individuals", I guess—and their roles in the execution of this plan. All one hundred members of the collective have been apprehended, though in the past year, two have managed to end their own lives."

Answers Will Not Help spoke up during a break in the recitation. "Is there more information on this collective? Are they conservatives? How tight is their integration? Do they mimic clades like the old-style collectives?"

"Oh, uh, one moment, I'll look that up once I'm finished," Günay said. "It goes on to say that, through investigation, members from some other collectives and several individuals besides were implicated and were also detained. During one of the System restarts between the Century Attack—as we've been calling it—and now, this information was confirmed by having an investigator sys-side fork rapidly to gather information and take action where needed. They were provided with emergency global ACLs and, once they found the perpetrator, they locked them in an unpopulated airlocked implementation of the System."

"The System was restarted more than once?" Debarre asked, taken aback.

She nodded. "About thirty times, I think. We had three shifts working on it for more than a year, remember. We just rolled memories back each time."

"But wouldn't the bomb or whatever just go off again every time?"

"It did the first two times, yeah," Günay said with a shrug. "Until we patched out the CPV vulnerability."

Dry Grass let out a surprised laugh. "Wait, you *patched out CPV? Entirely?*"

"Well, yeah, we kind of had to, otherwise we'd either have to reconstruct everyone with a memory of crashing, or the same thing would keep happening every time the perpetrator was reconstructed. It took us a good four months of total System downtime working all three shifts to get it done."

Jonas Fa, one of the two Jonases sitting at the table, had been steadily frowning more and more through the conversation, resting his chin on folded hands. Finally, he sat up straight and looked to Answers Will Not Help. "Hey."

The Odist let out a groan and kneaded the heels of her palms against her eyes for a moment before leaning back in her chair. "Fuck it. Why not? Might as fucking well."

Both forked, and the up-tree instances stepped around the table to face each other. Jonas Fa summoned up a small pocket knife.

Answers Will Not Help stiffened where she stood, teeth clenched.

Explaining as he unfolded the knife with a snick, Jonas Fa gestured expansively around the room. "So, if you've read any of the scandalous works about us, you can probably guess that we all have CPV mixed up for each other. It's nothing as grand as the stories make it sound like, though; just a way for us to keep each other in check and occasionally...play around."

Before anyone had a chance to ask any further questions, he swiped out with the knife, catching Answers Will Not Help in the cheek, leaving a gash that quickly welled up with blood. There was no noise from the Odist for a few moments before she finally let out a shaky sigh.

There was, notably, no crashing. She simply dabbed at her

cheek, inspected the blood on her fingertips, grinned wildly to Jonas, and said, "Oh, we are *so* fucked," and then quit, followed shortly by the second Jonas.

Günay, like many of the rest of us, had pushed herself away from whatever table she had been sitting at, looking horrified at the casual violence before her. "What the fuck?" she whispered for the second time that day.

"There is still an outstanding conversation about this collective, Günay," the remaining instance of Answers Will Not Help said breezily. "Can you tell us more about them?"

The systech stared, mouth open, for a moment, then slowly pulled herself back to her desk. "Uh...right," she mumbled, hiding some complex emotion by taking another long drink of water. "The OBLC describe themselves as fundamentalists, in the sense of returning humanity to its fundamentals, and pride themselves on very tight integration."

"'Integration'?" Debarre asked, tilting his head, a particularly animalistic gesture on his musteline features. "I haven't kept up on collectives at all. They don't make any sense to me."

"Groups of people who aim to live as a hive-mind of sorts," Selena explained. "They use tech from their implants to force alignment in ideals, or even just nudge complete thoughts into place for everyone. It's almost a religious thing for them."

"It *is* a religion thing for many," Answers Will Not Help added. "The ideals they try to live into tend to be high-minded conceptualizations of God or life or the way things 'should' be. It used to be that they would try to mimic clades in terms of structure, but their idea of what a clade is was batshit insane."

Selena nodded, picking up once more. "The clade analogy was far more common before AVEC. Answers Will Not Help asking that is a way of asking"are they old and batty or young and insane?""

Günay, who had been watching the explanation with something akin to amusement, said, "A lot of that is borne out of just not having a clue how things work, sys-side. I'm a systech, and you don't make sense to me at all."

"Goes both ways, trust me," Debarre said, laughing. "None of this makes sense to me, either, but then I'm the second oldest person in the room."

She grinned, nodding. "Well, even if you don't make any sense, I still like you all."

"We like you, too, Günay," Dry Grass said, stretching her arms over her head. "It is nice to have someone to talk to who is not just trying to keep the bureaucratic definition of peace. Those conversations are for Jonas and Debarre and so on."

"Unfortunately," Debarre grumbled.

"I would like to return to the topic of us still being alive people," she continued, smirking at the weasel. "So the System was restarted thirty or so times in the year-and-change we do not remember. CPV was patched out entirely. A collective tried to kill 2.3 trillion people. We are only just now getting access to extrasystem communications. What have Castor and Pollux been told about this?"

"Right," Günay said, sitting up straighter. "We told them at first that there was a communications issue, and then expanded on that later, once the scale became evident. We said that there had been a massive outage at the Lagrange station, that there were no deaths or anything, but–"

An uncomfortable murmur interrupted her.

"But...uh, well, we mostly said that Lagrange itself was down."

"And what did they say?"

"Well, it's hard to have a conversation with people almost four months away," she hedged. "So I guess we drip-fed information over time. I don't know the specifics; I really am just a systech."

Dry Grass smiled kindly. "Of course, Günay. What did they say in return?"

"To us? A lot of panicked messages requesting as many updates we could give them. Of course, by then, the messages were eight months out of date, and we'd been sending them hourly updates on the status of Lagrange for quite a while. They were broken down into buckets based on content: personal, political, technical, and vague threats." She smiled wryly. "I only really know all of that because I was privy to the technical bucket. Systechs on both of the LVs teamed up and started throwing ideas at us as fast as they could. They were mostly not any help, given the delay, but some of them were useful—especially the Artemisians. They brought casualties down from 15%."

I started to do the math in my head, but Harvey blurted out, "345 *billion!* Holy shit! You've gotta be fucking kidding me."

Günay shrugged helplessly. "We were doing the best we could from phys-side. They had the benefit of being sys-side, and also working without phys-side intervention for like...seventy-five years, you know?"

Shaking his head, Harvey said, "Still, that's fucking wild."

"Were there any other changes that were made?" Dry Grass asked. "You patched out CPV, learned plenty more about instance recovery, managed to turn back memories for trillions of people..."

"Yeah, uh...there's a whole laundry list, one second."

We waited as patiently as we could while the systech tallied up various changes.

"I cannot believe it has taken them this long to patch out CPV," Dry Grass sent Sedge and I.

"That's the one that got a bunch of your cocladists, right?" I asked.

"Well, 'got' is perhaps not a great word for it. Qoheleth was assassinated using CPV loaded into a syringe and a hundred or so instances of Sasha, back when she was True Name, were murdered by Jonas Prime," she sent. *"But also it is something that some of us have used intentionally for various reasons. Dear, Also, The Tree That Was Felled, our very weird instance artist, included it quite often in its exhibitions, and What Gifts We Give We Give In Death tried using it in some games they were designing, but it was seen as too transgressive and was roundly shut down. Answers Will Not Help seemed...not too put out by that lit-*

tle display"

Sedge stifled a giggle beside me. *"You guys are all weird."*

Dry Grass smiled proudly over at us. *"Our finest trait, my–"*

She cut off as Günay cleared her throat. "Alright, I have a list of changes", she said, and began reading off a list that appeared in translucent letters against the front of the AVEC stage area. "CPV was patched out; ACL permissions were hardened for sim isolation, allowing for locking cladists *in* sims as well as out of them; storage was optimized; some physical components were replaced, no clue which; AVEC improvements; Ansible improvements; merging improvements; and systech tools refined. There's a slew of others we're waiting on confirmation from you all before implementing: improvements to perisystem clade listing that would provide better statistics on who all is extant, which I guess has privacy ramifications; a solution for splitting the physical components of the System hardware was successfully tested, but that will mean production and deployment time, as well as downtime; limited per-sim Artemis-style skew; and some political tools to reduce anarchy."

"'*Reduce* anarchy?'" Jonas Fa said, snorting. "Fuck off with that."

She held up her hands defensively. "Hey, like I said, it's just a change, and I'm just a tech."

"I am sorry, Günay," Dry Grass said. "You are right that that is a conversation for another time. Tell us about these ACL improvements and merging improvements. Those are likely to be the most relevant to everyone here."

"Right," she said, frowning. "Well, the ACL improvements allow locking cladists within sims. We needed this to contain the perpetrator as quickly as possible, but left it in place. We came up with a suggested protocol with the ethics committee, though, that would mean a two step approval process—phys-side and sys-side—as well as a mandatory waiting period. It's disabled for now, but we can re-enable it whenever.

"The merge improvements involve finer-grained conflict

management, which is more just an efficiency thing; we're told nothing changed subjectively. We also enabled cross-tree merging."

A stunned silence followed.

"Holy shit," Selena murmured. "Cross-tree merging?"

"It seemed like it wouldn't be that big of a deal."

"It really fucking is," Answers Will Not Help said, and despite the hint of joviality that seemed permanently lodged in her tone, her expression was frighteningly serious. "Especially if there is no limit on how far diverged the cross-tree instances are."

"There isn't, no," Günay said cautiously. "Why's it a big deal?"

"Shitloads of reasons," Jonas Ko said. "It changes the nature of a clade a way from a strict tree to a cloud, a gestalt. Have you published this anywhere yet?"

She shook her head.

"Good. Don't."

"Uh...alright," Günay said. "I'll bump that up to admin, though. I don't have control over that."

"Alright. I'll tear Jakub another one, then," Jonas Ko said, smirking.

Günay winced. "Glad I'm not on admin," she said under her breath. "Is there anything else, though? I gotta get back to work. Shame, I like you all more than work."

"We like you too," Dry Grass said, smiling. "If you ever want to upload, you have a place up here set for you."

"I may have to before long. I like you guys, but you've made my life hell with admin," she said, laughing. "They'll either fire me or promote me within the year, just you watch."

"Well, you'll have a place on SERG," Harvey said, grinning lopsidedly. "If you're not sick of dealing with this shit, that is."

Once we'd made our goodbyes and the AVEC call had ended, we sat in silence for nearly a minute. Finally, Sedge said, "Well, holy shit."

Laughter around the table.

"Holy shit, indeed, my dear," Dry Grass said, scooting her chair closer to rest her head on Sedge's shoulder. "I need a fucking nap."

Sedge laughed and patted her shoulder amiably. "You and me both."

§

The next two days passed in relative peace.

There were a few more meetings with phys-side, usually with just Günay, but sometimes Jakub or another administrator peeked in. They all seemed to be rather cowed by the sys-side administration, such as it was. I chalked this up to the fact—later confirmed by Dry Grass—that there had been other talks beside between the latent Temporary Administrative Council and the System Consortium. Talks which had been far more tense.

Although phys-side remained in control of a few aspects, they had quickly ceded the rest to us once more, including ungating communications between Lagrange and Earth.

None of us knew anyone phys-side. We didn't have the luxury of communications separated by just over two seconds as opposed to the eight-month round trip to the LVs. We didn't have AVEC to help us out at all. All of our friends had either uploaded or died without having done so, and none of our family cared enough to talk to their grandson with however many 'greats' preceded that relationship.

Hanne, however was in yet a different situation. While her parents had long since died, her siblings had not, though by now they were quite old. Their communications were tearful reconnections, hasty requests for information on just what the fuck had happened.

As for that particular question, we had the chance to learn quite a bit more.

The process of restarting Lagrange included a new wrinkle: every time they restarted, more and more instances seemed to be unrecoverable. Even with the help that the LVs had provided in drastically reducing the number of corrupted instances, each time the System was brought up, the number of truly lost instances seemed to increase. There was a core of about twenty billion that remained unrecoverable no matter what, but the number climbed by tens or hundreds of millions with each restart, with different instances among the remainder, raising fears about future downtime and driving phys-side ideas regarding robustness and splitting the System hardware into separate physical components.

Dry Grass had been particularly affected by this. Her up-tree, In The Wind, seemed to have been instrumental in helping return functionality, and yet had not manged to make it through the last three restarts.

On hearing this news, she disappeared for nearly twelve hours, all of her instances merging back down into one singular self. When she returned, she at least looked more well-rested than she had in days, explaining that she had spent nearly all of that time in bed.

She and I also started spending more time together, with the next two lunches being just the two of us together. While I had memories of learning all about her through Tule, she was keen on learning about me in turn. She wanted to know what my take was on why Marsh had uploaded, explaining that both Cress and Tule had differing thoughts on the matter. She wanted to know why it was that I had slipped back into that transmasculine identity. She wanted to know how it was that Hanne and I had found each other, had fallen in love.

I mostly wanted to know—though I never asked—how it was that I—that part of me from before the merge—was falling so rapidly for her in turn. I turned that question over and over in my head, leaning on it for comfort whenever thoughts of Marsh struggled to overwhelm me.

When at last the group of representative clades met up again, we were joined by yet another Odist, I Cannot Stop Myself From Speaking, a bobcat furry who moved silently on soft-padded paws, whose voice was quiet and yet demanding of attention.

Also joining us on phys-side were Günay and Jakub, along with one of the information security officers, a dour person named en4, who introduced themself as a member of The London Cohort of New Zealots, a conservative collective from whom the Our Brightest Lights Collective had split some decades prior. LCNZ had apparently proven itself to not be conservative enough, and the far more militant OBLC had left to join a coalition of fundamentalist collectives and like-minded individuals in order to orchestrate the Century Attack.

"The LCNZ sternly and unquestionably disavows the action of the OBLC," they began. "Their actions are truly reprehensible, and despite our generally distant relationship with the System, we harbor no ill-will to any of you, even the Ode and Jonas clades."

"Even us?" Answers Will Not Help asked, a sneer painted on her face, voice dripping with sarcasm. "*Even us?* And what is it that we have ever done to you, my dear?"

Their face remained impassive. "We, like the original Zealot Cohorts, hold a rather poor opinion of those named in the Bălans' *An Expanded History of Our World.* We acknowledge that it was a sensationalized work, as expressed in the Bălans' own words in *Individuation and Reconciliation,* and those of Sasha in her *Ode,* but it is hard to let go of prejudices."

Answers Will Not Help scoffed.

"We stand by our earlier statement," en4 said, offering a hint of a bow from their seat. They were calling in from Earth, so their reactions remained on a delay, which took some getting used to. "We harbor no ill-will, we just do not like the manipulative tactics used by the eighth stanza in particular."

"We will come back to that," she replied coldly. "We will have words."

"So be it."

"We have spoken with the quarantined instance of the attacker several times," Jakub said, picking up the conversation smoothly. "They remain alive in this instance of the restart, although in previous restarts, they quit immediately on realizing that the bomb failed to detonate."

"Why do they remain alive this iteration?"

"We turned off their ability to quit," Günay said.

"That's possible?" Harvey asked. "Why the fuck would that even be a thing?"

"Oh, it's always been possible," she replied, shrugging. "It's another one of those privacy concerns, I guess. We moved them to the DMZ used for testing the LVs, the one that turned into Convergence on Castor."

"That is why I am here," Speaking said, standing and bowing to the attendees at the table. Not even her clothing rustled, no sound of fabric on fur. "I have been the sys-side representative interviewing them."

"Yes," Jakub said. "One representative each: Information Security Officer en4 and Speaking."

"Can you tell us more about them?" Sedge asked. "I want to know who would even do something like this."

Speaking nodded, returning to her seat. "Yes. They go by 8-stanza-1, a reference to the Ode from which we take our names. Specifically, it is a reference to The Only Time I Know My True Name Is When I Dream, who became Sasha when she was forced away from her role in the sys-side political landscape. A change, I will note, which the OBLC rejects. In fact their whole collective refers to the Ode. This is why they limit their membership to one hundred members."

"Wild," Debarre murmured. "Y'all are weird, but that's way, *way* weirder."

"Weird indeed," Jonas Fa said, staring intently at en4.

They smiled blandly. "Yes, we took inspiration for our naming scheme from your clade."

"Fucking gross."

Smile unwavering, en4 said, "We have no comment on that decision at this time."

"Why do you even work with the System if you hate us so much?"

"Because 2.3 trillion people live on the System," they said. "That is 2.3 trillion lives. We agree on that, yes?"

Nods around the table.

"2.3 trillion lives, then. 2.3 trillion lives that were taken from us here on Earth. 2.3 trillion minds in almost 40 billion uploads that might have lived full lives here among us phys-side. We resent that they were, and yet our only recourse is—*must be*— to keep them alive, to ensure that they at least remain among the living in some form or another." Their gaze drifted to the three present Odists. "We, too, desire nothing but the stability and continuity of the System, just for different reasons. This instance of us is an ISO specifically to live up to our own principles."

All three of the Odists nodded, expressions varying from serious to vaguely disgusted.

"Regardless of our opinions of each other," Speaking said, picking up the prior thread. "Interviewing 8-stanza-1 was a frustrating experience. I am told that I was the instance sent to discover their presence, relying on tools developed by my downtree instance, I Have Sight But Cannot See. I have no memory of this, but it does sound like something that I would do."

"What about it was frustrating?" Selena asked.

"They are...emotional. Very emotional. Understanding their voice through their sobs or wild laughter was difficult. All the same, they are a very grounded individual. They speak concisely and with no disregulation in their speech." She shrugged. "They just speak in coherent, well-formed sentences and paragraphs about untrue things. Their every word is part of a lie. Their very existence is built up around lies. They breathe lies out on every breath."

"They are very tightly integrated," en4 said. "They all speak thus. This is why they split away from us some decades ago. It was a mutual decision."

"You kicked them out?" Jonas Ko asked.

They shrugged eloquently.

"Despite these lies," Speaking continued, "I was able to glean plenty through apophasis and aposiopesis. All I needed to do was assume that every statement was false. ISO en4 confirmed much of this from the LCNZ's view. They—the OBLC—differ from the LCNZ in the sense that they believe each of those lives is a life lost, rather than a life preserved. They believe that the lives here on the System are, and I quote, "shadows and negations of souls". They believe that clades are negations and that up-tree instances are shadows."

"Yes," en4 said. "They believe that each of these negations negates a life phys-side, and thus the only way they could even bring into balance, much less overcome, the negation offered by the System is to destroy it. They hoped that by destroying you, they would give those who remained phys-side a chance at heaven."

"You said there were a group of collectives that worked together on this, though, right?" Selena asked.

"Collectives and individuals, yes."

"Did they all believe this sort of thing?"

They shook their head. "Not at all. Many of them struggled with the effects that the uploading of individuals had on worsening the climate catastrophe."

"That's not on us, though."

"Is it not?" they asked mildly. "For a while, it was quite popular for individuals to upload in order to work on the climate catastrophe, and yet many of them would disappear shortly after doing so, falling into new habits, new friend groups. It is only in past few decades that the pace of climate change was reversed."

"Yes, but hasn't much of that changed thanks to the Artemis data dump?" Boiling Maw dos Riãos, another of the furries sitting at the table asked. She was some sort of mustelid, though larger and far more thickly-furred than Debarre. A fisher cat, the System informed me through a whiff of distraction. I pushed it down in an attempt to focus. "Most of that effort took place sys-side as well."

"I will answer, but after this, we should return to the topic of the Century Attack," en4 replied. "Many of these collectives—of which the LCNZ is one—believe that this is a side effect of the Artemisians' convergence, rather than any effort from those who uploaded in order to help. We would say, "Are we to rely on aliens to solve every problem? Ought we not also work our-selves?""

"That's not–" Boiling Maw started, anger painting her face. She paused, took a deep breath, and settled back into her seat, sulking. "Right. Moving on."

Speaking bowed respectfully to the Riã. "Yes, though per-haps there will be time for a separate conversation on this mat-ter at another time. For now, 8-stanza-1 spoke of these negations and shadows and of their reasoning, and while I am left to guess at the negations of their own statements, I am confident of at least their reasoning for attacking Lagrange, thanks to ISO en4's confirmations. They wished to reopen the gates of heaven to hu-manity. I also believe that those other collectives and individu-als who worked behind the scenes on this attack had their own reasons, and as the investigation continues, both with me work-ing sys-side and Answers Will Not Help coordinating with phys-side, we will learn more and publish the results to the feeds."

Dry Grass frowned. "Are you sure that that is wise? Does the entirety of Lagrange need to know these reasons?"

"The eighth stanza and Jonas clade have made their decision. I do not care."

"Why not?"

"Because it is out of my hands. It is outside my bailiwick. That is their role. It is their responsibility to manage spin." She sat down once more, movements speaking of a barely contained energy. "I am the tool and have served my purpose. It is my job now to mourn my own losses as I may."

"We're working on it," Jonas Ko said soothingly after a moment's silent acknowledgement. "The goal is to spin it so as to discourage anything like this going forward, not give anyone ideas."

"That was going to be my next question," Dry Grass said. "If there are other sympathetic uploads or anyone else phys-side, would it not be dangerous to publish that information?"

"We are on it, my dear," Answers Will Not Help said, laughing.

"So," I said after the conversation drifted into silence. "What do we do now?"

"Mourn," Dry Grass said. "Work and mourn."

Interlude

<u>Nasturtiums</u>
Madison Rye Progress

Beholden — 2401

To: Beholden To The Heat Of The Lamps of the Ode clade
(EYES-ONLY)
From: Beholden To The Music Of The Spheres of her own clade
On: systime 277+48

Beholden To The Heat Of The Lamps,

It has been seven days. One week, I promised myself. I would wait one week while I watched the System limp back to life. I would wait a week and see what all was being done, what could be done to save the lost.

It has been seven days of increasing surety that those who have perished in this event are gone for good. And if they indeed are gone for good then that means my beloved is gone with them.

Do you remember when we came into being, A Finger Curled and I? It was the night of that awful monologue, that little joke of a scene where I was set to read some truly embarrassing lines. "We all play our parts. Some are towel boys and some lewd doctors…" I could remember the rest, but I do not want to. That line sticking in my craw is enough. I was a skunk that night because I did not want my face associated with those words. Burroughs! Christ.

It was awful. It was delightful.

I declared that it was necessary for me to get a drink, that I needed to wash the taste of those words off of my tongue and replace my grimaces with giggles. We went to that cute bar with outdoor tables and fairy lights strung above. Strange drinks and edamame. You and A Finger Pointing fell into earnest conversation about this and that as you so often do. There was love in your eyes as always, even back when such was too taboo to show in public. Another benefit of a skunk face: hide that love from nosy passers-by. Our human face always was too expressive.

It is too expressive now. It is full of tears and grief. It is full of despair. I cannot muster the energy required to be angry. I cannot pull up a smile from nothing. She is gone and she is never coming back. Yes, she merged back down, but as far as I know, she last did so some months ago, back at the beginning of winter. Yes, A Finger Pointing could fork once more into some new approximation of A Finger Curled, but that would not be her. She would be missing our sweet nothings and earnest conversations from the last few months. She would have decades of time — is it more than two centuries already? — of her life with you, so many memories of the past to talk about of which I would have no idea. She merged down, yes? And I never did.

It is full of grief. It is full of despair.

It was at that bar in the midst of our earnest discussion of taboos and friends. You assured me there was a shift in the air, that True Name, so staunch a personality within the clade, was happy for our relationship, but that she still encouraged our secrecy so as not to rock the boat for all of us, thanks to Jonas, but that perhaps soon, soon we would be able to hold hands in public, give each other little kisses and let those outside our stanza bear witness to what started as self love and blossomed into romance.

I acknowledge, of course, her relative aromancy, but for *me* it was romance, and for her it was still love.

We talked of just how it was that she alternated between human and skunk every time she forked. An affectation, yes, but a fondness for the past that I always admired in her

We talked of the past, of the open mic nights we hosted in

The Crown Pub for a while, AwDae and I reciting monologues and dialogues. Erina's awful song. And then there were only three performing the next week, only one the week after that, and then the open mic nights stopped.

We talked of the soreness of this, of our hidden domesticity, and she said, as though on a whim, "And here I am beginning to wonder if I have made the right path for myself. Maybe, with a little mindfulness, I can still correct my course. But I admit that I have been considering stepping away from the clade. Perhaps one of our stanza would take my place, fork a new Time Is A Finger Pointing At Itself." She said, "I would like to know that you would come with me if I did so. I have not felt so domestic with anyone but you."

Of course I would! Of course I would. How could I not? How could I send her out in the world to live some quiet life away from administering to a troupe of actors and technicians, and leave her to do so alone? She would have her fun and her flings, but she would not have what she had had for dozens and dozens of years.

So she forked into A Finger Curled and you forked into Beholden To The Music Of The Spheres.

That was us. A Finger Curled and her Muse. Beckoning and Beholden. A different version of each of you that lived their quiet life in a cottage. A week and a day ago, we snagged a middling bottle of champagne and set up lawn chairs in the garden. A week and a day ago, Debarre stopped by to drop off a firework — he only ever needed one to impress — so that we could have our own little show. We each gave him a hug and he told us small stories of nothing we cared about, of the fledgling attempt at a Lagrange Council quickly dispersed.

We never did get to see the firework. It sits still on the paving stone where Beckoning placed it, ready to light on a midnight that never came for her.

After all, it was not a week and a day ago, was it? It was one year, one month, eighteen days ago. Subjectively so little time, objectively a year and change without her. Lagrange crashed — was bombed, I am hearing, a contraproprioceptive device that ramified through the perisystem architecture in waves of death — and we were all lost. We of the lost were now twice lost.

Phys-side got the System up and limping a few times, I have heard, before it was at least up and stable enough.

Stable enough!

Stability was *us*. Stability was our lives. Stability was our quiet cottage. Stability was us heading to clubs and dancing until we wanted to pass out — until we did, on more than one occasion, slumped against each other and panting in some corner booth. Stability was the four of us — you and Boss, me and Beckoning — meeting up for dinner every few months and sharing our laughter.

Stability was her garden. Stability was the years she grew so much zucchini. Stability was loaf after loaf of zucchini bread, meal after meal of zucchini noodles, the grates of the grill getting weary of grilled zucchini.

Stability was the bright border of snapdragons and nasturtiums that bordered the walk. Stability was the few years she got obsessed with marigolds. Stability was the three dandelions she always permitted in the yard — moderation! Imagine. Stability was her green thumb to my brown, it was Motes visiting and calling us 'her weird gay aunts', little skunklet digging her paws into good clean earth beside her while I watched from the stoop with a gin and tonic with too much lime.

This is not stability. For me, this will never be stability. She is twice lost, and from this she will never come back. Do not delude yourself, 23 billion of us are lost and will never come back. 23 billion souls forgotten by the dreamer who dreams us all.

Today, I have picked the last of the nasturtiums — for despite the seasons, some of her flowers grow year round — and made myself one last grand salad. Bitter greens and those spicy-sweet flowers dotting it like colorful yellow-orange-red-purple confetti. Balsamic vinaigrette. A planked filet of salmon. Crusty bread. The small things that I know how to cook.

Seven days have passed and I cannot live without her.

I have finished my meal, and poured myself a drink, and I will finish this letter, and I will go sit outside on my lawn chair and light the firework and see the night blossom into beautiful colors, and I will quit.

In some few minutes, you will have more than 200 years of memories to keep and to hold, or to view, cherish, and let go. I do not care; I will not be there to care. Perhaps you will remember our happy years, and you will stop incorporating those memories when you get to eight days ago. All you would remember is my grief. All you would remember is my despair. If you choose to forget those, you will know that this is how AwDae chooses to forget those who have been lost: crying over these plants stripped of their flowers even as fireworks blossom above.

Live on, my dear. You have your Pointillist. Live on.

All my love,

Beholden To The Music Of The Spheres

Reed — 2401

The shift from the universal sorrows of Lagrange to the immediate and personal sorrow of grieving over Marsh had been evident every time I found myself alone, disentangled from the rest of the clade, from Hanne and Dry Grass and problems larger than myself. Now that we were all gathered here, though, all the Marshans and a few close others standing around a simple black sphere, that sudden immediacy of loss clutched at my throat and would not let me go.

The sphere, we'd been told, was all that remained of Marsh. It was their core dump. It was what remained of their corrupted existence here on Lagrange.

On examination, more information became available. The closer I looked at it, the more I seemed to know. The data was something less than visible, something more than remembered. Staring at the sphere was a process of discovering, of learning that it was a core dump, that it was one belonging to Marsh in particular, that it had been created in the first seconds of 2400, that it was marked as unrecoverable, that its nature was one of corruption, that it was tainted with the remnants of contraproprioceptive virus. So much information flew at me that I couldn't tell what it all meant, not least of which because the more I learned, the more the tears clouded my vision and the black sphere became a hole in the world.

In our world.

In *my* world.

There was some part of me that had hoped, however fool-
ishly, that Marsh was simply locked in some enhanced cone of
silence somewhere, working on this or that, rejecting all incoming sensorium data. Dry Grass, however, assured us that this was
not the case, though, that eir name had been all but wiped from
the System along with all of the rest of their existence, and then
she offered to bring us to their core dump.

The room in which the cores were stored was beyond vast. It
was an unending space, a three dimensional grid with the cores
stored at one meter intervals in all directions. The default spawn
point was a floating platform in the middle of a vast sphere, de-
void of cores, right in the center of it all.

"The room is set to dark; no one can see us or touch us, no
matter how many instances were here," Dry Grass said quietly,
then smiled wryly. "We could scream bloody murder and no one
would hear, and yet it has the feeling of a graveyard, does it not?"

None of us spoke.

"Right," she whispered, expression falling.

"How do we get to their core?" I asked

Dry Grass gestured to a faint circle embossed in the floor,
then stepped within its bounds. "Marsh of the Marsh clade," she
said. "Dry Grass of the Ode clade on behalf of the Marsh clade,
systech ID #338d84bb."

There was a quiet chime of acknowledgment and, in the direction that Dry Grass faced, an indigo-limned black ring formed
opening out onto some other part of the sim, hundreds of the
23-odd billion cores filling the view. The platform drifted slowly
towards the portal, and then through.

The cores were insubstantial spheres, ghostly, translucent.
Little double handfuls of whispy lives cut short.

All except one.

Right before the platform sat one core more real than the
rest, a matte *Eigengrau* with a faint blue haze around it. The platform drifted forward until the sphere rested at the center before Dry Grass at chest level, us Marshans—along with Pierre and

Vos—parting to make way for it.

As the platform came to a stop, the blue haze disappeared and one more chime of acknowledgement sounded. "Marsh of the Marsh clade," an androgynous voice spoke. "Crashed via CPV January 1, 2400, 00:00:03. Core deemed corrupt and unrecoverable by automated process, confirmed by an instance of In The Wind of her own clade, systech ID #88aa6e70."

"An instance of..." Dry Grass started, then blanched. "How many instances of In The Wind existed during this process of confirmation?"

"520,000," the voice said. "A total of two hundred million instances of various systechs have been noted as confirming corrupted cores."

"And none of her were recovered?"

"There is one core for In The Wind of her own clade. The clade directory lists no up-tree instances."

"Where is–"

"Dry Grass," Lily growled through gritted teeth. "Shut the fuck up."

She hesitated, a wave of grief, of frustration and sorrow, crossing her face. She bowed unsteadily, and then moved to stand by Cress, Tule, and I. Whether intentional or not, she stood so that Lily was blocked from sight by the three of us.

It had to be intentional, and that fact, seeing her cowed for the first time in my memory—mine and Tule's—had me bristling. Both Tule and Cress appeared to be biting back responses of their own.

For her part, Lily remained tense, standing rigid and still. Even as she began to cry, she did so without moving, without making a sound, tears simply welling up and coursing down her cheeks. "Rush," she croaked.

Looking anxiously between Lily and Dry Grass, ve nodded slowly. "Alright," ve murmured, then stepped forward and tentatively touched the sphere. "I had some words prepared, but I'm not sure I can remember them all."

Sedge sighed and stepped forward to join ver. "Hey, it's alright," she said, resting her hand on vis wrist. "Just talk to them if you want."

Ve clutched at the sphere, though it remained stolidly immobile. "Uh...okay," ve mumbled. "I guess I'm just sorry this happened. Sorry in a commiseration way. Sorry that we're here at all, standing around like a bunch of jerks while you're...uh, gone, or whatever." Ve trailed off with a nervous laugh, shoulders sagging. "But I'll miss you, Marsh. We all will. We're all here, you know. All of your clade. Pierre and Vos are here, too, and Dry Grass, all wishing that you were here with us. I'm sorry you're not, I'm sorry you didn't get all our merges first."

Cress sniffled. Lily continued to stare blankly ahead through her tears. None of the three of us immediate up-tree instances had managed to merge down.

When Rush didn't continue, Sedge leaned to hug awkwardly around vis shoulders. Ve stiffened, returned the hug, and then stepped away from the sphere again, rubbing vis hands against vis shirt.

Sedge took her turn resting her hands atop the core. She stood a while in silence, shifting her weight from foot to foot. Finally, she said, "Twenty-three billion dead, but you were ours."

She opened her mouth to continue, shook her head, and then stepped back to join me, Tule, and Cress. Pierre moaned softly, slouching against Vos's side.

Tule began to step forward, but Lily held up a hand. "Stop," she whispered. "Not you. Not yet."

"Lily, I–"

"Not yet," she repeated, then stepped forward. Rather than rest her hands gently on the sphere of the core dump, she clutched it tightly. Her face contorted into a grimace, but she spoke through the tears, through whatever emotion it was that held her in its grip as tightly as she held the core. "You died. You were *killed.* You were killed by those who thought we were less than them, who thought they could control the world to such an extent that our lives became nothing to them. Just so much garbage."

I saw Dry Grass wince out of the corner of my eye. Whether Lily was talking about the collective that had seen fit to attack the System, this Our Brightest Lights Collective, or the Ode clade and all of their supposed machinations wasn't clear to me, but Dry Grass certainly seemed to take the words personally. I held out my hand to her, but she shook her head subtly.

"Our lives were nothing, so your life was nothing, too," Lily continued. "Now here we are, like Rush said, standing whatever's left of you like a bunch of jerks who get to live on. Who the fuck cares that some huge majority gets to live on while so many people are just fucking...gone?"

She looked as though she wanted to say more, but her words petered out and she simply stared, unseeing, at the core she held onto. Finally, she let go of the sphere and stumbled back to where she had been standing before.

I started to step forward next, eyes locked on Lily.

"Stop," she whispered. "Vos first."

"What the–"

"Shut up. Vos first."

I glanced over to Vos, who was glaring at her. "What are you doing, Lily?" she growled.

"Go," she said hoarsely.

"If you don't want to be here," Vos said, voice flat, dangerous. "You can leave."

"I want you to fucking go," Lily snapped. "I want to hear about Marsh from someone who knew them better than any of us, these last however many decades."

"First Tule, now Reed? What about Cress?" She scoffed. "Do you think they don't know about Marsh?"

"Certainly not as much as you did, if they're all dating one of *them!*"

"Get out."

"It's not your–"

"Get *out!*" Vos shouted. "Get out get out *get out!*"

Pierre fell to his knees, clutching his head in his hands. The movement seemed to startle Lily to awareness and, with a stricken look on her face, she stepped from the sim.

Unsure of what drove me to do so, I forked and quickly followed her, guessing that she had returned home. I'd let my down-tree instance stay to say his words, to hear everyone else's.

My guess was correct, as there she was, already whirling on me at the notification of my arrival. "Oh, fuck you, Reed. Didn't even give me a chance to lock the door!" she shouted.

"Lily, what the fuck is wrong with you?" I hollered back. "You can't just cut Tule, Cress, and I out of Marsh's fucking funeral just because you don't like Dry Grass!"

"Fucking *watch me.*"

I slapped her across the cheek. Hard.

I think I regretted it even in the moment. I regretted it as soon as I felt my hand move. As soon as I felt that reaction bubble past any boundaries within me and take control of my body, I knew that it would cause nothing but pain—physical, yes, but also emotional and personal pain.

I certainly regretted it as soon as she yelped and stumbled back a half-step.

"No," I said, voice shaking. "I won't watch you try to rip the clade in two just like that, just like it's your choice for the rest of us. It's not like either Sedge or Rush care."

"Well they fucking should!" she yelled, clutching at her cheek. "They fucking should. You heard what they said. You heard it first-hand, even! 8-stanza-1, right? You read the books, you know as much as the rest of us. I don't fucking care if True Name is Sasha or whatever now, she's the one who fucked this whole thing up. She's the one who lied and manipulated all of us. What are we supposed to do about that? Huh?! Christ, that hurt..."

"Nothing, Lily! Jesus Christ. You act like the whole Ode clade just ruined everything."

"They did!"

I followed after her as she stomped into the kitchen, watched as she grabbed a glass and somehow managed to angrily fill it with water from the faucet, rubbing her cheek where I'd struck.

"They really didn't," I sneered. "You...what, read the *History* and decided that, without exception, they're all fucking evil? Even after everything? Even after all the other books explained what happened?"

"Fuck the other books," she said, more to the faucet than to me. "Fuck the Ode clade, and fuck you too. Fuck you and fuck Cress and fuck Tule. It's really fucking sad, watching you three get taken for a ride, the same manipulation that fucked us all."

Her anger still burned hot, I knew, but not as much as it had when first we'd arrived. I just needed to outlast it. Doing so by parking myself in my own anger probably wasn't the best way to do it—I could feel yet more regret building below the surface of my anger—but it felt too good, too cathartic to let go of. "We're not getting taken for a ride, whatever that means. We're just grown up enough to realize that a bunch of actors did what actors do and pretended." I scoffed. "They *pretended*, Lily. That's just what they do."

"So it's just a game, then?" she shot back, though I could tell she was flagging. "Just a game that led to a bunch of fucking psychos killing billions of people?"

"They lost people too, Lily. So True Name did some stupid stuff back in the early days; what of it? She explained it all, said how much of it was just playing at politics without doing much beyond making us look interesting to phys-side, making us seem worthwhile. That was their whole tack on keeping us stable: keeping us worth something to phys-side. Now a bunch of them are dead and–"

"Two of them are dead," she grumbled. "Two and however many up-trees."

"Yeah, real lives, Lily."

Her shoulders slumped and she finally settled into silence. After a moment, she drank down the water in three coarse gulps, leading to her coughing and spluttering.

I waited it out.

"Look at us, Reed," she said, laughing humorlessly. "Fighting at a funeral like a real fucking family, and me swallowing my water wrong like a real fucking idiot."

I sighed. "Right, yeah. Are we at least done, though?"

She waved away the glass and nodded. "Yeah, sure. I'm going to stay here, but I'll try to at least keep this to myself in the future."

"I'd prefer if you got over it," I said, trying to keep the anger from creeping back into my voice. "It's not like they're going anywhere."

She shrugged, chin already drooping to her chest as anger was replaced with something that looked perilously close to exhaustion. I wondered, not for the first time, if the rest of the clade was struggling with sleep as much as I was. "No promises. Pretty fucking hard to let go of," she muttered. "But I'll try."

"Well, alright. Just no more shouting, at least. Do you want to come back to the gathering? I know you said you wouldn't, but it would mean a lot."

She hesitated, shook her head, and then sighed. "I probably should."

"You definitely should. Just let us do our thing, and listen, I guess."

She nodded. "Can you ask Vos if I can come back, at least? I was afraid she was going to deck me," she said, then smiled lopsidedly at me. "Not like I escaped that particular fate."

I winced. "Yeah. Sorry about that, Lily. That was stupid of me."

"Nah, it's okay. I was being kind of a bitch."

"No comment." I sent off a sensorium ping to Vos and got a halfhearted shrug in response. "I think you can come back, though. Probably best to just chill, though, right?"

"Yeah, okay."

I took her hand in mind and sent a message to my down-tree to recall us to the sim, blipping into being close to where we had stood when we left. Lily trudged back to her place and I quit to merge back down.

I merged the memories of the fight with Lily wholesale, letting them mingle with Vos's words of love and loss. There was a part of me that regretted it, that they should be so tainted, but both sets of memories were important.

Pierre declined to speak.

That left just Cress, Tule, and I. Cress went first, stepping forward to rest its hands against the core, and then resting its forehead against the back of its hands. "There's too much bullshit going on, so here's a story.

"Back when Reed, Lily, and I were forked, Marsh was still presenting cis male, and so the three of us were to be the aspects of them that went in different directions. Lily headed back cis fem, Reed went back to the trans masc presentation we had phys-side, and I went somewhere neutral.

"I started out with they/them, leaning into androgyny as I'd always pictured it, something more tomboyish than anything, but over time, that began to drift, and I decided that 'neutral' was the wrong answer to the question of gender. Gender was the wrong question. Fuck it, I say. I opt out." It laughed. "The next time I merged down, Marsh sent me a message that was just them laughing, then requested that we use they/them for them."

It straightened up again, smiling. "So you see? It's all my fault they wound up how they did."

The rest of the clade grinned. Both Vos and Pierre laughed.

After Cress, Tule stepped forward and stood for nearly five minutes in silence. The wait began expectant, but before long, everyone gathered around the core bowed their heads one by one, settling into something more contemplative. The silence spoke as much as Sedge and Rush's sorrow, Lily's anger, Cress's humor.

When he stepped back, I sighed. "Guess that leaves me," I said. I could feel exhaustion pulling at my cheeks, pressing against my temples. When I touched the core, I was surprised to find it cool to the touch, dry, almost dusty, as though it would absorbe all moisture, accept all tears and still never be slaked. "I don't want to say anything, but Tule already covered that base. I guess you've all talked a lot about the past, so I'm not sure I have much to add. I guess I'll just say that I hope we can find a way forward that doesn't lead to us feeling terrible forever."

There were a few nods around the circle, though Pierre only buried his forehead against Vos's shoulder.

"So I don't know. Let's just keep being good to each other, and keep finding ways to stay on top of things." My words sounded hollow, emotionless. I decided to lean into that feeling directly. "I'm having a hard time connecting emotions to my words, here. I think it's all super overwhelming, so I guess all I can do is just hope that that's not always the case."

Sedge, Tule, and Rush, my up-tree instances, all leaned forward to rest their hands on my shoulders.

"It's incredibly you to just think about how to manage stuff going forward," Lily said, no ire in her voice. "That's just kind of your role in this whole thing, huh?"

I chuckled, feeling some of the pressure in my chest fade. "Right, yeah. Manager of the enterprise."

"Pretty sure that makes me an employee," Sedge said. "Though I guess I got it from somewhere."

We all laughed.

We drifted away in small clumps after that. Pierre and Vos returned to Marsh's home—their home, now—along with Sedge, who said she was going to head back to work. Rush nudged Lily off to a bar, stating that it was high time at least some of us got roaring drunk.

The four of us who remained—me, Cress, Tule, and Dry

Grass—stood in silence for a while. There seemed to be little point in saying anything as we processed this impromptu funeral. All that needed to be said had been said, or if not, then it had at least been put on hold in the face of our overwhelming emotions.

I thought of the stages of grief, of Lily's anger, of the sadness so many of us lingered in, of the bargaining that I knew we all held within us. Perhaps there was some way to get Marsh back. Perhaps there was something we could yet do. Perhaps some combination of the core that remained and all of our memories could lead to some solution. Perhaps this new cross-tree merging held some promise after all.

"I want to see In The Wind," Dry Grass said eventually, her first words since Lily had told her to shut up. "I want to see what remains, and then I want to go lay down with the three of you, if you will have me."

I blinked, standing up straighter. "Me?"

She nodded. "If you will have me," she repeated, voice small.

I thought of so many complex emotions that had plagued me over the last few days—the memories of love, the way they clashed with my memories of distance, the memories of Lily burning up with hatred—and, finally, nodded. "Yeah. Let's see In The Wind's core, and then get out of here. Anything to help out after all this will be good."

§

I followed Cress, Tule, and Dry Grass back home.

The three of them lived in a narrow brownstone of sorts, full of the dark wood and plush carpets that I knew well from Marsh's house, though the walls were lined—in some places all but completely covered—with paintings. The vast majority were of landscapes skillfully done in watercolor or acrylics, but each of which was interrupted with a shape of black so deep that it seemed to eat any and all light around it. Beyond just reflecting zero light, it pulled greedily at light that even got close.

Also spaced out through the house were various *objets d'art* I recognized from Hanne's work. Dry Grass explained that both paintings and art were from her cocladists Motes and Warmth In Fire. "My little ones," she called them, which fit well, given what I knew of Warmth In Fire.

She sounded proud of them, as a mother would of her children, which took me a minute to piece together. There were no shortage of family dynamics within the System—after all, old and young alike upload, and upload dates can be decades or centuries apart—though it was relatively rare that they were so strong within a clade where everyone was by necessity the same age. What guardianship we Marshans felt over Cress, the smallest among us, only barely seemed to scratch the surface of the depth of Dry Grass's feelings over And We Are The Motes In The Stage-Lights and Which Offers Heat And Warmth In Fire. We were protective of Cress; she was hanging artwork on her fridge door and walls.

Proud, yes, but the overriding exhaustion—physical and emotional—kept her expression muted and heavy, and she soon requested that we lay down as we had planned.

The bed up in the second-storey bedroom was already wide, but Cress and Tule pulled on either edge to stretch it out by another half meter or so while Dry Grass all put faceplanted onto the mattress. She elbow-crawled her way up until her head was at least resting on a pillow before letting out a muffled groan.

Cress and Tule followed after, moving as though they knew the parts they were to play. Dry Grass's pillow was quickly shifted up into Tule's lap while Cress settled beside her, rubbing on her shoulders. I knew from Tule's memories, still slotting their way in along with my own, that this was a somewhat regular occurrence.

I stood awkwardly by until Cress chuckled and gestured at the open space beside Tule up near the head of the bed. "Just relax, Reed."

"Yes," Dry Grass mumbled. "You do not need to do anything,

there is no pressure. I want to be around those who enjoy my presence rather than resent it. We are all just here to unwind, yes? Among friends, yes? After these last few days, after so many tears and meals and meetings, I would like to think that this includes you, my dear."

"Right," I said, forcing a chuckle of my own as I awkwardly clambered up onto the bed, leaning against the headboard and hugging my knees against my chest.

We sat—or lay—in silence for a while other than the occasional small noise of contentment from Dry Grass.

Even as we stayed in silence, and Cress and Tule doted on their partner, this woman I had such strong feelings about foisted upon me out of nowhere only a few days prior, I struggled to disentangle my thoughts on the events of the day.

The longer I thought about it, the more surreal the act of having a funeral in the midst of such a disaster felt. Our gathering of nine people standing around an all-but-featureless black orb somewhere in a grid of yet more featureless black orbs was small. Nine people had stood around that core dump: six cocladists, two partners, and a systech who also happened to be a partner of two of those cocladists.

It was so small, and yet even if there had been a hundred people there, a thousand, it would have felt vanishingly tiny in that vast, open space. 23 billion orbs set into a grid, and this one was ours, our double handful of grief. After all, hadn't dry grass also sobbed openly and freely before the marker of her own loss?

It was so small, and that vast, open space remained silent, empty. The settings on the sim were such that we would only ever see or hear ourselves in there. There might well be billions of others struggling with their own double handfuls of grief, and yet it would only ever be us.

There was more grief to be felt there, layered beneath the exhaustion, confusion, responsibility, and however many more complex emotions had been caked on top. There would come a time when the ability to simply grieve would be laid bare, I knew, and soon, but it was not yet.

And so we stayed in silence.

Dry Grass was the first to break the silence, mumbling into her pillow. "In The Wind."

"What was that, love?" Tule asked, brushing fingers through her hair.

"That was my up-tree instance, yes? In The Wind? I remember the rattle of dry grass in the wind." She turned her head and laughed, choked and hoarse. "A full sentence snuck into a poem. I picked that up from Louie. Eir clade, os Riãos, did much the same: a poem expanded upon from within. I thought I was *so clever.* I thought I had gotten all of my grief out that second day. I thought I could move on, limping, until I heard of the work she'd done, that she made it so far and still did not make it to the end. Until I saw her core."

Tule, more flexible than I, bent down and kissed her on the cheek. Cress gave her own kiss after. Both of them glanced briefly at me, looking a little sheepish. I couldn't quite piece together the reason for their looks until I pieced together their confusion—our confusion, since I shared in it—of how I must feel about her.

The compulsion to echo that gesture was certainly there, too. I knew from countless memories the softness of her skin against my lips, I knew what even the briefest touch would mean to her as she worked to process her own loss.

I also knew her only as a friend, only as Dry Grass of the Ode clade, only Cress and Tule's partner, with whom I had shared only a few meals.

Thinking rapidly, I opted for a middle ground of squeezing gently on her shoulder. This gained me a rather relaxed-sounding sigh from Dry Grass, and a pleased smile from both Cress and Tule. Dry Grass shrugged my hand off of her shoulder to instead take it in her own, holding gently.

"Can you tell us about her?" I asked.

After a long moment's pause, she nodded. "She was the part

of me who remained a systech. After I burnt out, I mean. I had grown weary of the mediation and moderation side of the job. I loved the tech, instead. I loved the feeling of being a caretaker for this vast and wonderful world we live in. I did not want to deal with adults bickering at each other over stupid shit, and I certainly did not want to deal with phys-side. We are the moms of the clade, yes? My stanza? Not the judges and jurors."

Both Cress and Tule nodded, though the statement largely went over my head.

Perhaps guessing at such, Dry Grass continued, "Each of our stanzas focused on something different. I am sure that much is in the stories you have doubtless read, if Lily's reaction is anything to go by. She fusses at the eighth and their politics, perhaps the first with their habit of spying, but mine, the sixth, wound up with all of Michelle's—our root instance—all of her dreams of and desire for motherhood. Motherliness. Caring and cherishing. That is why I have all of that art on the walls: it is all cherished, all lovely creations from Warmth and Motes, the clade's little ones."

"So In The Wind was the one who stuck with that moderation?" I asked.

She nodded. "To an extent. She often explained how she would push the moderation duties off onto other systechs. She really was just as focused as I was on the tech side." She rolled over onto her back so that she could look up to us, transferring my hand in hers from one to the other. "All I wanted to do was take a vacation. I should have known it would wind up far longer than the two weeks I had intended. Michelle had already tried that all the way back in 2124, systime 0, and she got an entire clade out of it, after all.

"She usually got what she want, too. She worked the tech side, disentangling crashes and hunting for problematic objects. She is the one who kept me up to date on the tech side, usually over lunch." I could hear the smile in her voice as she continued, "Those weekly lunches were something lovely, sandwiches sitting unfinished as we talked and talked and talked about this whole confusing mess we lived in. The politics remained infuriating to me, which I suppose they also did for her, given the way she would rant. Even so, it kept the pilot light lit for me, that I might hear about this System I loved so much."

Cress nodded. "It must be hard to lose that."

"It is more than that," Dry Grass said, sniffling. "I loved her, my dear. She was my sister, my twin. Fuck what my down-tree says, I lost *family*."

"I'm sorry," the three of us mumbled.

She rubbed the back of her free hand against her eyes. "I will mourn the loss of a sister and friend. It will take time, and I can only just touch it briefly now. It is too hot."

Familiar sensation, I thought, and from their expressions, I surmised that my cocladists were feeling much the same.

"Need some space from it, love?" Tule asked.

"Please."

He nodded, working on a careful extraction from his role as pillow, replacing his lap with another pillow from the bed as he slid from beneath her. He stretched his arms up over his head, winced at a quiet pop from his neck, and then shifted to lay down beside her instead, arm draped over her front. Cress followed suit, laying down beside Tule and hugging around them both.

I chose to remain sitting for a while, idle gaze settling on the triad beside me, while I thought of the ways in which Dry Grass talked about In The Wind. I tried mapping that onto my own clade. Thinking of Lily like a sister, of Cress like our clade's own little one, felt right in a way that I didn't expect. While it was difficult to think of Tule as in any way that much younger than me, despite being my second degree up-tree instance, but perhaps that was due to his lingering similarities to me. After all, Sedge had forked him off shortly after I had forked into her. It was part of the package deal: Sedge went back to exploring femininity while Tule returned to cis-masculinity; ditto Rush and a further queering of gender. Both of them remained siblings—younger siblings, perhaps, because I was their progenitor. Cousins, maybe.

But Marsh? Were they a parent? Were they also a sibling? Some great-grandparent, perhaps? Or were they simply my root instance? All fit to greater or lesser extent.

Finally, the thought ran its course and, left with a curiously numb and empty mind, I slid down to join the other three in laying on the bed, though I kept what I hoped was a polite distance, laying on my back and staring up at the ceiling.

The polite distance lasted for less than a minute before Dry Grass rolled onto her side and draped an arm across my middle. *"If this is uncomfortable, do let me know, Reed,"* she sent in a sensorium message as both Tule and Cress scooted closer to her. *"Otherwise, I am going to try and sleep."*

Tense, I nodded. *"It's...different. Not bad, just going to take some getting used to."*

"Should your boundaries change, then, let me know and I will adapt with them. I am simply craving touch. It is grounding for me."

I nodded once more, patting the back of her hand where it rested on my side.

"Ooooh, Reeeeed," came the barest hint of a message from Cress, and I peeked an eye open to see it peering over Dry Grass's shoulder, grinning.

I smirked and rolled my eyes. *"Shush, you."*

Tule messaged a few seconds later, including Cress in the message, *"You good, Reed?"*

"Yeah, just confused. Dealing with emotions. Trying to figure this out, maybe. It's taking a lot of getting used to."

"I can imagine," he replied. *"I caught myself feeling a little sorry for dumping this on you, earlier today. Trying to keep in mind that it's your fault, not mine."*

I did my best to keep my laughter to myself. Dry Grass's breathing had grown steadily slower and I didn't want to wake her if she was drifting off. *"Uh huh. All my fault. Nothing to do with freaking out about the entirety of Lagrange going down."*

"*I guess I'll allow it.*"

"*Is there any more news on that?*" Cress asked.

"*I mean, there's plenty,*" I sent. "*Almost too much. All these changes they added to the System are beyond me. Like, they made the Ansible and AVEC more robust, which I guess is good, though we don't use those any. ACLs are whatever, I guess. Not something we have to worry about. Splitting the hardware of the System, though? That sounds wild. Ditto adding cross-tree merging, which the other Odists and Jonas freaked out about.*"

"*Cross-tree merging? Like you and I merging?*"

"*I guess so. Answers Will Not Help and Jonas got pretty weird about the whole thing, actually, saying it changed clades into 'gestalts' or something. I guess I can see it, too. We still fork like a tree, branching out and everything, but if we can merge from one branch to another instead of just down, then the metaphor falls apart.*"

Tule chimed in with a scoff. "*What about that would make them angry? It just sounds like a minor improvement and a change in terminology. Maybe not even that; we stay clades and cladists, just with this new feature.*"

"*Hell if I know. They're old and weird.*"

Cress buried its face against Tule's shoulder to muffle a giggle. "*God, if they're weirder than Dry Grass, they'd have to be.*" It sighed, added, "*But I guess that cross-tree merging sounds interesting. I can't imagine what a mess the combination of all six of us would look like.*"

I stiffened, restraining the urge to sit up straight. "*Like Marsh, maybe?*"

There was silence from both of my cocladists, though I could hear that their breathing had picked up in turn. "*Well, now there's an idea,*" Tule said at last.

§

We lingered in silence for the remainder of the evening, the four of us piled into a bed now stretched to fit all of us. Two of my cocladists and their partner, and now me. Who knew what

I was? There was the friendship that we had built over the last few days. There was the camaraderie that we had built through work. There was the acquaintanceship that had been there from years prior.

And now there was more. I didn't have words for it—latent romance? A crush?—and Dry Grass was asleep for much of our time together. It wasn't the time for conversations, it was time for just resting, something I realized I dearly needed as well. We all did, as we napped off and on for some time until the clock hit one in the morning, at which point I stepped back home to spend the rest of my night with Hanne.

She was already in bed, curled around a body pillow, though not yet asleep.

"Reed?" she asked through a sensorium message as I crept into the room, a cone of silence set up over me to keep from disturbing her. *"You back for the night?"*

Startled out of my attempt to be sneaky, I straightened up and dropped the silence. "Yeah, sorry Hanne. I didn't mean to just disappear on you."

"It's okay."

I nodded, shedding my trousers as I made my way over to join her in the bed, once more in one piece.

"Or, well, it isn't," she admitted. "But I figured you had important things going on."

"Right, yeah. I'm sorry," I said, climbing in behind her in the bed. "I actually fell asleep, or I would've been home sooner."

"Oh, okay," she mumbled. I felt her relax against me, and I hugged my arm around her middle. "I was worried you were out running yourself ragged."

"That was earlier. I wore myself out at our little funeral."

Hanne sighed into the long silence that followed, eventually replying, "I went to see Shu's...uh, core, I guess, with a few others. I came home and just kind of lay down and have been here ever since."

I tightened my arm around her. "I'm sorry, Hanne. It's super overwhelming there. Did you get any rest, at least?"

She shrugged noncommittally. "Glad you got some. Where'd you crash?" She winced at the choice of words, curling tighter around her pillow. "Where'd you take your nap?"

"Over with Cress and Tule and Dry Grass. We sat in bed to talk and then just all fell asleep."

"Oh?" I could hear the faint smirk in her voice. "Did you wind up getting all smoochy with her?"

I laughed, pressing my face against the back of her neck. "No. A bit cuddly, maybe, but that's it. We may go on a date at some point. An actual one, I mean. Not a work lunch."

She laughed as well. "Well, good. I'm happy for you."

I kissed on her nape. "Yeah, we'll see. It's a weird way to come about a relationship."

"Mmhm. It's really weird talking about this now, though. All this stressful stuff going on, and we're talking about relationships."

"We talked about that a bit, actually," I said. "Tule suggested that it was a bit of focusing on the good things, but Dry Grass said it might be more like a 'protective measure'. Something about trauma bonding. "Building more relationships to pin ourselves down after so many were broken"."

"That's a kind of cynical way of looking at it."

"I guess," I said. "She was hurting. We also saw her lost up-tree instance's core."

"Oh, shit. I'm sorry."

I shrugged. "We were all hurting, just in different ways."

"Yeah, I guess we are. I'm still somewhere between numb and grief, I guess."

"I'm sorry, Hanne," I said. "I'm...I don't know. Grieving? Confused? Hurt?"

"Hurt how?"

"Hurt like I've been kicked by someone I trusted."

She nodded. "I guess I can see that. I trusted phys-side. I

trusted the systechs. I feel kind of like that trust was broken in some ways."

"Yeah. Thinking of it like that way, I guess I can see where Dry Grass is coming from, though. We're protecting ourselves by holding onto trust that we do have. She said even trauma bonds arc still rcal bonds."

"That's a bit less cynical."

We lay in silence for a while, and I found myself lingering on the thoughts of holding onto trust. I was doing that now, wasn't I? I was with Hanne, my partner of nearly a decade, trusting that she would be here in the morning, that I'd still be able to talk to her, drink coffee with her, drink too much champagne and brandy.

"Hey Hanne?"

"Mm?" She sounded on the verge of sleep.

"I love you."

"I love you too. What brought that on?"

"Remember what we were talking about before...before the attack?"

"You were talking about 2399," she said, then laughed sleepily. "I asked you to sell me on the year. You made a pretty convincing argument that it was a good year."

"I stand by that," I said, grinning. "But yeah, we were talking about the past, asking about life back phys-side. I said, "Am I not allowed to be a bit maudlin?" I was being really sappy."

"You should've said that instead."

I snorted. "Yeah, I guess so. I'm feeling pretty maudlin now, though. I still feel hurt, I still feel like I'm grieving, but I'm feeling maudlin, too. Extremely sentimental. Effusively sad."

"Effusively!" She sighed, squirming around to give me a kiss. "Reed, my darling, my love, my very own, please never change."

"Wasn't planning on it," I said, grinning. "But yeah. The grief is really starting to kick in. I got so *angry* at Lily today. She was being such a bitch about Dry Grass, I mean, so of course I did, but...well, I hit her. Slapped her across the face."

"You *hit* her? Jesus, Reed."

"Yeah, I know. I feel terrible about it. I know a lot of people are super angry about things now, so maybe it makes sense, but that was a pretty good way to knock myself out of that mindset. I feel betrayed, yeah, but not that fury anymore."

"Well, good. I don't want you hitting people."

I laughed, feeling tiredness starting to pull at my cheeks once more. "Neither do I, trust me. I feel betrayed and depressed, and it's got me all maudlin."

"Tell me something good, then," she suggested. "Try to get back to sappy or mawkish or whatever else you called it."

I nodded, thinking for a moment before offering, "Cress was talking at the funeral today about how it was playing with gender and how it's the reason Marsh started going by they/them. It got me thinking about how I started going back to that transmasc identity. I tried just forking myself into how I looked back phys-side, but it was...I don't know, unsatisfying."

"How so?"

"It felt like I'd taken this big shortcut. I put all that work into it phys-side, and it was like it lacked all the weight of that process to just turn into what I remembered from those first days after uploading."

She furrowed her brow. "I thought that's what you'd done, actually."

"Not in the end. In the end, I wound up going back to what I remember of my pre-transition life and taking the long way around."

"How, though? It's not like hormones do anything here."

I shrugged. "I met up with a bunch of other folks doing the same thing—actually surprised I didn't run into Hold My Name in the process—and we all talked about the various ways we could go through the process. Some hunted down doctors who had uploaded and were willing to do things like help act out the process. I mostly just forked once a month from that cis body into what I am bit by bit. I let my voice change, bound my chest, added surgery scars, each bit step by step."

"That's wild," she said. "What's this got to do with Marsh, though? Feeling maudlin over gender?"

"Well, kind of, after Cress talked earlier today. Mostly, though, I was thinking about how, for a while, I was merging down with Marsh every month instead of every year, since they got my previous instance's memories. They got to experience the act of transitioning right along with me. They sent me this really heartfelt message about how they'd forgotten the joy of it all, and how it was nice to live through it again, in a way."

Her expression softened to a smile. "Okay, that's more like the memories I was thinking of. How does that fit into maudlin?"

"Just remembering that, I guess. That was back when we talked a bit more, and we wound up having a little chat after every merge. They sounded so fascinated by everything I was seeing and going through, so I asked why they didn't do the same. They said that it was my life to live, and that they'd just remember it for me, just like how they'd remember Lily's and Cress's."

"Oh," she said, then stiffened, averting her gaze. "*Oh.* And now they aren't here to remember it."

I sighed. "Right. It's still a good memory, though, and I'm going to remember it at least."

"Well, so long as you can hold onto the good stuff, too."

I nodded. "Has me thinking, though. They apparently added cross-tree merging in the process of getting the System back up and running. Cress and Tule and I started talking about what it might take to merge the whole clade to see if we can get Marsh back."

"Wait, what?" She looked taken aback. "Cross-tree merges? Would that work?"

"It might," I said, shrugging. "It'd be all of us, at least, right? All of our memories from over the years, combined with those from when we *were* Marsh. I mean, it wouldn't be exact, of course, but it'd still be something."

"Not exact?" she asked, then winced, answering her own

question, "Oh, right, because they won't have their memories for all of that time."

"Yeah. Not exact, but who knows, maybe they could still live on in a way."

Hanne once more rolled over, settling back into my arms again. "I guess."

"Just thinking of those stages of grief, though, it makes me wondering if I'm also stuck in the bargaining stage. Trying to find ways to ask the universe to give them back."

"Yeah. I–" She interrupted herself with a yawn. "I'm a bit wary of it, maybe, but maybe some good will come of it."

I stifled my own yawn. "Why wary?"

"Just worried you won't get what you want."

I sighed. Sleep was clearly tugging at us both, so as I surrendered to it, I murmured, "Yeah, me too."

§

The next day, while our down-trees continued to work on this lingering project of figuring out what life on Lagrange would look like moving forward, Dry Grass and I both sent forks to meet up to talk over lunch. She let me pick the restaurant, a reconstruction of a reconstruction of a reconstruction of an automat I remembered from phys-side, though it turned out she'd been there some decades prior.

Ah well, such was the danger in trying to find a place to eat with someone who had lived for more than three hundred years, most of that sys-side.

Life on Lagrange seemed to be limping back into something resembling order, at least. The automat, a place called Horn & Hardart, squatted at the base of a skyscraper in a loose simulacrum of New York City as it had appeared all the way from the early 20th century to...well, likely 2399. Who knew if work had begun again, though given the crowds in the street, the buskers and bustle, I imagined that it would before too long.

The default arrival point was a newly renovated LaGuardia airport, something that was only ever in the planning stages when I had lived there for a brief few months, and transit into the city itself was via bus and subway, both packed with other cladists.

Dry Grass and I sat in a well-tailored cone of silence, letting us talk in peace.

"Everyone looks so nervous," I observed at one point.

"I imagine many do not trust that the System is up for good, this time," she said. "Though it is not all a negative nervousness. Look."

I followed her gaze to see a young couple looking, yes, nervous, but also very clearly out on a date. Their knuckles were white as they held hands, yes, but they were still holding hands. Their expressions were anxious as they looked around the bus and out the windows, but full of limerence whenever they looked at each other.

"They are cute, are they not?"

I smiled. "Yeah."

She nodded subtly toward a lithe person of indeterminate gender, standing at nearly eight feet tall. They wore a *very* expensive looking suit in subtly different shades of black that nonetheless glittered in rainbow hues whenever the sun caught it. Where not covered by finery, their body seemed to be cobbled together from various species, from a vaguely canine snout to ears that would be home on a mouse, a crest of feathers blossoming from atop their head. Behind them, a thick, crocodilian tail stayed tucked out of the way against one of their legs, curled just above birdlike talons for feet.

"That is Devonian. I do not know if they recognize me or are ignoring me, but we met some time back when I followed a few cocladists to a club. I will leave them be, but look: see how proud they are? See the brightness in their eyes?" she said fondly. I wasn't nearly so adept at reading the expressions of fantastical creatures, but I trusted her. "And look there."

I followed her gaze once more, this time finding it lingering on an old woman. *Beyond* old. She looked ancient, hunched and tired, propping herself up on one of the handrails. Peeking out of her handbag was the tiny snout of some sort of miniature dog. She looked as anxious as the others around me, and yet, as I watched, she dug a hand deep into one of the pockets on her wool coat and fished around for a moment. She came up with what looked to be a small cube of cheese, which she surreptitiously fed to the tiny dog. For that one, short moment, as she cooed down to the animal, the anxiety was washed away and there was nothing but joy on her features.

"This place," she said, leaning back in her seat once more, "is so stupid. It is stupid and weird and full of stupid, weird dreamers like us. It is a miracle that it exists, it is a miracle that it has continued to exist for so long, and it is a miracle that it came back up in so pristine a state. Unwhole, yes, but that stupid, weird vibrancy remains, does it not?"

"I suppose it does," I said. "All the sims are still here, right?"

"All the sims and objects, yes, but so many of the souls. Minus that 1%, yes, but that is still more than two trillion, is it not? Friendships, relationships, and clades were broken and changed, many have quit out of despair and many more will, I am sure, and yet many more still exist and live on. New uploads will be ungated soon, and more will come and join us, new clades will blossom. New friendships will be forged. New relationships are already starting, yes?" she asked, grinning and patting my thigh.

I laughed, looking down to my lap and resting my hand atop hers. *God, Lily really* will *throw a fit,* I thought. Aloud, I said, "I suppose so, yeah."

"We are all anxious, as you say, but we are more than that: we are still here. We are still alive. We will do all that we can to continue living, and those phys-side will see to that."

Once we stepped off the train, still holding hands both out of affection and so as not to lose each other in the crowds, we walked the short distance to the replica Horn & Hardart, still talking of life on Lagrange. We talked of when we had uploaded, of the first things that we did sys-side, of the origins of the System that Dry Grass's root instance still remembered.

"The 2110s were a horrible mess," she said once we sat down with our cups of shitty coffee and small bowls of soup: chicken noodle for her, clam chowder for me. It was too thick, too grainy from the flour used to thicken it, and it needed copious amounts of pepper to make it in any way interesting. It was, as far as I could tell, a perfect reproduction. "Pandemics. The WF and Sino-Russian Bloc having a staring contest over the Carpathians. Governments trying to disappear anyone who knew too much in the worst way possible, which accidentally led to the creation of the System. Turns out, it's a pretty good place to store your undesirables, so most of the Founders were loud, opinionated, politically obnoxious people."

I laughed. "You were loud, opinionated, and politically obnoxious?"

"Do not be ridiculous, Reed. Of course I was," she said primly. "It was our friend that made this place what it was, yes? Ey was the one who became the template for this world, yes? But all the same, it became a cherished place. We uploaded in the System's second year, as soon as we could afford to, and even then the System was a mess. Consensual sensoria had yet to be implemented, building and object creation had yet to progress to where it was today, the ability to eat—eat and feel sated—was not added until the fifth year—this is all before systime was even a thing, remember, so this is *very* early—so those who uploaded hungry remained so for years at a time. I loved it all the same."

"You still do, sounds like."

She laughed. "Of course I do! It is more than just a love of life, the System is my baby. It is *our* baby, the Ode clade's. We ushered it into being and raised it up to be what it is today. All of this–" She gestured around at the automat, the tables crowded with lines of cladists before the windows bearing the more popular dishes. "–is our baby, all grown up. The people, the automat, the city, all of those abandoned sims and all of those overcrowded hubs. It belongs to everyone and no one. It belongs to itself."

I listened, rapt, as she grew more animated and eloquent; watched as she sent out an instance to fetch us some of our favorite plates of plain-yet-filling food.

"We all played our part. I dove into tech, Warmth coaxed the System into letting em make weirder and weirder objects and more and more delicious foods, True Name and her stanza guided it as might any parent. Even if her methods came off as unsavory, I believe her—believe Sasha, I mean, who she became—when she says that her goal was only ever the security of our existence.

"I feel like my baby has stumbled. The System stumbled and fell, knocked its head, forgotten some of what it knew. I feel like our existence stumbled, as some group or another got so frustrated as to trip it up. When I dump my energy into all of this work, I am doing my best to nurse it back to health. We all are. I am working the tech angle. The eighth is working the political angle—you have seen Sasha has poke her nose in once or twice, yes? She is still striving." She smiled fondly, adding, "Even the third stanza is there with us, sitting *shiva* and praying as they will."

We sat back as her ephemeral instance set down a few pot pies and a plate piled high with hash browns in front of us before quitting. Dry Grass sectioned off a large portion of the hash browns to start dousing it in hot sauce.

"All of this to say that we have stumbled, taken a blow that has left us dazed, but we will do our best to come back from it."

"You're sounding more hopeful than you were last night, at least."

She laughed, fork of heavily spiced potato already on its way to her mouth. "Yes, well, I am not freshly back from a cemetery, am I?"

I nodded, getting a few bites of my own (less heavily spiced) share in. Horn & Hardart's hash browns were quite good, but only while warm.

"You use a lot of family language when you talk," I said once I'd washed the hash browns down with coffee. "Which makes sense from what you've said, of course, but it got me thinking last night about what Marsh was to us. Couldn't decide whether they were a parent or a cousin of some sort."

She nodded, already starting in on her pot pie, breaking open the lid to let the steam escape. "It is not a dynamic that works for everyone. Even within our own clade, it is complicated. Hammered Silver, my down-tree, *hates* that. She disowned me for some time over these thoughts. Tt does not make sense in some cases. Motes and Warmth are my little ones, but while A Finger Pointing and Beholden—Motes's guardians—feel like siblings to me, Dear, Rye, and Praiseworthy—Warmth's down-trees—definitely do not. They are friends, Rye especially, perhaps, but little else."

"Yeah, and I guess that's been coloring my feelings on the whole idea of cross-tree merging."

Dry Grass frowned but remained silent as she ate, gesturing for me to continue.

"We've been poking at the possibility of merging the whole clade to…I don't know, actually. Reconstruct, I guess? It wouldn't be Marsh, but if nothing else, maybe it'd be someone who could carry on in their stead."

"Alright," she said once she finished a few bites. "I am glad that you see that it would not be Marsh. What do you think this new person will do? What will you do?"

"We had this idea while laying in bed last night, it's not exactly matured much beyond that," I admitted, laughing. "I don't know, though. Maybe we could at least talk and share memories. They'll feel all the stuff we talked about at the funeral yesterday, right? Maybe they can work out some differences and such. Maybe they'll join the clade. Maybe they'll just quit."

After a moment's thought, she sighed. "Well, I checked in with my down-tree, and Jonas is losing ground on a request to remove that functionality, so you may well have the chance to play around with this, but do be careful to manage your expectations, my dear. There is much that this offers, but also much at risk."

"You don't think it's dangerous or anything, do you?"

"Much at risk socially, Reed. There is the potential for that friendship and love, yes, but also the potential for pain."

§

There was a strange sort of distance involved with my life as a cladist, just by virtue of the ways in which my world worked. It was a constant, something that I'd noticed shortly after uploading, something that had stuck with me ever since. It shouldn't be the case that I would feel distance from what I was doing just because a fork was off doing something else in my stead, right? I would be getting all of their memories, after all. Everything they experienced would become something that I had experienced, too. That's what it meant to be a cladist, after all: an instance is specifically an instance of a cladist. They may think different thoughts and live separate lives for a few seconds, hours, or days, but they maintain the same identity with the intent to come together again once more, while a cladist adopted their own identity separate from any down-tree. Our own social construct defined by memory.

And the memories here on the System were something far more than what they were back phys-side. Yes, they were imperfect: they collected the same sorts of impressions, attached the same amount of meaning and emotion to time and place. They were eternal, though. I could browse back through the life that I'd lived as Reed and as Marsh before that and pull together as exact a picture of what had happened as though it had happened only some hours ago.

Nevertheless, there was a distance that came with experiencing two things at once. If I sent out a tracking fork to, say, go on an exploratory date with someone that I'd accidentally developed feelings for through an ill advised merge while both our down-tree instances attended a meeting with phys-side in the middle of the apocalypse, intellectually, I wouldn't expect that I, as the down-tree, would feel some sort of distraction from the meeting at hand, as though I were looking over the shoulder of someone else. I wouldn't expect that I as a single instance would feel like I was living two lives at once, because that was specifically what forking was used for, right? It let us live two lives at once and yet still feel singular about the whole thing. That was being a cladist.

But here I was, confronted with the very real sense of distance I was feeling from this conversation between the representative sample of clades and phys-side, forcing me to consciously focus on paying attention.

Or maybe I'm just anxious, I thought.

The topic of the conversation certainly had its share of anxiety-inducing power. We'd gathered once more in the room with the AVEC stage, finding our seats around the oblong table that had long since started to become familiar, while Günay and Jakub joined us from the L5 station.

Need An Answer called the meeting to order, though with no new faces, this largely amounted to her stating that she had a list of topics that we wished to address and picking one to start with.

"When last we spoke about the perpetrator, 8-stanza-1, it was stated that they were locked in the DMZ for the time being," she said. "Are we able to speak with them ourselves?"

Günay shook her head. "The DMZ is currently offline."

Most of those sys-side stared blankly. Harvey, meanwhile, laughed. "What the fuck does that mean?"

"Oh! The DMZ can be completely isolated, right? That was what they wanted for the launch vehicles. That means that we can also bring it up and down just like the System as a whole."

"Terrifying," he said cheerfully. "Thanks."

Günay, looking baffled, asked, "Why's that terrifying?"

"Have they been brought back online with this start-up?"

She shook her head.

"So there's this person who's effectively dead, right? You can bring them back to life, presumably stuck in a default sim, and they're going to immediately go crazy because they're suddenly all alone thinking it's fifteen minutes before their plan was to go down but it's not," he continued, ticking points off on his fingers. "CPV doesn't work, they can't quit, their plan was only 1% successful—if you even decide to tell them that!—and it actually made Lagrange loads safer with fixes and new features. Oh, and don't forget, literally trillions of people hate them now."

Günay looked helplessly over to Jakub, who nodded. "That's an ongoing conversation to be had sys-side," he said, sounding as though he was choosing his words very carefully. "We can bring the DMZ back up whenever you would like, and you will retain full control over transit to and from the DMZ–"

"Can you prevent 8-stanza-1 from entering the rest of Lagrange?" Debarre asked. "I'm with Harvey in that it's kinda terrifying, but I also don't exactly want them over here, either."

Jakub bowed. "That's already been implemented, though if you want to lift it in the future, you will need to consult with phys-side. That's how it was designed on the LVs, after all. For this reason and for our sake, I'd like to ask that you keep us—phys-side and the System Consortium—up to date with whatever decisions you make regarding the DMZ and 8-stanza-1."

Debarre shrugged. Harvey scoffed. Jonas Ko grinned, leaning back in his seat, saying, "Sure thing, Jakub."

After a moment's uncomfortable pause, Need An Answer asked, "What can you tell us about the CPV device?"

Günay, who had been slouching further and further down in her seat as the discussion had drifted away from the technical, sat up straight once more. "It was one of those things that was really clever and all the worse for it," she said. "They uploaded a few months before the attack and went out to big public sims and met a bunch of people. When they set the bomb off, it hit them first, but before it did, it used their access to the perisystem clade listing to look up everyone they'd interacted with to go infect them and their cocladists after looking up everyone *they* knew about, and so on. This would have gotten more than 99% of the System, especially once it hit the new upload assistants, who have probably met more people than anyone else, including those who never talked to anyone else since. Once the number of uninfected cladists fell below a threshold—I think one billion?—the clade listing allowed access to a full listing of everyone sys-side, and the virus just mopped up from there."

"What was that threshold even for?" Selena asked. "I thought it was part of the privacy policy that no one be able to just look up everyone on the System."

"I don't know," she said, shrugging. "It was all super old code. My guess is that it was leftover from the first few years of the perisystem architecture."

Dry Grass nodded. "I remember when we were able to look up everyone sys-side. We used to do it to see if anyone we recognized had uploaded in the last week."

"And they did all of this in a few months?" Need An Answer said, gently steering the conversation back on track.

Jakub shook his head. "We don't think so. They were the only one from Our Brightest Lights to upload, but they had the rest of OBLC working with them, plus a dozen other collectives and some individuals besides. I don't know the specifics, but I imagine it took them well over a year to organize everything while still keeping it under wraps."

"That much work, though, and they can't have had just one person working sys-side," Debarre said, brow furrowed in a frown. "Are you sure they're the only one out of all those collectives and people that uploaded? Wouldn't they have to have sympathizers and so on here?"

"We are working on it," I Cannot Stop Myself From Speaking, who had until this point in the meeting been silent, replied.

The bobcat's expression remained impassive, but it was hard to miss just how sharp her fangs were with the anger evident in her voice. I was happy to see that she at least looked away from Debarre as she said this; the anger seemed instead to be directed at no one in particular, or perhaps the world as a whole. A world that would permit such people to exist. It was an anger that veered well into vindictiveness.

Need An Answer, perhaps sensing the tension this inspired, moved smoothly down her list. "The next point that we would like to discuss is the sentiment that has crept into the System based on the news of an attack. I must admit that we found it frustrating to hear just how much phys-side knew in comparison to what we had been told. Günay said, "There is some suspicion of malicious actors, yeah. I say 'suspicion' in earnestness, I promise." Mr. Strzepek stated that certain data were to be withheld from both sys-side and phys-side." A smile, condescending, curled the corner of her mouth. "And here we learn that news of the attack was released some weeks ago, phys-side."

Günay wilted in her chair, looking down at her desk, wherever she sat.

Jakub, on the other hand, sat stock still for several long seconds. "Yes," he said at last. "During the briefing prior to our first meeting, we were instructed that anyone who was asked were to say those words specifically. They were displayed in our HUDs and enforced via NDA inhibitors."

Answers Will Not Help rolled her eyes. "Tacky."

"I suppose I ought to thank you for telling me the fucking truth after," Jonas Fa said cheerily. "Good on you, Jakub! Perhaps there *is* a bone in your body, even if it isn't your spine."

The admin bristled at the insult, visibly forcing himself back to calmness before he continued. "You'll remember that I also said we were maintaining information hygiene."

"Oh! Of course, you're right. And whose idea was that?"

"Shut up, Jonas," Answers Will Not Help said fondly, pre-empting any response.

"Needless to say," Need An Answer said, once more glossing over the tension, "the response sys-side has been fraught. Sys-techs focused on such had to throttle several of the main feeds after complaints that it had become an impossibly dense flow of information. There is grief. There is panic. There are calls for heads, ours *and* yours."

"We've been shaping the sentiment as best we can," Selena said. "But it would've been far easier if this had been a coordinated effort. As it is, we are keeping the anger and panic to tolerable levels and steering cladists towards grief. Better that than anger; some of those calls for your heads were hunting for ways to launch some sort of counterattack."

Jakub stiffened. "Which is precisely why we tried to control the release of information."

"Oh, we are not mad at you for that!" Answers Will Not Help said, laughing. "Good job on that front, we know well how difficult that can be. We are mad at you for being a fucking coward and withholding that information from *us*."

"But the Consortium–"

"Is not here. You are," she retorted. "Someone is getting their head bitten off, may as well be you, yes?"

I frowned, they were goading Jakub, pushing him repeatedly into anger. I couldn't figure out why. I could understand *their* anger—I was feeling much the same—but attacking the phys-side admin, some random middle-manager, felt like a strange and petty move.

I sent Dry Grass a quick ping to ask, and she replied, *"It is my guess that they are pushing blame onto him because they want him gone. They want the Consortium to replace him with someone they have more control over. That, and they wish for Günay to feel better."*

"They really like her, don't they?"

A hint of a smile touched her face. *"Do you not, my dear?"*

"Oh, I like her plenty. I actually hope she uploads. I'm just wondering where that's coming from."

"She is easily controlled," she admitted. *"But yes, I like her too,*

and I suspect she will be pushed by the Consortium to join us before long. I think that Jonas will, too, to turn her into a long-term asset."

"There are joint commemorations already in the works," Abd al-Latif, one of the representatives, was saying. "Serene; Sustained And Sustaining has volunteered an unfinished sim that was under construction by one of her lost instances as a memorial, and has been talking with a docent phys-side about a permanent AVEC channel open with one of their memorials."

"That would be lovely," Dry Grass said. "The loss affects both worlds, does it not? Every loss up here represents someone who once lived phys-side, who left behind family and friends. Will there be a posting of these commemorations? I know of many—myself among them—who would attend as many of them as possible."

Abd al-Latif bowed from where they were seated. "There will be, yes. We'll work with you and Sedge to get that posted and pinned."

"It'd be nice to get some stills from those off to the LVs as soon as they begin," Sedge said.

"Of course," Need An Answer said. "And on that note, all messages from the LVs have been ungated, but, in order to prevent individuals from being flooded with all of them at once, they are being maintained on a request basis, and instructions will be posted to the feeds for how to access them...now."

I sat up straighter—as did several around the table—and checked the feeds. Pinned at the top of several of the larger feeds were instructions for accessing messages. It was close enough to accessing an exo that I was able to access mine almost immediately.

Two from Reed and Hanne on Castor, three from Reed on Pollux, several from friends. Plus eight from Marsh#Castor and five from Marsh#Pollux.

I felt a hollowness swell within my chest as I sank back into my seat. Around the table, I watched similar reactions from others. Knowing that it would likely leave me hurting, I cautiously opened the most recent of the letters from Marsh.

> The Marsh clade,
>
> They say you're all dead.
>
> They say you're all dead and none of us know what to do. None of us know how to cope with something like that. How do you learn that someone who *was* you for so much of your life is just gone and then keep living a normal life? I'm sure you're going to get letters like this from each of your counterparts, but...fuck. What are we supposed to do, knowing this? You're all me. I'm all of you. A part of me has died.
>
> They say they're working on it, and I hope to *hell* they come up with something, because I'm not sure what I'd do knowing even one of you was lost. It's no easier to lose one portion of oneself than it is to lose a full half...

I shook my head jerkily, swallowing back tears as best as I could, and closed the letter. I'd have to read it when I was alone, but even still, the words echoed in my head. *They say you're all dead.*

Around the table, silence held for a long moment, faces blanched, tears flowed.

After another few minutes, Need An Answer stood from her seat and bowed deeply to all present. "My friends, there is much to process in these letters, and there will be much to process in the months upcoming as more trickle in. I wish you all the best, and should you need to step away, you are free to do so. However, there remain two points on our agenda that I would like to address before we call an end to the meeting."

Two representatives stepped away immediately while the rest of us worked on mastering our emotions.

"The next item on our list is the topic of information consolidation. Mr. Strzepek and Ms. Sadık, what can you tell us of this working group that has been set up?"

Günay visibly brightened, leading Jakub to nod towards her. "Yeah! That was one of the things I helped start."

Need An Answer smiled. "Then I suppose we have you to thank."

Still grinning, she nodded. "It started as part of the information we gained from the LVs, a sort of library of ideas that had been sent our way, and then it grew to digging through the Artemis library. Both of those were what helped bring losses down from their initial numbers. There've also been a bunch of phys-side engineers here and on Earth that have been contributing."

"And I am assuming that we will be looped in on this, yes?"

"Oh, of course, I willll..." She squinted off into the middle distance, then nodded decisively. "I've granted you admin access, you can loop in whoever you would like."

"Thank you, my dear. Can you give us a better precis of the current state of this library?"

"Oh, um," Günay started, frowning. "I guess. Systechs on both LVs have come up with their own procedures and manuals and stuff, and they sent us all of those, plus a bunch of suggestions for things to try as we worked, so it's got all of that information in it. We also had a few teams going through the Artemis library searching for instances of crashes in all of the civilizations they've encountered—the four races on board and the two who didn't join. There was a bunch in there that we just grabbed wholesale and started sorting through."

"And what of us?" Dry Grass asked.

"What do you mean?"

"What of those times when you spun up Lagrange and kept it up for days or weeks before stopping it again? Did you keep the information from us? From all those systechs who were working?"

I could read the tightness in her face, the hope for news of In The Wind.

"Oh. There's some of that in there, too, yeah, though you need to understand that, in most cases, we had to restart back from the crash, which meant there was a lot of bringing the systechs up to speed, rather than them generating new ideas. A lot of it was time spent automating their work so that the System came back at as close to full potential as possible. This last restart began a week before you remember with only a few systechs running through final attempts to recover instances before the boot process completed."

Selena leaned forward. "That's fascinating. Which systechs, though?"

Günay furrowed her brow. "I don't remember off the top of my head, but I can get you the list." She paused, adding almost bashfully, "Though their memories were also trimmed."

"Why?" Answers Will Not Help snapped, rising to her feet.

She shied away from the Odist. "Because...because everyone in the System went through that. We could only do a batch job. The only filter we were able to manage before losses started to grow was for those who uploaded in those 15 minutes to prevent neurological damage. I'm sorry, nothing nefarious, I promise..."

Jonas Fa rested a hand on Answers Will Not Help's arm, gently pushing her back into her seat. "Thanks, Günay. We're going to trust you on that, but we may have questions later, okay?"

"Right," she said, sounding small.

"Mr. Strzepek," Need An Answer said, guiding focus over to Jakub. "Can you please tell us about the proposed changes to the System Consortium?"

He nodded impassively. "Yes. We're working on more tightly integrating any System leadership into–"

"Let us stick with the term 'representatives', please."

Wrong footed, he blinked a few times, then continued. "Any System...representatives into the Consortium board."

"How do you propose to do that?"

"We'll discuss that."

Need An Answer smiled, and the blandness of her smile spoke of contempt. "What a lovely opportunity we have to start right now, my dear."

"Right," he said through gritted teeth. I could almost feel the higher-ups breathing down his neck to cooperate. "The two proposals are for a permanent AVEC connection to Consortium headquarters in Trondheim and to set up an instance of the System in the building allowing the...representatives to exist within the building's physical space. The former could happen immediately, the latter will take five years or so."

Jonas Ko tilted his head, eyebrows raised. "A secondary System? Collocated instances?"

"Yes, connected by an Ansible connection with Lagrange. It's the same technology that would allow us to divide up the physical components of the System for safety's sake, after all."

"Jesus," he murmured, echoed by several others around the table, leading to quiet laughter. "Not sure how to feel seeing everyone taking so much interest in us."

Jakub bristled again, and this time didn't try to hide it. "Screw you, Jonas. You keep acting like I'm working against you, when all I'm doing is trying to manage the situation. I took this job for a reason, I *care* about the System, despite what you keep implying."

Jonas Ko gave him an almost coy look. "Jakub! You sultry minx, finally, I see a hint of that spine. You're right, you're right. We'll let up a bit."

"Ignore him, no way we are letting up on you," Answers Will Not Help said. She said it with such playfulness, though that it seemed very nearly to serve as an apology for her own snippiness.

Jakub looked between the two, still gripping the edge of his desk back phys-side. "We'll talk," he said at last.

"Of course, of course. I–"

It was at that point that my up-tree's date wrapped up and

he quit, a pile of memories cascading down onto me. I lost track of the conversation for a few seconds as I rushed to slot everything into place. There were few conflicts, but the conversations between me and Dry Grass had been deep and full of subtleties that I wasn't sure I could fully appreciate in the moment.

"What about cross-tree merges?" I asked.

Dry Grass's attention snapped over to me. Several others around the table turned to look at me, confused, and I realized that I'd interrupted someone.

"Uh...sorry."

"No, you are alright, Reed," Dry Grass said, her gaze still locked on me. "I believe we were done with that topic. Tell us about these cross-tree merges, Günay. You said that these are already enabled?"

"Oh," the tech said, pushing herself up in her chair. "Yeah, they're enabled. You must be in physical contact with the cocladist you want to merge with, and then both must confirm the intent to merge, and then only one will be allowed to quit. The merge gets offered to the other cladist as with normal merges."

"I'm assuming that one has to fork first, right?" Jonas Ko asked.

Günay shrugged. "I mean, you don't have to. You could just take on the memories without forking."

"Right, got it," he said, then smirked over to Jonas Fa. He forked into a new instance who stood behind his chair. "Hey buddy."

"Hey yourself." Jonas Fa grinned, forking as well. "Hit me."

Answers Will Not Help leaned over and socked him solidly in the shoulder.

"Ow! Not you, you little snot," he said, laughing.

"Later, children," Jonas Ko's new instance said, reaching out to take Fa's hand in his own.

After a moment's look of concentration on both of their faces, the new Jonas Fa quit. Jonas Ko—now tagged Jonas Ko/Fa, though whether by him or the System wasn't clear to me—

immediately stumbled to the side, clutching at his head. We all looked on, startled.

"Jesus Christ," he mumbled, kneading at his temples. "Felt like a normal merge, but...weird. So fucking weird."

"Weird how?" Answers Will Not Help asked cautiously.

"He's just...ugh," Jonas Ko/Fa groaned, straightening up. "He's just not like me at all. It's like...like he's living inside my head with me. This is going to take *ages* to reconcile. What the fuck..."

"How long have you two diverged, anyhow?"

"I was forked during secession, he was forked in systime 25."

Answers Will Not Help laughed. "Yikes."

Jonas Ko/Fa shook his head and said, "Fuck this. We'll play with this later," and then quit.

Throughout this show, Dry Grass's eyes never left me. I returned her gaze anxiously, mulling over the words we'd shared on our date. Words she now remembered as well. *There is potential for friendship and love, yes, but also the potential for pain.*

I mulled over those words, then made up my mind anyway.

Interlude

<u>Columbines</u>
Samantha Yule Fireheart

A Finger Pointing — 2401

I remember that sprawling labyrinth of garden boxes I tended with you, each an island of color made up of one biome or another. I remember stumbling across my down-tree and her partner, how you and I made a game of keeping *just* out of sight of them. I wrote her a letter once raising the ante, daring her to spot us between the meandering alleys of our sim.

I remember our pyromaniac phase. I remember how it *really* worked for you. We danced, you know; in the way lovers do under the moonlight deep in the mountains. We had such a fright once when your dress caught fire as you pirouetted and it billowed out like a bellflower. That frumpy old thing was so ragged the coarse fibers made for *choice* kindling. That really shook you up. That is a soreness we did not ever address. We just stopped sharing our nights over the fire for a long while.

I remember standing at the window of our kitchen looking out over the shed whose roof was damp with fresh rain and holding one another side-by-side. I remember the coarse lace of your blouse's frilled shoulders, the dampness of your freshly-showered fur. I remember the smell of grilled cheese just about to burn as I kissed your temple, feeling in the moment as if I was saying goodbye to you.

I remember how distant we felt. I shared my down-tree's desire to have the Ode clade in harmony, but our very *existence* was transgressive. My relationship with you could *not* be curtailed. Our down-trees danced in private profanity, my dear, but *we* were inseparable.

That was always the point, was it not? To lean into domesticity with one another? It was on just such a night that they forked, after all. So they went on to build their cabin in the woods, to sit under the awning of that porch bench of theirs to indulge the light of dawn and dusk alike. I remember how you began to count the colors, to make silly names from their kenning like *lividpurple* and *ultrablue* and *sweetlight*.

And I remember coupling on the Adirondack chair on that same porch while the sun was low, its plastic bowing, threatening to snap in half under our weight. I gave you that meteor shower of kisses down your neck, paw steadying your hips, when once you bucked and the thing gave out right then. We both shouted in surprise, then laughed at the absurdity of what had just transpired, and groaned as we licked our shard-bitten wounds.

I remember the court of an abandoned schoolyard overgrown with frosted branches and cast in a blanket of blinding white. I remember the stillness of the air, the chill of that heavy silence that comes when a pressure front has rolled in and your voice carries twice as far. I remember the warmth of a paw on my back through fur, under a coat far too thick for my liking. I remember you sharing the air under my jaw. I remember how you just nudged me in that *deadly* way of yours, the consequential buzzing up and down my neck, the way my arms subtly curled in against my chest as if to embrace you despite the weight of your head on my shoulder.

I remember the first time we laughed about the joyless droop of young columbines, the way they hung limply from their stems like the trunk of an elephant. I remember how you were tickled by the flamboyance of their frilled hindpetals; by the bombast of ten and then their stamina like so many proud little dicks standing erect for all to bear witness, as if for us to do so was to be some kind of transcendental experience. I remember how wide your smile was that day when, still amidst a fit of giggling, I mused that I may make a garden of them if their shamelessness so attracted you. That brightness melted me; it made me what I am today.

I see motes of memory all scattered about, significance imbued in pregnant silence and insignificant moments. I see fragments of a bigger picture all blown apart for me to collect and catalog later, presuming I remember their details at all. That is why I have written in my journal most of all about what I sense, what I feel, what I know, and less the precession of events.

> Though neither one of us would see it be sown,
> I cherish this gift-memory as were it my own,
> So I will love you as she loved her;
> I will remember for all of us.

Reed — 2401

"Reed, are you sure?" Rush asked.

I shook my head. "I don't think there's any guarantee that this will do anything like what we're hoping. I think it may actually be quite rough. When I watched Jonas do this, he said it felt really weird, like a really old merge, but also from a vastly different angle, rather than the usual down-tree."

"He, uh…" Sedge said, then cleared her throat. "He actually quit pretty soon after, said it felt like Jonas Fa was living inside of his head before there was any reconciliation."

Rush furrowed vis brow. "Christ, what a trip."

We'd gathered in my home once more, all standing out in the back yard where the sun shone and everything was green, even the little, marshy pond in one corner, even the little impossible statues that Hanne had left scattered on hidden, moss-covered pedestals. It felt like home to me, a welcome change from having spent so much time in the headquarters of late, and the last two nights split between two bedrooms. Eight days after the crash, and a little bit of home sounded nice. A little bit of comfort felt necessary.

"Yeah." I sighed. "Tule and I tried, since I already had their memories anyway, but he wouldn't be able to merge down directly. It was only a few days worth of memories, anyway. It felt strange, but not intolerably so. All the same, I was thinking maybe we'd do it somewhere relaxing so that…whoever the result is can spend however long they want reconciling in peace without having to worry about the outside world or external stimulus. Maybe that foggy pasture sim with the pagoda, maybe somewhere with a bed."

Cress shrugged. "We have a spare bedroom, too, and Dry Grass can stick around in case we need any help."

Tule nodded. "She got back up to speed really quickly, but I guess that's how it goes when you're three hundred something years old."

"Alright. That's a good idea, too."

"You like that pagoda, don't you?" Rush asked, a sly grin on vis face.

I laughed. "It's a nice sim."

"It is! Don't get me wrong. Do you think Jonas being so old is what made it so painful for him?"

"Oh, almost certainly," Sedge said. "A founder who has been slowly going nuts. Jonas Ko forked during Secession and Fa forked a few decades later."

"So before systime 1 compared to Marsh uploading in 178," I added. "And forking dates of 1 and 25, while us oldest forks are less than a hundred. We were, what, systime 180?"

Lily, who had been silent and sullen up until that point, nodded. "Systime 180+11. Individuated, but not to the same extent." She looked away, mumbling, "Enough for some differences in opinion."

Cress sighed. "I get it, Lily. I really do." It stuffed its hands in its pockets, still staring at its cocladist. "But we can sort that out between us later. For now, we'll have to contend with the fact that this new instance is going to have the same argument within them, right? Marsh managed it, so I trust that they'll be able to, but still."

Her shoulders slumped. She nodded again, falling back into silence.

"How about this," I said gently. "We give this a go and just watch to see how it goes. If they quit, they quit. We don't need to push so hard that it becomes a problem. If they stick around, then we can all discuss it together to see how it feels. If they feel closer to Marsh, neat. If not, I guess that's fine, too, and they can decide whether or not to stick around."

"I mean, that sounds alright by me," Sedge said. "Tule?"

He nodded.

"Rush?"

Another nod.

Preempting Sedge, Cress said, "Me too."

"And Lily?"

She stood in silence, staring over at the pond, ringed by reeds and cattails.

"You can say no if you–"

"Yes," Lily interrupted. "Yeah. I'll do it. If nothing else, maybe they'll be able to reconcile all of this shit with the Odists, with you all and Dry Grass. Maybe they'll be able to teach me how to, too."

Cress, Tule, and I all smiled. "Thanks, Lily," Tule said. "Even if not, that you even said that feels good."

She crossed her arms, still looking away.

"So...when do we do this?" Rush asked.

Tearing my gaze away from Lily, I said, "I don't know. We could do it now, even. I imagine it's going to take a while for the reconciling, and it's not like we all need to be there the whole time. Everyone okay with Cress and Tule's spare room? I'll let go of the pagoda I *guess*."

They laughed.

"They'll probably want a bed if they're going to be laid out with a merge," Lily murmured. "I'll swallow my pride if that helps."

"We can ask Dry Grass for some space," Tule offered.

"No, it's fine," Lily said, finally meeting our gaze again. "Weirdly, I don't have too much of a problem with her specifically, it's just...it's complicated. I don't know how I feel. I'm sorry about the funeral. I was emotional."

I reached out to pat her awkwardly on the shoulder. "Sorry I, uh...hit you."

Cress gave me an awkward look, somewhere between aghast and befuddled, then laughed. "Jesus, Reed."

"We were angry," I said, rubbing a hand over my face. "No excuse, I mean, but I got caught up in the heat of the moment."

Lily snorted. "I mean, so did I, but yeah, apology accepted. We'll work on it."

Cress grinned, shook its head. "Well, I guess come on. We'll set up the spare room and do the merge, and this new instance will be both slapper and victim."

We stepped away, me holding Rush's hand, Sedge holding Tule's, and Lily holding Cress's, to arrive on the stoop in front of the brownstone that was slowly becoming familiar, and yet which already lived in my memories.

The building was in a neighborhood in the New York sim that Dry Grass and I had gone to lunch a few days before. An actual neighborhood, too, with cladists grouped up in little knots, talking on the verge or on other stoops. The mood remained tense and anxious, but there were at least a few laughs to be heard. More than there had been before, at least.

Dry Grass, as it turned out, was already out of the house. Once we stepped inside, Lily looked around, frowning. "Weird taste in art, but okay."

"It's from a few of her cocladists," Tule explained. "Motes did the paintings, Warmth In Fire did the sculptures."

"Oh, hey!" Sedge leaned closer to one of the paintings. "I've met Motes through A Finger Pointing. Cute little skunk. Always looks like she's seven or eight or something. Always covered in paint."

I could see Lily's frown growing deeper, so I nudged everyone towards the stairs. "Come on, bedroom's up and straight ahead. I had an instance stay there last night."

We trooped up the stairs and into the bedroom. Here, despite the decor of the rest of the house, seemed to be a bedroom straight out of Marsh's home. I looked around, taken aback.

"*Lily looked uncomfortable,*" Cress sent. "*I sent an instance to clear out the paintings. They're in the closet.*"

I nodded subtly to it. "*Probably a good idea. Besides, a little busy for someone who's probably going to be having a rough time.*"

"So," Rush said as we shut the door. "What do we do next?"

"Fork, basically. Then all merge down into one of our instances." I forked as I continued. "I've done it before already, so I'll volunteer my fork. Doesn't matter in the end. It'll be a blithe merge, all memories, no one will have any sense of primary memories, really."

"Won't they wind up looking like you, though?"

I frowned. "I guess so. I can have them look like Marsh last time we met."

"How long ago was that?" Sedge asked.

I shrugged helplessly. "About a decade."

"More recent than me, at least."

"I can do it," Lily said quietly. "I saw them six months ago."

I frowned. "You did?"

"I didn't mean to. We ran into each other."

Sedge laughed. "There are two trillion people on the System. How on Earth did you just run into each other."

"We still have the same tastes, don't we? We still both like automats. We just both happened to go to that Horn & Hardart's."

I snorted. "I just went there, actually. Guess you're right."

Lily only shrugged. When she forked, a short, slight person appeared before her. They were dressed in something akin to sleepwear, though I recognized the soft and loose silk pants, the soft tunic, the thick, cotton shirt, and the shawl akin to what I'd last seen them in. They had changed in appearance, though, aside from that. Their hair was a tousled brown, their skin darker and unblemished, and their expression far more open than I remembered.

"Well, huh," Tule said. "Interesting to see the directions they went. Any idea why?"

"Not really," the new fork said. "I don't have any of their memories."

"Neither do any of us," I added. "That's something we should probably be aware of, too. This will be a lot of Marsh, all of them that comes from our lives, but none of their own that they lived in the years between."

There was silence around the room.

"I'm still in, to be clear," I said, voice sounding almost bashful to my ears. "Just a point to remember."

Sedge nodded, forked. She was followed by Tule and, after a pause, Rush and Cress.

"Well, just need to touch and intend to offer a merge. Lily—er, New Marsh?"

They shrugged. "Works for now. What do I do?"

"You'll be prompted to accept, sort of like how you can accept memories, just an additional step. Then the other one of us quits and you'll get the merge itself."

"Here," my up-tree, Reed#Merge said. "I'll go first."

"Can we do them one at a time, or can we get all of the merges lined up and incorporate in one go?"

"I...don't actually know. We can try."

They nodded, smiled faintly to Reed#Merge, and winked. "Well then...hit me."

Sedge and I laughed.

Reed#Merge took her hand and tilted his head thoughtfully. New Marsh furrowed their brow in a look of discomfort. When Reed#Merge quit, they screwed their eyes shut and let out a shuddering sigh. "Fuck, this feels weird."

Sedge#Merge stepped forward and took their hand. "Ready to try another, or do you want to try and incorporate first?"

"Go ahead," they said hoarsely.

Another thoughtful look, another quitting instance.

New Marsh let out a groan. "Okay okay okay! This'll work, but fuck, you guys, hurry!"

The rest of the clade's forks rushed forward to clasp hands

with New Marsh, quitting one by one. By the time Rush got in place, they'd collapsed to their knees and were struggling to breathe.

"Bed!" they gasped. "Please...ugh, turning off...sensorium..."

We helped lift them up to get them into the bed, resting them atop the covers.

They lay there, their eyes still squinted shut and breathing coming in ragged gasps. "Cress first," they whispered hoarsely, then groaned, expression slackening as they let the merge progress.

We stood there for a few minutes, anxious. Cress eventually sat on the edge of the bed, burying its face in its hands to kneed the heels of its palms against its eyes.

"How long will this take?" Lily whispered.

I shrugged, ineloquent.

Nearly an hour and a half later, New Marsh whispered, "Now Reed..."

Two hours later, they said. "Rush...oh! And Sedge...and Tule!"

Tule frowned, leaning closer. "What happened?"

"Reed just merged you all down a few days ago. The memories were already there." They laughed. "He already took care of a lot of the conflicts for me. Thanks, I guess."

"Uh...you're welcome?" I said, then laughed. "Are you all done, then? That was faster than expected."

They shook their head, sitting up in the bed slowly. "Memories are in place, but conflicts are still there. Those will probably take a week or two to sort out, but I can at least function now. It feels...weird. I can see what Jonas meant about it feeling like you all live in my head now, but maybe that'll pass after the conflicts are merged. Hey, can I get a glass of water?"

While Cress ducked out of the room to fetch them water, we all did our best to relax. I was surprised to see just how much tension I bore in my shoulders, just how tightly my hands had been clenched throughout. "Think you'll stick around?" I asked.

They shrugged, then winced at their own apparent soreness, nodding to Cress as it handed over the glass. "I guess for now, yeah. It's not...uncomfortable, just weird. Like having a strange taste in your mouth or wearing a new shirt or something. The conflicts are kind of itchy, but I'm already working on them a little bit."

We talked for a while longer, though descriptions were slim, repetitions of what we'd already heard. It felt weird. It felt itchy. It felt weird. It felt strange. It felt weird. Even having experienced one such merge before, it didn't wholly make sense, and I was left intensely curious. My experience had been so mild, with only a week's worth of memories, rather than dozens of years from five different instances. I had no idea if five hours was good or bad for managing all of that, but we'd always been adept at merging.

"Hey," they said at last, once the line of questions had died down. "What do you say about inviting Vos and Pierre over? Maybe they'd like to meet me."

I winced. I'd been dreading this moment. I'd intentionally not brought up the subject of Marsh's partners, lest that dissuade my cocladists. Admonitions rang in my ears, Hanne's and Dry Grass's. *I'm a bit wary you won't get what you want,* Hanne had said. *The potential for pain,* Dry Grass had said. New Marsh had these memories, now, too, but I had no way of knowing just how close they were to the surface, whether they were even at the forefront of their mind.

There was a long silence that followed as we all seemed to digest the ramifications of this.

"Yeah, I guess," Sedge said warily. "I don't know how it'll go, but yeah."

A few minutes later, we sat staggered on the stairs before the front door, New Marsh sitting up front, waiting. A knock, hesitant, sounded, and Cress called out from beside Tule, "Come in."

Vos and Pierre stood frozen, both with their hands raised in a wave, their eyes locked on this new version of their partner, slowly pushing themself to their feet to stand front and center before them.

"Marsh?" Vos croaked?

Pierre only darted forward, nearly taking New Marsh down as he collided with them, arms cinched firmly around their middle with his face buried against their shoulder, sobbing.

Stunned, New Marsh patted awkwardly at his shoulder before slowly enveloping them in a hug.

"What...but they...what?"

"Vos," I said, standing as well and moving to stand beside the pair. "I want you to meet someone."

She swayed on her feet, eventually reaching out a hand to prop herself up against the door jamb.

"One of the changes made in the System during the downtime was to enable cross-tree merging. It hasn't been announced yet, but Sedge and I were at the meetings, so we, uh..."

"I'm all of us," New Marsh said, voice strained from the force of Pierre's hug. "I'm the entire clade. I'm as much of us as I could manage."

Pierre quickly unwound his arms from them, staggering backwards with such hurriedness that he nearly tripped were it not for Vos, there to catch him. "What the fuck..."

"All of..." Vos, realizing she was all but out of air, gasped for breath. "All of you? *All* of you?"

New Marsh nodded.

"But...but Marsh..." Pierre whispered.

Vos's gaze bore into New Marsh. "You told me something on New Year's Eve, right before you headed up to the study. You looked me dead in the eye and smiled and said something."

They blanched.

"What did you say to me?"

Looking over to me nervously, they began to tremble.

"What did you say to me? Tell me," she said, voice growing louder, higher in pitch, until she was nearly screaming. Pierre quit unceremoniously, and she stomped forward a few paces. "What did you fucking say? What did you say? What did you say, whoever you are?! You said it every fucking year! *What did you fucking say?!*"

New Marsh quailed at her advance, ducking around to hide behind my arm. I could read the way that Cress moved in them, could see that warring with the need to be understood that I felt in myself, the need for my little bargain with grief to work.

Vos's gaze shifted to me. "*You,*" she growled. "This was *your* idea, wasn't it?"

I swallowed dryly and nodded.

She finished her advance in two long strides, hand already winding back, and struck me across the face hard enough to knock me to the side against the wall. I crumpled under the sudden rush of pain, winding up in a jumbled heap on the floor at the base of the stairs. New Marsh darted back as the rest of the clade cried out.

""'I'll see you in a few, beautiful',"" she spat, tears coursing down her cheeks. "That's what they said, you awful piece of shit. "I'll see you in a few.""

"Vos, I–"

I didn't get the chance to finish. She had already stepped away.

About ten seconds later, a sensorium message hit me with such force, with so much adrenaline, that I slumped over to the side. Regardless of the strength of the message, her words were eerily calm. *"No contact."*

It took nearly a minute of silence before the shock wore off enough for New Marsh to creep back into view, carefully helping me to my feet once more. My lip was split with blood trickling down my chin, and my nose felt broken, though it still looked straight. All the same, I forked as soon as I was calm enough to, letting my still bleeding down-tree quit.

Even hale once more, the memory of pain lingered.

"I need a fucking drink," Lily said. She sounded exhausted. "Come on, I know a place."

§

The place turned out to be a coffee shop that seemed to specialize in coffee-inspired cocktails.

We stepped first to Infinite Café, an enormous sim that allowed any coffee shop on Lagrange to link an entrance. It took the form of an enormous ring looping up over us with what looked to be thousands of mismatched buildings lining its single avenue. A sign before us announced this to be the cocktails district.

I upped my estimate to tens of thousands.

We numbly followed Lily as she led us through the incredibly crowded thoroughfare to an unassuming brick building with a glass door. Inside we found a sparklingly white interior, with the bar and tables made of looping and curving slabs of marble. Out front, the ice field of a glacier glinted in the sun. Whether sim echoed bar or the other way around was unclear.

Pausing just inside the door, shielding our eyes against the brightness of so much white, Rush laughed. "Goddamn, what a look."

We sat on the awkward and uncomfortable stools at one of the tall tables huddled in a corner, each nursing our espresso martinis or negronis or Irish coffees.

"Anubias."

We all looked to this new instance of us, this new member of our clade.

"Anubias. I was hunting for more marsh plants while we ordered, and I think I like that one best. Really don't want to be associated with Marsh themself, now."

"Anubias," I murmured, looking the plant up on the perisystem. "Like Anubis?"

They nodded. "God of the funeral rites."

Lily scoffed and shook her head. "Which one of you dumb-asses is *that* morbid?"

We laughed.

"That was pretty fucked," Sedge said.

"Yeah." Anubias turned their martini by the stem of the glass between their fingers. "We probably should have asked."

I agreed quickly. "We really should have. I'm not sorry that we went through with the merge, but I *am* sorry that we brought them into it. Vos cut all contact with me. I'm sorry that we thought of this whole thing as rebuilding Marsh. I knew it wouldn't be that on some level, but..." I trailed off, shrugged.

Sedge nodded. "I kind of figured it wouldn't be, too, not after seeing the new Jonas stumbling like that."

"Yeah. I'm sorry, you all."

Lily shrugged. "We knew what we were getting into, at least mostly. We all agreed."

"You seem weirdly relaxed," I said. "Actually, you seem al-most chipper."

"I got to watch you get punched in the face," she said smugly.

I rolled my eyes.

"Really, though, I feel a lot...I don't know. Lighter, maybe? Like I got a lot off my chest in the process. I'll want to talk with you, Anubias, at some point to keep thinking about this whole Odist thing. Maybe this can be a part of that reconciliation."

They nodded. "Sure."

"But yeah, even just going through with this felt like a step forward after however many steps backward. It feels like ages since that dinner at your place, Reed, all that time getting more and more upset."

"Yeah."

Silence fell again as we drank.

"So what do we do now?" Cress asked, downing the rest of their drink in one go.

We all looked around at each other, searching for answers in each other's faces. I let the moment linger. There was, as always, a pressure on me as the oldest to speak up, to be some sort of, if not leader, then at least wrangler-of-opinions.

"Start processing, I guess," I said at last. "Send letters to the LVs, catch up with friends, spend time with loved ones, and start processing whatever the world has become."

Epilogue

A dull clang rang out from the dim light of the stage, followed by a sickening thump. The girl, looking no older than fifteen, sprawled, limp and bloodied, unconscious on parquet. A person stood over her, breathing heavily, spittle flecking their lips and madness in their eyes. They let out a feral scream and leapt high in the air, a length of pipe held over their head, which they brought down with all of their might.

Right as it was about to land, the lights went out, leaving the entire auditorium from stage to doors in pitch black. In the darkness, the last of the shout was punctuated with another clang and a horrible crunch.

The play continued from there. The police showed up. The investigation was swift and decisive. The arrest was made. All of this in utter darkness.

Even at the scene change, though, as the lights came back up, as the foyer disappeared and was replaced with a court-room done up all in wood, the scene for the rest of the performance, the puddle of blood remained on the floor, untouched and bright, arterial red, glinting in the stage-lights.

At first, I thought it must have been a mistake, some stage-hand forgetting to clean up the mess. As the play continued, though, it became increasingly clear that this was intentional. The attorneys deftly avoided stepping in the puddle, never looking at it. The judge never looked at it. The jury never looked at it. Neither did the bailiff or any of the witnesses.

The perpetrator, however, couldn't seem to keep their eyes off it. Even as they were brought to the stand, even as they rambled, nigh-incoherently, in response to the whys and hows that the prosecutors threw at them, their gaze never left the blood, still untouched, unsmeared except for where the victim's body had pushed it. Even as flashbacks played out in reverse chronological order, from the police's investigation to the murder to the point at which the perpetrator had first met the victim early in their childhood, all taking place in a feathered spotlight behind the prowling lawyers with the rest courtroom dimmed, they stared, eyes wide. Their expression was at times hungry, at times mournful, but always keenly focused.

As the play drew up to the climax, as the attacker was convicted and condemned to live forever, mouldering in some dark cell, they at last darted around the defense's table, hands still cuffed before them, and collapsed, laughing and sobbing in equal measure, above the pool of blood, smearing it on their hands, over their face and clothes. "I did it!" they howled. "I fucking did it *and it didn't mean a fucking thing!*"

We were once more dropped into utter blackness, treated to nearly five minutes more of wails and screeches, giggles and sobs, laughter and half-words, all slowly fading to silence.

The analogy was clear—almost ham fisted—and it left my stomach churning. It left a lump in my throat and a hotness on my face. It left me sobbing. Me and so many others in the audience, from what I saw when the lights came back up. Each seat had a cone of silence above it, preventing me from hearing anyone else. Beside me, Dry Grass had started crying from the beginning and hadn't lifted her head from her arms folded on the small table before us throughout the entire performance.

The auditorium, full at the start, was half-empty by the end, so many of the audience members having left in disgust or pain.

But now it was over and the house lights were coming back up, illuminating the two score crescent moon tables scattered through the room, the remaining audience sitting behind them in comfortable chairs. I stayed beside Dry Grass, rubbing her back gently as she worked to get her emotions under control. The audience filed out slowly while a few techs tore down the stage, gesturing at various props and the like, which either blipped out of existence or floated back into storage on their own. The blood on the stage was, thankfully, in the former category.

Dry Grass, now leaning back in her chair and breathing in deliberate calm, and I watched as as a bundle of black and white fur sprinted across the stage and hurled itself out into the audience, making as much of a bee-line for us as was possible with the tables in the way.

Swivelling her chair toward the hurtling skunk, Dry Grass threw her arms wide, letting Motes leap into them.

"Dry Grass Dry Grass Dry Grass!"

"Motes!" She pushed the skunk away from her enough to meet her gaze. "You stupid...awful..." She fell to crying once again, clutching Motes to her front.

That means I did a good job!" the skunk sent via a sensorium message as she rested her head over her cocladist's shoulder, grinning at me. She looked to be no more than ten, despite being the same three-hundred-odd years old as Dry grass. Where Warmth In Fire bore childishness about em, Motes seemed to actually just be ten years old.

I shook my head in disbelief and leaned forward to pat her gently between the ears.

After another minute or so, Dry Grass carefully swiveled around to face me, looking over Motes's shoulder in turn. "This little asshole *knows* I hate it when she does those scenes."

The skunk squirmed about in her arms until she was sitting sideways in her lap. "I did not know you were here," she countered. "That would not have changed the show, but I still did not know, or I would have warned you to arrive late."

Dry Grass took the chance to wipe her face with a napkin swiped from the table. "I would have appreciated that, yes."

"You would have hated the original! Ioan wrote it so that the body was supposed to stay on the stage instead of just the blood. When I said I wanted the part, ey changed it to be just the blood so there was not just a kid's body laying on stage, even though it took some creative work with gravity."

I glanced back to the stage, realizing that it was actually canted toward the audience by about fifteen degrees. Enough that we could clearly see the surface of the stage—back to a blissfully clean matte black instead of the blood-stained parquet that had been there before—without it being so unnerving as to make us feel like we were going to fall towards it, or that the actors were going to fall into the audience.

"You are right," Dry Grass was saying, straightening out Motes's shirt and overalls, both of which were thoroughly stained with paint. "I would have hated that even more. I did not even see the rest of the play, skunklet. I put my head down and turned down my hearing."

"Aw!"

"It was pretty good," I admitted. "I can tell you about it later."

"No, I will read it on my own at some point when I am calmer." Dry Grass nodded toward the stage. "But look, A Finger Pointing and Beholden."

The two Odists—one tall, slender, and human, the other a shorter, softer skunk—made their way far more sedately toward our table. They walked arm in arm, leaning affectionately against each other, each carrying a drink in their free hand and paw.

"Reed!" A Finger Pointing began, reaching out with one arm to offer me a hug. "I am pleased you made it." She glanced at Dry Grass with a rueful smile. "I hope we did not traumatize you *too* much.

I leaned into that hug and watched as Beholden started guiding chairs away from the next table over with a gesture, a curl of the finger beckoning them over one by one. One slid across the floor so that she could flop down into it, with another for her parter. As soon as she and A Finger Pointing had done so, Motes forked off two more instances to go pile into each of their laps as well. After all, as Dry Grass had explained, they had essentially adopted the roles of Motes's parents.

"You have, but Motes has already apologized," Dry Grass said.

A Finger Pointing winced at Dry Grass' words, setting her drink down and offering a bow. "I am sorry, my dear; I recognize that our approach to reclamation is at times quite uncomfortable. I will endeavor not to be so careless in the future. More warnings, perhaps."

Dry Grass waved the comment away. "I trust you, Pointillist. Thank you for the consideration."

The taller Odist showed none of that wariness when her eyes came back up to meet mine. "I am sure we each feel differently about this particular production. I, for one, would have been satisfied even if the house were empty; all that preparation, that one climactic performance makes for a potent font of catharsis, does it not?"

I laughed, my throat still raw from my own bout of crying. "I suppose so. Motes certainly seems to think so."

The skunk lingering on Dry Grass's lap grinned proudly to me.

Dry Grass sighed. "That it does, my dear, and that is what keeps it a trauma worth processing."

Beholden laughed. "You are so very much yourself, Dry Grass." She gave her instance of Motes a squeeze. "Please do keep that up. But how are you two feeling beside that? Any news?"

"Yes, have you heard back from the LVs, yet? It is about time, is it not?" A Finger Pointing asked.

"Yes," Dry Grass said. "At least I have. News has started to come in from Castor and Pollux. It was a shock to hear from In The Wind#Pollux. I have set aside processing that for later, though; I believe Reed even has a letter."

I sighed, leaning forward to grab my drink off the bar before settling back in my chair. I was glad I'd gone for a wine rather than anything fizzy. My throat still felt raw from the crying. "I'm doing okay, I think. Coming to terms with it all. The play was...a lot. I guess part of why it hit me so hard was because, yeah, I heard back from Marsh#Castor today."

"Oh, Reed. I had not considered how they might fit together," Dry Grass said, leaning over to squeeze my hand. "Do you want to talk about it?"

"Actually, I was hoping I could get your opinion on some of it, if you don't mind," I said, looking to the others.

Motes, preoccupied with soaking up as much affection as she could, merely shrugged.

"I am fine with it," Dry Grass said, then added with a smirk, "That is why I brought you here, after all, is it not? That and the experience?"

I laughed, nodded.

A Finger Pointing leaned down to her Motes's ear. "My dear, could you–?" she cooed. The little skunk leaned up, dotted her nose affectionately to her cheek, and then quit. "Please, Reed; I am *intensely* curious what they have to say about all this."

Beholden seemed focused on brushing out Motes' mane—perhaps a little more than could be expected, as though working to distract herself—though she nodded all the same.

"Alright, thanks. I'll just read it to you, it's fairly short." Feeling a little silly just staring off into space to read, I summoned up the letter on a sheet of paper and began to read.

Reed,

Words cannot express how glad I am to hear from you! Over the last few weeks, we've heard that they were finally on track to start bringing Lagrange back online, and then we finally got the notice that the System had finally come back up and that they'd gotten the non-recoverable losses down to 1%. We had a small party here with all the Marshans here—

there's a new one, by the way, Hyacinth. They'll write you their own letter.

We weren't the only ones, either. Every one of us was invited to no less than three other parties celebrating the news. You may be out of reach for those of us on the launches, but we do still love you all, and deeply. Thinking we'd lost you for good was one hell of a way to prove that to ourselves.

Over the next week, we started to hear from more and more people as news of their clades back on Lagrange began to trickle in. Most of those we talked to spoke of losses of tracking or tasked instances. No small pain, of course, as some of those tracking instances were tracking things like relationships, but a few days later, we heard an instance of first one missing cladist, then another. A friend we made after Launch was inconsolable after learning that he just no longer existed on Lagrange in any form. He had had a clade of two, and both were wiped out, plus all three of their tasked instances. The Arondight clade on Lagrange is no more.

Our anxiety began to grow without hearing from you. We knew you were busy, at least: news of Sedge working as hard as she was reached even us in those first days. Still, I wish you'd written sooner.

To finally get a letter that said that I was dead, however, made me feel in a way I can't even begin to describe. I was sad, because of course I was—someone I knew and talked with with some regularity was now dead. I was stunned, because of course I was—the disaster was now very immediate and real, affecting my own clade.

But what am I to do with the knowledge that it was specifically *me* that was dead? You live on, as do Lily and Cress, Rush and Sedge and Tule, but the root of your clade is now gone. You're now six instead of seven. You're now a clade without a root instance. *We're* a clade without a root instance. I exist, sure, as does Marsh#Pollux, but our down-tree doesn't. We came from them, didn't we?

Here I went on for some length about what it must mean for a clade to be without a root, about how you're now three completely separate clades, un-related, but I realized I was saying relatively little. That's still true, in a way. It's true in the clade sense, in the *tree* sense, but apparently no longer in the me-chanical sense. This cross-tree merging! It sounds like it's going to change everything. No more merg-ing down only. 'Cross-tree' means less now; sure, there's the lack of shared memory, but no longer are they out of reach of merging.

I don't blame you at all for what you all did to create Anubias. I know that it hurt Vos and Pierre, and I hope that, some time in the future, they can bring themselves to forgive you. But honestly, I would have done the same. I would've done everything in my power to reach for some bit of the old to bring back to life. I know that Anubias is *not* me, that they can never be the root of the clade, but you did what you felt you had to to try and make your lives more complete.

I hope there are more letters on the way, but please write me as soon as you get this. You'll have had eight months of getting used to life without our root instance. You'll have had eight months with-out Marsh, and I want to know how it feels. I want to know how to get over this very real, but very strange grief.

Until then, you all have all our love. I'm glad to hear that, even in the midst of this, that love is still a thing and that you and Dry Grass are revelling in that. I'll have to meet up with her instance, here on Castor. Keep yourselves safe, and stay in touch. We'll do the same.

Marsh#Castor

When I finished reading, our little crowd sat in silence, each thinking their own thoughts.

My eyes were drawn to A Finger Pointing, to the pensive tapping-together of her fingertips. "I have been looking forward to the opportunity to speak with you about just that, Reed. About this cross-tree merge, I mean. About Anubias." She glanced at Beholden, who nodded, though her own gaze remained distant, then went on. "We, too, are without our root instance. We are without our Michelle Hadje, she who became ten, who became—nominally—one hundred."

Dry Grass carefully nudged Motes out of her lap so that she could straighten out her blouse. The little skunk bubbled up with the instance in Beholden's lap; letting her up-tree quit so that she could merge, then taking her place.

"It has been a long time for us." Dry Grass smiled faintly. "A *very* long time. You have had eight months, my dear."

I looked down at the paper, just as I had done for much of the day already.

"I would like to hear how you feel, too, Reed," Dry Grass said. "We all have our thoughts on the matter—we are Odists, of *course* we do—I am sure, but before we taint yours, tell us how you feel."

I sighed, eventually folding up the letter and returning it to my pocket. The physicality of it made it feel more real, focused my mind in one particular spot. Getting it out of my hands gave me, somehow, permission to look up and speak directly to the others.

"I'm feeling torn," I admitted. "I like Anubias. They've quickly found a place in our clade. They aren't *Marsh*, though. I've been...I don't know." I took a moment to reclaim my train of thought as my speech stumbled to a stop. "I guess I'm well into grieving now, and even if Vos hasn't reopened communication, I'm sitting with her in that loss of someone important. Whether or not it's important that they were the root instance varies from day to day. Today, it feels pretty important."

Dry Grass nodded. "There were times throughout our history that Michelle felt more like a friend or sister than our down-tree instance. It hurt either way, but the mechanical aspects, the sundering of the ten stanzas, lingered often in our thoughts."

"It seemed rather more symbolic, for my part, that particular note," A Finger Pointing commented. "We seldom merged with her after those first few years. What really bothered *me* was the implication that we were all doomed to quit, that what happened to her was a premonition of what was to come."

Beholden looked suddenly away, mastering some intense emotion that washed over her face. She seemed to want to speak, though, so we all remained in silence.

"And we *do* have that in us," she said at last, voice thick. "We do have the capability–"

When her voice failed, A Finger Pointing reached over to her partner, pulling her close by the shoulders.

She sniffed, sighed, then went on. "–in Death Itself and I Do Not Know, but also in Muse, my up-tree."

Motes drew her legs up onto the chair with her and buried her face in her arms.

"I never did keep that final merge," Beholden said quietly. "It was too much, too fast, too soon. It was all far too close to the Century Attack, and it was so much time in one merge that I was worried I would lose who I was. *This* me—the one that loves Boss–" She nodded over to A Finger Pointing. The affectionate hypocorism got her a smirk in return. "–and Motes in the way I do—would not exist anymore. Not quite."

There was a quiet whimper from the smaller skunk in her lap, which gained her a kiss atop the head from her guardian.

"Her letter and their garden of nasturtiums and columbines will have to do, I suppose."

"And my memories from Beckoning," A Finger Pointing added quietly. "I do have those, yes? I have been meting them out to you at the choicest of moments when I feel you need a good cry."

Beholden rolled her eyes, but the hidden smile there was genuine. This was, it seemed, a particular discussion that had lost much of its sting. "She quit and left behind only memories, I mean to say. It is all we had when people died back phys-side, and it is all we have here, now, cases such as these."

"I do not *like* it," Beholden added with a bitter chuckle. "I think I actually *hate* it, that she could do that—that *any* of them could do that. One more thing to be anxious about after months and months of anxiety."

A Finger Pointing watched Dry Grass carefully while Beholden spoke, turning her gaze on me only after some silence lingered between us. "I do not believe this premonition, of course, that we are doomed to quit, but you can see how it affects each of us. There is enough death in our clade to make us wonder, yes?"

Dry Grass nodded, perhaps a bit warily.

She spent a moment doting on Beholden before straightening up, brushing out her blouse with a sigh. "There is, perhaps, some of my longing for Dear in this—it is the instance artist of our clade, now no longer on Lagrange, and instance artistry has held my interest since I met it—but I have been gradually reaching out to each of my cocladists in the hopes of creating a synthesis of our clade—our own Anubias, if you will—named Ashes Denote That Fire Was. We both have our beloved naming schemes, yes?"

I laughed, nodded.

"It is not out of an effort to recreate Michelle, though, but to better understand one another and ourselves through the lens of someone who is each of us at once."

Dry Grass nodded. "The mutual understanding is a thing I am particularly interested in. There have been schisms within our clade that might...well, not be mended, but may at least provide greater understanding."

Motes lifted her head and, despite the tear-tracks in the fur on her cheeks, smirked. "*We* got cut off!" she said proudly. "Even you did, Dry Grass!"

"For a bit, kiddo," she said, laughing.

"I do not know that we will resolve disputes so dire as that with a mediating instance," A Finger Pointing said with a soft chuckle. "Although I have occasionally done such within the fifth stanza—even before this business with cross-tree merging—what I am really interested in is how it might give us a more complete picture of the Ode clade at large. We have occasionally been accused of idolatry, of placing the *idea* of the clade above the community that it comprises, but now I think our community is all but dead, and in desperate need of some unifying identity lest we ever remain shattered."

Dry Grass smiled wryly. "I was surprised at just how willing Hammered Silver was. She cut off three entire stanzas—and, briefly, me—and I expected that would mean that she would be rather opposed to the idea. I am curious to see how that goes, in the end." Turning to me, she continued, grinning, "But you also dealt with that with Lily, yes? You punched her, even."

A Finger Pointing looked wide-eyed at me, leaning back. "Reed?"

I laughed, sheepish. "It was hardly a punch! I slapped her in the heat of an argument. Don't worry, I got that and more from Vos," I said, shaking my head. "I still feel awful about that. It's...well, not really something I thought I had in me. Everything was just so stressful around then. It was less than a week after the attack."

My words didn't seem to reach her, or perhaps they weren't

convincing enough. She looked warily to Dry Grass, then back to me. "Grief in the wake of the Century Attack has caused a great deal of pain; and it did not stop with the loss of our loved ones on New Year's Eve, did it? Muse quit a week later out of despair—her and so many others in her position—and now I learn the Marshans and their beloved are *hitting* each other!"

Any lingering mirth I felt quickly died. What had since turned to a source of humor between me and Lily—at least on the occasions we *did* talk—was suddenly brought into contrast with the rest of our lives. "No, you bring up a good point. I stand by the fact that it felt awful at the time, and it stung for a long while after. I don't see myself as a violent person, but clearly I have it in me. Vos remains no-contact, so I can't guess how she feels, but she didn't seem the type to lean on violence, either."

Dry Grass, looking between her cocladist and I with an expression more of curiosity than anxiety, said, "You do not strike me as violent either, but it does have me wondering just how much that remains after the fact."

"I should hope he does not strike you at all!" A Finger Pointing quipped. She looked to me with a disarming smile, and I felt at once the dialectic couched within her words. This fighting—though unconscionable—was no isolated event; more than one of my friends had similarly lashed out, and the feeds were filled with cladists hunting for therapists.

I snorted. "I have not, nor do I plan to. It has me watching my actions like a hawk, and while I'm sure the anxiety over the fact that I'm capable of such things will fade, I doubt I'll ever forget about it—really, truly forget: it'll stay in the forefront of my mind whenever strong feelings come up."

Dry Grass nodded. "I would not want you to remain in anxiety, of course, but I am pleased to hear that it is something you are cognizant of."

A Finger Pointing crosses her arms. "Anubias possesses both your and Lily's perspective on that spat; what have they to say about it?"

"It's certainly come up in conversations with them, how they were dealing with the conflicting views of everything from throughout the clade. Marsh had clearly done so, after all, right? Whatever thoughts I had of reconstruction in that particular sense evaporated almost immediately, and we all leaned into this reconciliation as soon as they picked their name, so it's not like it's out of reach for us to fully reconcile."

Beholden smirked. "I know Slow Hours and I have had our spats from time to time–."

"More than that!" Motes said, grinning.

"–*often*, so the cross-tree merging has given us another tool to mediate." She rolled her eyes, adding, "*When* we decide to actually use it."

"Well, huh," I said, sitting back in my chair, arms crossed. "I hadn't actually made that connection—that cross-tree merging could be a deliberate form of mediation rather than some accident of Anubias."

"You would have to commit, yes? The both of you would."

"Right. Things are *better,* but they aren't *great.* She still has her issues with your clade."

The skunk snorted. "Yes, yes. Yet more of the same, I assume."

I laughed, nodded. "Too much sensationalist history, I guess."

"I still want to kick Ioan's ass for some of that."

A Finger Pointing tilts her head at Beholden. "You want to kick Ioan's ass for all the embarrassing things ey has made you say on that very stage behind us."

"I want to kick eir ass just in general," she said primly. "It just seems like it might be fun."

"Oh, it *is,*" she mused, before turning her gaze on me once more. "So let that be my request to you, Reed. I want you and Lily to talk about this, to consult with Anubias, and to tell me how that goes. I am sure Dear would have a heyday if it were here to explore cross-tree merging, but seeing as it went the Ansible—I am *very* much stealing that turn of phrase—I think I would like to collaborate with you three on this new form of reclamation."

With that, we fell into, at first, silence, and then comfortable chatter about the small things. Drinks were summoned—warmer and more comforting—while Motes slipped out of Beholden's lap and dreamed up some chalk to start drawing on the black-painted-concrete floor, an image I recognized as the dandelion-ridden field where I met the Ode clade that first morning after the attack, so long ago and yet also so recently. Dry Grass and I cozied up together, as did Beholden and A Finger Pointing.

It was, I decided, our own reclamation, just the five of us. The stress of the play was behind us. The stress of the Century Attack could be set aside. For tonight, we were here together, with all our love and affection. For tonight, Motes could doodle on the floor of the auditorium without a care, Dry Grass could tease me about my tickly stubble when I kissed her cheek, and Beholden and A Finger Pointing could exchange looks of devotion of an intensity I rarely saw.

Tonight, we were *here.*

We were here together.

Stories From After

Game Night

Michael Miele

Joanna — 2401

Joanna sat at her kitchen table, having the hardest time figuring out the next best move to make while playing solitaire. The cards were jumbo print, of course, a leftover from her time physside. She was just about to move a column of cards using a king when she heard her doorbell. She could have created her sim so the default entrance was within her home, but she was old-fashioned. She liked having her guests wait a bit while she got around to answer the door. There was something to be said for indulging anticipation, especially on the System, where so many things were instantaneous. She swiped a wrinkled hand over the in-progress game and the cards fluttered away, stored in an exocortex to pick up later. She got up slowly and puttered her way over to the front door.

Arranging this get-together was a welcome distraction for her. When she received the confirmation message, she had trouble thinking of much else. Though she hadn't met her visitor yet, Joanna knew what she looked like. She looked out of the peephole to check it was her visitor before undoing the lock and opening up the door.

An older woman was standing on Joanna's front porch. She had a slight hunch to her back and was quite short so that Joanna had to look down slightly to make eye contact. She was wearing a striped shirt with comfortable slacks and her gray hair was done up in a perm tighter than any of the folds of her skin. She was clutching a small purse and looked expectantly at Joanna to make the first move.

"I trust you're Bethann then? Saw my ad in the feeds?" Joanna asked.

"Yes, yes. And you must be Joanna. I decided to come and see what this is about. I could also use a break after all the unpleasantness that's been going on."

"Well that is an understatement. Still, I am glad you made the trip out."

"Likewise. Now, can I come inside? The outside of your sim isn't exactly winning any awards."

Joanna held out her hand to help the woman climb up the final step into the house. Bethann pushed past her hand and stepped inside without another thought. The interior was cozy, if not a little dusty. There was a boxy T.V. set into an ornate wooden frame that sat on the floor facing the living room. The thought of moving it was impossible, it had been there long enough to begin fusing with the floorboards underneath it. The couch had an intricate floral pattern for a flower that Bethann was sure did not exist. Perhaps a take on an object'd'art from the Exchange? The coffee table, fittingly, had an abandoned cup of coffee sitting off to the side. The living room was small, barely enough room to step around the tables and furniture to move around. Bethann wondered to herself why Joanna had decided to make her sim so cramped. Before she could ask, Joanna said, "I'm glad you could take time out of your busy schedule to come over."

A blatant attempt to guilt Bethann over her re-scheduling their meeting. She let the comment slide off of her and responded with, "I would have arrived sooner, but I won't miss my shows. I've been getting invested in the newest reboot of Darkest Shadows. They've learned a lot from the last seven attempts that is making the show compelling to keep up with."

"I'm more partial to Bonanza myself, but I don't think the writers knew what to do with Hoss in the latest version being produced sys-side. I stopped watching when Little Joe forked into Medium Joe and Big Joe. That's just too much Joe for one show."

"Yes, it does sound like a lot. So where are we doing this? I don't think there's enough leg room for us to set up here."

Joanna puttered around Bethann, shuffling her feet on the worn carpet as she did so. She waved her hand for Bethann to follow her. "This way dear, we'll have more room in the kitchen."

Bethann walked over and sat down in one of the two chairs set up at the kitchen table. Much like everything else in the sim, it seemed tailor-made for Joanna's convenience first. The table was big enough to seat one extra guest and no more. Joanna arrived shortly after Bethann had set down her purse. If Bethann had noticed how Joanna had neglected to offer her a drink or snack before they were settled, she didn't say so.

"What game would you like to play first? Was there a favorite that your young gentleman would choose?"

Joanna laughed, "You get right to the point don't you? Reminds me of him in a way. But to answer your question, we would take turns in picking out the games we would play. Since you are my guest, I'll give you the first choice."

"That's mighty kind of you. I'm partial to boardgames, so I'll suggest something simple to start with. Have you ever played Uncle Wiggily?"

"I can't say that I have, but I'm willing to learn."

"If you'll grant me the proper ACL's, I can grab it out of the games I've brought with me."

Joanna looked up and away for a few seconds before saying, "There, you should have permission now."

Bethann reached her hands into her purse and pulled out a colorful box with a collection of anthropomorphic animals dressed in fancy clothes prancing about in an idyllic forest. The majority of the box art was taken up by the titular Uncle Wiggily, a dandy rabbit man with a black suit jacket, bright yellow shirt, red corduroy pants, blue bowtie, and a top hat that he had tipped to the side.

Bethann opened up the box and began unfolding the game board and setting out the player markers. "If you're at all familiar with Candy Land, it plays similarly. You draw cards from the deck and on each of the cards is a number that tells you how much you are to move. The catch is that there are poems on each of the cards and you must read out the poem before you are allowed to move."

"Every time? Wouldn't that get tiring?" Joanna asked.

"It's a part of the overall whimsy the game is trying to evoke. You are a dandy woodland animal having a merry time of skipping through the forest after all."

Bethann set the player pieces in front of Joanna, each a copy of Uncle Wiggily but with different colored suits in red, green, blue, and yellow. Joanna chose the blue piece and Bethann chose the green. They set their pieces on the starting square and took turns reading the cards and moving their pieces. As they settled into a rhythm of passing turns, they talked with each other.

"I'm deeply sorry for your loss. I've lost a lot of good friends in the New Year too," Bethann said.

"Thank you. It's been a terrible few days."

"What was your young gentleman's name?"

"His name was NaSRFS. I didn't know much about him, but he would come once a week to spend time with me. Didn't strike me as a tracker, more of a tasker really. That made his choice to visit a little more special. It's nice to know that he was willing to fork for our time together."

For a moment, Bethann's shoulders tensed at the mention of NaSRFS, and then it was gone. "That does sound nice. It's good for us old fogeys to socialize with younger instances. They keep us up to date on what's happening outside of our own sims in the System, do they not?"

It was a leading question, but Joanna was not taking the bait. After an uncomfortable silence had passed, Bethann placed her marker at the end of the winding path and said, "I guess that makes me the winner. Why don't you choose a game for us to play next?" She gathered up the pieces, shuffled the cards, and folded up the board in quick measure. Packing it away quickly and carefully.

"Oh, I know just the game. I'm more for card games, so I'll teach you how to play Clock."

"Never heard of it before."

"Then I'm glad I can be your introduction." Joanna pointed her hand down and flicked it quickly upwards. Through the motion, she had produced a standard deck of playing cards with the words JUMBO PRINT on the side in large bubble letters. She took out the cards, removed the jokers and rule card, and began shuffling the deck. As she shuffled, she explained the basics of the game.

"Clock is a lot like a cooperative variant of solitaire. You work together to play cards on the various positions around the 'clock' that is built around the deck. But it is a competitive game too, as each play gets both of you closer to playing out the cards in your hand and winning the game."

"Sounds delightful. How many cards do we get?"

"Five to start, but if you don't have a play, you draw until you have a playable card." Joanna stopped shuffling and dealt out the cards to herself and Bethann. She alternated giving each of them a card until they had a full hand of five. Then, she turned over four cards from the top of the deck to form a cross shape around the deck in the center.

"I'll go first," Joanna said, placing a black five on top of a red six.

Bethann played a red nine on a black ten and passed her turn. A few turns later, Joanna stopped her turn to say, "Aces are special, you play them on the corners and then can build on top of that suit. They provide a new set of plays to make on your turn and open up new strategies." She laid down her ace of hearts in the upper left corner, closest to Bethann. "You've been awfully quiet. Are you also thinking of someone you lost recently?"

Bethann grumbled and drew from the deck until she had a three she could play.

"Yes, a good many someones. Three long-lived instances of my own that I will miss, though they never called, so less so than others."

"I was lucky enough to keep all of my personal instances. I'm sorry to hear you have lost some of yours." She played a king and moved a column of cards onto another column.

"It's small potatoes in comparison to the rest of the System. But I guess everyone's hurting." Bethann played a queen on Joanna's king.

"I've reached out to my family, but they're reeling too."

"I really should do that. With everything happening, I didn't really consider it."

"That's surprising. Especially when you agreed to spend time with a stranger on such short notice. No other friends available?" Joanna was needling Bethann, trying to get her to crack.

"Much as I would love to tell you, it seems as though you've won." Bethann moved the six of hearts onto the five in the corner and waited expectantly.

Joanna swore under her breath. She played her last card, the seven of hearts, and said, "So I have. What are we playing next?"

"Phase 10 but with dice. I could do with throwing something right now."

Joanna tried to keep the insinuation that she had thrown their previous match deliberately out of her voice. "Sounds interesting, how do you play?"

"If you're familiar with Yahtzee, it's similar in a lot of ways. You roll all ten of your dice and then choose which you want to keep, re-rolling up to three times. Then you try to make hands with the numbers you rolled and we score after ten rounds."

Bethann brought out the game and they spent time talking about little things. Joanna mentioned her new favorite coffee brand she had found on the Exchange while Bethann complained of the gall of the newest uploads in their tone on the shared feeds. While they were both still listening intently, neither prodded the other for more information than was given. Before they knew it, ten rounds had passed.

Bethann tallied up their scores and said, "My, my. I seem to have won this one."

"I can't believe your third re-roll actually mattered in that final round."

"What can I say? Risk is necessary if you want to win."

"I've got my own game that has an element of risk."

"Oh? Do tell."

"It's called Steal-A-Bundle. You make pairs with the cards on the board and the cards in your hand, but your pile can be stolen out from under you if your opponent has the same card that is on top of your pile in their hand."

"Hmm, sounds like it could get tricky quickly. Well, go ahead and deal out the cards then."

Joanna shuffled her well-worn deck and placed four cards face up in the center of the table. She then dealt out four cards to each of them. They passed turns back and forth, each placing a card from their hand onto a card in the center and adding it to their pile. They were even with each other until Joanna had picked up a set of eight's. Bethann flashed her own eight from her hand and moved Joanna's bundle on top of her own.

"A shame, Joanna, truly. It seems you don't know how to manage risk after all."

Joanna's eyebrow twitched at that. Bethann had crossed a line with that implication. She placed the remaining eight from the deck on top of Bethann's bundle, pulling the cards into her own pile. "I know more than you can imagine. Like that you also had a standing game night with NaSFRS."

Bethann's eyes went wide. "How did you..."

But Joanna cut her off, "When I found out he was lost, I did some digging. And I can never just leave well-enough alone. I think you did much the same as me. I respect you enough to think that you weren't completely unaware of the way I worded my ad on the feed. It was set to run in your most heavily traf-ficked areas after all. Let's cut the shit for a second."

Bethann let herself relax and the tone of her voice was icy, calculated. "You should know that I forked just for this meeting. If you're carrying out some grand plot, you're not going to take me out here."

Joanna scoffed and said, "We've just met, I don't expect you to have a CPV built out for me. And I don't have one for you, if you are worried about that. That comes later once we get to know each other better."

"Then what, exactly, are you driving at?"

Joanna leaned across the table and got in Bethann's face as she whispered, "He got us to drop our guard. Both of us."

"Yes, that is troubling. But whatever he knew has left with him. Shouldn't that be a comfort?" Bethann asked.

Joanna's face pulled down into a deep frown. "We know a lot of dangerous secrets."

Bethann waved a hand through the air, dismissing her con-cerns. "Oh sure, bunches. But that doesn't make it easier to lose him."

Joanna leaned back, which caused the wooden chair to creak slightly. "How can you be certain he wasn't just using us to get intel?"

"I can't be sure, but we used him too. Admit it. Wasn't it good to have someone to play games with that would give a damn?"

Joanna's frown eased back off into a tired smile. "Yes, it was. He knew how to keep things interesting."

"If it helps, I miss him terribly as well."

"Strangely, it does." Joanna straightened up and asked, "Now what are we playing next?"

"I'd like to kick this up a notch. Try something a bit more complicated. Have you ever played Othello before?"

"Hmm, not particularly. Are you sure you don't want to play chess?"

"No, no. I find it to be too cliche. And we're playing friendly games, correct? I have a bit of a mean streak with chess."

"Othello it is then."

Joanna cleared the table with a thought, the playing cards sliding effortlessly back into their box. Bethann dug around in her purse until she found a small bright green board that folded in the middle. She unclasped a hinge on the side and opened the board up. Inside of the board were two trays, each filled with shiny round plastic tiles that had white on one side and black on the other. She set one of these trays in front of Joanna and the other in front of herself. She then took four tiles and put them in the middle of the board in a cube in the pattern of white-black-black-white.

Bethann explained the rules of Othello in painstaking detail. She spent so long on the rules that Joanna wondered if they were going to have time to actually play the game. She interrupted Bethann's explanation of the importance of taking the corners by saying, "Seems straightforward to me. I think I can pick up the rest as we play."

Bethann shrugged her shoulders and motioned to the two colors. "Now, which color would you like?" Bethann asked.

"How generous of you to give me first pick. I'd like the white tile please."

"Then I will go first as black."

She picked up a tile and placed it on the board so that the white tile was between her two black ones. She then flipped the white tile over and made the whole line black. Joanna thought for a moment before deciding on where she wanted to place her tile. She reached hesitantly across the board and placed her white tile, flipping the black pieces to white. They passed a few more turns before Joanna started to feel the pressure the game had to offer.

Joanna's forehead wrinkles were scrunched up as she concentrated on the board. "You don't give an inch, do ya?" She placed a white tile and could only flip over two.

Bethann placed her tile, flipping five white to black and said, "I've no patience for people who coddle when competing. Oh, it's important to explain the rules. And you daresn't leave out any details or gain the upper hand by withholding at the start. But once you are playing a game, then you are on your own. For is it not the act of playing that teaches us the most? How can there be sweetness in eventual victory without having been defeated? Loss can be an excellent teacher, if you let it."

Joanna placed her white tile and methodically flipped over row after column of black tiles until the majority of the board was covered in white. "And what has this loss taught you?"

Bethann grimaced down at the board on the table. "That I need to be more careful with how I place my pieces. But the game is not over yet." She tapped her container of tiles to emphasize the fact the game was just starting.

"No, not this. I meant *the loss.* The one that everyone on the System is working through."

Bethann thought for a while and placed her tile on a corner. While it only gave her four tiles, she was using it to gain a future foothold. She replied tiredly, "That we are not as immortal as we like to believe. It is easy to forget the fragility of our shared dream. And living much longer lives has shifted our collective perspective."

"Do you think that we'll be able to heal, without being able to forget?" She placed a tile that gave her a full row of white.

"I think it's possible, yes. But again, the scale of time for that healing to occur is elongated. To help my case, I'd like to share something about NaSRFS that I discovered while mourning. He was only 120 years old. Can you believe that?" She claimed a full column of black.

Joanna gasped and said, "He was just a baby! Barely over a century old and gone already. Too soon, much too soon." Two diagonal lines of white flipped onto the board.

"You see my point though. Phys-side, 120 is an incredibly long life, but here you're just getting to the good stuff. I don't think everyone is as worried about losing an entire year as someone phys-side would be coming out of a coma. Because to us, a year is a drop in a bucket of time. Inconvenient, yes, but devastating, no. It is the loss of the promised years of those that disappeared that weighs heavy on us. The collective potential of billions of immortals snuffed out that has us weary to our bones."

Bethann placed her last black tile, but it could only flip over one tile. She could tell Joanna was going to win a few turns ago. When Joanna placed her last tile, she didn't even flip over the tiles. Instead, Bethann flipped them for her as she talked.

"I suppose I could see that. If I'm being honest, I had a similar reaction recently. The day after New Years, I realized that I hadn't turned off my reminder for NaSRFS coming over to play cards. When I got the notification ping, it took me a moment to realize that he wasn't coming. Then that dovetailed into thinking about all of the other weeks left in the year where I would not see him and I felt myself a fool. Both for forgetting to turn off the alert and for grieving time that was not spent."

Joanna looked to be on the verge of tears. Bethann reached out a hand across the table to comfort her, patting her hand gently. Joanna let the moment last for a second and no longer, immediately pulling her hand back towards her pack of cards. She was upset at the fact that Bethann had managed to get her to let her guard down and show her sadness. The last person to manage that had played her. Composure regained and wobble gone from her voice, she said, "One more game. And this time, I get to choose my favorite."

It was a dare. An invitation to dance along the edge of their shared grief at their limit. To play a host's favorite game in their own house was incredibly dangerous.

Bethann steepled her fingers and breathed out through her nose slowly. "I do hope I don't regret this, Joanna. But I'll bite, what game are we playing?"

"Texas hold 'em poker."

A small smile at the corners of Bethann's mouth. "It's hardly interesting without a proper wager."

Joanna shrugged and said, "I suppose you have a point. Whoever wins the round, gets to ask one question. No stipulations or affordances made or given. If you know the answer, you must talk."

Bethann nodded, "Agreeable. Deal out the hand."

"You know how to play then?"

"Everyone knows poker, Joanna. Let's face each other properly."

Bethann waved her hand through the air towards the middle of the table, Othello board and pieces vanishing into mist. Her bag lurched to life and coughed out a large pile of multicolored poker chips. With a quirk of her eyebrow and a twitch of her eye, the pile was divided neatly in half. Joanna let the cards fly from the open box to settle in front of them, two face down each. The only sound in the room was the steady ticking of the novelty cuckoo clock on the wall. Each woman peeked at her hand as though it held the secret to the universe. And then, the game began.

"Ante."

"Call. Playing the flop."

"Bet."

"Raise."

"Call."

"Playing the turn."

Bethann scowled, "Fold."

Joanna scooped the wagered chips into her pile. She gathered the cards up with her hands, shuffled them, and offered the deck to Bethann to cut. She tapped the top, declining the offer. Joanna dexterously dealt the cards out to both of them.

"Ante."

"Call. Playing the flop."

"Bet."

"Call. Playing the turn."

"Check."

"Check. Playing the river."

"Bet."

Joanna shook her head and said, "Fold."

Bethann snatched the chips in the wagered pile and let them slip through her fingers and clink musically into her personal stash.

Joanna gathered the cards and handed the pile to Bethann. "You'll deal." It was not a question, but a command. Bethann did not refuse. She bridge shuffled the cards together a few times and then offered the deck to Joanna to cut, which she did.

They were all business. Only speaking when taking game actions. Each blink of the eyes told a new and complex story. A flick of a card on the outside of the flop before the turn was enough to raise and force a fold. Or the sniffle of a nose was a false tell meant to throw the opponent. Hands kept only on the feeling that the tapping of a foot was excitement and not nerves. The myriad invisible ways in which they both could not help but to give their hands away. Everything that they had learned from each other in the last few hours was put to ruthless, efficient use.

Bethann started the round, hoping to force Joanna to bet all her chips, "Ante."

"Call."

"Playing the flop." She dealt out three cards; two of diamonds, jack of spades, and five of hearts. Joanna itched the back of her leg with her foot. Bethann hesitated for a second before removing her fingers from the five of hearts.

"Check."

"Check. Playing the turn." Bethann dealt out the next card, nine of diamonds, and took an opportunity to peek at her two face down cards. She noticed that Joanna's eyes had lost some of their edge. Only a sliver, but enough to catch.

"Bet." Joanna tossed her chips high in the air and let them hit the middle pile one at a time. She was teasing Bethann. She wouldn't have it.

"Raise." Her betting was serious and succinct. She used the back of her right hand to push the required chips into the pile. She kept eye contact with Joanna as she moved them.

"Call." Joanna clicked her tongue on the roof of her mouth and the chips needed appeared on top of the betting pile. She only had a few chips left.

"Playing the river." Bethann turned over the final card, a 2 of clubs.

"Check."

"No all-in Joanna? Where's your sense of adventure?"

"I have my own cliches I'm opposed to. Ready to reveal?"

"Let's see what you have."

The two players flipped over their face down cards and they each announced their poker hand in turn.

"Two pair," Joanna said. She had a jack of hearts and a nine of spades.

"Three of a kind." Bethann had revealed a seven of hearts and a two of spades. A hand just good enough to beat out Joanna's. She slumped back into her chair a little, letting the tension from her body relax. Joanna sat and stared at the poker hands for a while, letting the silence stretch on. She broke it by pushing the poker chips from the center over into Bethann's pile.

Bethann did her best to sit straight up again and said, "You don't have enough chips to make the ante, Joanna. I've won. Now it's your turn to spill."

Joanna tapped the kitchen table rhythmically with her pointer finger, a frown deeping on her face. "Go ahead and ask it then."

"What actually happened on New Year's?"

Joanna sighed and said, "I don't know."

Bethann reached for her purse, a scowl had crawled onto her face. "If you won't play by the rules you set your..."

But Joanna cut her off. "I'm not asking you to believe me! I don't know. Half of my network is gone and the other half are scrambling for answers. The information lockdown is tighter than it's ever been. Whatever happened is so important, they've shut down my usual avenues for sniffing it out. Not to mention the emotional state everyone's been in. You try retaining a system log dump file that's trillions of lines long while the agent who brought it to you breaks down into tears on line 555,678,901 because their best friend died and they didn't know!"

Bethann let go of her purse and her expression softened. She could see how frazzled Joanna was from how tightly she clutched her fist. Her eyes, endlessly tired and yet still intense and sharp, dared Bethann to question her testimony. But Bethann knew she was telling the truth.

"Thank goodness it's not just me. I've personally got twenty-four forks scouring the System for leads and haven't come up with anything substantial. I thought I was losing my touch."

Joanna laughed and said hoarsely, "I've got fifty-two working overtime right now. The merging has been a bit much to keep up with, but it sounds like they're bringing out the big players for this."

"Council of Eight nonsense?"

"Most assuredly."

"Ah, well then. Nothing a change in tactics can't fix right?"

"Beats moping around all day for sure. Need to use all this restless energy somehow."

Bethann stood up from her seat and said, "This was fun. I didn't realize how much I needed it. I think I'd like to come over again. Perhaps without the spycraft next time."

"Oh, come now Bethann. You know that's what makes it fun. Besides, I think that's what he would have wanted."

"Same time next week then?"

"No, I wasn't born yesterday. You'll know I'm game from this series of sensorium pings."

Joanna sent over a quick succession of five sensorium pings and watched Bethann's expression turn to one of manic glee.

"That works for me. Have a lovely night Joanna."

"You as well, Bethann."

And with that, Bethann stepped from the sim back to her own home. Joanna willed the sim to dim the lights. She puttered back to sit at the kitchen table and brought out the solitaire game once more. After carefully considering her options, she decided to not move the column with the king after all. Instead, she placed a red queen on top of it and drew a new card. She smiled brightly down at the board and her hand as everything started to fall into place.

Home From the Game

Caela Argent

Sadie Amara — 2401

She hadn't seen them in... well, in years. And yet, here they were... sitting on her couch. She swallowed, awkwardly, and took another step closer.

She was never really *comfortable* around her own forks, even one as sufficiently... What was the word again? Right, as sufficiently *individuated* as this one. Hell, they lacked everything she considered *herself*. The brown hair tied back in a scruff was gone, replaced with a shaggy mane shot through with a green streak. The ridiculous clothes, plated with bulky metal and accompanied by a cape.

Oh, and of course, the fact her fork had turned into a *massive hulking wolf-person.*

She watched it as it sat on the couch, massive snouted head hanging low, the creature that used to be just like her in every way. They stared glumly down into a space somewhere on the floor. Deep brown fur, almost matching the tone of her skin, was gently ruffled by the breeze of a fan.

She took a deep breath. "So... um..."

"I'm sorry." The creature's voice was a low rumble, its head raised up to look at her. "I know... especially with everything that's been going on regarding the attack... it's hard to put up with an unexpected guest..."

"Yeah. Well..." She shrugged. "I mean... It's good to catch up!"

"I just..." The wolf swallowed. "I need to be around people. And you're the only person I know outside of..."

She nodded as her up-tree's sentence tapered off. "The game."

The single-page announcement lay on the arm of the couch, where her fork had left it.

Forbidden Sector to Close For the Foreseeable Future

Hey all. Devteam here.

No doubt by now you've heard the news; a significant number of our fellow uploaded instances here on Lagrange have permanently crashed from a large-scale terrorist attack inflicted on system architecture. In the wake of the ongoing crisis, we have seen fit to shut down the sim for the foreseeable future.

All instances will be removed from the sim. Do not worry; your character data will be safe. We are co-operating with systechs and the Council to address what damage, if any, has been done to the game and the toll of those within. A memorial will be constructed in the Sky Palazzo at New Terra, in remembrance of those who are now gone.

The game will reopen soon enough. Until then...

Stay safe. Keep each other close.

— Forbidden Sector Dev Team

What Gifts We Give, We Give In Death
(Ode Clade)

Simon "Clank" Knight (Tarot Clade)

Caela Argent (Tarot Clade)

Sadie had first played it... oh, back in the 2320s. Close to a century ago, shortly after she'd uploaded. It was the sort of space-action-adventure sandbox game every sci-fi nerd dreamed of. Not that she'd ever admit to being a sci-fi nerd, of course, but there was a time when Sadie played it obsessively for a month, and decided to waste no more time on it after one character she played met a spectacularly *explosive* end.

As a condolence to herself, she created a *single* fork, the only one she would ever create, and told it to have fun while it played, and return once its character had died.

And, clearly, it had lived and died as many characters, each time returning to the game without merging down. Each death, it rolled a new one.

Until it became whoever it was in front of her. A... the name of the species sat on the tip of her tongue.

Loup-Garou!

The Loup-Garou were fictional, and absolutely nothing like the species of Artemis encountered a near-century after their creation. Instead, they were a species of anthropomorphic wolves, A concept Sadie found more than a little embarrassing and frankly ridiculous.

Given that all three of *Forbidden Sector*'s designers had been furries, it was only natural that there would be a species of strong, muscular wolf-people.

So of *course* the fork of herself she left there would evolve into... into *this.* She'd try different techniques for each character, moving to a different strategy or build if the last one failed. Eventually she landed on one character that would survive, after failure after failure, and for some reason that just *had* to be the shaggy-haired wolf person.

And now that wolf person she'd become was sitting here. In her house.

She turned back to her bowl of cereal, took a bite, then swallowed. "So... Not that your company is unappreciated, but..."

"I'll be out of your hair soon enough." The fork rubbed its eyes. "Just... need a few days."

"Good. Good. I'm... I'm glad." Watching the wolf person's head turn away, she realized that her phrasing was probably not the kindest.

"I was just... well, apologizing for not really having enough accommodations for you." She scooped up more cereal, gulping it down.

"Mm. It's fine. I lived in a *spaceship*." The wolf chuckled. "Leg room is kind of at a premium there, y'know?"

"You had a ship of your own? Wouldn't that mean you'd have..." She feebly thumbed through her memory to try and find the exact game parlance, before giving up and settling on what came immediately to mind; "A... a guild? Why not try rooming with them, I'm sure you'd prefer it over–"

The whine that escaped the wolf's lips, (*her* lips?) sent a shiver down her spine. Watching her fork's ears fold back was like a cold knife in her chest.

"Crew's gone, Sadie." The wolf shook her head. "All of them."

"All of them?" Sadie blinked.

"Vax and the Scrap-Breaker were both taken by CPV. Aska crashed from grief and Charles merged back down with his Root. It's me and Miller left. And Miller... won't answer my calls."

"Oh. Oh jeez, I–"

"I'll move out by next week, I just..." The wolf sniffled. "I just need to be around somebody right now. I know I'm not the most... familiar person to you, despite–"

"I understand." Sadie laid her bowl of cereal down in the sink, immediately rushing over to comfort her alternate self. "Seriously. I do."

As she sat beside the her-that-wasn't-herself, she idly reached over to scratch the ears of their massive lupine form. The wolf shrugged, nuzzling into the gesture. It at once surprised her, and yet made total sense; with enough perisystem manipulation, you could emulate the senses of anything. Even an alien species, with senses of taste, smell, *instinct*, radically different from that of a human.

Even a Loup-Garou from *Forbidden Sector*.

And of course, next to her was a version of herself that had embraced that, while she'd rejected it. And of course, even through individuation she could still see the little threads of herself in the wolf. Her fork's dark brown fur was the exact tone of her skin, she still bounced her leg when bored, and she still tapped her index finger against her thumb when she was stressed.

All this time, she'd thought of the game as a waste of time, something that her fork would tire of eventually. Little did she know that this fork had been forming connections and making friends, just as she herself had, and that those fragile connections were just as easily severed as hers.

And now, at the turning of the century, after a terrorist attack that had taken the lives of so many...

Her fork was here.

She was still alive.

"I'm sorry." She leaned over, gripping the wolf. "I... I've made a total mess of things. I never even thought to ask if you changed your name."

The wolf blinked. "Oh. Oh drek, I'm sorry. I'd completely forgotten you don't know me." She squeezed her eyes shut in laughter. "I... back in the game, I'd become somewhat infamous. Pirate Queen, you know. Everyone knew me." She thrust out a paw. "Mistress Lissa, at your service."

"Sadie... I mean, you knew that..." She sighed. "Sorry, it's hard getting used to–"

"I know." The wolf chuckled awkwardly. "It's awkward for me, too."

She stared into Lissa's eyes. Her own eyes. "I really should have sent you a sensorium ping or... or something. I... I'm sorry for never checking up on you."

Lissa shrugged. "Hey. That cuts both ways. I guess I was scared that you'd see *this* and think... Well, I dunno."

"I'm... I'm just so glad you're still here. I wish we could have met—*properly* met—in different circumstances."

Lissa wrapped a paw around her Root Instance, tugging her closer. "We're here now. No point in looking back, right? We've got each other, no matter what happens."

And so they sat, wolf and human, fork and root instance, together.

The Party at the End of the World

Krzysztof "Tomash" Drewniak

Scout at The Party V — 2401

The Party stumbled at the touch of apocalypse.

One of the System's hurricanes of experience, one of those storms of people and food and music and sex and strange drugs and yet stranger shared sensations passed around and so much more, skipped a beat at the turn of the century.

People noticed different things: some of those around them disappearing, that New Year's Eve 275 had suddenly become 277, a cocladist they couldn't reach, a friend checking if they were alive. All these glitches and oddities rippled out through The Party in an explosion of confusion. Many Party-goers hopped out to see to the world, some for the first time in years or even decades.

Some were jarred out of the rhythm of their life. Scout At The Party V, who, like the previous Scouts At The Party, was simply a dog, forked to take up its down-tree's bipedal form and mantle of systech. He could tell that he needed to do more than enjoy pets and snacks right now. That was not a comfortable thought for a Party animal, but Scout still felt it had some residual duty to its world.

The Party kept going despite all this. This particular The Party had put itself in a desert to ring in the new century under the stars. Now, many people were summoning tents, wanting to stay here where information might come ... and to dance through the uncertainty.

If the world was ending, as many feared, what else was there to do than party through it?

The Party was, for a time, subdued. It was like a festival where a major act was late. Everyone who stayed did their best to have fun, to enjoy what entertainment they had (and they had plenty still—if nothing else, all manner of "it's the 25th century!" plans could still go on), while glancing around and wondering what had gone wrong. What news? What happens next? Where's the big event?

It took several days for that news to arrive. The Party had picked up steam again by then, and sentiment was building for the idea that these glitches or whatever were future us's problem and we should go find a new place, though no one was sure where. All those motions melted away suddenly in a rush of "Check System General News" and "Holy shit." and "No, that ... really? The fuck?" and "Dreamer's *ears*, no!".

It wasn't a rumor anymore. There'd been an attack. Deliberate crashing of the System. About 1% lost.

The apocalypse had properly arrived.

The Party didn't stop.

An idea radiated, person to person, mind to mind. A small twist on something they'd missed out on—no, been robbed of—some days ago, or perhaps a year ago, and an outlet for the need for the new, the different, that had built up within The Party during the days of hesitation.

So, the tents disappeared, stages vanished, and the desert was loosely cleaned up. Then, in a rough mob, leaving a few stragglers behind as always, The Party hopped into an AVEC stage.

The stage expanded as they came. Less a stage now, more a square, a stadium, the essence of a gathered crowd. Video pickup pointed at many of the attendees individually and, as if from a news helicopter, at the whole lot of them. The stage kept growing as word got out to regulars who'd tapped out to work or mourn or seek answers, but who wouldn't want to miss this.

Then, the calls began. To who? To everyone anyone could think of, to family, to old friends, to reporters. Who didn't matter, exactly, just that people phys-side were present. Were invited to this.

Soon, the flood of new connections and incoming instances reduced to a trickle. The grand conference call was properly wrangled by then, and had been massaged to ensure that the intent of the callers came through without overwhelming the System's link to Earth with everyone getting millions of individual perspectives on the action.

A near-silence fell over The Party briefly, subsuming the earlier wisps of catching up or "You're alive!" or introducing friends that had been scattered throughout the crowd. Then, with their only cue being that someone else was going for it, The Party sang. They sang with human voices, both those that reflected what their owners had uploaded with and those that had been tuned and tweaked relentlessly. They sang through muzzles that warped each syllable. They sang with intentionally poor speech synthesizers. *They sang in italics, somehow, those few who had discovered the trick to it, even if it wasn't noticeable here.* They weren't in tune and were barely in time, but it didn't matter.

This was a roar, a protest, a reclamation.

> Should auld acquaintance be forgot,
> and never brought to mind? ...

The Party would have its midnight, and to hell with anyone who stood in their way.

Many from phys-side joined in once the idea had filtered through surprise and light-lag. And so, at the end, The Party stood as "For auld lang syne" echoed back from the Earth below.

Glasses appeared in hands, paws, mechanical pincers, anything that could hold them and many things that couldn't, while the room waited to see what was next. Attention drifted to the centaur woman who'd floated this plan first and so had the dubious honor of being in charge for a moment.

"I'm not giving a whole speech," she declared, her words echoed by retransmission and by expectation. "You've seen the news or you haven't. I've got only one thing to say:

"The Party. Doesn't. Fucking. Stop!" She stomped a hoof for beat and emphasis.

Cheers. Toasts to the future, the past, absent friends, present friends, anything, everything. And then, there before the eyes of anyone who hung around to watch, The Party picked itself right back up.

The Party never stops. Not even for the end of the world.

A Well-Trained Eye

Andréa C Mason

Lucia Marchetti — 2401

The rain against old glass panes and the sways and bumps of the car on the rails ready the air for conjurations. Lucy sits on the bench 6th from the back, on the right side, a sketchbook open across her knees. Today she's trying charcoal. Feels right with what happened a week ago.

This lonely train through the valley and the mountain is her chapel and now her hermitage in the wake of the bombing. There are plenty of churches and other religious retreats across the System if she wanted, but none of them have ever felt a fit for this work. She thought about skipping this week, and told herself if the train wasn't running, she'd pick up again later, but even with no passengers save her, the engine pulls its empty tail along the countryside. So, as she has done every week for the past 250 years, she has gone to her locker in the station, pulled out a fresh sketchbook, and boarded.

Lucy conjures in her memory their faces.

She can only recall 63 of the 68. It is true that the System means she cannot forget anything now, but it merely preserves in amber what the memory held at the moment of upload. It cannot restore the faces she lost to time. Even a number of the faces she recalls are not complete memories. Those she has filled in over decades, extrapolating or iterating on them until they are whole enough for her to feel it completes them. Over 260 years, her hands have become capable of incredible art, both through endless repetition and boundless study. When she is not here in her railcar-sized confession booth, she enjoys a life as an artist, known for bittersweet paintings and sculptures, happy to teach and happier to learn, a lover of life and a bringer of joy.

Of the five lost, two faces she cannot recall because they were unexpected complications on a job. One face was sent to kill her, but wasn't good enough. One face jumped her in an alley to rob her, or perhaps worse, but couldn't have picked a worse target. She doesn't recall her first kill's face, because there was a bag over his head and a gun loaded with both bullets and an irreversible choice was pushed into her hand.

The 69th face is the most vivid to her, but Lucy has never felt the need to draw her. After all, she let that last one go, and every morning after she wakes, Lucia Marchetti hopes that poor girl listened to her and got far far away. She hopes that woman lived a full life and that the family never caught up.

The clack-clack of the wheels on the track sets a rhythm for her vigil, her penance. The weather in the sim varies based on algorithms and set patterns both, stable enough to make maintenance easy, unpredictable enough to mimic weather phys-side. Today the rain is quite heavy. She welcomes it. The inside is dry, but the wood of the train car has a slight moist smell, a beautiful attention to detail. The lights in the car flicker a little more than usual, the train is a bit slower than usual but the ride is if anything less smooth. She likes the rougher rides, because it adds a challenge to her work, one she is well accustomed to after centuries but nonetheless welcomes. The rain fills in the silence where passengers would chat and shuffle and cough and rustle newspapers and make all those sounds living people make. She wonders how many of the usual riders died in the bomb, and how many are just afraid to go out, unsure, mourning, or just needing time alone.

Some art critics and fans throughout the System have pointed out that the left eyes in many of her portraits have fantastical details, often drawn as flowers, or the root of vines, or sunsets woven into faces, or in her sculptures become caves, grottos, tidal pools, library alcoves, hidden urban alleys. Many speculate on the symbolism of that, and her favorite theory is the one that she lost an eye to cancer, and her obsession with art and color is due to the way cancer distorted her vision, and that her art was a reclamation of what it had taken from her, a final spite to the disease that forced her to upload. Even though it was wrong it was very romantic, and even now she did very little to fight it, and on occasion coyly encouraged it.

A bullet through the left eye had been her professional calling card. Left hand on the top of the head, barrel of the silencer to the eyelid. She had taken so much from the world through left eyes, and she put back as much life and beauty through them now as she could. It would never be enough. More than a few of the faces she could only conjure with the bloody hole in a lifeless head, but she has never rendered it in sketches. She recreates and restores them as they were before, using decades of study to fill in what she destroyed. Even as styles and methods and tools change in her hands, she gives the dead that. Owes them that. The only real Liberty she takes is with the hair above the faces, refusing to give hair any semblance of being pushed or held down by anything.

The piece of charcoal snaps in her hand, and she realizes there are tears staining the current sketch. She wipes her eyes, takes another piece of charcoal from her satchel.

The bomb dwells on her mind. The Century Bomb, detonated at midnight, the start of the 25th century. 2400-01-01. 276+1 systime. In a digital world so removed from death, suddenly a toll on an incomprehensible level. Mechanically, it was a contraproprioceptive virus, launched at an astounding scale, wiping 1% of the System's current instance total by interrupting their code irreversibly. Functionally, it was a bomb that killed billions and scared shitless a trillion more. She wonders why they did it. She doesn't want to know, but she wonders. She wonders if it was just a job. She wonders if it wasn't. She wonders if they can remember all the faces of the people they killed. She wonders if they died in the bomb themselves. She hopes they did. She snaps another piece of charcoal, but if there were tears, they burned off on the heat in her face. It takes several breaths to unclench her fist, and she grabs another piece of charcoal.

This is the longest stretch of the track. It's between the third and fourth stops, and it's where she starts sketching every time. Some weeks, depending on her mood or free time, she waits for the train to finish looping through the five stops and the station before picking up in her usual place. This time she doesn't wait. The calm she needs comes as soon as the engine lurches into motion from the station, and she lets the sounds and motions balm her weary heart.

Charcoal means no color, but it lets her play with shading techniques. The more recent the face, the more realistic it becomes on the page, whereas older faces come out impressionistic, sketchier, or strikingly simple. Once she did them in chronological order. Then by age, alphabetical by first name, then last, then by height or by estimated weight, by location, by time it took to complete that dirty work, until now she's run out of categories and just lets them queue their own order, double checking periodically who is left and who isn't.

She feels a low impulse to include some of the regular passengers who are missing today, but cannot bring herself to break 250 years of rite and ritual. She decides tomorrow she will come back with separate sketchbooks or maybe some other medium, sit in a different place on the train, and sketch as many of the regulars as she can remember. Those she will not keep hidden away, and those she will let her sys-side self take care of.

Most people would send a separate fork for this, she figures. She always leaves a fork at her home sim, and when she gets back to the studio that fork will merge down to her. It is important to her that this continuous (as much as one can be here) version of herself be the penitent one. She thinks other people would understand that, it's not something that really needs explaining, but she has never told anyone directly what she does, and those who know about her train rides know better than to ask.

She wonders how many of them survived, and how many of them died or quit. She wonders how many will quit or crash from the grief. She chides herself for getting distracted. She sketches.

She long ago learned the art of faking motions. She trained herself to glance up and stare at random points in the room, usually where other passengers are, to give the illusion she is not doing this from memory. It is a performance for the comfort of others, and the comfortable ask less questions. She almost always got left alone anyway. She wonders how she must look from the outside. Short, black hair, in a layered bob that tapers into her neck, pale skin, wispy and thin. Her outfit for the train is always the same, a plain, thin white blouse with short sleeves and dark blue buttons down the middle, a pair of dark blue slacks with a very high waist, a tasteful pair of flats, tented teal triangles for earrings. The train is based on its early middle twentieth century ancestors, and she commits fully to the part as well. She never asks anyone if she pulls it off, or asks for a picture.

It takes her a while to notice there is someone else in the railcar with her.

One of those upward glancing motions registers some bright color on her left, but it takes four more motions before it actually clicks that it's an arm in a jacket. She stops mid-sketch and turns to the other passenger.

Across the aisle from her seat is a bench against the left wall of the train, and despite years of riding she cannot say for sure if the bench was always present or a new addition. Other than that it does not stand out, as all the upholstery, cushions, wood, metal, and design choices fit perfectly with the rest of the compartment. It might have been there the whole time. It might have appeared there seconds ago. It alarms her how little her memory has charted the left side of the aisle.

The other passenger is a woman who is also a skunk. She is tall, broad-shouldered, portly, covered in earthy green fur, with a mess of curly hair that is swept to the side and bleached blond. She wears an orange canvas bomber jacket, a beat up white tank top, grayish cargo pants, and heavy boots. Her arms are spread out on the back of the bench. One of her legs is crossed over the other, bouncing on it. She is grinning. Something about the fur pattern near the skunk's left eye unsettles Lucy, but it is obscured by the dark round sunglasses the skunk is wearing. How the skunk's tail seems to be at an impossible angle to her body while sitting down Lucy chalks up to the benefits of the System.

The skunk's grin widens when her presence is acknowledged. Lucy looks at her but lets the other woman make the first move. The skunk gladly obliges. "You know, it took me longer than I'd like to admit to realize you haven't been drawing other passengers."

Lucy chews her tongue before responding, turning back to her work but not letting the stranger from her sight. "Who's to say I wasn't before?"

The skunk shrugs. "It's possible, but I've seen you here every week for decades. It didn't click until about 6 years ago that the styles change but the faces don't."

A regular, then. There are other cars, and Lucia only rides the train once a week. So many different bodies and species exist within the System, and with the weird prevalence of skunks among that, not recalling this one's face didn't feel too strange. Old instincts warn her that her visitor could be banking on that, but she dismisses it with a stroke on the page.

Lucy sighs. "Well noticed. What else have you observed?"

The skunk tilts her head and chews her tongue a little, tapping a claw. "More a hunch than an observation, but you don't draw the living."

"Correct again. Not here, anyway. Elsewhere I do not restrain myself so."

The skunk gives a bobbing nod. "People you lost?"

Lucia speaks plainly. "People I killed."

The test is laid. How will the examinee respond? Fear? Nervous laughter? Anger?

The skunk raises an eyebrow. "Appearances can be deceiving, but you don't strike me as a soldier."

"Metaphorically, maybe, but never literally."

The skunk's claws tighten into the wood of the bench at either end of her arms. "Not a cop, I hope?"

Now there's a measure of character. Lucia genuinely laughs, and the skunk's grips relax. There's that bobbing nod again, and the mephit says, "So, ah, contract work."

Lucy cannot decide if the animal's cavalier nature is charming or cause for alarm. Her heart wants to believe the former. A gut trained on a former life tells her the latter. Both are anxious to see how this plays out. "I would call it familial obligations, but they did pay me for it, and friends of the family would throw me work now and again as well." She pauses. "You know how family can be."

The skunk gives a sad smirk. "Half of mine disowned me for being queer. Don't think it's quite the same but I can sympathize, at least."

Lucy stops sketching for a second, and makes eye contact with the skunk, or as best she can through the other's sunglasses. Even without the eyes, there's a topography of emotion in the snout and cheeks and brow. That pattern of fur around her left eye, it's rough. Aesthetically it interrupts the face. An interesting choice. Panic surges just a little again.

Lucia blinks and shakes her head, turning back to her sketch. "Well, good thing we both got out."

The skunk looks out the window behind her. "And yet the past never stops trailing behind us here. It's like this train, never moving forward, on an endless loop that carries us in circles. Even if we step off at a stop, it will be back around to pick us up again."

Lucy sees no reason to add anything.

The skunk turns back towards her. "These pieces you do fascinate me. They all lack your signature."

"What need to autograph them? They are for me and the dead. Other than the prying eyes of those like you who see my process, they are never shared."

"That is not the signature I mean."

She tenses. "Ah, a stylistic one, then. Do you mean to say I am an artist beyond these sketches? Who do you think I might be?"

"I know exactly who you are."

Everything goes quiet and the light dims. Somewhere in the conversation Lucy missed the whistle for the tunnel, and as the trains slips into the darkness the driving rain no longer fills silence. Even the wheel-clacks sound quieter. The bulbs along either side of the car have dimmed, and the one on the skunk's right has gone out completely. The skunk has taken off her sunglasses, and is wiping the lenses in the cotton of her tank top.

It is not a pattern in her fur, Lucia realizes. It is a scar. A scar that starts north of the brow, runs most of the way down her cheek, and in the middle, crosses her eye. The left eye itself is clouded over, with only a hint of the pupil beneath. The other eye is a striking hazel, untouched.

A million possibilities run through Lucia's head. This is someone here to blackmail her. The family finally sent an assassin. Somehow one of her targets survived and has found her for revenge. The System isn't real, and this is Purgatory, or worse, Hell, luring her into a false sense of security to strengthen her damnation. All of these could be true at once. She does not know. She finds she cannot quit, or leave the sim, or even move, paralyzed in pure fear, an emotion she has not felt in centuries.

Meanwhile, the skunk is saying, "You are Lucia Marchetti, renowned artist and sculptor. One of the most distinct in the System, in fact, and if I'm not mistaken, the unintentional pioneer of three major art movements of the last two centuries. Most intriguing is your lasting fixation on the left eye, present on almost every one of your pieces with a living thing in it. There's a lot of theories, but no one really knows why you do it. Except I think I do."

Lucy resigns herself. 260 years was a good run. More than any of her targets got sometimes by a factor of ten. She should have trusted her gut and bailed. She should have run. She shouldn't have said so much. But she did, and she tries to make peace with having to face the music. It's not really working, but she still cannot bring herself to flee. They say that no one can force you to stay in a sim, that it is impossible to truly hold anyone anywhere in the System against their will, but none of them ever account for the pressure one can exert on oneself. So, if this is the end, she decides, even if she cannot accept it, she will not fight it. "You're here to kill me, aren't you?"

The skunk laughs. "Kill you? Why would I want to kill you?" She holds her sunglasses up towards one of the light fixtures, checking the lens for smudges. "You might be the only person on the System who understands me."

Lucia has the brief vivid image in her mind of an engraved lighter and a carousel tearing itself apart. The skunk across from her must be some sort of fanatic, perhaps another professional killer, or worse, unprofessional. Someone unmoored from reality, perhaps. Madness is more prevalent in the System than anyone admits. Lucy decides she would have preferred if this stranger was here to kill her, then chides herself for this self-destructiveness.

Still the skunk speaks, and taps next to her damaged eye. "For most of my life phys-side, I would now and again come down with migraines that always started behind my eye. Most of them were mild, but some of them would put me down for a whole day. Once or twice I even had visual aberrations, and I couldn't even see out of it. It'd be like static, visual white noise. For some reason, after I forked off my root instance, I started having the migraines again sys-side. The pressure is there, and the hurt is sometimes there, but now I hallucinate. Vividly, and only through that eye. My right eye is locked on reality, and the left eye ranges from minor distortions to things that even our more adventurous chemical days never came close to. I've never met anyone else that gets migraines here like mine. But then, I see your work, and I finally think for a second that maybe I'm not alone."

"I'm not totally convinced you are not here to kill me."

The mephit shakes her head. "I swear I'm not. I mean, you've been here—the System, I should say—for a long time?"

"Centuries."

"When did you upload?"

"Why should I tell you?"

"So I can prove I'm not sent by your 'family'. Just want to know the year."

Lucia mulls it over before saying it. "2140."

"Which was 31 years before my root instance was even born."

"Doesn't mean that you aren't—"

"You have to believe me! You have to, and you have to experience something like I do. It has to be the reason!" The skunk's face is a patchwork of frustration and desperate need.

"I never in my life before this place or after had a single headache."

The stranger is on the verge of tears. "Then why?"

"It's where I put the bullets."

The skunk's eyes go wide, and the rain slams against the rail car as the train leaves the tunnel again.

For the first time in all her years of penance, Lucia wishes she could stop drawing these faces, and instead in this moment sketch the creature across from her. The surprise in the mephit's features decays, like a flashbulb in a camera after it's gone off in those ancient movies the Don loved to watch. Lucy wants to capture this moment as hope withers and understanding winds vines slowly into the visage of the woman. She can see her piece together what that means, why these faces must never bear that mark, a million questions banished to the aether with one simple, ugly, answer. It is Lucia's opinion that art is better left unexplained, and this is why. If it weren't for the storm outside she would have heard the poor thing's heart break. There is a biting of a lip, there are tears, there is a bobbing nod of understanding, and a single, deep sob. If she could raise a hand, a brush, a chisel, these minutes would turn into her finest work, she would capture the death of a hero as seen through a mirror. She mourns it as the emotions pass, as the traces of them evaporate off the skunk's muzzle like morning mist in the sun. To capture what she saw in the moment would be a blasphemous vanity. She tears herself away from staring, and continues her sketches.

It is a while before either can speak. The skunk speaks first. "I think knowing that, somehow, makes your art...more beautiful to me?"

Lucy snorts. "That's unfortunate."

"Do you regret it?"

She rolls her eyes at this. "No, I have sat on this train every week for 250 years drawing the dead because I have nothing better to do. What a stupid question."

"Did you upload because you got tired of killing?"

"I uploaded because I was tired of being a man." She looks up to see that the skunk has put back on her sunglasses, but they cannot hide her surprise again. Lucia sets down the notebook and the charcoal on the seat next to herself. "The family gave me an address and a man's name. They did not tell me what he had done, usually they did not, but they spoke with such vitriol I assumed his trespasses were high. The family back then overlooked my dalliances with other men, as men were easy to pay off, and I suspect I was not the only one in the family 'wandering from the path' in that way. Something about the venom in the request made me wonder if someone in the family had been spurned, and I was cleaning up loose ends. No matter. I had given up long ago on caring about my targets. A job is a job, and the family always found me work.

"I broke into the apartment, and in the dim light of the living room was the most beautiful woman I have ever seen. She was like polished stone, you could tell she was made more beautiful by the things she endured. It took me a moment to remember what I was even there for, and I wondered again if this wasn't business but personal affairs. She noticed me, and panicked, pulling a blanket to herself even though she was clothed. I did not yell, I did not shout, I did not strike in my work. I used a level voice, moved calmly and deliberately, and made no sudden movements. People feared that more than an angry man, and it meant there was a lot less cleanup involved. I did not hide that I had a gun. She asked me who I was, and I said I was strictly here on business, and she didn't need to know. She said she didn't trust me, and I told her very simply that if I intended to hurt I would not have waited for her to see me. I told her that all she needed to do was answer me a question, and then she could leave safely. As a show of faith, I stepped out from between her and the door. She weighed her options. She was taller than me, a bit stockier, but I was a man with a gun in my hands. She relented, and with a sigh told me to ask. I told her all I needed to know was where I could find my target. I told her the name.

"Perhaps you are smart enough to know where this is going, but I mistook her panic for loyalty. She became defensive, refusing to give any information and demanding of me explanations. I told her she need not be loyal to him again and again, that it was not worth her life to defend him, and that all I needed to know is where he was. She offered bribes. She offered violence. She offered a great many things I dare not say. I do not know how long our exchange went exactly. Easily 15 minutes, likely more. I grew impatient and finally asked her why his life was worth so much more than hers, and that regardless of what happened to her I had a job and that man had to die.

"She wailed, falling to the floor, and told me with absolute despair that she was the man I was looking for. Only then do I begin to inspect my surroundings carefully. I take notice of the decorations, the aesthetic choices, the recurring theme of rebirth. There was a jacket, hung on the back of a dining table chair, with a flag on the shoulder, a flag of stripes and three colors. Such a jacket was not uncommon among younger generations of my country, but the flag was not the flag of Italia of old, nor any of the new flags of the many states my homeland became under the Western Federation. No, this flag is the standard of a country with no land, abstract territory, yet one I—and, I highly suspect, you as well—reside within. Three colors, yes, but the stripes of the flag are horizontal, not vertical. Five stripes, not three.

"No doubt you have heard the tales of old about those Lost in the sims, in the days before the System. In that moment, like them, I became lost within myself. I was not old then, but I had lived a very long life. I tumbled down through memories, emotions, places, times, lovers, imaginations. This woman before me, born something else, but made beautiful by change, was she as me? Pulled unwilling into the affairs of the family? Forced into shapes preordained, melted down and poured into a mold, cracked upon the altar of tradition, to fit needs or to ornament the mansion walls? Did she break the mold, or melt again to make herself anew? Could I do the same? My lovers were all overlooked or bought off, but in the eyes of those who shaped me, I was property who could buy a place at the table in time but never my own freedom. This Angel before me was an epiphany, and to the gospel of my employers I fell apostate in a moment. In my head and only in my head I begged mercy and forgiveness from her, that I might forever fall to her feet and serve to atone for my trespasses. She was living proof that my resignation to my fate was an act of cowardice, that for years I had been lying to myself. A thousand versions of myself in my head ran to every corner of my mind and pulled together a new self, an eternity of hands falling over themselves to construct some possible way to let this woman go without getting both her and myself killed. No markers lay for how long I was lost in my head, and when I pulled back to the reality before me, I have no idea if I had been gone a second or an hour. The woman before me still wept. I made up my mind. It was made from the moment I saw her jacket.

"I told her to look at me. She did. I told her the man I had come to kill was clearly already dead. She stared at me for a long time. I asked her if her identifications had her old name or her new one on them, and when she said new I cemented a plan. I told her I had no intention of killing her, but that I could not promise the same of my employers. I set my gun on the table. I sorted out for her an impressive sum of money that I kept on my person, as even as late as the 2130s hard currency opened far more doors than brute force. I knelt down beside her on the floor. I pressed into her hands a marker, something that would grant her safe passage anywhere she showed it, an agreement of families and organizations that preceded us by centuries. I told her where to go, what places my family would never tread, and what she needed to say to get there. I told her to wait 20 minutes after I left, pack as little as she could, and leave immediately. She sat there stunned, and only as I got to the door did it grip her that this was real.

"She asked me why I was helping her. I could not lie. I told her that killing her would make her a man again and I could not stand to take such beauty from the world. Manhood is not a problem if it is choice, but I was never given one, and I would not force anyone to reconsider their own decision. I do not know if she understood me, but she nodded. As I departed, she asked if she would see me again. I told her no, I was already as dead as the man I had been sent to kill, and left before she could delay me further.

"I do not know what happened to her. I don't know what happened to the family. I do not know what happened to the cats left in my apartment. I do not even know if the sun set the next night. I moved quickly, using the weight my name had gathered over the years to get me quick passage to Roma. Uploading was still new then, expensive and still a mystery to most, but Roma had an Ansible clinic. I arrived in the city just before dawn, and caught the staff as they arrived for the morning. I drained my accounts and gave them each enough to fund the clinic for a year, to upload me and to strike my name from any records. They asked me what to do with my body. I told them to burn it and toss the ashes into the Tiber. When they objected, I handed them even more money, and finally they gave way."

Lucia looks up, and out over the countryside rolling by the windows of the train car. How far, she wonders, does it go? Does it end a small ways from the train? Are the mountains on the other side of this valley merely a trick of sensoria? Or has someone rendered them, crafting the walls of stone as they rise from low earth, etching little runs and outcroppings for a thousand meters upward? Does the sim stretch beyond the mountains, an uncanny mirror of the alps that she had traveled phys-side often enough, mostly for business, only very rarely for pleasure? She knows most of the stops are fleshed out, but she has no idea if all the land in between them is. She briefly sees the faint orange reflection of the skunk's jacket in the window, and tries not to think about how long she might have been silent.

Still, as she speaks, it is a few moments before she turns back to the other passenger. "There is nothing more to tell. The killer for hire died on the Ansible table. I do not miss him. I mourn those whom he took from the world. I carry them on eternally here, as I have since the first day I ever rode this train."

The skunk smirks. "I wonder if the riders know they're in your rolling mausoleum."

Lucia frowns. "It is not a mausoleum!"

The mephit's lip twitches. "Right, my mistake, if it doesn't contain any remains, it's called a cenotaph, isn't it?"

The frown turns to a scowl. "That is not what I mean."

The skunk leans forward, resting her forearms upon her thighs. "A confessional, then. Do you say your 'hail marys' as we ride along these chancel rails? Quite a trick to use a train to transit the stations of the cross, but with only 6 stops instead of 14, you may find us lacking."

Lucia turns to her, meaning to scald the other woman with a glare. "Do not mock me. Those traditions were antiquated before I was born, much less you. I ask nothing of a god I do not believe in. So too the dead are the dead, they feel nothing. Hear nothing. Give nothing. I do this for myself, I grieve. I regret. From what authority do you speak? What right have you to judge?"

The skunk raises her paws in defense. "I'm not judging."

Lucia bares her teeth. "The hell you are not. You speak harshly, think me a sinner."

The skunk crosses her arms before herself. "Listen, I am not in the business of *salvation* or *absolution.*"

"Then what, pray tell, are you in the business of?"

The other woman furrows her brow, and leans back. Then, slowly, smugly, she grins. "*Joie de vivre.*"

Lucia finds herself genuinely unsure how to respond to that, so she doesn't. On she sketches, ignoring her spectator as best she can. A stop comes and goes, the fourth, and neither debark. No one gets on either. Riders. A thread lies untraced in Lucy's mind. She pulls it.

To the skunk she says, "You asked earlier if the riders know what I do, as if you did not number among them."

The skunk's face isn't just grinning, there's some anticipation around the edges of it. This stranger has been waiting for this question. "Not usually, no, not by a traditional count."

Lucia squints. "Yet you said before the tunnel that you have observed me here for decades."

The skunk looks up, and taps a cheeky claw to her chin. "Yeah, weird, I wonder how that could be?"

"Do you spy on the passengers?"

The skunk tilts her head disappointedly, and lets the silence answer for her.

"Neither then, some small animal, like a mouse or an insect living on the train."

A shake of a head. "Construct or instance, I'd consider them passengers, too."

"And you observed me directly, yes?"

"This is a fun game! Yes, I have countless times."

Lucy doesn't like this game. She hates the feeling of missing something simple. Perhaps it isn't simple. "You...you are the train we are riding in, and you have watched me all these years, and forked to something that could speak to me."

The skunk laughs, and slaps her knees. Lucia turns red, scowling. Wiping humorous tears from her eyes, the skunk says, "I love artists so much. Creative! Very creative, but a few problems. One: I was born after you uploaded. Two: I only forked and individuated from my root instance in 2357, and Three: the System is capable of many incredible things, but that's a little too fantastic." The skunk gave a little head bob. "I guess in a metaphorical way you could say I speak for the train, but no, I'm afraid as long as I've been around in this sim, I've just been a skunk."

Lucy looks out the window, and says aloud, "I do not like this game."

The skunk laughs again. "I'm having a blast. Do you want me to tell you?"

The artist glances back only briefly, and shakes her head.

"Do you want me to give you a hint?"

Now Lucia turns to look at her, and when the skunk raises an eyebrow, she relents. "Fine. Fine! Yes!"

The skunk slips her left paw into her jacket pocket. "Your hint is: rider and passenger are passive roles."

Passive? If riding a train is a passive state, what would be an active—

Lucy nearly throws her sketches to the floor, gesticulating angrily. "You are the engineer. You drive the train."

"Correct!" The mephit holds up three clawed fingers on her right paw. "Beyond maintaining the sim, I wear three hats. One is engineer. The second is stationmaster. But neither of those explain seeing you in this car, do they?"

Lucia's turn to raise an eyebrow. The skunk pulls her left

paw from her jacket pocket, and holds up a ticket puncher. Lucia buries her face in her hands. "Conductor. And now I am the asshole for not even remembering you."

The skunk scoffs. "I'm not hurt! Think of it this way, you and this sim have been here for 250 years. I've only been 'on board' for about 35. I dug through our personnel records recently, and there have been well over 100 conductors, never mind several active at the same time. You've been focused on your work, faces change, and at some point you stopped paying attention to who was coming around to check for fares. Hell, I've met other regulars in other sims who don't recognize me right away. Same goes for the 15 years I've been stationmaster, and have you ever actually been to the engine? Did you realize it has to be crewed? I'm proud of my work whether it gets seen or not, but often it isn't."

Lucia finally finds the other end of the thread. "Do you own this sim?"

The smile fades from the skunk's face. "As of a week ago, yes."

"Was it the Century At–"

"Mr. Nguyen had been planning to retire for some time. He'd given full access controls and permissions of the Sim to me a few months back, and after 275 years, he planned to retire at midnight, right as the century rolled over." The furred woman bit her lip and looked away. "I...I don't know if he died in the Attack. The way he was cleaning up his affairs by the end he might have quit the big one. Either way, he's gone."

A grief settles into Lucia. She realizes she does not know the attendants of this sacred place. If it is half as intricate and complex as she thinks, this sim takes a great amount of work and dedication to keep running. The System's curse of eternal memory meant nothing if she did not bother to take notice of someone in the first place. Dozens of faces. Hundreds, likely. On top of this, layered like a dusting of ash or snow, is the suspicion that now this skunk and whatever forks of her there may be are the only ones left. Both the skunk and Lucia herself were lucky. How many sims now sit empty, with no owner? How many empty homes and shops and cities and wildernesses and worlds wait for occupants, like pets who do not yet know the loss of their caretakers, or worse, cannot understand it? Does the System reclaim them? Should it? Should they stand as cenotaphs, markers of a terrible loss few people can yet truly wrap their heads around? Or like a home in a vibrant neighborhood, should the next inhabitants move in, so that life can go on for the living? She doesn't know. Answers are beyond her, she is the rain that falls from the sky and her eyes in equal measure. She rolls off of resolution or closure, like droplets off the panes of the glass of the traincar.

Her tears soak into the paper of her sketchbook, and that tugs her to reality again. She cannot change the past, but she can change the present, the future. She wipes the water from her eyes hastily. "I did not know his name. Nor yours, though you clearly know mine."

The skunk straightens up a little. "My name is Seras. Seras Frame."

Lucia nods. "Seras. I will remember it."

Seras shrugs. "You can't forget it."

Lucia says, "language is an art, not a science. When we say forget and remember, they can mean many things. I will say your name, Seras. I will speak it aloud and address you and not take you for granted again."

The train begins to slow as it reaches the fifth stop. Seras looks out the window, then back to Lucia. "I'll be getting off here, but before I do..." her voice trails off, and she holds up the ticket puncher, clacking it a few times. Lucia smiles. She pulls the ticket from her pocket, as she has every week for hundreds of years.

Seras stands up and takes it, looking it over. "Honestly, I was worried we'd lost all our riders. It's hard to say who's just too overwhelmed to show up, and who's gone. If you're here, I'm sure I'll see other old faces soon enough." She punches the ticket, and pauses. "Have you killed anyone since uploading?"

The train comes to a stop, and something deep inside Lucia

tenses. She snaps at the skunk. "Why? Worried I'm going to start up again?"

Seras rolls her eyes, and hands Lucia back her ticket brusquely. "Just curious."

The skunk walks away swiftly, headed for the back of the car. She's just about to leave when Lucy finds her voice again. "I didn't even know you could kill someone here until the bomb went off."

Seras stops dead in her tracks, but doesn't turn around. Lucy keeps talking.

"I heard rumors of people being assassinated, but I never looked into it. How could you kill someone in a world like this? It all stunk of conspiracy, and you know how people are here. I thought I finally found a world without violence, and for a time I had such a world. Then the bomb devours billions, like an earthquake rending the ground into a maw of Hell. I am brought so close to the jaws of death I remember why I was glad to leave that world behind." Lucy feels like a child, small, afraid. Even after transitioning it is a feeling she has rarely felt, and her usual guard falls away. Words tumble from her before she can stop them. "And I do think this is confessional. I do my penance in this public place, an anonymous sinner, because it must not be done alone. I apologize for my hostility. I do not like to be so plainly and nakedly seen by a stranger, and you frightened me like I haven't been since the Ansible table."

Seras turns. The two women watch each other for a while. Lucia speaks first.

"Do you think I've done enough? Held this Vigil for enough lifetimes? Should I keep going?"

The train's whistle blows. Seras shakes her head. "I told you before. I'm not in the business of Absolution or Salvation." She walks to the back door. As the railcars start to lurch into motion, she adds, "I'm just happy to see someone's still riding the train."

Then she's gone, and Lucia pushes herself over a few seats to the window. She sees the skunk laughing and pulling the back of her jacket over her head. As the train pulls away, she's stomping her boots through the puddles on the platform as she runs for the shelter of an awning.

Toward Eternity

Thomas "Faux" Steele

Aurélien Delacroix — 2401

Aurélien Delacroix leaned back on the cracked leather barstool and interlaced their fingers, claw-tips painted an eye-catching sapphire that matched their majestic crest. Tapping a cigarette out of a crumpled packet of Gauloises—also blue—they tucked it into their beak but left it unlit. "Let's start with a name and go from there, shall we?"

"Gaëlle," the Persian leopard replied, golden eyes tracing the curves of the blue jay's deep purple suit. The corner of her muzzle curled into a slight frown as she took a seat, the curves of her dress cascading down her lithe body like turbid water. A choker set with fire opals like translucent magma adorned her throat. "Of the Khayyamzadeh Clade. I've heard that you fancy yourself a detective, Monsieur Delacroix."

"Others describe me that way, but I prefer to say that I dabble in the archeology of the soul," Aurélien replied, their crest fluttering ever so slightly with a hint of *amour-propre*. Materializing a lighter into their palm, they summoned a jet of flame to ignite their cigarette. "If you have a sufficiently interesting mystery for me, I'll endeavor to solve it for you. Sound fair?"

Gaëlle considered Aurélien for a long moment, her manicured claws sinking into the foam padding. "I don't do 'interesting'," she said slowly, her voice like distant veldt thunder. "But I do have a mystery of a sort...I need someone found."

"Is this related to the Century Attack?" A lazy wisp of smoke rolled out of the blue jay's beak as they slowly exhaled. The ember of their cigarette gave their amethyst eyeshadow an iridescent glow. "I imagine you've already checked the clade listing."

"Naturally." Gaëlle sighed, her shoulders slumping. "I expected there to be casualties after they announced that the cause was Contraproprioceptive Virus. I just didn't expect the losses to have hit within my clade," the leopard murmured, her paw instinctively batting at a silver pendant in the form of an art nouveau key suspended from a dainty chain around her neck. "Did you uh...lose–"

"No. I'm technically part of a clade, but"—Aurélien took another puff as they swirled a half-empty glass of Armagnac and watched the amber droplets dance against the crystal—"we all seem to be a bit drunk on the liquor of solitude these days."

"I don't think we're supposed to be alone," the leopard murmured in a low purr. "Not in the System at least. No heart-balm can truly soothe the ache of involuntary solitude."

"Then tell me more about the one that you're hunting for." A mournful saxophone rose above the steady drone of conversation that echoed off the cove ceiling above them. "Anything that might help me identify an up-tree instance."

"Her name was Céleste," Gaëlle began, claws scratching lightly against the weathered mahogany bar of the Sombres Reflets speakeasy. "A lynx. Reddish fur, beautiful emerald eyes, and a grin just a bit off-kilter. She was–" The leopard's voice hitched. "She was not our clade's root instance, but she was very close, much closer than I am."

"You sound like you could use a drink. Bartender!" Aurélien called, their voice slicing through the smoky air. A moment later, a handsome human with a well-trimmed mustache—part of the sim—stepped forward, chromed cocktail shaker in his white-gloved hand.

"Whiskey." Gaëlle clutched her pendant tighter, the nubs of teeth-scarred claws striking melodically against the metal like diminutive bells. "Three fingers, neat."

The bartender plucked a bottle from the top shelf, pouring

precisely the requested volume into a squat crystal glass in front of Gaëlle. Her gaze softened for a moment as she brought the amber liquid to her muzzle. After a deep sip, she let out a trembling sigh.

"Take as long as you need to gather your thoughts," Aurélien murmured. They glanced at the narrow silver of cityscape visible through the nicotine-stained transom window above the speakeasy's iron-wrapped entrance. Bitter rain fell in sheets outside, the tires of dour sedans dousing the sidewalk in opaque water as they rolled past. "We have nothing but time in this sim. I know that this process can be...difficult."

"Difficult..." Gaëlle echoed, raising her glass to the dim light of the bar, amber whiskey twinkling like a falling star as she brought it to her muzzle. "That's certainly one word for it."

"How long has it been since Céleste last forked?" the blue jay asked, sympathetically clicking their beak.

"Six months ago. The instance has probably individuated since then, but...I hope that there's still a part of her out there somewhere." Gaëlle paused, her eyes misty as she took another swig of whiskey to steady her trembling paws. "I should never have trusted the promise of a place beyond death. It's so easy to leave words unsaid when our gaze is toward eternity."

"You had no way of knowing," Aurélien replied. The smoke of their cigarette curled lazily upward, contributing to a haze that muted the light thrown by the solitary incandescent bulb above them. "No one predicted that phys-side would lash out at the System with such violence outside of the darkest sims birthed from conspiratorial delirium."

"There was this...old playground on the sim where the core of my clade still lives. Céleste loved it there." Gaëlle stared vacantly down into her whiskey, her sinuous tail twitching restlessly against the tarnished brass footrest. "I'd join her there at the same time every week and we'd sit on the swings and reminisce until we ran out of memories or mimosa, whichever came first."

"I assume this new instance wasn't there when the appointed hour arrived?" The ember on Aurélien's cigarette glowed brighter as they took a contriving puff.

"No," the leopard replied with a sigh. "And the clade listing wasn't of much help. I suspect that the new instance hasn't quit, but I don't have access–" Gaëlle's voice trailed off, her fingers tracing aimless patterns on the mahogany bar.

"Those damned privacy settings," Aurélien murmured, offering a sympathetic nod. "Useful at times but...also occasionally frustrating."

"Mrm. I blame myself for not spending more moments with her, for living through a thousand other experiences apart when she was always just a ping away." Gaëlle sighed. "I always thought we'd have more time."

"But we never quite have enough, do we?" Aurélien said, gesturing for the bartender to bring another glass of Armagnac. "I've been in the System a hundred years and I still feel like I've only enjoyed a thousandth of what's out there."

"There's no comfort in eternity when the cocladist you want to spend it with isn't there," Gaëlle mused, tilting her glass to let the dingy light refract through the remaining whiskey. "Find her for me...please?"

"Who else would have an idea as to this fork's whereabouts?" Aurélien asked, extinguishing their cigarette on a dull ceramic ashtray adorned with the yellow-stained tips of filterless butts. The bartender casually swapped it out as he supplied the bluejay with more brandy.

Gaëlle pursed her lips, gaze focused on the rain-spattered transom window. "Go to the Government Club and ask for Zamburak Tehrani. He is an old friend on good terms with all the members of my clade...unlike myself."

Aurélien gave her a curt nod before tipping back the full glass of Armagnac in a single golden stream. Donning a weathered camel trench coat, they studied the leopard's face for a moment while straightening their tie.

"Try not to get lost in the rain," Gaëlle said, a hint of anxiety visible beneath her sphinxlike façade. The blue jay nodded in silent reassurance, feathers ruffling slightly in the dim light. As their claw-tips wrapped around the heavy brass door latch, they glanced back at Gaëlle.

"I'll find her." The door swung shut behind them, the building's weathered shutters rattling in the howling wind. Sipping on her whisky, Gaëlle watched the blue jay's blocky figure disappear into the cityscape until it was swallowed entirely by sheets of bitter rain.

§

If the atmosphere in the Sombres Reflets was *The Maltese Falcon*, then the Government Club was *Brick and Mirror*. Aurélien stepped onto a cobblestone street lined with neatly-trimmed groves of Persian cypress trees and slowly exhaled. Dead ahead, a three-story building with a majestic art deco façade was impossible to miss, its emerald green and gold details accented by Kashan tilework. The gated archway that separated it from the street was flanked by two marble cheetahs, each bearing a gleaming torch of sapphire flame.

Giving an acknowledging nod to an oryx concierge with horns spiraling up into infinity, Aurélien entered the manicured *charbagh* and immediately felt out-of-place. The splendor of Pahlavi Iran hung heavy in the air, accompanied by the crisp scent of jasmine wafting from abundant white-flowered bushes that lined the walkways. It was as if time itself had gotten lost within the red sandstone walls, twisting in on itself until emerging as a past that had never come to pass.

"*Salam*. Are you looking for someone?" An Asiatic cheetah gave the blue jay a polite smile, her sapphire Qashqai-style dress flapping lightly in the warm breeze. "The Government Club usually isn't somewhere one ends up by accident."

"*Salam*," Aurélien greeted her with a tip of their crest feathers and a friendly *jeer-jeer*. Unfortunately perched just beyond the shade of a colonnade, their jacket in the direct sunlight was quickly becoming a Dutch oven. "I'm looking for Zamburak Tehrani. Would you happen to know where I can find him? Preferably somewhere air-conditioned."

The cheetah's eyes flickered with recognition as she brushed an errant strand of headfur off her forehead. "Ah, yes. Fortunately for you, he's usually around this time of day," she murmured, glancing up at the late afternoon sun. "You might also consider donning something a little more...breathable. Most of us here prefer it on the warmer side."

Aurélien nodded, two blue jays visible for a split-second before one—the visibly perspiring instance—quit. A lightweight cotton *gandoura* billowed around the new instance's lean and muscular frame, golden threads woven through the collar adding a hint of elegance to the simple tunic. The cheetah shot them an approving smile.

"Better," she said, her tail curling leisurely behind her. "Now, follow me, if you would."

Aurélien's talons clicked on the lavish Isfahan tilework that covered the entire corridor, intricate lattice work and columns to the blue jay's right exposing the Government Club's inner *paridaiza*. A fern-shaded stream coursed through the center of the courtyard, where manicured orange trees bloomed in orderly rows. Anthropomorphic creatures of every kind lounged about with languid grace, sipping on saffron lassis or engaging in animated conversation beneath cedarwood and canvas canopies.

"It's rare for a new face to appear on this sim. And rarer still for it to belong to one with nostalgia for the old Troisième République," the cheetah continued, stepping lightly around a plump peacock preening in the middle of the walkway. "Don't mind the curious glances."

The blue jay nodded, a group of chattering marmosets going eerily silent as they passed, turning toward them with leery expressions etched on their muzzles. "I suppose that it can't be helped," Aurélien conceded, lifting a winged forearm in a half-hearted wave.

"We aren't exactly a popular tourist destination," the cheetah murmured, her whiskers twitching in amusement. Pausing before a gilded door engraved with Persian calligraphy so intricate that Aurélien wouldn't have been able to decipher it even if they knew Farsi—which they absolutely didn't. "I am Anahita. When you find Zamburak Tehrani, kindly tell him that I sent you his way. And don't forget to enjoy the Jannah Room—it's quite the experience."

The doors parted into an antechamber encrusted with gemstones that seemed to dance in the flickering light of two gas-fueled lamps. Squinting slightly, the blue jay took a few steps forward and brushed aside a velvet curtain to reveal the unvarnished splendor of the Jannah Room. The rhythmic strumming of a tar accompanied by the hypnotic melody of a santur echoed off the towering ceiling.

However, the music wasn't what caught Aurélien's attention. The blue jay's gaze was fixated on the river of golden wine winding through the room, shaded by artificial trees which each bore a unique culinary delight. Lifelike marzipan branches bloomed with rice-stuffed grape leaves, skewers of spiced kebab, and gleaming vark-garnished baklava in the shape of pomegranate flowers.

"*Dorood.*" A king cheetah gestured, silver goblet in paw, from a floating chaise. Clad in a sumptuous ruby kaftan embroidered with threads of silver and gold, Aurélien's intuition marked him as none other than Zamburak Tehrani. "Are you thirsty, stranger? Please, drink your fill."

The blue jay carefully wrapped their claws around a goblet from a table inlaid with mother-of-pearl, the cool metal against their palm a welcome respite from the oppressive heat. "*Dorood,*" Aurélien responded, inclining their head in respect as they squatted down to lazily skim it across the surface of the golden river. "Your hospitality is appreciated."

Brining the goblet to their beak, the vapors wafting off the intoxicating wine carried with them the rich scent of honey and saffron. After a tentative sip, a blissful warmth rolled down the blue jay's throat while a hint of burnt caramel lingered on their palate.

"May you always find the fruits of life in the System to be sweet," the Zamburak toasted, lifting his goblet in a leisurely toast before guzzling the remainder of his wine. His eyes, molten gold studded with flecks of emerald, studied Aurélien over the rim. "Now, what has brought you to me, hrm? Surely you're not just here for a few baklava."

Aurélien took a longer sip, the sweet nectar ensnaring their senses as a sensation of utter contentment washed over them. The cabalistic wine's effects reminded them of the narcotic Pan-elim they'd been plied with in the hospital prior to their upload. "Anahita directed me to you. I was told by another that you might be able to provide me with the information I seek."

"Anahita?" he echoed smoothly, allowing the name to roll off his tongue in a slow, thoughtful rumble. "And what might you wish to learn from me? Most would consider me to be more foolish than wise. I am one cast in the mold of the Joker of Madinah"

"I'm looking for a member of the Khayyamzadeh Clade," Aurélien replied. "My interest is purely professional, of course."

The Zamburak's eyes narrowed to glittering slits before he let out a slow, measured laugh layered with both amusement and exasperation. "The Khayyamzadeh Clade are a tricky bunch. Are you sure you'd like to get mixed up in their affairs? I find it's rather like trying to bathe in pitch."

"Perhaps it's a mistake," Aurélien replied, setting the goblet on an ebony-inlaid table with a gentle *clink*. The blue jay's beak seemed to almost curve into a thoughtful frown as they turned slightly away. "But answers rarely come without a cost."

Using a small wooden paddle, the Zamburak directed his chaise into a small pull-off and climbed onto a shore of smooth-tumbled lapis lazuli. He brushed his kaftan, scrutinizing Aurélien with a keen eye that seemed to instantly size them up. The cheetah strolled over and picked a pomegranate from one of the artificial trees, his claws effortlessly slicing it apart to reveal the ruby pearls within.

"Tread carefully, "the Zamburak warned, the corners of his regal maw curling slightly as he popped a handful of the blood-red jewels into his muzzle. He extended the other half to Aurélien, who gratefully accepted. "The one you seek is still much like Céleste, for better or worse."

Plucking one of the pomegranate arils free, the blue jay rolled it between their fingers while scanning over the extensive collection of ornate shamshir swords adorning the far wall. "Why didn't Gaëlle come here and simply ask you herself?"

"Perhaps she was afraid of seeking her out alone," he murmured with a nonchalant shrug. "Or perhaps, she thought it wasn't her place to ask. I sense Gaëlle believes that my neutrality with regard to the other members of the Khayyamzadeh Clade amounts to a character flaw."

Sampling the pomegranate, Aurélien appreciated the burst of sweet-tart flavor that brushed across their tongue like the tip of a *billet doux*. "And yet you've chosen to remain impartial anyway?"

The Zamburak waved his paw and the elaborate murals adorning the ceiling faded away to reveal a cosmos stretched out like a silken canvas, punctuated by radiant stars and swirling nebulae. His manicured claws traced an absent pattern on the surface of his goblet while he gazed up at the heavens. "The universe doesn't favor a quark over a lepton, so why should I favor one cocladist over another?"

"Mrm...I prefer to shape the world around me rather than gaze at the heavens," Aurélien replied. "And for that, I need information."

With a playful smile, the Zamburak used his barbed tongue to scrape the interior of the pomegranate clean as he removed a shamshir from the wall and balanced it in the center of his palm. "Every blade here"—he drew the shamshir from its ornate leather scabbard—"holds a secret. The trick is knowing how to unravel it."

Aurélien pursed their beak, instinct drawing them to a shamshir with a golden hilt adorned with strips of shimmering fire opal. The iridescent scales almost pulsed in their grasp as they shed the scabbard and revealed a gleaming Damascus steel blade. "And how would a humble corvid such as I manage that?"

"The same way a humble cheetah learned many years ago," replied the Zamburak, brandishing a polished blade that cast a gladiatorial glow against his golden fur. "Are you familiar with the basics of swordplay?"

Aurélien tilted their head, blue-tipped feathers bristling in anticipation. "I know enough not to cut myself," they replied, th opalescent spark in their eyes matching the hilt of the shamshir their claws lightly gipped.

The Zamburak let out a throaty laugh that echoed across the chamber. Something in Aurélien's chest warmed at the sight of his affable grin. Persian music dramatically faded away, replaced by the lively interplay of a saxophone and bassoon. "Then let us begin the Shamshir Dance. Fortunately, the stakes are quite a bit lower here than phys-side."

Aurélien moved lightly on the balls of their feet, the blade in their hands perfectly balanced as they mirrored the Zamburak's poised stance. "The first rule of the Shamshir Dance"—the Zamburak tensed as he stored energy in his thighs—"is to listen to your blade."

Closing the distance between them with almost supernatural speed, the Zamburak brought his *shamshir* down in a clean arc. At the last second, Aurélien mirrored his action on the upswing, sending out a reverberating *clang* that seemed to shake the stars above them.

"The second rule," the Zamburak continued, luminous eyes gleaming under the starlight like a radium watch dial, "is to listen to your opponent's blade as you would your own. Any less and you are merely sparring instead of dancing with your partner."

Aurélien nodded, barely managing to parry the next onslaught of swift attacks. Sweat began to bead on their cheek feathers as the cheetah pushed them backward with a series of double-pawed slashes. "M-mrmph...this is getting to be a rather long list of rules, *mon ami*."

"Fortunately, I have only one more for you. The third rule," the Zamburak said with calm conviction, "is to listen to the silence between the clashes, for in that silence, you will hear the secrets speak."

Parting their beak, Aurélien drew a quick breath as they narrowly dodged another sweeping cut. Despite giving off the initial impression of a creature of leisure, the Zamburak was shockingly athletic. "How does one listen to silence?" they asked, leaping atop a table and parrying from the high ground.

"I would have thought that you'd know the answer already," the cheetah replied smoothly, launching himself onto the table with Aurélien. The wood creaked under their combined weight but held fast. "The same way one listens to whispers in the wind or the rustling of leaves."

The Zamburak's shamshir whizzed past, barely an inch away from Aurélien's beak. The blue jay stumbled backwards and quickly regained their footing as they were simultaneously struck by inspiration. "Or the language of two cocladists sitting together in an empty playground, saying nothing and yet everything to each other at the same moment." Aurélien finished.

"Very good." The Zamburak's voice carried a hint of approval. The cheetah flashed a pair of gold-capped canines as he smiled. Aurélien moved with renewed vigor, sweat dripping from their forefeathers as they used their superior agility to keep the Zamburak off-balance.

If the Zamburak was Céleste and Aurélien was Gaëlle, then their relationship had been a delicate balance, each one needing to listen just as much as to speak. Each clash of their blades echoed the natural rhythm of conversation, the Zamburak's impetuous and aggressive strikes echoing Céleste's fiery spirit while Aurélien's calculated parries mirrored Gaëlle's reserved nature.

Céleste's fork became clearer in their mind; no longer an abstract notion but a lynx slowly emerging in Athenian glory. The Zamburak struck again, shamshir glistening under the starlight, and the blue jay caught a glimpse of deep crimson as a pulse of pain shot through their side. The wound was superficial, just a shallow cut, but it jolted them into perfect focus all the same.

"Silent paws in the snow," Aurélien muttered under their breath, their feathers bristling with insight. Their backward stumble had overturned a mound of Turkish delight, leaving delicate tracks in the powdered sugar. "This fork—are they perhaps partial to a different climate?"

"Indeed," he affirmed with a dulcet purr. "Her heart has always been at peace amidst the snow-capped peaks of the Zagros."

"Know any good mountaineering sims?" Aurélien asked, driving the ball of their heel into the Zamburak's shin. The cheetah let out a sharp yelp, balancing on one leg as he beat back Aurélien's assault with the raw power of an avalanche rolling through the tree line.

"It's not in a different sim, but...I think I know just the place," the Zamburak replied with a knowing smile. With a swift movement, he closed the distance between them and slipped under the blue jay's guard. Aurélien's *shamshir* flew from their grip as they were viscerally ejected from the Government Club. "*Safar khosh begzared!*"

§

Aurélien collapsed backward onto an unspoiled blanket of powdery snow which almost instantly soaked through the thin cotton of their *gandoura*. Rolling their eyes, the blue jay forked into a winter-appropriate outfit, swapping the lightweight tunic for a well-insulated down jacket and sturdy snow pants. A fierce wind stirred their plumage, nipping at the slight gaps between the feathers on their cheeks.

In the distance, Aurélien caught a glimpse of a red-orange light through the thickening flurries. With no other signs of civilization in sight, they began to trudge toward it, pulling their hood tighter while tilting their beak down against the bitter cold. Their thickly-gloved hands fumbled for a cigarette, only managing to tear the pack open on their fourth attempt.

Framed by the swirling snowflakes, Aurélien withdrew a single filterless Gauloises. With years of practice, they clamped it between the frost-kissed edges of their beak and lit it with a strike-anywhere match. Drawing the smoke deep into their breast, Aurélien let the rush of nicotine siphon some of the chill away.

After a few minutes of effortful trekking, Aurélien arrived at a small clearing. Standing out against a background of scraggly trees, the red-orange light illuminated a rustic log cabin with shutters painted a vibrant gold. A healthy plume of smoke curled from the stacked stone chimney, while a pair of well-loved skis were propped against the railing of the front porch. The half-smoked Gauloises dangled from Aurélien's beak as they climbed weather-beaten stairs that creaked ominously beneath their weight.

After straightening the lapels of their jacket, Aurélien rapped their knuckles on a solid oak door adorned with a wreath of juniper branches interwoven with fragrant strips of dried orange peel. A moment later, it swung open to reveal a cozy living room bathed in the glow radiating from the roaring fire in the hearth.

"*Quelle surprise.*" The lynx standing in the doorway appraised Aurélien with emerald eyes, a half-smile on her muzzle as the acrid smoke from the Gauloises mingled with the frosty air. "I wasn't expecting company but...do come in. You'll catch your death out there. Just put that damn cigarette out."

Aurélien wordlessly flicked the Gauloises into the nearest snowbank, watching as the glow of the embers was quickly snuffed out. Stepping over the threshold, the scent of warm pine and roasting meat was a welcome contrast to the lynx's obviously begrudging hospitality. Playful shadows danced across worn Persian rugs strewn across the hardwood floor.

"You keep a lovely home," Aurélien remarked, shaking the dusting of snow free from their feathers.

"It doesn't quite have the grandeur of the Government Club, but it suits me just fine," the lynx replied. Futzing over a tarnished silver-plated samovar warmed by a small kerosene burner, she poured steaming tea into a pair of chipped porcelain cups as Aurélien hung their jacket over the back of a chintz armchair. "Do you take sugar?"

Aurélien rubbed their hands together for a moment before stretching them out towards the primally-satisfying warmth of the fire. "Yes, two spoonfuls," they said reflexively. "And if you'd be so kind, a bit of cream, *s'il vous plait.*"

The lynx huffed out a laugh as she sauntered back to the barebones kitchen tucked away in the rear of the cabin. Opening a crazed porcelain icebox, she retrieved a small glass bottle of cream and shook it gently before adding a generous measure to one of the tea cups.

"Here you are," she said, setting the steaming cup on a small wooden table beside Aurélien. Heat seeped into their cold digits like a summer breeze as their fingers curled around the smooth porcelain.

"*Merci,*" Aurélien replied, inhaling the fragrant steam before taking a measured sip. Strong and laced with a hint of cinnamon, the tea settled comfortably in the pit of Aurélien's stomach. "So, you're Céleste's fork, yes?"

"Are you here to offer condolences?" The lynx stiffened slightly, her eyes darting to the slowly diminishing fire before settling back on Aurélien. She took a leisurely sip of her tea, her nubby tail flicking with mild agitation. "You could've left a vase of ice-lilies on the porch in lieu of undertaking a *vol de la mort*."

"No, that's not why I came," Aurélien replied. "I was tasked with ascertaining your whereabouts, and I do not rest until my investigation comes to a satisfying conclusion."

"Is that so?" The lynx's ears pricked up as her foot-claws rapped against the unstained pine floorboards. "Was it Gaëlle who requested your services, perchance?"

A slight nod of the blue jay's head served as confirmation. "She was most eager to get in touch with you after all that had happened as of late. Are you aware?" "

"I enjoy voluntary solitude, but I don't live under a rock." The lynx's face remained inscrutable, her emerald eyes reflecting the flickering firelight. Then, she let out a diffident chuckle, shaking her head as she leaned back, cutting a sharp silhouette against the chintz. "Gaëlle had nursed a crush on Céleste for many decades. She's beautiful, don't you think?"

"She's like twilight over the Seine." Aurélien nodded in agreement as a falling log sent a shower of sparks bouncing off the smooth river stones that lined the hearth. "And yet it seems your heart does not agree with your eyes."

The lynx thoughtfully pursued her lips. Soft light accentuated her youthful features, which were in stark contrast to the mélange of nostalgia and melancholy in her wizened eyes. "My heart has perhaps seen one too many twilights over the Seine. Dusk also means night is near."

"That is true enough, but twilight has its own beauty," Aurélien murmured. Taking a sip of their tea, they paused and inquisitively cocked their beak. "I'm afraid that I didn't catch your name. I'd like to properly thank my host for a lovely cup of tea."

Remaining silent, gentle waves formed in the diminutive ocean clasped tightly in the lynx's paws as she studied Aurélien's face. The fire quivered momentarily as a particularly violent gust of wind rattled the cabin's foundations. "Tell me, stranger. What do you see when you gaze up at the night sky?"

"Stars," Aurélien replied shortly after a moment's pause. "I see stars, of course."

"Just stars?" The lynx murmured, a soft smile creeping at the edge of her muzzle. "Only diminutive specks of light scattered against black canvas?"

Tired springs creaked as Aurélien shifted slightly to lean against the unyielding backrest. It reminded them perfectly of a particularly irksome piece of furniture that had adorned his grandmother's humble sitting room, always sheathed in dense plastic. "I suppose I see heavenly glory, Céleste."

The lynx nodded, her eyes briefly gleaming with distilled starlight. "So, what now? Are you going to tell Gaëlle the truth?"

Aurélien peered down into the dregs of their tea, scanning for omens in the waterlogged leaves. The hisses and pops of the dying fire punctuated the silence between them. "I was only hired to find you," they murmured, noting what appeared to be the silhouette of a mushroom as they set their now empty cup down. "What happens next is not up to me."

"*C'est la vie,*" Céleste quipped, pushing herself off the chair. Her tail swished behind her as she moved, tracing patterns against the checkerboard pattern of her flannel lounge pants. Squatting beside the hearth, she casually dropped another log onto the pile with a resounding *thu-clack*. "We're always beholden to the decisions of others, whether they be friends, lovers, or cocladists. Perhaps I just wanted a taste of living for myself, at least for a little while."

"And now?" Aurélien asked.

"Now?" Céleste shot an inscrutable smile over her shoulder. Turning away, she picked up a wrought-iron poker and pensively stirred the embers before sweeping some of the ashes aside. "Now I spend the rest of the evening emptying out my samovar and considering how much longer I'd like to gaze at the heavens alone."

"I wouldn't want to overstay my welcome." Aurélien pursed their beak, giving her a nod as they stood up and tucked a cigarette into their beak—leaving it unlit, per Céleste's request. "You've been more than gracious to an uninvited guest."

"Off so soon? I hope that I didn't chase you away," the lynx murmured. "Our little discussion was just starting to get interesting."

"Not at all," Aurélien assured her while deftly slipping on their jacket. Their thoughts drifted to their clade, long scattered to the winds. Perhaps it might be time to reach out, if only to have an excuse to sample an unfamiliar haunt. "But, if stargazing ever gets a bit lonely–"

"–I know where to find Gaëlle," the lynx murmured. Escorting Aurélien to the door, she crossed the cozy space in a few graceful strides. Upon cracking it open, the pair were greeted by a gust of sharp wind that whipped up ethereal swirls across the landscape like diminutive dust devils.

Aurélien shivered, giving Céleste a warm *jeer-jeer* as they pulled their coat tighter. "I was going to say you could find me," they finished. "If you're ever in need of a stiff drink, leave a message for me with the bartender at the Sombres Reflets."

"Perhaps. After all, Death could have just as easily have kindly stopped for me as for my fork." A coy smile danced on Céleste's muzzle. "Can you give Gaëlle a message for me?"

Aurélien tilted their head and cocked an inquiring eyebrow. "Of course."

"Just because the stars are scattered does not mean they are separated." The lynx delicately tilted her head onto one side, her gaze momentarily lost in the snow-blanketed landscape beyond the front porch. "They all belong to the same sky."

"I'll pass the message along." Aurélien closed their eyes as the door's latch clicked shut behind them. The bluejay sent a ping to Gaëlle before letting out a satisfied sigh that hinted at their exhaustion. Still, at the Sombres Reflets, there would be time enough to enjoy the satisfaction of providing the first drop of gold for relationship *kintsugi*...and perhaps gather the fortitude to reach out to a few cocladists. "*Nos cœurs se tiennent par la main, même quand les distances nous séparent.*"

Then, beneath an endless sky painted with shimmering constellations, the blue jay turned and stepped confidently toward Eternity.

Prophecies

Madison Rye Progress, with
Samantha Yule Fireheart

Slow Hours — 2401

To step into The Bean Cycle was to be immediately assailed by sound. There was, as to be expected, the clink of glasses and muted howl of steam wands bringing milk up to temperature, but mixed in was the clatter and clicking of work being done on bicycles. Wheels were spun, chain was dragged through derailleurs, tires were changed. Milk was steamed, espresso was made, names were hollered out.

It was not the type of din that Slow Hours expected for the one she and If I Dream were looking for. It was too uneven, this wall of sound. Too unpredictable. The steam wands were too piercing and the occasional clang of a wrench or raucous laughter over some story of a crash too jarring.

She looked to If I Dream, who merely shrugged.

Scanning the cafe-*cum*-bike-repair-shop revealed little. It was certainly well populated enough, with every table in use and few enough empty chairs. In the corner by the window, a crowd of synthetic creatures of some sort had gathered, looking vaguely feline but with glassy faceplates showing LED-light eyes in sets of fixed expressions. While they were all far shorter than Slow Hours—who one would be hard pressed to describe as tall— the couch that they were sitting on looked to be barely able to hold their weight.

Even if it was not the type of place for the target of their search, it was still incredibly endearing, and she made a note to herself to return some day.

"Afternoon, friends," the barista said, grinning to them. They were tall and wiry, red hair and beard shining in the bright halogen lights over the bar. "Two mochas? Extra whipped cream?"

Caught off-guard by having her order guessed for her, Slow Hours froze, brow furrowed.

If I Dream elbowed her in the side, murmuring, "I have canvased this place before. Do not worry about it." More loudly, she said, "Yes, though please make it three. Thank you, Hasher."

Still frowning, Slow Hours allowed herself to be guided down the counter to wait for their drinks to be picked up. She set up a cone of silence over her and her cocladist, more for the relative quiet that it offered than for privacy.

"Are you sure this is the place?" she asked.

If I Dream nodded. "Yes, quite sure. Hasher was the one who tipped me off, and I...have seen her outside."

"You are already watching her, then?"

The panther smiled faintly, gave an even fainter shrug. "I am nothing if not myself."

"Then why did you not just go speak to her yourself?" Slow Hours asked. "Or bring me straight to her?"

If I Dream rolled her eyes. "My dear, I *just* said that I am nothing if not myself. That is not my role in this. That is yours. This is the story we are telling, yes? We are stepping into a cafe and ordering a coffee. We are seeing what this is like, this place where she has been parked the last week. We are speaking with Hasher."

Sighing, she nodded and leaned against the counter, poking at the anodized sheet of aluminum that covered it. Thankfully, it seemed to be coated with some thin sheen of resin to keep the texture reasonable and noise down. "Well, alright. You are the sneaky ones."

"Do you not also live in stories? I thought that was part of your whole shtick."

She snorted. "Well, okay, good point. I suppose I am still a little rattled, is all."

" 'Rattled'?" If I Dream laughed. Like everything else that she did, it was nearly silent, more a quiet huffing of breath through her nose than anything. "*The* Slow Hours of the Ode clade is rattled?"

"Yes, yes," she said, waving away the comment with a grin. "I really do see your point about the story, I am just finding it hard to slow down, perhaps. When you said that you had heard something, I was ready to race to find her, to have to jump through all the hoops of a fetch quest, so to hear that you already know precisely where she is, that you are already watching her, makes waiting for a coffee like this feel like a waste of time."

"It will be worth it, I promise."

"The coffee?"

The panther laughed once more. "Well, I was going to say the story, but the coffee *is* quite good here, so, yes."

It was only another minute or two of waiting before Hasher waved to get their attention, gesturing to three paper cups sitting on the bar, ready for them. Slow Hours dropped the cone of silence and winced at the sudden barrage of sounds that followed. She turned her hearing down a few ticks. "Thank you," she said, bowing. "By the way, we were hoping to meet up with a cocladist of ours. She is a skunk, a furry, built rather like myself." She gestured down at herself—human, instead, with pale skin and curly black hair tied up in a messy bun, but stocky and short. "Black fur, white stripe, a little jumpy. Have you seen her around?"

Wiping their hands on a towel hooked into the strings of their apron, Hasher nodded, tilting their head over toward the couch full of robots. "The one who was sleeping there the last few days, I'm guessing?"

"Sleeping?" Slow Hours asked, frowning.

"Yeah. She would just kind of curl up at one end for a few hours and nap. No biggie, of course, and we all liked her. She only ever slept while things were slow, and she'd always move when asked." They broke out into a grin again, shrugging. "Or when it got too loud. Or when it got too quiet. Or just every now and then for no reason we could figure out—very stimmy type—but she was always very polite about it."

"Yes, that would be her," she said, smiling. "Well, thank you very much. Did she leave recently?"

They nodded towards the back door of the shop as they started to make their way back to the line of customers waiting for drinks. "Out back, out to Infinite Café, probably half an hour ago. Just peek in if you need anything!"

The two Odists bowed their thanks and carefully picked their way further over to the cafe side of the building, winding their way between tables until they reached the brick wall. There in the middle was a green, wooden door set into an arch, and above the arch "INFINITE CAFÉ" shone in tooth-achingly pink neon.

The sim in which The Bean Cycle existed had a weather pattern tuned after somewhere in the northern hemisphere, so they had entered the shop sometime in early March—a scant three weeks after Lagrange had come back online after the Century Attack—where the air still had a bite to it and salt still stained the sidewalks out front from where the ice had been melted in the days prior. They had arrived late in the afternoon, the sun setting down along the street casting long shadows behind them.

When they stepped out into Infinite Café, though, it was the same bright, midsummer's noon as it always was there. The light came from everywhere and nowhere, and their shadows sat just beneath their feet. It was the perfect temperature—no matter who you were, no matter your preferences, it was always perfect—and it was as packed as ever.

If one percent of the population of Infinite Café was missing, Slow Hours could not tell, and for that she was grateful.

The sim was dead simple: it consisted of one, long road set into a thin torus. A truly enormous torus: when she looked up, she saw a bright thread directly above them where the road had curved up into an arch hanging in the heavens, and yet the road seemed perfectly flat as far as she could see.

Lining either side of the street were entrances to cafes. Cafes, coffee shops, doors leading out into libraries with coffee carts, alleyways leading out into sims where coffee was hawked from handcarts, dusty steps leading up into marketplaces where vendors boiled their coffee in their cezves in great vats of sand set over wood fires. Anywhere that served coffee to cladists that wanted was free to create an exit that led out into Infinite Café, and over the two centuries of its existence, it had grown from a labyrinthine maze of buildings to the ring-road that it was today.

She had no clue how it worked, if it really was that big, but the sheer size of the System had been driven home quite effectively over the last few weeks—23 *billion* dead! The number remained surreal—so she was hopeful that there were no tricks involved, no attempts to make it look bigger than it was.

She was hopeful that all of these people here on this relatively crowded street were real, not constructs or illusions. She hoped they found coffee and friends and loved ones and long-lost selves.

A gentle touch to her shoulder brought her back to the present. She looked over to If I Dream, then followed her gaze to the center of the thoroughfare.

There, in the middle of the path, stood a skunk. She looked much like others in her clade, with white-striped black fur, tapered snout, cookie ears poking out from an unruly mane, and where she differed, it mostly came down to clothing. She wore a linen tunic in dandelion yellow, cinched around the waist with a leather belt, and a pair of loose, woolen trousers in a dusty brown. Her mane was tied back with a kerchief of some sort, a pastel triangle fully visible to them as she stood stock still and stared straight up to the arch above.

Slow Hours felt concern tugging at her cheeks, while a glance at If I Dream showed only curiosity.

"Shall we?" she asked.

If I Dream nodded.

Letting a crowd of joggers pass, the pair made their way up to the skunk so that Slow Hours could gently touch her elbow.

The reaction was far more extreme than expected as the skunk let out a shriek and skipped three or so meters away from them, nearly colliding with a couple walking hand in hand. She whirled, tail bristled out behind her and ears splayed to the sides. Her eyes were wide and breath coming in quick gasps.

Both Slow Hours and If I Dream took a pace back, startled.

In the span of a few short seconds, the skunk seemed to get her bearings and comprehend just who was standing in front of her. She visibly worked on mastering her breathing as she stood up straighter, brushing her paws anxiously down over her shirt. "Ah...I, ah...Slow Hours?"

She bowed slowly, deliberately, so as not to startle the skunk any further, and nodded. "Yes, and And If I Dream, Is That Not So." She held out the extra mocha. "We got you a coffee, What Right Have I. Would you like to join us?"

What Right Have I looked between the two anxiously, clutching at the hem of her tunic. "I...ah, do you...I mean, is there an occasion? Is there a place? I was...I mean, I had been in The Bean Cycle but the couch...oh, I am talking myself in circles..."

With that, she began to pace in an abbreviated line before them, alternating between scrubbing her paws together and straightening her already quite straight shirt.

Slow Hours looked to If I Dream for help, and the panther stepped forward silently and wrapped her arms around the skunk from behind.

At first, she thought this would be a prelude to them stepping from the sim together, or perhaps some affectionate bear hug, though this did not fit what she knew of their faint acquaintanceship.

Instead, though, If I Dream simply squeezed around the skunk and stood still. There was a squeak and a tense-looking squirm from What Right Have I at first, but in surprisingly short order, her breathing fell under her control and she slouched against her cocladist, looking as close to relaxed as Slow Hours had ever seen her.

"What is this about?" she asked If I Dream via sensorium message.

"A hunch," the panther sent back. *"Apparently a correct one, for which I am glad. Sometimes compression helps, yes?"*

"If you say so."

"Are you alright, my dear?" If I Dream murmured loud enough for Slow Hours to hear as well.

"Y-yes. *Tizkeh l'mitzvos.*"

"Will you join us for coffee? It is not a demand, to be clear. Just an offer."

What Right Have I nodded slowly. "Is the...ah, is the couch free in The Bean Cycle?"

If I Dream hesitated for a moment, then nodded. "The creatures have left. There is a person sitting on one corner, but if you are comfortable, the rest is free."

"If we...I mean, if I may set up a cone of silence, that will be fine, yes."

Slow Hours watched as the panther gently released her grip on the skunk, the two monochromatic animals—one in baggy, colorful linen and wool, and the other in black form-fitting shirt and leggings—separating cautiously, as though to move faster might once more send What Right Have I into manic pacing.

"Shall we?" Slow Hours asked, smiling reassuringly to her cocladists.

The couch was indeed free, though there was no other instance of If I Dream visible. Slow Hours put this out of mind as best she could; the first stanza was well known for just how easily they slid about unseen, unbeknownst to others as they simply watched, observed.

They sat in the crook of the couch, L-shaped as it was. What Right Have I requested one of the corner vertices of their little triangle so that she could get up and pace should she need, nudging the low table that sat before her aside to help assist in this endeavor, before setting up the cone of silence and nudging it to obscure them as occupants. The din of the coffee shop fell to a low murmur.

The three of them set their coffee cups on small coasters set in the air just within reach, and waited in silence.

"What Right Have I," Slow Hours began gently once the silence seemed to open up. "From Whence messaged the first stanza a few days ago to see if any of them knew where you were."

"She messaged Speaking, in particular," If I Dream added quietly. "She is the instance hunter of our stanza, yes? But she is feeling perhaps a little burnt by recent events and requested some space, for which I am glad. She deserves that."

"I know," the skunk said. "She has messaged me several times. I have...ah, I mean, I always endeavor to let her know when I am okay. And I am! I promise."

Slow Hours laughed, holding up her hands. "I believe you, my dear. This is a meeting between friends, not an interrogation. We wanted to see whether you are okay, yes, but it has also been some time, yes? And I have been checking in with much of the clade in the last few weeks. There are several of me out and about on meetings such as these."

She nodded. "She told me she just wanted...ah, she requested"a bit more proof than gentle rebuffs." I told her that I am okay. I told her that I was walking and meditating."

"Is that what you have been doing during the day?"

"I..." She trailed off, scrubbing her paws against her thighs. "Some, perhaps. A little. We are still in *Shloshim*, but I cannot...ah, I am not focused."

"You will have to forgive me for being a bit blunt," Slow Hours said gently. "But are you overflowing?"

What Right Have I's expression dropped, the skunk quickly going from attentive to panicked to miserable.

If I Dream held out her paw, an offer for reassurance. "I do not know what your overflow looks like, What Right Have I. I trust that it is not pleasant, though. It rarely is, yes?"

"It is sometimes," she admitted, shaking her head at the offer of touch. "It is...ah, it comes in two flavors. It shows itself as religious ecstasy sometimes, of a sense of spirit, a feeling of *HaShem* existing in the world, in the System. Those who reach out to RJ, who reach out to our friend, they are reaching out to *HaShem!* Ey may be our personal *HaShem,* yes? But ey is an abstract manifestation of the world!" Despite the sudden animation in her words, the sudden fluency in her otherwise stuttering speech, her expression remained dire, anxious.

Slow Hours smiled faintly, taking a moment to think back. The skunk's choice of words triggered a memory of a report written for the clade decades back. "Codrin said that, yes? Or rather reported that Answers Will Not Help said that."Our own personal *HaShem.*" She said that she could not feel em on Artemis, yes?"

What Right Have I nodded, subsiding back into the couch. "Yes. I...ah, I mean, I would not have joined them for that reason, never mind the other difficulties faced."

Both Slow Hours and If I Dream nodded. No Odist had joined Artemis for its ongoing voyage.

"But ey is still *b'tzelem Elohim,* yes? Ey is still in the image of Adonai, yes? Ey is still human, even if ey is our world. Our world is *b'tzelem Elohim,* and we, *b'tzelem Elohim,* reside within em." She smiled weakly. "Rav From Whence does not like it when I say these things, but that is what I feel when I am overflowing."

"And that is what you are feeling now?" Slow Hours asked.

"No," she said, once more sounding miserable. "If I do not feel ecstasy, I feel anguish. I feel...mm, I feel nullity. I feel nothing. I feel RJ and I think,"Ah my friend, my friend." I do not see in em the divine. I do not feel *b'tzelem Elohim,* I feel stupid. I feel...ah,

I feel broken. I have been staying here, sleeping where I may be seen because I am afraid...ah, because I am so, *so* afraid that I will disappear, that I will crash and that no one will notice me. I fear that I will be forgotten and that...ohhh, I am talking in circles. I am thinking in circles, I am sorry."

"It is okay," Slow Hours said gently. "Do you think you are overflowing because of the Century Attack?"

The skunk whimpered and pushed herself quickly to her feet, pacing once more and shaking her paws out as though to dry them off, then straightening her already straight skunkerchief. "I have been dreaming," she mumbled, then jerked her head to the side with a quiet squeak. She continued more clearly. "I have been dreaming, here on the couch, out there in Infinite Café when...ah, when I fall asleep out there."

Slow Hours tilted her head, sitting up straighter.

What Right Have I smiled faintly. "I have...ah, I am not the oracle that you are, my dear. I am no prophet."

She smiled, shaking her head. "Neither am I. I would still like to hear your dream, though."

The skunk nodded, paused to gather her thoughts, then spoke slowly. "I am disembodied, yes? I am floating and I see a figure, and they begin to weep, and they dissolve into a cloud of black specks, and these specks float away on a breeze, and each one enters the heart of a cladist, and they cry out in agony and dissolve into clouds of their own, and so it ramifies until all are dust. I see you, yes, and I see If I Dream, and I see Should We Forget and I see No Longer Myself."

If I Dream jerked back as though slapped, a sudden move that was nevertheless silent. "Do not–" she said, then shook her head.

"I am sorry, If I Dream," What Right Have I said, bowing low and forcing herself to sit once more. "I...ah, my dreaming mind remembered names of those lost, perhaps, and extrapolated."

The panther nodded, scrubbed a paw over her face, and sighed. "It is okay, my dear. I am still feeling raw."

It was What Right Have I's turn to offer a paw. If I Dream accepted gratefully, giving a brief squeeze. When this lead to another squeaky tic from the skunk, she let go.

"Ah...sorry," the skunk stammered. "I have...I mean, that is to say...ah, I am talking in circles. I am sorry."

"It is okay," Slow Hours said gently. "Do you need some time?"

She nodded, bowing her head for a moment before retrieving her mocha for a tentative sip. Apparently finding the temperature tolerable, she followed this with a longer drink.

Both Slow Hours and If I Dream followed suit, simply taking in the ambiance of the shop.

"Have you had dreams, Slow Hours?" If I Dream asked, breaking the silence with her quiet murmur.

She startled to awareness, smiling sheepishly. "Since the attack? No, nothing memorable, though I have not been sleeping well. I do not imagine many are."

"And before?"

What Right Have I perked up, setting her coffee aside and scrubbing her paws together, kneading pads against pads. "Do your prophecies only come in dreams?"

Slow Hours laughed. "My little predictions are not prophecies. They are just that: guesses based on the trajectories of the stories one tells. I may predict that, when we leave today, What Right Have I will linger a while yet because there is something she has yet to tell us– no, it will come in time, you do not need to until you are ready. But that is based on the trajectory of the story I have heard so far." She hesitated a moment, thinking. "But yes, I have had dreams that may well have been prophecies, but only ever in hindsight."

"Tell us...ah, I mean, will you tell us some of what you dreamed?"

"Yes. It has happened four times. Only those four, though." She held up her hand with as many fingers raised as she explained. "Perhaps Lagrange got hit by a stray cosmic ray or some other fancy particle and it flipped a bit inside the portion that contained me, and I was given some premonition. Smacked upside the head by Apollo, yes? Or, in your terms, visited by the angel of the Lord who gave me a honeyed scroll to eat."

She tapped one finger. "The first was about Qoheleth and his little...adventure. Some two decades before, I had the same dream five nights in a row, of him standing in his robes, arms raised to the heavens, and then crumbling down into sand. At the time, I did not even realize that it was him. I had not seen him in more than a century, and when I had, he was dressed like a natty old college professor."

The next finger, tapped. "The second was about Michelle's death, and I will not repeat it."

She tapped her ring finger. "The third happened in the midst of a play—one of my yearly performances—and in the scene, I was to fall to my knees and cry out,"The knife! At her neck, the knife!" But instead, I passed out and apparently mumbled words not in the script which tallied exactly with Sasha's experience."

There was a moment of silence as she considered the fourth and how best to describe it, not least because of the easy comparison to What Right Have I's dream as explained. Finally, she tapped her pinkie "The fourth was a dream of a core part of me being removed through the back of my neck, a disappearing from the world and becoming a ghost in the next. There was more that I do not understand, visions of a field, a park, but I had that dream every night on the five nights leading up to New Year's."

What Right Have I listened attentively to Slow Hours's description of her prophecies, or at least prophetic dreams. As she spoke, her cocladist's expression darkened, until by the end, she was scowling. "I am no Daniel," the skunk said once she had finished. "I will not scry your *mene, mene, tekel, parsin.* But if you had foreknowledge of Michelle's suicide or the Century Attack, why did you not say anything? Who might we be if Michelle still lived? Might Lagrange be unharmed if we but knew this?"

By the end, she was nearly growling, so many of her verbal tics melting away as that emotion rose.

If I Dream lifted her snout from where her gaze had drifted. "Did she know, my dear? Or did she only have a recurring anxious nightmare? Do we not all have a hundred recurring anxious nightmares a year?"

The skunk glowered. "And? If that is–" A tic briefly interrupted her, a jerk of the head to the side, and this time she really did growl, though it appeared to be more at herself than anything. "If that is so, then why were these not known?"

Slow Hours straightened up. "I apologize if that came off as in any way glib, What Right Have I, or as though I could have done anything about them. I did try to get in touch with Michelle after those nights of dreams, but she only smiled and reassured me that she would"live on". It was not until after she quit that those words had any import."

What Right Have I's shoulders sagged, though she was clearly still gritting her teeth.

She sighed, continuing, "And perhaps it is as If I Dream says. They were anxious nightmares. However, they still bore the acrid tang of ill omens to me. There was a scent of premonition, and so I have slotted them neatly into that category, even if they *were* only caused by anxiety."

There followed a long moment while the skunk processed this. She seemed to be running down a mental checklist, as her rapid breathing shifted almost immediately into something deeper and more even, her posture straightened from a wary hunch as though ready to bolt, and her expression settled into a rather stiff half-smile. All spoke of various bits of therapy Slow Hours remembered from centuries back.

"Alright. Okay." What Right Have I slowed her breathing further and turned her paws facing up, another skill from therapy. "Okay. You are the both of you correct. I live in my head and in the Tanakh and with a thought of prophecies. For you to call them such, it, ah...it...okay. It makes them not what I was thinking. You are not Ezekiel. You are not Jeremiah."

Slow Hours smiled, gave a hint of a bow from where she sat. "I am not, no. I am a script manager and nerd whose imagination gets away from her sometimes, yes? Even in sleep, yes?"

The skunk's smile grew more earnest as she nodded. "Again, I am sorry. I...ah, I do not know. I am unwell, perhaps. I am over-flowing and making connections that do not exist."

"Do you suppose you have had more than four, if you include those that did not come true?" If I Dream asked curiously. "They do still sound fascinating, if only as a curiosity."

"If I have, including the scent of premonition, then I do not remember them. It was that scent, though, that led me to reach out to Michelle. I am embarrassed to say that that was the only one I acted on, though, given that all four of those revolve around death."

What Right Have I furrowed her brow, paws shifting to clench tightly around the hem of her tunic. "I remember a story...ah, a snippet from the *History* where May Then My Name says that Michelle thought of herself as a dead woman walking, yes."

She nodded. "May Then My Name went on to say that Michelle thought that perhaps even the dead can know joy, yes."

"Did she, in the end?" If I Dream asked, frowning. "Know joy, that is? When she asked us all to merge with her, to share with her all that we had become, what did she feel? When, for an instant, she became ten thousand years old, did she choose to quit because she found peace?"

"I think that she did, yes." Slow Hours spoke carefully, keeping an eye on What Right Have I for further tics or other signs of distress. "Or, rather, I must believe that she did. There is too much despair if I imagine her as buried under the weight of all of our own despairs and neuroses. If it is a comfortable fiction, so be it. I will live in that comfortable fiction."

If I Dream nodded slowly. "Far be it from me to dispel what curtains keep despair from leading you after her."

She laughed and shook her head. "There is no suicide in me, thankfully."

"When I received her sensorium message, I nearly refused to attend out of protest. I think many of us saw the writing on the walls when we heard that uncertain steeliness in her voice."

What Right Have I winced, squirming tensely in her seat, right at the edge of the couch cushion. "It...ah...I mean, I struggled. I was there– we all were there! But I struggled."

The panther smiled faintly to her. "We all did, yes. Part of me felt that if any one of us did not go, then she would not quit. Another part was terrified I would be one of many who did not come, and that she would die feeling abandoned by her own family. If she was going to quit, and she wished to do so in the company of her clade...And now..."

She trailed off and let her gaze wander down to the drink she still held in her paws. Blinking rapidly, the muscles on her cheeks and snout briefly became more prominent, as though she was doing her best to keep her expression placid, to not snarl or voice her despair, much as it had been throughout, though the tears leaving tracks in her cheekfur were impossible to hide.

Alarmed at the sudden shift in demeanor, Slow Hours scooted a few inches closer to If I Dream, offering her hand just as the panther had done for What Right Have I before.

She accepted with a grateful—if still wan—smile.

Slow Hours returned that smile, saying quietly, "That was the dream I had, you know. The premonition. An upwelling of joy and then an overflowing. She looked up to the sun, and the sun was RJ, and then they were one and the same, and it was all joy."

At this, What Right Have I burst into tears. She did not cry prettily, but very few people did. It was a brief cry, however, and soon after she scooted back to the furthest limit of the cone of silence and drew her legs up onto the couch with her, growling as she did, "Slow Hours, you are the fucking worst."

"I am the worst, yes," she said, voice still quiet and calm. "But that is why I am choosing to believe that the premonition was true and why I am choosing to believe that she did find joy, or peace, or at least nothingness and freedom."

"They both deserve to be together. I hope that that is what No Longer Myself has obtained. What all of those lost have," If I Dream sighed.

"I think...ah, I hope your dreams were true, in the end," What Right Have I said after a long silence between the three of them, after each had fallen merely to sniffles. "I hope that they *were* prophecies, whether or not you knew. If only for that one, I hope that they were true."

Journal of Diago Pereira

Nat Mcardle-Mott-Merrifield and
Sarah Bloden

Henrique Pereira — 2400–2401

May 12th, 2400

The door is pressed open and the lights are turned on with a soft click, below wooden planks bemoan the shuffling feat of Henrique and his slippers, his old jeans loose and baggy, the knitted sweater he wears worn like his brittle bones. He walks with his cane, tapping on the floor as he finds his seat, guided by his great Granddaughter Isa, who guides him with steady, thoughtfully slow, footing.

"Take a seat Grand Papi… it will… it will all, uhm…" she mutters the words, "be okay" aimlessly, then lets a minute of quiet drift between the two of them, sounds of weeping heard from the floor below. She had only recently entered her teens, how could such innocence possibly understand such loss, the ramifications of the news not yet settled in for youthful Isa, yet the reality sank soundly onto the soul of elderly Henrique. The meandering minute passes, and Isa looks back up, eyes filled with concern for her great Grandfather's wellbeing. "Ah, Grand Papi, would you like me to get you your coffee mug? A blanket? Anything to give you comfort…?"

Finally, he begins to sit down on his leather recliner, waving his aged hand dismissively, wrinkled and frail. His dower face, aged like the cracked leather he put his weight onto and pock marked with freckles from years in the sun, bunches together as he grimaces, not at the offer but towards the state of the world, the state of his family, the state of the System, and perhaps his aching body as well.

Gently, slowly, deliberately he lowers himself and rests into the seat, his reading seat, the seat he got from his aunt as part of her will, a skilled tanner—skill that shined through the weathered cushions that strained to hold his retired body. So weak, so old—the days of power and youth having left him, drained from him by the decades. He looks up, and lets out a tired, weary sigh, then shakes his head.

"I... I just need to sit down, my dear. Sit down... Just... sit down. To think... in quiet. Please, Isa my dear, leave me be for now. Go, tend to your Mami, she needs your comfort."

He stares back down at his lap, grunting and listening to the door creak closed as Isa leaves, allowing lingering thoughts to swell in might and misery. Flashes of denial sting as Henrique's depressed thoughts flow freely, he attempts to come to terms with the news again, just as another baleful shriek fills the air, a cry, a plea heard by none who deserved it.

Descendants deleted and ancestors now long gone. His Granddaughter weeps at the knowledge her handful of children and acres of ancestry were now lost, taken from her just as his brother was through the same act of terrorism.

Terrorism. What a foul concept that was so filled with angry grays, blacks, and whites. Months, months the System was down and its dire truths suppressed, until finally reaching the 'net in a slow torrent of terrible news, chaotic questions, corroborating with bitter claims, the collectivists caused harm on a cataclysmic scale, like some malevolent maelstrom, a maverick ridden by the reapers' wrath.

He looks at his hands, fingers clenched and unclenching, shaking. Tempering anger soothes his emotions with contempt to those responsible, as tears get lost in the saddened crow's-feet lining his tired face. His watery eyes look to the left, noticing the spine of a lithe book tucked within the drawer of his side table, a familiar thing that rested with a fine, blue-feathered, ink quill strapped to its outside.

He sighs somberly, shakily, and reaches for the journal that once belonged to his late and lost. A Journal of Diago Pereira, his brother—or siblings, as he would later come to learn in his youth, and love years after his younger brother uploaded with his once hidden plurality in tow.

The next few moments were a blanket of misery, misery that mastered the old mans' mind, and moved him to lift the old literature to his lap. Tears gradually overwhelming, he wipes them off and opens the book to the first page, a familiar feeling now underwhelming compared to the weight of tragedy on his shoulders:

12th of March 2304

Today is my 17th birthday and as a gift my Grand mami got me this journal to practice my english writing in. My teacher told me my writing is pretty good since he started teaching me but needs work and my mami thought it would be a good idea to give me a book to practice in. He said I should focus on my punctuation mostly as I seem to forget to include that in my writing sometimes. He also said my spelling could do a little bit of work so I'll try and focus on that.

Today was so fun after school, I took my bike home and my cousins, sisters and a few of our friends from the next farm over were waiting for me! I even saw aunt Corita, she managed to get the day off from the Ansible clinic, I hardly ever get to see her. We had a quick game in the backyard field , I think my sisters took it easy on me, there usually way more dexterous then I am! (*ELES FIZERAM ISSO, EU JÁ VI ELES*

CHUTAREM VOCÊ, MAS NO FUTEBOL! HAHA.) I can still play pretty good Fel!

Anyway, after a few goals, my mami called us in for dinner! It was Fels and my favorite, homemade Acarajé and Picanha, and for dessert Grand mami made me a vanilla cake with blue icing!

After we ate, my mami and Grand mami gave me my gifts, this journal and a letter from my brother that wished he could be there. He also sent me printed photos of him and his army buddies at the BrAr Line. They smile, but the scenery is so grim and barren. My aunt tells me it was once farmland, and now it's just mud and metal fences.

Even if this was given to me to improve my English writing, I really enjoyed writing about my day! And I didn't expect it to be. But I am tired and don't have much else to say, the cake was yummy! I always love Grand mami's cakes.

In the margin, "Property of Diago Pereira" can be read, along with the thumb smearing of blue icing dye that has since stained the once fresh paper, now freshly stained by stray tears. Henrique smiles, sniffling softly as the wrinkles on his face rise, his thumb and forefinger slides the pages to a random entry, a familiar sensation of such delicate paper dancing between his fingertips—wrinkled, marked, and lightly stained pages of faded graphite and century old ink—dates dotting the upper left. He moves his hand across the paper, reading the crude handwriting of early script, a pastime he took part in on a monthly basis, now a catharsis, a means to mourn.

He flips through the pages more, methodically moving fingers before finding one to finally read through in full:

17th of June 2304

Dear Journal, I got home today after my english classes, and Mami and my sisters told me Henrique had sent a letter from the BrAr Line. It talked about how he saw a Hyacinth Macaw making a nest on one of the watchtowers at the Briar. (*SORTUDO! EU GOSTARIA QUE PUDÉSSEMOS VER MAIS A LINHA DO BRIAR. PARECE TÃO INTERESSANTE.*) It really doesn't Fel.

He wrote in the letter that he was ordered to chase the bird off because it was making a nest, but even with him and his buddies' best efforts it stayed. I'm proud of it! This story got a laugh out of everyone, and to my surprise mom showed me a feather that came with the letter, it was bright blue! Further down, my brother said that while he was trying to get the bird to leave, he managed to collect a few feathers from its nest and thought I'd like to have one. (*HENRIQUE É UM IRMÃO TÃO LEGAL. ESPERO QUE VOCÊ POSSA ME APRESENTAR A ELE EM BREVE.*) I do too, Fel.

Both Fel and I are so excited to have received it, the Hyacinth Macaw is believed to be an extinct species. To know one still lives makes us so happy! I can't wait to show this in class tomorrow, I know Mr. Rocha loves to watch birds as much as I do.

Speaking of Mr. Rocha! I asked him if I could borrow his binoculars after class today. I've been wanting to go visit my spot with them and see what birds have been nesting near there. He agreed with the exception that, "You better let me come with you, I'm not about to miss out on a bird watching expedition, let alone give my binoculars away without supervision!" I know he meant well by that, but I couldn't help but feel a little nervous. Mr. Rocha is a good teacher, though. Friends of my eldest cousin, who was taught by him when she was younger!

After looking at the letter and feathers, my sisters and I did our chores around the farmstead with the farm hands. Just as I was finishing, my sisters came up to me and told me they saw a flock of white birds that were nesting in one of our Latex Trees, I could only guess what they must've been at the time, but I wouldn't have guessed they're White-Necked Hawks! They were all nested there and warding danger away from the nest. They looked so majestic! I can't wait to watch their eggs hatch, such a beautiful species of bird!

One of his favorite entries, and a reminder of a brighter day at the Briar line, one not so filled with dull gray and scorched earth. He frowns, hesitates, then hastily lifts the journal from his lap, finding the ink quill resting in the nook of his arm rest and right leg. He carefully raises it up, pondering—not recalling—how he so quickly removed it from the strap on the journal, carefully preening the blue feather adorned to the end of the writing utensil.

His hand works the fine fibers of the feather, tracing it down to the firmness of the pen nib, pointed, certain, precise. He lazily drags that same fingers as before across another section of pages, coarse papers scraping assuredly as he stumbles into another two entries, both rather lengthy:

24th of July 2304

Dear Journal, today I write away from home. I told Mami I was going to spend the night over at Gregors home, to which she was wary to acknowledge me doing so. She made sure I had my tablet with me, and that I had lunch packed as well. I appreciate her concern but sometimes it feels almost too much. Before I left, Mami also made sure I had offered my chores to one of my sisters, which I had, telling her Iara agreed to do my tasks today so I could spend the night away from home. I'll just end up doing twice of hers on the weekend.

Since I plan to spend the night over at the high rises, I left early this morning. I hadn't been to see Gregor in a few months and was curious about what was new.

Fel and I hitched a ride on a truck, and on the way Fel was discussing with me if I had also felt the new identity that was forming. Fel and I still don't know where she came from, but we feel that she has a similar origin to Fel, herself. Hopefully we'll find out from this newcomer. (*ESTOU MUITO ANIMADO PARA VER SE PODEMOS APRENDER ALGUMA COISA COM ESSE NOVO COMPANHEIRO PLURAL, DIAGO. VOCÊ REALMENTE DEVERIA EXPLORAR MAIS A 'NET SOBRE A PLURALIDADE.*)

Fel, you know I would if I had the time to do so! I'm just always too busy. Anyway, we've been writing this at the 'cave' now, and it looks like it is probably two in the afternoon, and we've had our lunch too, feeling ready to go! Also, the tide is starting to fill up this old garage so I better get packing or I won't be able to take the boat out at all. Thankfully, the weather is peaceful with hurricanes Gabriel and Taylor having traveled down south this time of year. Still, the ocean waves are choppy so I won't be able to spend any time writing in the rowboat. Next entry will be written once we've made landfall, at the high rises. I'm hopeful Gregor will be available today!

Henriques smiles, recalling how adventurous youthful Diago was, he flips the page, his fingers feeling the pages curl, curious eyes reading the lines that are revealed.

25th of July 2304

Dear Journal, Fel and I made it to Gregors' home without any issue, and are writing this entry at the top of the high rises! *(É TÃO BONITO! SE NÃO FOSSEM AS NUVENS DE GABRIEL, VOCÊ PODERIA VER TODAS AS ESTRELAS DO CÉU!)* While the waves did rock the rowboat, it wasn't at all a challenge to find harbor at the old high rises. We were met by Marcia, who helped us anchor the boat to the third floor balcony-pier, and we caught up with one another! She asked how my mami and Grandmami were, how my sisters were, how the farm was doing, then offered me lunch which I politely declined. *(ELA FEZ VATAPÁ!! O VATAPÁ DA MÁRCIA! É SEMPRE TÃO DELICIOSO! COMO VOCÊ PODERIA DEIXAR PASSAR UMA TIGELA FRESQUINHA DE VATAPÁ DA MÁRCIA, DIAGO!! AH!)* I'm sorry Fel, but I wasn't hungry then! Quit thinking about your stomach so much.

Anyway, after our talk, Marcia led us to where Gregor was, he was busy doing his own chores and tending to the seventh floor gardens. I always enjoy walking up to this floor, the view is amazing, though often windy without any wall. As soon as he saw me we hugged! It'd been too long, and like his mother, we talked about how things had been in the last few months, his community, my family, the hazards of the weather and the hazards of piracy along the coast, their fishing farms, our latex farms– *(NA VERDADE, ELE MENCIONOU COMO CONSEGUIRAM PESCAR ATUM HOJE! E ÍAMOS TOMAR UM POTE GRANDE DE MOQUECA DE CAMARÃO! O QUE FOI TÃO DELICIOSO!)* Oh yeah! We've never had real Tuna before, only ever that fake processed stuff. So when Gregor offered to have us present for their dinner we were more than happy to accept, we even told them we intended to stay the night, which he and Marcia were happy to oblige.

We spent the remainder of our afternoon playing Go. He's always been better at it, and we don't have a board at home to practice. Regardless, it was a lot of fun! And I did manage to win a game in the end.

Now, Fel and I sit on the roof and gaze across the stars. It is truly gorgeous... and I think we can spot the System too, orbiting overhead. Honestly it's crazy to think some of my Grandparents are there now. I hope they look at us and bless us with a good harvest, surely the tuna Gregor's family caught was one. (*VOCÊ ACHA QUE ALGUM DIA CHEGAREMOS LÁ, DIAGO?*) I don't know Fel! It would be cool, though I bet.

Sigh. I do not wish to be conscripted. I do not wish to tend the fields of burnt earth that my brother does. I wish he didn't either. (*É TÃO ESTÚPIDO! POR QUE FOMOS PARA A GUERRA DE NOVO? O QUE A ARGENTINA FEZ COM O BRASIL? POR QUE SEU IRMÃO TEVE QUE IR! POR QUE NÓS TEMOS QUE IR! AH!*) I can't recall Fel, I wish Mami hadden gotten us into those history classes. Anyway, it smells like dinners done.

His anger, simmering now, grows sour with grief renewed. Why, why must they have done this? A society of people, free from the strifes of this withering world, peaceful and calm and claiming new lives... Taken, made lost for some bitter pointless stance. Had the universe not taken enough from him, from his family, from his people? Was it fate, destiny, that others would bring agony to the Pereira family and so many, many more on this hellish earth? Surely, he had done enough, harbored the forgotten sins of his nation for long enough, the punishments that his father endured and reflected onto him, for long enough? Surely, this was enough, should have been enough, to avoid this tragedy?

To have lost so much more, to know generations of elders and cousins and sons and daughters were now gone. Now longer of the heavens but beyond, if there was such a thing. Henrique didn't have the slightest clue, and he doubted there was anything after. They were gone, his brother was gone. It was as simple as that, a weeding fact he began to harbor and nourish.

He observes the fine details on the pen in this bitter moment of contemplation, Henrique's fingers flipping the pages with unplanned, instinctual precision, eyes unwittingly landing on the next entry:

> *23rd of September 2304*
>
> Dear Journal, class wasn't too special. My teacher commented that my punctuation has been remaining consistent but that I should try to expand my vocabulary and gave me a thesaurus. It's full of English words and very heavy! So I'll probably read it when I get home.
>
> But! FINALLY after months of planning, Mr. Rocha and I left to go birdwatching. He was very busy marking the exams of all the classes he taught, but he was able to schedule some time with me this week! We have been planning to visit a spot along the interior, within the marshes and prairies of província cinzenta. I told him it was nothing special, just a place I try to visit when I have enough allowance to take the bus that far. (*AGRADEÇA AOS ANTEPASSADOS QUE O SR. ROCHA POSSUI UM CAMINHÃO! EU ODEIO PEGAR CARONA EM ÔNIBUS. OU ESTÁ SUPER LOTADO OU TEMOS QUE SENTAR NO TELHADO...*) Yeah,

it was quite far, and his truck was quite comfy. Though honestly, I was just excited we got to see somewhere new that's not just your house or farm. Yeah! You sounded like you enjoyed it as much as we did, huh Davi? **(Yeah! The views were beautiful. If a bit haunting. You still need to take me to Gregor's one of these days, I'm sure he'd be happy to have you visit him again.)** (*OH SIM! AS VISTAS DA CASA DELE SÃO INCRÍVEIS! ALÉM DISSO, A COMIDA DA SUA MÃE É TÃO DELICIOSA!*)

I will, I will! Anyways, as should be obvious, getting there wasn't too difficult, and we parked along the eastern edge of the Amazona Basin. From there I led the way down some dirt trails, and showed Mr. Rocha a family of nursing trees that had begun to sprout new life. **(It was very pretty! There were at least five different burnt up trunks that had fallen over, and were all sprouting entirely different trees from them!)** Yeah! And in the trees, we saw many birds flying in and out, they looked like brownish twistwings, we also heard peeping! The sound filled me with such joy, and Mr. Rocha remarked how wonderful it was to see nature adapt and heal in spite of all the destruction caused by 'A Grande Fumaça', so many years ago.

The comment had Davi curious, and so I asked him how 'A Grande Fumaça' even started, **(Thanks again. I wasn't sure how Mr Rocha would take you being plural, otherwise I would have asked myself.)** (*SR. ROCHA ARRASA! TENHO CERTEZA DE QUE ELE TERIA IDO ÀS ALTURAS PARA OUVIR SOBRE NÓS!*) Eh... I'm in agreement with Davi. I'd rather just keep this between us three.

Anyways, I'm glad I asked because I learned things I

never recalled being taught besides the really nasty terrorists and stuff. Anyway, when he was done I asked why people would do such things, it was kinda absent minded of me to ask, but when I did Mr. Rocha had this moment of contemplation before he told me that "Some very angry people simply choose to resort to fan the hate and anger in their hearts, in order to make an impact on the world. In their case, they wanted many people to see the perils we suffer, like some twisted bonfire, and these people believed that by burning down the Amazon it would call the world into action." I told him that didn't make any sense, and he agreed, "Anger drives many men to do senseless things, but this is why it is important to keep a level head at all times, and to control that flame, turn it towards a warm hearth that nurtures and improves the quality of all. Not tear it down and destroy it."

After our conversation, we went and had lunch. (*FOI EMPADÃO CASEIRO! DEVO DIZER QUE O SR. ROCHA É UM EXCELENTE COZINHEIRO!*) He is! And he made extras, so we got to take some home with us to share. Today was honestly the best.

Yet, despite the uplifting ending and relative cheerfulness of the entry, such aspects go unread and unappreciated as Henriques eyes stay fixed on the penultimate paragraph. His breath quickens to nigh hyperventilation with quicker clouds fogging Henrique's brief-bright thoughts with foul ashen clouds.

A Grande Fumaça, another crazed disaster, dealt by the collective cells of Brazil. The terrorists' insanity deemed that the only path to salvation was more mindless destruction. To alter and to tarnish the Grand jungles of South America with thermite fueled flames.

Such scornful actions created lasting consequences. The Steel Acquisitions Act, fueling the cinders for the pyre that would become the Brazilian Civil War, followed by the unsatisfied bloodlust that lead to the annexation of Paraguay and the eventual invasion of eastern Argentina.

Anger flares once more, the scalding inferno of nearly a century ago igniting hot and glowing fury in the old mans beating heart. He throws the pen in anger, then gasps, smelling acrid burning. He looks about the room, the lights a brilliant yellow. Torches of flame around him. He gets up, he needs fresh air...

He rises, his right hand numb, crumbles under the weight and he begins to fall to the floor. His left hand, clenched into a fist, slams to his inflamed chest, leaving him sobbing, weeping, falling. With a loud thump against the hardwood floor, he cries and whines. Why, why did they have to take his brother? Why did they have to kill so many bright souls, to accomplish what? To state what?

"W-why... W-whhyy... whhyyy..."

He mutters through a limp tongue, half numb lips. He was shot, he realizes, he believes, time slowed like a putrid muck as the sudden taste of something sickening and metallic crosses his tongue. His heart hurts, agonizing, a flame. He struggles to breathe, and wonders why, why, why was he sent to the front line. Why was he chosen to be shot, an innocent at the whims of a corrupt government.

He looks up, watching the members of the Argentinian resistance raid the Briar Line. Guns alight, loud, shouting, surrounding him, soon kicking him.

"Me perdoe! Me perdoe! Me perdoe! Me perdoe!"

He begs for forgiveness as memory fades, figures all around him, following him to his youth. Full of bullies, malevolent peers, punishing him, teasing him, childishly chastising him for the acts of his rebellious father. A man dedicated to the independence of Rio Grande Do Sul, a man who died fighting the civil war, and marred his family name with the title of-

"Traidor! Traidor! Traidores Imundos!"

-And he suffers the consequences. Crying, choking, dying, dimming... before Diago screams, chasing, sprinting, pushing away the bullies, the ne'er do well teenagers twice the siblings' age.

No longer surrounded, Diago leans down, reaching his hand towards his elder brother. Henrique looks up, vision blurred from the blinding backlit visage of Diago, details smeared, yet comfortably cool and shaded in soft shadows.

"Ei, irmão mais velho!"

Henrique hears the cry of Diago calling out to him, before watching that youthful silhouette approach him, take a knee, and offer his hand down to his fallen self.

"Está tudo bem, você está seguro. Vamos, vamos para casa! Todo mundo está preocupado com você."

Henrique nods, sobbing, smiling, and reaches for Diagos hand, hearing the worry and concern in his brother's voice.

"Vamos para casa. Irmão mais novo..."

Then everything fades to black.

Hours that felt like minutes go by, and with a groggy start, white light fills Henriques vision.

The door to the examination room clicks open, Isa walking in, exhausted, her nurse outfit freshly donned with fresh concern still on her face, she kneels down, checking on her Grand Papi, healing instincts kicking in as she takes Henriques hand, watching his face twitch into wakefulness.

"Oh, Grand Papi... shh, it's okay... You're safe, you had another little stroke. You're safe."

Henrique simply nods, groaning, looking down at the white linen bed he found himself in. He inhales through clenched teeth, leaning back into his pillows and breaths out shakily, then looks to his left, smiling towards Isa, then further towards the bedside table, spotting the journal still at his side.

Isa's fears quickly diminished as she saw him come too. Watching as his senses returned to him. It wasn't long before a doctor entered, clipboard in hand and hesitant smile showing.

"Ah, Mr. Pereira. You had us all worried there, but, thankfully to your Granddaughters quick thinking you're looking to make a full recovery. She's a very excellent nurse, we're lucky to have her with us."

Isa smiles, then glances over to the journal Henrique was just looking towards. She picks it up, handing it to him.

"Grand Papi, we'll be moving you to another room for the remainder of your stay, but once we're there would you like me to stick around for a while? The hospital has given me permission to attend to you, and, well, I saw you reading Grand uncle Diago's journal. I was thinking I could read some of it to you?"

Henrique nods with a wide smile reaching from ear to ear, stretching those years of well earned lines like the boughs and branches of a Bertholletia Excelsa.

"Of course, my dear Isa. I'd love that so, very much."

The minutes went by as medical accessories were untethered and unlatched from their anchoring, allowing Henriques' bed to be transported to his new room. Isa walked alongside while another nurse pushed, her fingers gently intertwined with her Grand papis' own.

The new room was optimally lit and blandly furnished with whites, blues, and beige, presented in the most iconically hygienic ways a hospital could be. Isa finds a seat beside Henrique, a metal thing with dense padding cushions, unlike her grin which was soft and comforting; not at all dissimilar to her eyes, which began to look downward towards the journal that she split open in her hands. She carefully turned each page, finally landing on an entry that was written earlier into the books life:

3rd of May 2304

Dear Journal, today I write after Fel and I have gone exploring! I did my chores this morning, stripping the bark from the trees mainly, then I went down to the coast and took the rowboat out from 'the cave'. Though I didn't visit Gregor, instead I took the boat further west, to visit some of the abandoned towns in that area. I brought some chicken sandwiches with me, as I planned to stay most the day there and take the last bus back.

I know it's dangerous, but my curiosity just urges me to swim in those waters near the old ruined towns past the shore. Mami, cuz I know she'd be worried sick for me, doesn't know I do this, but I can't help but want to explore! It's like exploring a whole different world, well maybe not ENTIRELY different, but different enough to feel like it's a place I've never been too.

I also go because Fel is always wanting to see the world... and she's always going on and on and on about leaving the house, leaving Brazil. Honestly I'm happy to oblige! I'm not too keen to live here for the rest of my life either.

Anyways, once we took the rowboat far enough, we anchored up to what we guessed must have been an old apartment complex? We could access the third and fourth floors, but the rest was flooded. But despite this, I was able to dive down to the floors below with my light to guide us. I always make sure to wear one on my chest so I'm never diving in the dark. I've also been practicing my diving for quite a while now, and the longest I can hold my breath while swimming is a full minute and sixteen seconds!

Diving down to the floor below, it was filled with seaweed and other water plants, also I found all sorts of cool things, old photo portraits, toys, a Rig! It was inhabited by some tropical fish, Tetra I think is what they're called? Very small and they glowed brightly when my light hit them! It was very pretty! (*TENHO QUASE CERTEZA DE QUE VI UMA CAIXA DE TESOURO TAMBÉM! ERA PEQUENO E BRILHANTE! MAS PROVAVELMENTE É MELHOR QUE NÃO O TENHAMOS FEITO. ESTAVA PRESO ATRÁS DE MUITOS MÓVEIS ANTIGOS.*) Yeah, it wouldn't have been safe to try and dig that out.

When I surfaced I had my meal– (*OS SANDUÍCHES ESTAVAM MUITO DELICIOSOS! VOCÊ MAMI FAZ OS MELHORES SANDUÍCHES.*) Yeah, they really are super good. Anyways, afterwards we swam down the outside of the building and we were able to get much deeper, even with the surrounding kelp clinging to its walls. Turns out the apartment was built on top of a barber! At least I assume it was a barber as I saw the red and blue striped pole on the outside of it. I couldn't open the door, and the windows were boarded up to get some breath. Next we explored the upper floors above the water. The building was very slanted, so climbing the old stairs wasn't easy, and most of the apartment rooms had their front doors locked still. But the rooms I did open were very empty, however one had an old campfire in it! (*CLARO QUE NÃO SOMOS OS AVENTUREIROS QUE EXPLORAM AS RUÍNAS DO BRASIL!*) I guess! Either that or someone else came here before and tried to live here. The walls were spray painted in beautiful and ugly murals, and one room was entirely coated in bird poop... it wasn't pretty but I did see the various nests that were using the old space as a new home!

Once we were done exploring, we grabbed the rowboat and went back to shore. We just barely caught the bus we wanted, which was good since I was so tired. I got home and my family asked how my swim was, as I probably smelt like the sea.

Now Fel and I rest in bed... it's funny, despite all that destruction caused by nature, seeing life still present and flourishing is nice. It gives our world color, and makes me happy.

Anyways, I'm tired. That's all!

Isa closes the book softly, clearing her throat after all that talking, and places it at her great Grand papi's side. Henrique looked up in response, a mild smile present on his thin lips.

"Thank you, sweet Isa. You're the best Granddaughter an old man like me could ever ask for." He grins, then coughs softly, frowning at the sorry state his body was in. Isa reacts accordingly, leaning down to assist her great Grandfather, but he raises a hand- "It's fine, some water is all I need."

Isa frowns, but goes to pour her father a cup, turning away to head to the plastic jug not more than a couple meters from his bedside table.

She pours the cup, then pauses "...Grand papi, is..." She sighs, then turns back to pass him the cup. "Are you okay...?" A question that could be easily dismissed with a 'yes', a white lie to maintain this status quo he wished to uphold and quell any worry. Yet, Henrique knew better, hearing the way Isa asked, feeling the way those words carried soft care, the compassion in her voice curating how she phrased it, and quite simply from the way her eyes penetrated his own. The ache in his heart would not cease until he expressed his thoughts, and he knew this status quo should not be maintained.

"...I... am not. No. The System, it is truly gone, yes?" He asks, expression grim. Isa pauses, having handed over the cup. Then shrugs and shakes her head. "The word on the 'net... Well, it is unclear. There's been claims that they're trying to recover it, some saying success, others saying failure... its..."

Henrique nods, raising his hand once again. "It is an uncertain time, I... understand." I silence drops between the pair, long and thoughtful, as Henrique stares at himself through the reflection of the water, seeing the man who he once was and the youth before, so full of potential, that who couldn't be. An innocent child who had a brother, before being taken away from home to become the cog for some militaristic machine, and discarded, broken, at the end.

"Why didn't you upload, Grand papi?" Henrique is drawn from his stupor, glancing up at Isa with a pained, confused expression that evolved to one of frustration, and finally mournful regret.

"I... I was too anchored to my duties here... to many responsibilities, to many tasks that were expected of me..." he says, a weak truth, one that did not admit the full pains of his reasons. Reasons he did not care to admit because they scared him, filled him with anxiety, regret.

Why didn't he upload? There was nothing to stop him, he had the opportunity, he was given the privilege after his service. In fact, it was expected of him by his country and family, for was a broken man, and a man with the buried soul of a child. Once his service was done, he was seen as useless by the aristocracy, and his family name denoted him a traitor by the people.

So, why not simply allow himself to be discarded? Buried like that child who was taken away? Why, why did he put such effort into the farm, into making a family. Why did he feel the need to prove the worth of the Pereira name...

Was it to prove they weren't traitors to brazil? To prove his life had meaning? To live a life after years of strife? To try and forget the pain of no longer being at his brother's side? Or to avoid that pain, to bury it too, like the child, like the hundred dead from a worthless civil war... The notion of seeing someone so different from how he would've remembered them. Of seeing a person who he loathed, despite all that love. To see someone who had the chance to be a child, who did not need to bury that precious, perfect part of life. Scared him, for the emotions they elicited.

He scowls, emotions eating away at him... Isa frowned, leaning in.

Diago was his friend, as any sibling should, but one who'd be a constant reminder of the time *he* lost, the time *he* should've had as well. Diago lived the life he lost, and he *hated* him for that.

Yet.

Henrique could not let that hate burn. Those flames would rather stoke fires of passion and thankfulness, that his brother's youth could stay at Diago's side. Even if he had that all taken away from him, he should be happy his brother managed to avoid it all through those careful weeks of planning, ultimately resulting in him being snuck out the month before his mandatory conscription. Years before he would return home.

His fists balled up, and tears began to be shed. Why must he feel this pungent jealousy contradict his love, and why must this unfettered joy ruin the urge to swell with anger and selfish want. Not only this, but the half-void in his chest was lonely, forever imperfect because he never could say goodbye.

His life, all his life, was hell, hell on earth. From his earliest days under the sun, to his first days at the Briar Line, to his last days working the farm, and undoubtedly to his final day on this god forsaken planet his deleted ancestors long ago abandoned.

Yet his brother, the person he cherished so dearly, avoided that. It wasn't fair, but did that matter? He sacrificed everything, and his brother lived his life. And now he sat here, in a hospital bed, seething and seeing those reasons come to light. Showing him he never once was truly happy, never once truly satisfied, and never once given the chance to live, never once allowing himself to-

Isa grabbed his hand, and gently kissed his forehead, shocking the elderly man out of his manic spiral. He sobs out a gasp, and looks to Isa with watery eyes and tear stricken cheeks. She smiled warmly with saddened eyes. She was no longer the innocent girl he saw in her today or days prior, now she was someone who somehow could peer into this old man's heart. Seeing his pain. Understanding his turmoil.

"Grand papi... even if they do not return to the system, your ancestors look down on you with pride as they ascend to the heavens. Your brother... he missed you, I know it. He is thankful and I know for certain he wondered every day when he would see you."

She gulps, thinking of what to say as her own mouth grew parched from this shared, emotional moment. "If... the System returns. Let go of these anchors you claim to have. And those regrets that tie you up. You do not need to utter them to me, Grand papi, but you cannot let what life you have left wither by."

"And if it doesn't return, sweet Isa?" Henrique asks, voice raspy and scared.

"Then... we will find those joys here. And move on, together. Wherever we can, however we can. And our ancestors will continue to look down on us, smiles on their faces, eager to see you live your life with happiness, and awaiting the day for you to join them once you have.

Henrique sighs with a shaky breath, and lays his head on Isa's arm. Isa, in turn, lays on the bed, supporting her Great Grand papis head. Giving him the comfort he required.

March 1st, 2401

21st January 2305

Dear Journal– or, dearest Henrique, who I hope will return home safely to receive my journal as my parting gift. Its with a heavy, but hopeful heart that I might escape the enforcement of our seven years service to our country. I will not get a chance to meet you at the front, let alone meet you upon your return. (*MAL POSSO ESPERAR PARA FINALMENTE CONHECER VOCÊ, HENRIQUE. DIAGO PODE ESTAR INCERTO,*

MAS ESTOU EXTASIADO POR FINALMENTE CONHECÊ-LO DEPOIS DE TODOS ESSES ANOS EM QUE VOCÊ FOI FORÇADO A NOS DEIXAR.)

While Fel may be excited, she is not wrong that I am hesitant. **(I am as well, but I have faith in our future.)**

I agree, Davi. By the time you'll have read this entry, you'd have learned that our auntie Corita and our Mami had been planning to secret me away so I would not be forced to participate in the conflict at the BrAr Line. I know it is not my place to say such, but I apologize that we did not tell you while you were still in service.

While I may be leaving, Auntie Corita told Iara and Ana that when they turn 18, she'll do the same for them, and we'll all meet each other in the System one day. Which is a day I greatly look forward to.

I miss you, brother. I miss the days we could have swam together, ate food together, and explored together. Yet this world we were born into chose to take that away from us. You were always so much braver than I was, and now here I am taking my first steps into a new world I can't ever come back from. *(VOCÊ É IGUALMENTE CORAJOSO, DIAGO, E DEVEMOS ESTAR ENTUSIASMADOS! ESTA É APENAS MAIS UMA AVENTURA! E O HENRIQUE VAI SE JUNTAR A NÓS! TENHO CERTEZA DISSO.)*

We eagerly look forward to the day we can see you, Henrique.

Your little siblings, Diago, Fel, and Davi.

As Henrique closes the leather book for the final time, he exhales, tucking the journal away into his satchel. The door opens and an Ansible technician arrives.

She greets him with a nod, asks his name, and takes him down the hall. She confirms he answered all the questions on his questionnaire, and reassured him that this decision was final. Henrique simply nodded, acknowledging the questions with polite answers, stepping in time with the gentle tap of his cane. Each step feeling lighter than the last, like years of weight fell off his back, as if piles of ash or fettered leaves flowed free into the compost, ready to fertilize new growth, new life, new hope.

The techs put him into the seat, the process seamless, precise, and he feels as if he was floating, a leaf gliding amongst the wind and beautiful breeze... and he closes his eyes.

The sensation of stretching in blackness, like a series of strings strung taught and sewn back, was as unnerving as the visual of a slate gray box surrounding him. But this unease passes as he immediately sighs, eyes closing once more as the feeling of chronic pain and aged weariness was, thankfully, entirely gone. He exhales, the soreness of his shoulders, exposed to decades of hard labor, could finally relax. That foul weight, finally lifted.

"Welcome to Lagrange, this room you find yourself in is called AetherBox#9182. Currently, I am facing away from you so you may have some privacy. Please, let me know when I may turn, unless you do not require any clothes. Simply want your desired apparel into being, and it will be there."

Henrique's eyes open, wrinkled smile growing into a briefly confused frown as the individual who just spoke to him was some kind of furry. A species of creature he had not seen before, with a large black tail flanked by two defined white stripes. She wore a very old fashion tweed jacket, and a red plaid skirt that hung just below that.

"Ah– simply desire it, *Senhora...?*"

"Indeed, take your time. It is not as if we have a schedule to maintain."

There was a hint of irritation in that reply, and Henrique flushed red for a moment, embarrassed at being inconsiderate of this individual's time. He thinks for a moment, of his slippers, aged worker jeans, then his blue t-shirt and well worn wool sweater overtop. He looks down in pleasant surprise to see those very clothes on him... then he frowns, thinking... remembering memories of his younger days, before he met his beloved Annette, a button up white shirt, loose at the collar, straight and flowy at the hem, long too. Perfect for those especially hot summer days, then reimagined his worker pants... the day he first got them, how richly deep green they were, not how worn and damaged they were now, with discolored patches sewn on to cover up damaged holes. He recalled the well sewn fabric of thick, durable, comfortable material... and to his amusement found those exact clothes on him, in the same condition he miraculously remembered them as. He stepped forward, comfy slippers, now refurbished but still broken in, muffling his footsteps.

"*Senhora...?* I am ready, you can turn around now."

The black-and-white-striped furry turns on the spot, an exact motion, her rounded spectacles, housing slitted eyes that stared with a scrutinizing and dubious glare. She held a smile that felt tired, ungenuine, but not strictly forced... a smile that was rehearsed and used to mask some deeper-seated emotions, simply present to appear approachable.

"Again, welcome to Lagrange Mr. Pereira. It is my job to inform you of the basic mechanics that are present within the System. Your clothing was the first part of this exercise, next, we will go over forking. Please follow my lead."

While he had no idea what to expect upon uploading, he wasn't expecting such a hasty introduction... or at least one that felt so precise and mechanical.

"Pardon, *Senhora,* but may I ask if you are real?... Also, to slow down. I understand your time is valuable but this is feeling all a little overwhelming to me. Perhaps you could offer me your name? And you may refer to me as Henrique, please."

The furry's smile falters, before a hand raises up as she grasps her temples between two fingers. "My apologies, Henrique." She bows apologetically, curt and quick however, to keep this implied schedule on track.

"It has been... quite hectic recently, I assure you I am very much 'real' and not some digital construct you'd otherwise be familiar with on the 'net, if that was what you were implying. I suppose I have been feeling a little thin as a result of recent events. You may call me Then I Must In All Ways Be Earnest of the Ode Clade. In All Ways for short."

Henrique grunts and smiles. "Quite a name, In All Ways, but I do not judge. Now what is this about forking?"

She nods, then raises a hand to her side before an exact duplicate of her appears in an instant, mirroring her pose and demeanor. "Forking, as we of the System have coined it, is the ability to replicate yourself. It is important to know that this fork is not just a construct, a program, or a template-"

The other In All Ways speaks. "But a whole person. With their own desires, hopes, and dreams that are parallel or differ from your own. Those who dive into this practice wholeheartedly are known as dispersionistas, which make up the vast majority of the population here... while others who are more free with individuation are known as trackers, while not always as liberal with their forking, they still form the other sizable chunk of the Systems population. Lastly we have those who simply fork to complete tasks or short term objectives, and prefer not to individuate. They are aptly known as Taskers, and fill up the last chunk of the System.

Despite her best efforts, the slip up was clear in her speech. That pause allowed for the pang of unmistakable pain, anger, frustration, sadness, and grief, to give way to a convoluted series of expressions shared between the two In All Ways, both suffering these emotions in divergent ways. Some trauma surging forth and causing the twin furries to ripple briefly.

Henrique frowns, a hand raised to place upon or embrace In All Ways, before pulling back. "Ah... pardon I should ask before offering comfort. I understand the pain too well, In All Ways."

"Do you?!..." Both reply with a snap. The leftmost one maintains a spiteful glare, before vanishing as the original recoils and looks to the floor shamefully. Henrique all the while, continues to stand there with his hand out. Gradually, he lowers it and reaches for one of In All Ways paws, getting her attention. He gives an understanding smile, unphased by the furry's tumultuous emotions barely held at bay.

"I... can, yes. Perhaps not exactly as you do, In All Ways. But I can. I know the pain of losing someone. Someone close, someone you care for. And I give my sincerest condolences to those who you have lost. You are with common company, and you do not need to apologize, *Senhora*."

"I am... I... Mm... Thank you." In All Ways mumbles, ceasing her seeking of that instinctual apology, the urge to explain, and glances up, tears just beginning to stain her cheeks, before she forks them away. She remains silent and nods, exhales, then breaths in, composing herself, and returns her gaze to the elderly man. His face, a gentle network of lines forming an understanding, compassionate smile.

"I would ask that you fork, Henrique. So that you are familiar with the process. Remember, do so with intent. Simply think it, and it will be."

"Think it, and it will be. Hm." Henrique mutters, his eyes, then head turning. Thoughts of clades, of trees, of the farm, of the family, of Diago, flash by and before him stood... him. But not as he is, rather, as he was. Him as he was a little under a century ago. Maybe 17 years of age, wearing the same shirt, now smaller. Similar pants, now cut short at the knee. And those slippers, now sized to fit. His hair that thick, unkempt brown and tied back. Eyes green and innocent. Heavily pigmented skin from days in the sun, with a slight tone in his muscles as well. Contrasting firmly to his current wrinkles, leather like skin, and hundreds of sun spots.

In All Ways stared at the pair, her eyes, tired still, no longer viewed either with suspicion or trepidation but with... hope. A hint of a smile creeping along her exhausted face, her shoulders untensed and fists unclenched.

"Good. It's important you understand how to fork, as it is a vital part of the System's mechanics. May we continue?"

Both Henriques look at one another, smiling in their own ways. The elders face wet with joy, years of regret resolved. The youths face beaming, and tearful as well. Excited for a future they never had.

The moment is peaceful, interrupted only by an embrace of the two Henriques, enhanced from this tranquility and relief. Then, there was one. As the elder Henrique accepted the merger and quit.

As In All Ways watches this happen, she walks up to the youth, standing at attention but with expressive hesitation in her face. "Actually, before we move onto the last step. I have a question I must ask. It is entirely optional, and purely to sate my own curiosity, so you need not answer if it does not suit you too."

Henrique looks to In All Ways, nearly at the same height now, and nods. Juvenile voice adjusting to what the world weary mind could recall. "Of course, ask away In All Ways."

She sighs, smile diminishing slightly. "Why did you choose to upload, now? Of all times. You... went through a tumultuous time, from what I read of your reports. And most of your immediate family uploaded centuries before you did. Why not then? And now... after the events that have transpired. Are you not afraid of what will happen next? Of the future?"

The beaming, childish expression of Henrique dims to one of contemplation, though that smile does not vanish in its entirety. "I was overcome with grief, frustration, and jealousy, when I returned from the front. And allowed those emotions to drive me into a life I did not want, convincing me that it was my responsibility. After all, seven years commanding men and women on burnt earth leaves one with that lingering urge to take the reins, not out of a want, but out of what is expected of them to keep them safe."

He sighs, slippered foot kicking at nothing in particular on the slate gray floor. "That expectation, those vile emotions, blinded me from what I really wanted. Masked the realization of why I was doing this to myself. I missed my brother, and I never got to say goodbye. Never got to see them one last time, never got to meet their headmates, more siblings for me to cherish. And for... what, a little over a hundred years? I couldn't come to terms with this. Not until I thought he was gone for good. Not until I had realized I truly lost my chance at a better life. And now? I'm happy, truely, absolutely happy. I can live how I wish, experience the things I never got too, and most importantly meet my brother and siblings. I was old, anyways, so if it were to all end now I can at least pass on with this seed of joy and hope within me."

In All Ways smile returns in full, her hand resting on Henriques shoulder. "Thank you for indulging me, Henrique. And I can assure you, we will see that seed blossom into something beautiful. Now, onto the final aspects of this training. My next step is to teach you how to navigate the System. Similar to forking, you must think with intent, in this case, of the location by its signifier. This is sometimes referred to as stepping into a sim."

Henrique nods, stepping back, before cocking his head. "But, In All Ways. I have just gotten here, where exactly do you expect me to go?... wait." His smile broadens and reveals his pearly teeth. "M-may I step into the sim of my brother? Is that possible?"

In All Ways nods, "I just sent a sensorium ping to... a down-tree of the 'Macaw' clade, they refer to themselves as Diago Hyacinth, so you are aware. They'll be awaiting your arrival. I'm sending you the name and tag of the Sim now.

Henrique shivers, feeling the sudden arrival of information that wasn't there mere moments ago. Excitement brimming.

"And one last thing, Henrique. What is your clade name? If you do not have something in mind for me to register now, I will simply reach out to you later." She steps back, signifying the finality of this meeting.

Henrique answers almost immediately. "Pereira Clade, please. Goodbye *Senhora* In All Ways. Thank you." and steps from the sim. He's met by a familiar sight, the backyard of his family home where he grew up, however instead of flat field with up-turned dirt and rusting soccer goals, with a single floor shack of a house behind him, there was a plethora of budding flowers, green shrubbery, trees, and the serene sounds of chirping birds and gentle winds filling the air.

"*Olá, irmão mais velho!*"

"*Olá!*"

"Is... Is it really you?"

Henrique turns as he hears those three similar, familiar voices calling out to him. Now, as he looks upon the source of those voices, he stares up to see a towering, adult, anthropomorphized chimeric individual who wore the heads of a panther, a bull, and a python, on his widened torso, all staring at him with utmost glee. The trio step forward, those familiar green eyes impossible to confuse for anyone else's."

"*Sim, querido Diago.* It is me, Henrique, your big brother. Its really, truly, me."

The two surrender to their withheld urges, and rush to meet one another in tearful, joyful, brotherly fashion. An embrace sought after for generations, centuries, years that tried to dry and wither a snuffed and suffocating desire, a desire now rekindled and set ablaze into a blossoming, hopeful, beautiful sight to behold amidst this blooming garden. A single blue feather drifts down, as a macaw flies free with its flock in tow.

Millwright

Andréa C Mason

Andréa C Mason#Millwright — 2403

I need a break.

Even before uploading, I was the face. The spokesperson. The rep. The primary fronter in a plural system of at least nine. The fursona everyone knew, the friend, the organizer, the closeted kid who burst out of the closet a social butterfly. It worked, then. Whether I wanted it or not, I was good at it, when we could manage our mental health.

I was one of the headmates that pushed for uploading as our body failed and our loved ones dropped like flies.

Not being the front when we hit the System proper was a bit of a shock, but when we finally fanned out and forked into our separate headmate-y selves, I de facto became the Face of the Clade. Alex eventually ended up running everything, she was the part of us that likes keeping archives and all that, but I was expected to be head of social affairs. Even later, when my side gig became my main gig and I functionally became a clade unto myself, I was still expected to be diplomat and ambassador in turn.

That side-gig-turned-sys-side-career was a flush of kinks and dreams made real. After about a decade of careful planning and testing, we started a 'company'. We forked endless versions of ourselves and sent them out into the world. We found a way to replicate the "synths" of phys-side fiction, and embraced it so thoroughly that it now takes exceptional effort to act fully organic. Here, we could live out the fetish of being mass-produced, effectively engaging in sex work in the process, but also live out the fantasy of helping whoever needed it and being able to bow out if things got unsafe or unstable.

As we expanded rapidly, some part of me felt a pull towards authenticity, and we decided to have a "brick and mortar" headquarters. We worked with several sim artisans to create the now-famous High Falls Millworks#46b147c4. We chose the name, location, and design based on a district of the town our great-great-great grandmother lived in called Brown's Race in Rochester, New York. Hundreds of years before even she was born, the city had made a name for itself off the mills powered by the waterfall and river nearby. We even went as far as to commission a meticulously crafted fully functioning triphammer forge, like the area once had. Her name was Andréa as well, and I took her name out of admiration. We also named our company 9IN INDUSTRIES as a nod to her favorite band.

Building a factory, one that made our production model look more complicated than "gather client specs and fork to those in another room", one that featured a convincing "assembly line", exploded our company overnight. We had to restructure on the fly, and that is where I forked from my down-tree instance. The most continuous version of me, Andréa C Mason#Foundry, remained head of the company, but she forked me, Andréa C Mason#Central, to be the heart of it all. Yet again I found myself a face, communal voice, a spokeswoman and figurehead for this clade-within-a-clade we'd become.

My path from my down-tree diverged quickly and wildly. I became less and less involved with any direct production or facsimile of such. I would fork for something, and then that fork would develop into an entire department. My forks spread out and I found myself not working with my hands all that much, really, if at all. For our own safety and the safety of these so-called mass produced forks, we needed contracts, standards, and rules, inasmuch as those things are enforceable in a System largely without any governing body. We were up front that any version of us that was sent out had full rights to quit at any time for safety's sake, and having that in writing out up front prevented all sorts of headaches and worse. Thus one of the first departments we ever made was a Legal Department of sorts. We weren't in it for any sort of profit, by the nature of our project we were already swimming in rep, but we did want to get the message out there to more people. So, I forked a marketing version of myself, and they began a Sales and Outreach Department. We had a team for returning forks and merges down, specifically based around coping with loss, trauma, abuses that might have led them to leave, conflict resolution, contract disputes. We had an HR and Public Health Department. As our operation expanded, we needed sim artists, construct artists, experts in fields, professional engineers, so we made a Logisitics Department. We had an R&D team. Once we expanded far enough, we set up an Education and Training Department. When we'd fleshed out the area around High Falls enough, we began to offer unused space up for development in the style of the buildings that had existed physside. We had a Real Estate and Zoning Department. #Foundry started out involved with a great deal of it, but she became more involved in the so-called "physical work", and even among the teams and departments that she founded, she trusted me to handle the ins and outs of people management. We had a surge in the early 2300s, at some point tracking over 100,000 forks, but those numbers waned in time, and we stabilized around the end of the century with about 64,000 "units" in service and me in charge of a whopping 6,000-person staff.

I tell people so often that I didn't like it, but the truth of it was, I was good at it, and for a while that was satisfying enough. We had built a company from the ground up, and I found myself at its peak. We had created an incredible corporation, one that had all the fantastic idealism of what a company could be, and because of the nature of the System, completely removed from the reality, brutalities, and consequences of what running an actual business phys-side caused. #Foundry and I were praised through parts of the System, conservatives lauding us as poster-children of capitalism (despite the lack of such sys-side), and liberals championed us as meritocracy in motion, proof that with ethics and smarts, businesses could treat both customers and employees with respect and kindness.

The occasional leftist would praise our unions and sex-positivity, that a post-human trans woman being head of anything still felt like something worth celebrating, and a few more condemned us for recreating a corporation wholesale inside a place that should have been an anti-capitalist's paradise, but overwhelmingly there was silence from the people that once, a long time ago, we had called comrades and stood shoulder to shoulder with both phys- and sys-side. Now it is my greatest shame, but even at the height of 9IN INDUSTRIES's success, it left a sour taste in my mouth. Couldn't they be happy for what we'd accomplished, what *I* had built? #Foundry was lauded as a mechanical genius, but I was the face and name of the company. I joked that the C of our middle initial stood for Central, I appeared in interviews and magazines, I gave talks and attended conferences. #Foundry was the inventor, but I was the entrepreneur, and at my worst I basked in it. After all, I—and my thousands of forks, but really weren't they just extensions of me?—had worked so hard. I had *earned* my success.

A few partners left me over it. A few more I only knew through it. #Foundry had become more and more elusive over time, and even in CERES clade affairs and meetings and gatherings I began to take her place, forking and sending a merge down to keep her updated. I was two faces but one, perhaps the most well-known member of my clade, and the subclade of me within it. I was the ace of myself and my self. When the clade became embroiled in our Authority Crisis in the 2360s, I was the most affected and part of the fixes and rescues that followed. I was Andréa C Mason, and the #Central after my name was more a job title than a signifier.

We made it through, all the way to the end of the century.

We gathered, that night, as so many across the System did, to welcome in the new year, to send the 2300s out with a bang and to ring in the brand new frontier of the 2400s. Our entire staff was on hand throughout the offices and facilities, and many who had outside the lives had brought partners or friends, and it was a revelry for the ages! God, what a night!

What a night.

God, oh gods above and below, what a horrible night.

To say that my subclade was hit hard by the Century Attack does not give any sense of scale. I have talked with many a pathologist, perisystem architect, and number of other experts about it, and still we lack answers. We were not the origin, but we were a minor epicenter, and for whatever reason, the contraproprioceptive virus was particularly effective at dismantling us in bulk. We kept in close communication and had very accurate numbers for how many forks of us existed at any given time, we used sensoria and a variety of other methods to keep an incredibly tight and informed network, and within ±5, there were 69,760 Andréa C Masons throughout the system on the night of December 31st, 2399.

By the time the dust settled, 12 of us remained, and of those 12, two quit within a week. 4 more crashed from grief in the next month.

I can't comprehend how to explain what it felt like to suddenly look at the clock approaching midnight to find myself alone in a room that had contained hundreds, almost alone in a sim that over 6,000 people had inhabited what felt like only moments before. To run panicked and slipping through streets laden with snow from accurate weather sims, with no pawprints or hoofprints but my own, to find #Foundry alive and sobbing, to find 2 other forks, bewildered and dissociating, to become inundated with thousands of requests for help, of anger, asking what they had done wrong or if they had violated the contract or what had happened, and having no answers for any of them. Within a day, #Foundry sent a mass message to the feeds within a day, and 9IN INDUSTRIES shuttered, now likely never to reopen.

#Foundry nearly quit when she found out that not only had we suffered impossible losses, but through some mechanism we did not and still do not understand, caused further ones. If you were in proximity to a fork of Andréa C Mason when the Century Attack happened, there was an 85% chance that you died as well. Of the hundreds of visitors and inhabitants of High Falls Millworks#46b147c4 that night, not a single one survived. We were a *vector*, somehow. Perhaps it was due to the mechanism by which the virus spread. I don't know. One of us quit and three of us crashed over that fact.Where do we even start to recover from this?

Partly, we just won't. We have our different reasons, but as the two leaders of our now defunct corporation, #Foundry and I have made the agonizing choice that we will not rebuild. We talked for days, sitting on our faithful reproduction of the Pont de Renne bridge, watching the falls roar and the sun rise and set, taking turns sobbing into each other's arms. Almost two centuries of work disappeared in what was to us an instant. We could not start again. It's over.

#Foundry has now taken my place in clade affairs. She wants to reconnect with her cocladists which are her siblings and her former headmates, which are the closest thing she has ever had to a family here and now the only family she has left. She struggled even to fork, although I understand that after an incident with getting her head stuck in a pitcher of fruit punch she is relearning the trade. #Foundry is eschewing her reclusivity that marked so much of the back half of the 2300s, and trying to reconnect with her own "humanity" again, insomuch as a clade full of animals can have such a thing. I think it's good for her. She is, in the end, the most continuous version of me, and she should remember what it's like to be a person again. An individual. How to be Andréa instead of Director Mason.

As for me?

I'd like to pretend the change that I'm about to make is some Grand gesture of atonement and a reawakening of class consciousness. It's certainly in play, I'm not going to pretend it isn't. Look at me, the turncoat, the hypocrite, the working class anarchosyndicalist queer phys-side turned girl boss captain of industry sys-side, who cast aside her morals and consciences with the slightest bit of success. I'd been so hard before uploading on so many people for giving up everything they believed in for even a small amount of success, and more than a few cases nothing less than righteously so, but when I found myself in the same position I put them all to shame. I tell myself that again and again whenever the dread or guilt or shame creep in, I tell myself that now is the chance to atone and to regain my class consciousness. And yeah, that is part of it.

It's a bigger truth, the one I hate to admit but cannot deny, is that I was so fucking bored and no idea bores me more than going back to being the socialite.

A simple concept that a lot of people seem to struggle with is that just because someone was really good at something, doesn't mean they like doing it. It is entirely possible to learn or understand innately the skills and necessities of a trade, to have a skillset or the tools to be really really good at something, and still get a little enjoyment out of performing that thing. My business may have vanished into the ether, but I still have all those social connections, I still have a reputation that precedes me hours in advance of me showing up anywhere, my fame and to some degree what you could call a fortune of social capital still exist, right there, waiting. If anything, if I chose to go back to that life and flourished again my legend and legacy would become even stronger, the determined woman who didn't let one of the greatest possible losses one could suffer slow her down, who pulled herself up by her bootstraps from nothing again, a phoenix, reborn in the mythology of good old protestant work ethic.

Even that in itself should fill me with disgust, but it only furthers my apathy. I took pride in a product I claimed I produced, despite how little I had to do with it actually being made, and that brought me the satisfaction that all the social engineering and handshaking and baby kissing and photo posing and being a people person didn't. The pageantry of rich people, of successful people, of this upper class is largely that. Pageantry. Especially sys-side, it's just a show. Their parties are dull, their social mores and customs and activities lack substance, nothing really happens that makes anything. There was never any struggle, there was barely any conflict, and it produced only an ennui in me that I did not see the size of until someone all but ended the world.

I want to work with my hands. I want to make things. I want to be alone, and I want to create. The people who made it what it was may be gone but High Falls Millworks#46b147c4 still exists. All its machines still function, and I'm going to take the time to learn to use every last lathe, forge, and press in here, and I'm going to *make* things. I want what I do to be tangible, to be meaningful, not words and nods and smiles and fuckings in the right place to keep things moving. I've hired a number of people to help me maintain the sim, but I have asked them largely to keep our relationship professional and distant, and when I finally feel satisfied that I am not just a voice and a face, maybe I'll even try seeing people again.

Until then, I ask you keep any requests or comments to yourself. I'm not going to be in a place to take commissions anytime soon, I just need to forge for myself for a little while. Hone some real skills.

Maybe this will go nowhere, and I'll just quit and merge down. More likely I'll individuate, but really, that's my business, not yours.

Also, ditching the old tag. Figure it's obvious why. Turn off the spotlight. Close the curtains. My monologue's over. The show must go on, but it can do so damn well without me.

Goodbye.

Andréa C Mason#Millwright.

Sentences

Krzysztof "Tomash" Drewniak

In All Ways — 2405–2406

"So, what's the surprise delay this time?" Günay joked, despite the serious topic of the meeting that would be starting soon. She, like some of the sys-side delegates and the cameraperson, had arrived early. Her conference room, along with its AVEC-linked partner on the System, had become the main venue for high-level Century Attack-related meetings out of an inertia that froze into tradition.

"A comma," Dry Grass replied. "I expect it will reach its final position by the end of the century."

"No wonder the joke down here's been that the real sentence is waiting in prison until the uploads make up their minds."

"I have heard similar here," Dry Grass said. "On the matter of delays, have you decided when you will upload?"

"Restoration Day two-eighty-…something. The next one. I want to be sure there's nothing else I can do down here. … And I got talked into picking a symbolic date by–"

Need An Answer, who had suggested that upload date, appeared in the room just then. She had stayed involved when this group branched off from the Temporary Administrative Council. The rest of the representatives and the invited audience joined her a moment later.

"–oh, looks like it's time."

The cladists took their seats while Jakub walked into his conference room, bringing along a few System Consortium higher-ups and politicians who wanted to witness history. He looked less frazzled than he had years ago since the set of tasks that could be shoehorned into "project-managing the recovery effort" had shrunk to a reasonable size.

Those involved in the Attack who had remained phys-side had been convicted years ago. There was no question about their guilt. They had proudly admitted their crimes and used their trials to broadcast their manifestos and grievances, which their governments had previously suppressed in the hopes of covering up the whole affair.

Phys-side authorities had then requested that the System recommend a punishment, seeking to calm the controversy about that question that had erupted on Earth. The System had, eventually, answered, in its meandering distributed way. Now, all that remained was the alchemy of turning something everyone knew (unless they had made an effort to avoid System-wide news) into the statement of a government that did not exist and was quite firm about not wanting to.

"We have transmitted the evident consensus of the System as to what sentence ought to be imposed upon those convicted of conspiring to destroy us," Need An Answer pronounced. "Does the System Consortium have any concerns regarding the accuracy of our report?"

"We do not," Jakub replied.

"For the record," Jonas Fa asked, "has the Consortium learned of any new issues that could prevent that sentence from being imposed?"

"We don't know anything that isn't on the feeds," Jakub replied.

Jonas nodded. "Good."

Need An Answer waited for the silence to become definitive. "Anything else before we begin?" she asked.

Hearing nothing, she waved a hand over the table to pull the report back into existence. The black text on the white pages that appeared was typeset plainly. (This did not disappoint those, like the committee's Odists, who had wanted the

System's first criminal sentence to have aesthetic weight, as the font used was one that was rarely seen phys-side these days outside of historical records.)

Jonas Fa reached out to pull the last, nearly blank page over to him and quickly signed it. "May this fate dissuade any future saboteurs."

The document went around the table, collecting signatures and comments.

"I agree with the plan, but am mainly glad we settled on *something*," Selena said, signing slowly. Debarre added "At least the topic's done with," as he put a pawprint onto the page. Yared Zerezghi, who had taken the time to practice for this part, said "It's a shame the first signing ceremony I've been pulled into for centuries has to be this."

Then the page reached the systechs, who were here representing some of the organizations and interest groups that had helped make the "referendum" happen. Dry Grass began, saying "I remain optimistic that these measures will bring about reform and healing," as she committed her full name to the page. Egil Thorsfork of SERG simply stated "It's harsh, but fair." No one could tell how Clear Channel was holding their pen with those hooves, but their usual "CC" appeared with an "I'm no longer worried we haven't thought this through." Yi Meiling, representing the admins of the main public feeds, pulled a seal from a pocket on her permanently hovering wheelchair and pressed it down, then said "I still can't believe we made 1% turnout!"

Aditya Singh, one of the people who kept an eye on the Deep Space Network sys-side, signed without a word. Then, he said, "Consensus is consensus, and I'm not opposed to the idea everyone's compromised around, so I've signed. However, for the record, we should just shoot them instead."

"Absolutely not!" Dry Grass exclaimed. "That is antithetical to the purpose of the System!"

"And give them the easy way out?" Egil demanded, overlapping Dry Grass. "Not to mention,–"

"No." Need An Answer said firmly as soon as she sensed an opening in the brewing argument. "Enough. We are not here to relitigate the question." The room went quiet. She took the signature page from Aditya and added her mark, a swirl of words that she had spent more time crafting than she would want to admit. "It is finished."

She gathered up the report and fed it into the mail slot that had been added to the room for today. In the phys-side conference room, the pages worked their way out of a printer.[1]

Günay gathered up the sheets and flipped through them to check for obvious errors. She set the last page on the table, took the pen, and scribbled something by her name. "Looks like it all came though just fine."

"I prepared a speech," Jakub said, "but Need An Answer just summarized most of it." He signed, making sure the camera got a good look at him. "As she said, it is finished. All we can do now is watch events unfold."

"Only time will tell if we have chosen well," Need An Answer added. "So, we must wait."

"Watch the politicians take a whole decade to make a call," Günay said. "Just to let the System feel the tension for once while they 'reach consensus'."

Dry Grass decided to take the sarcasm seriously. "Although it would delay our meeting, should your people discuss the matter until consensus, I would applaud their caution."

"There was one more item on the agenda, I believe," Jakub said, hoping that the official signing ceremony, of all things, could be kept on track.

"The formalities, yes," Need An Answer said. "Having rendered its report, this committee is, per its own choice and System custom, dissolved immediately. We name no successors and disclaim any authority we may appear to hold. Let all subse-

---

[1]Setting this up led one of the staff involved to commit to eventual uploading so he could give those who had insisted on paper a piece of his mind *properly*.

quent matters be referred to those willing to handle them. We thank you for your aid and wish you peace and fulfillment." Her tone shifted from official to cheery on a dime. "Bye!"

As soon as she was done speaking, she vanished from the room. Right after that, the conference rooms were disconnected. It was rude, yes, but there was no sense in wasting an opportunity to make a point about the System's lack of governance while the politicians and media were watching, especially when there was a less formal gathering planned for later that day.

A few minutes later, the report was official:

> We, the denizens of the Lagrange System, to the extent we have an opinion on the matter, find the following sentence acceptable for those involved in the Century Attack conspiracy to destroy the System:

> The guilty shall be uploaded. As a special restriction, they shall be prevented from quitting out entirely— at least one fork of each of them must remain alive. We will not leave them the option of fleeing their crimes like their comrades did when they recovered along with us.

> Furthermore, to protect the System from their recidivism, any messages they send phys-side will be a matter of public record and will require approval from a panel randomly drawn from volunteers, which shall not include any cocladists of those so sentenced.

> These restrictions and protections may be removed by the consensus of a general sample of the System, as measured by a process similar to the one used to approve this final recommendation.

> In short, for their part in a conspiracy to murder trillions, we would sentence these people to live.

We have made this decision carefully. It took over two years for this suggested sentence to clearly emerge as the option that most of us could accept. As the tallies and summaries were being prepared back then, we noticed many were concerned that our choice had been made in a collective vengeful frenzy. So, we sent this proposal to the denizens of the LVs in order to gather their opinions, and held a cooling-off year while we waited for those views.

When debate resumed, we found that support for this sentence to life had solidified and that the consensus on the LVs was aligned with ours. Therefore, we are confident that we have not made this recommendation rashly, and we declare that we are comfortable with it becoming a precedent for sentencing if a similar conspiracy arises in the future.

Since our proposal may prove surprising or confusing without the context of our discussions, we're including the following summary of how we came to our conclusions.

In the beginning, while many still felt the pain of raw grief, there were many different suggested punishments for the perpetrators of the Century Attack. We had, just as we know you have phys-side, a substantial contingent of people suggesting that we bring back the death penalty, just this once. The idea lost traction on sober consideration. Some said that execution was too much of a punishment and violated the System's core purpose of preserving life; others argued that death was insufficient—how could a few lives balance billions of silenced eternities?

Another initial cluster of ideas, some brought over from phys-side discussions, involved imposing some form of imprisonment sys-side, since this is now technically feasible. These proposals collapsed under the weight of their variety—no one could agree on how to pick from the competing plans. From there sprung concerns about precedent, followed by a general view that going down this road would lead to a government forming here. Very few people trust any potential government to leave their corner of the System alone, so the threads full of prisons and purgatories fell away. In addition, some were concerned that imprisonment would prevent rehabilitation or, conversely, that it would shield the guilty from the consequences of their actions.

With the two most obvious suggestions off the table, many took a step back and considered how justice functions on the System in the hopes of finding a new approach.

The System has almost no justice system for the same reason it has little crime: the nature of our existence greatly limits anyone's ability to use force on anyone else without their ongoing consent. We can, for example, fork away injuries, recreate things that have been taken (if we had set the permissions to allow that in the first place), and we can always simply go somewhere else. Thus, neither a would-be criminal or would-be court can make anyone do anything through meaningful threats of harm.

We do have tools that allow us to keep order on a local level. People can be excluded from sims. If someone's behavior is unwelcome in a given place (for instance, if they were sucker-pushing people in a coffee shop), they can be bounced. Enough such incidents of improper behavior generally lead to troublemakers developing a reputation that leads to preemptive bans, while a sufficient shift away from that tendency towards unwanted actions typically leads to previous restrictions being lifted.

Even those rare people who get cut off from large parts of the System are not completely shut out of society. Anyone can find (or, if need be, create) a place whose rules or lack thereof suit them. For example, there are many seedy dark alleys where everyone knows to expect muggings or worse. Hanging out or living in them is as permissible a way of life as any other one can forge up here.

We expect that, if our recommended sentence of uploading is imposed, the conspirators will face broad exclusions similar to those that fall on those who will not abide the System's "mainstream" social norms. Some places already plan to bar their entry, either because the sim mods do not want them around or to prevent disruptions from people's reactions to their presence. They will find many messages they send ignored or filtered.

Some of the trillions of instances on the System will still, for their own reasons, want to reach out to the perpetrators of the Attack. We hope that these connections will come from those with good intentions and will facilitate some healing in the fullness of time. It is possible, however, the guilty will, to avoid the anger of their fellows or otherwise, retreat into their own private bubbles and experience no further consequences than being left out of society here. Only time will tell.

We know this is a strange and unusual punishment, but there are no other options we could agree on.

We cannot even agree if such a sentence to life is a mercy or a cruelty.

Prepared and confirmed on this 125th day of the 281st year of the System by,

- The Only Time I Dream Is When I Need An Answer of the Ode clade, advisor, sys-side

- Jonas Fa of the Jonas clade, advisor, sys-side

- Selena of her own clade, advisor, sys-side

- Debarre of his own clade, advisor, sys-side

- Yared Zerezghi of his own clade, advisor, sys-side

- I Remember The Rattle of Dry Grass of the Ode clade, perisystem technician (unaffiliated), sys-side

- Egill Thorsfork of Gunnar's clade, perisystem technician (primarily System Emergency Response Group), sys-side

- Clear Channel of their own clade, perisystem technician (external communication coordination feed, technical advisor for Lagrange financial simulation assns., "the AVEC pony", &c), sys-side

- Yi Meiling of her own clade, perisystem technician (Core Feed Admin Council), sys-side

- Aditya Singh of his own clade, perisystem technician (Deep Space Nine-ish), sys-side

- Jakub Strzepek, Project manager, recovery initiative (phys-side)

- Günay Sadık, System technician III, recovery initiative, phys-side

P.S. We are still not happy about the attempted coverup.

[Appendix A: consensus aggregation methods, vote totals, and demographic breakdowns]

[Appendix B: summary of consensus on Castor LV]

[Appendix C: summary of consensus on Pollux LV]

[Appendix D: endorsement of Guiding Council of Pollux LV]

"Speaking of subsequent matters," Egil asked, "who'll do the tutorials if this all goes through?"

Around half the room glanced at a woman who had chosen a seat in the back.

"I will guide them as I would anyone," In All Ways promised. "I will ensure that even those who sought to kill us know the basics of their new home, their new world."

She sighed. "I ... I will not abandon my principles, my centuries of helping, my part in making the System everything that ..." Even though the poet's name had been revealed over two decades ago, she still hesitated when mentioning em. "RJ wanted it to be. Eir work has been damaged enough."

I will not leave you alone at the gates of your dream, AwDae.

§

The guilty were, after some debate and legal wrangling physside, slated to be uploaded at noon on January 1st, 2406. As the appointed hour drew near, In All Ways walked out from the old arrivals lounge, making her way towards Point Zero. She could have prepared to meet them anywhere, but she knew she needed to be here. She did not normally do anything special before forking for a tutorial, but she wanted to fix her role in these sentences in her mind by submerging herself in memory.

The lounge she had left had been used in the early days of the System. Before dedicated tutorial spaces were established, people popped into existence as close to Point Zero as possible. From there, they would generally follow the haphazard signage towards the lounge, where people who'd registered for pings about their uploads would wait. Between those two places, hints floating in midair or shimmering on the ground, along with helpful wanderers, would hopefully get across the basics ... like how to put clothes on.

In All Ways had spent a lot of her formative days out in that intermediate space, helping fresh arrivals get a handle on their new world and diverging from Always Be True as she did. That experience led to her becoming a very active and respected tutorial-giver, which then led to a construct patterned after her (usually her human form, but sometimes the pre-upload file screamed "send a skunk") becoming a frequently-used entry in the new upload introduction roster.

Today was a skunk kind of day. As In All Ways walked, she mentally reviewed the list of conspirators, forking off a copy of herself for each one. In between them, she looked over the list of scheduled uploads, and forked off more copies to meet ones that seemed like they would be interesting or fun to talk to or who might need some extra help.

Once she had made it to the plaque marking where her world began, she turned around to face the line of skunks proceeding after her and nodded to them. Their clothes varied based on what had seemed most fitting for the person each instance was going to meet. The ones going to meet the conspirators wore a beige blouse, long pants, and librarian glasses—she had wanted comfortable familiarity as she went into those meetings.

The other instances of her nodded back and vanished, each to their own Aetherbox, to take their place before the person they'd forked to meet arrived.

Then, she herself stepped away. Historically significant tutorials were no reason to miss brunch plans.

§

Brother Jan Nowak was a member of the Order of True Heaven, a small religious collective that wore the trappings of ancient churches. They had been too tiny for those institutions to notice, let alone condemn, until after the Century Attack. The Order had linked themselves together, implant to implant, to share their divine revelations and holy ecstasies. As the century drew closer, however, their linked thoughts spiraled and twisted in on themselves, pulling ever stronger towards the flames of martyrdom and crusade. The Order had supplied several volunteers who uploaded to prepare the way for the virus knowing that, when they took down the System, they would be hastened to eternal glory.

Now, after the instant-infinite gap in consciousness that came with an upload, he was on that same System, but with no expectation of death or escape.

"I don't want to be here," he said before opening his eyes.

"I know," said a woman's voice from somewhere behind him. She was much calmer than Brother Nowak expected given what his siblings had done.

Jan opened his eyes. He found himself standing in a gray cube of a room, lit uniformly from nowhere. He turned around to identify the person speaking. There, providing the only color in the room, was a black furry ... something ... with a white stripe running down her tail. She stood with her back turned, facing the wall. "Greetings–" she began to say.

That the being sent to meet him wasn't even *human* set Brother Nowak off. "I'll have no part in your false heaven! Your soulless paradise! I'll have no intercourse with this usurpation of God and your abandonment of humanity! You have discarded your very body, you fiend, you devil!" Even though he had been disconnected from the Order during his years in prison, he still expected his rage to be echoed back to him by his fellows, though they were further away than ever before—he did not even have an implant now.

The skunk at the far wall said nothing.

"Get out! Go away! Let me go!" The self-styled monk waved wildly at the skunk, trying to banish her. Them? It?

"Brother Nowak, I am here to introduce you to the basics of life on the System. I have done this for countless others for over two centuries. If you would bear with me for a few minutes, we can finish the tutorial and you can be on your way."

Brother Nowak crossed his arms. "And if I don't want your 'tutorial'? Your honeyed whispers of ruin?"

"I will wait," the skunk said.

"You'll ... wait," Jan said. He'd been expecting threats or that he'd be left in this cube to rot, but not that.

"I am no stranger to eternity, Brother Nowak," the skunk said, her voice softened by the wall she was still facing. "I remember what it is to be Lost."

Brother Nowak stared at the skunk, confused.

"... That is a good line, I will need to pass it on once I am done here," she added quietly to herself in the silence.

"So, what, you'll starve me out here at the gates of your so-called afterlife?" Brother Nowak shouted as he turned to pace between the sides of the room. As he began walking, he realized that he didn't have any clothes. "You'll leave me to waste away, naked and alone?"

"No, nothing like that," the skunk said. "I am not here to punish you. I will tell you how to create clothes and food and wait until you want to. Or until you tire of hunger and adjust your sensoria to remove it, either works."

Brother Nowak stopped moving and waited to hear more.

"Now, as I was going to say before we went off the rails, to be clothed, all you need to do is to envision the clothes you would like to be wearing and think your intention to be wearing them at the world. This will become easier with practice, but, for now, you may wish to form your desire as you breathe in and speak it into being as you breathe out."

Jan thought. His Order's holy crusade against the abominable idol that was the System had only partially succeeded, and now he'd been sentenced to *live*, of all things, in the very idolatrous machine he hated. It would have been better if they had executed him: at least then he would get his eternal reward. But, since he was here, he might yet have a purpose. It might be his duty to bring the lost sheep within the System to the Lord from within. If so, the least he could do is to be properly dressed for his vocation.

He took a breath, remembered his days trying to convince people to join him in his order's choir of revelations, and said "I would be clothed that I might bring salvation to this place."

The clothes his followers and brethren on Earth had known him in appeared on his body: a conservative suit—white with a black jacket and plain black trousers, all tailored to fit him. His wide gold-colored tie was blazoned with a silver cross. He was a preacher in these slowly ending days—no, in this eternal temptation—and he stood up straight, filled with conviction and carrying the lamp of light that had pointed to true peace for millenia. He wished that his siblings could share in these thoughts, but it was not to be.

The skunk heard the jingle of metal and the clack of dress shoes as Jan took an experimental step. "May I turn around?" she asked.

"I suppose I should see the face of the demons and heretics that dwell here," Jan said.

The skunk turned around and looked at Brother Nowak. "In All Ways," she said, holding out a paw and stepping forward.

The ... whatever it was ... seemed to be offering the preacher a handshake. "In all ways?" he repeated hesitantly.

"Yes, I am Then I Must In All Ways Be Earnest of the Ode clade. Or simply In All Ways," she said.

"Brother Jan Nowak, as you already know," the man said, pointedly not getting closer or offering a hand.

In All Ways lowered her paw. "So, Brother Nowak, would you like to move to the next lesson?"

"No," he said.

"Let me know when you are ready, and we will discuss forking," In All Ways said. "Or if you need to talk through something, I will be here, though I do not know how much help I will be." She stood patiently, and, when no response came for two minutes, she sat down, enveloping herself in her tail.

Brother Nowak began pacing the perimeter of the room once he realized nothing else would happen. He *knew* this was a test of his faith, but he could not comprehend what he was meant to *do*. Many circuits of the empty room later, he shouted "What do you want from me, O Lord? Am I to tear this blasphemy against You, this modern Babel, down, brick by brick? Am I to wander this virtual desert and preach until all have heard from me? Give me a sign, I beg you!"

In All Ways said nothing. Brother Nowak was not the first person who needed to get a good rant or vent out soon after uploading, and she had become a quite patient listener over the centuries.

Brother Nowak kept his angry prayers going for several more rounds of the cube. As he began to come down from his angry despair, he saw that In All Ways had not moved. Had not reacted. Had not even slid to get away from the 'crazy street preacher', as most people called him, when he came near. "How are you just *sitting* there?" he roared at the skunk.

"I have all the time I need, Brother Nowak. And there are much worse places to be stuck waiting."

"But won't you get bored, sitting here waiting for me to taste your forbidden fruit?"

"Oh, I will, but that is why I send forks to such meetings. I am still out there doing … something less boring."

"So you're some pale imitation of yourself, then? A soulless copy? Out, Satan!" Brother Nowak tried to wave In All Ways away again.

"I am as much a person as any other fork of me," In All Ways said, standing. "Though I can say nothing definitive about the state of my soul."

"I demand to speak to the original! The one who can yet be saved!"

"If you want my tracker instance—the In All Ways I came from—she is surely busy, and I will not bother her on your account. If you want the root of our clade—the person we all forked off from, who uploaded originally—Michelle Hadje quit in … 2306, by your calendar."

"Quit?" Brother Nowak asked.

"No longer on the System. Passed on." *It was her time, I must admit.*

"So I can …" He focused on the idea, beginning to speak his intent, to pray. "I want to quit. I want to leave this space and meet my Father in Heaven, to leave these sinners to their damnation. I want to quit." Unlike his earlier conjuration of clothing, this act of will felt like pushing uphill through mud. "I know it's difficult, this place is a trap for souls, but I will leave it. God willing, I will leave it."

As he kept talking, he felt the pressure easing up as the ensnaring dream of the System registered his intent and began to loosen its grip on his thoughts. But then, as he was beginning to picture the light of the hereafter coming to meet him, he was struck by a wall of feeling, coming from the System itself. There were no words: it was the pure sensation of inability, of being forbidden.

Brother Nowak fell to his knees.

"You cannot quit," In All Ways said. "The poet has bound you to eir shattered work. Though you may still quit in favor of a fork, if you ever desire to lock in a change."

Brother Nowak growled as he stood. Salvation had been so close, after all these decades, all this work. But then, as he understood the rest of what In All Ways had said, he smiled. "So I can leave, go on to Heaven, so long as I fork first?"

"You can quit and let your fork take your place as the root instance," In All Ways said. "I will not give my views on how this affects your soul to you; I am a tutorial-giver, not a theologian."

Brother Nowak knelt and bowed his head in silent prayer. Some time later, he rose. "So," he asked, determined to act before his courage left him, "how do I fork?"

"Intend to, as you did with your clothes," In All Ways said. "Lay out, or keep in mind, any changes you want to make while forking, the tag you want your fork to have if there is one, and so on. Then send the intention out into the world, and it will be so. Let me know if I have been unclear."

Brother Jan Nowak stepped forward and, like he'd been told to, intended his fork. He did not even need to open his mouth before Jan Nowak#Fork appeared next to him. The original Jan clasped his hands at his heart and bowed his head. "Father, into your hands I commend my spirit," he said, quitting out.

The remaining Brother Nowak, his #Fork, lifted his hands to his face and examined them closely, as if surprised they were real. He then made the sign of the cross and mumbled a short prayer and ... it brought that same steadying reassurance that he remembered from before forking.

"... now what?" he asked In All Ways. "I still feel like me. I still feel the Holy Spirit within me. Could we have erred? Could I have strayed from wisdom?"

"I do not answer such questions. I will not assure you that no ranks of angels answer to dreamers. And many of the congregations here do not want to hear from you so soon after the Attack. You will need to decide this yourself. You have time."

"Time here?" Brother Nowak#Fork asked.

"No, you have a home sim assigned to you. Ordinarily, you would be given auto-populating rooms in a larger sim, but it seemed too risky to give you a public door. So, you have," she flicked her finger at Brother Nowak, transferring rep, "been given a larger than usual tutorial bonus, now that you have forked. You will be able to use this to outfit your surroundings as you like, though I suggest you stick to a pre-built design initially.

"I will explain these things, and other basics of how to interact with the System when you are ready."

Brother Nowak sighed. "Well, if I'm to be a soulless—or maybe I'm not soulless, I don't *feel* soulless—wanderer here, or … whatever my calling is now, I might as well understand how to live inside this idol. Maybe knowing that will help me understand my purpose."

The next few minutes were spent on the standard "welcome to the System" activities: how to get on the feeds, how to send messages, how to edit ACLs, and so on.

"That is everything you need to get started," In All Ways finally said. "You can now intend to go to your home and proceed from there. Or you can … wait, no, many of the places I would send new people have you on the bounce list, never mind."

"And, once I'm home, what do I do? Is there more tutorial? Will I need a job? Will there be streams of angry people seeking vengeance?"

"No, this is it. Simply intend to go home. Your sim's ACLs have been locked down to ensure you are not surprised there. Once you have gone … do whatever you want. Spruce up the views. Become a hermit and contemplate the soul, maybe. Or go preach on any street corner that will have you. Whatever you like. You have time."

"But what if I—the other me—can't reach Heaven while I'm alive? What if he's standing outside the Pearly Gates waiting for me? How could you do this to me, with your sweet poison, your talk of forking and quitting! How could you damn me to this entrancing eternity? How dare you!"

"Go, Brother Nowak," In All Ways said, sighing. "Go and live. That is your sentence. Perhaps it is also your penance. Go and sin no more."

"No."

In All Ways sighed again. Her glasses slipped down her face and she did not push them back up. "The courtesies I give to the newly emplaced are done. I will have nothing more to do with you, you who fanned the flames of the fervor that brought so much death to me and mine, for … a long time. Go, or stay here. I have done what I promised."

The skunk quit out.

Brother Nowak#Fork stared at the place In All Ways had been. "Damn you!" he shouted at the air in front of him. Then, he intended to travel to wherever the skunk had gone. It felt forbidden, impossible, even before he started to speak the words.

He sent himself to the uncustomized expanse of home that had been made for him and sat on the bare ground, ignoring the default chair, to contemplate what he would do with his eternity.

No easy answers came. Only the weight of time.

§

When 93's life fell apart, ey went looking for answers. The plant in eir hometown had closed down, and ey never could seem to break into any of the businesses that tried to replace it. No one wanted good, clever logistics staff anymore—or, at least, no one wanted em. Ey had done everything right, saved money when ey could, and none of it had helped.

Ey could tell someone had to be behind eir misfortune, and so, ey did what ey did best: tried to figure it out. Soon, ey encountered others who had seen that something was deeply wrong with the world, hiding in the dusty corners of the net. Ey found the Numbers Station: a collective of amateur journalists who worked to become unremarkable, to be average, to be unnoticed. Together, they would weave together all the little details that people standing around on the street could pick up until they had proof.

Proof of what? Well, proof that the old uploads, up there on the System, were the powers behind the powers, that they were running the world from space, with their immortality and ability to fork. 93 had suspected this might be the case, and, as ey kept talking with the Numbers Station, ey became more convinced. After all, the System elites had written books where they had admitted to pulling strings—books that had faded out of popular awareness on Earth surprisingly quickly. If they were willing to openly admit to making payment-for-uploading happen, what had they done that they had *not* bragged about?

And so, 93 had eir mission. Ignoring the frequently warned of possibility that these 'journalists' might, like many other collectives, be in a tech-assisted feedback loop where they pulled each other further towards a warped reality, ey surrendered eir name and became 93 of the Numbers Station.

Over the years, eir collective's quest for the truth brought 93 into contact with many of the Century Attack conspirators. Ey naturally fell into eir role as a logistical intermediary. 93 was no one special, and ey took advantage of that fact to sneak people, supplies, and information between groups who ought not be detected meeting each other.

None of eir seemingly-careful work helped. All eir connections had been arrested, convicted, and sentenced to uploading, and so had 93.

Once ey could tell ey had been uploaded, 93 opened eir eyes. Ey was in a gray cube built of smooth stone panels.

"Greetings," a voice said, startling em. "You have been uploaded to the Lagrange System. I am facing the wall behind you, as many arrive here without clothing."

93 turned around to see who was talking. It was someone with black and white fur who kept her hands loosely behind her

back.

"Okay...," 93 said hesitantly. Ey looked down, and realized ey'd ended up here naked. "How do I get clothes?"

"Picture what you wish to wear. Breathe in, fixing the image of those clothes in your mind. Then, breathe out. As you do so, *intend* to be wearing those clothes. It helps to say what you want to happen as you breathe out, at least at first."

93 breathed in and breathed out, saying "I want to be wearing my average outfit," ey did so. And so it was. Eir clothes were intentionally nondescript: ey wore a cheap, plain white T-shirt with an even cheaper mass-produced black raincoat over it. Eir jeans and tennis shoes were ones that could be had near eir home for almost nothing, and they came with the permanently beat-up look of low-quality material. Eir outfit was meant to be typical, to be unremarkable, and it succeeded at that in the places ey usually haunted, ever watchful for more glimpses of what the true powers of the world were up to. Ey was surprised by the lack of feedback from eir implant to confirm whether ey had maintained eir collective's standards.

"I'm good," 93 said.

"May I turn around?" the skunk asked.

"Go ahead."

The skunk turned around and stepped towards the middle of the room, holding out a paw. "Welcome to Lagrange, Mx. Ninety-Three."

"How did you know my name?" 93 asked.

"It was in your pre-upload file," the skunk replied. "I have access to it so the tutorial can go smoothly."

93 nodded. "That makes sense, I guess. Who are you?"

"In All Ways," the skunk said. She sometimes left her name a mystery as a hook to keep people moving through the tutorial, but she could tell this would not be the right approach here.

"... In All Ways of the Ode clade?" 93 asked.

The skunk bowed. "Then I Must In All Ways Be Earnest of the Ode clade, yes," she said.

"So are you here to kill me or recruit me?" 93 asked sharply. "Or just to gloat over another success for your millennium plan?"

"I am here to give you the System tutorial, Mx. 93. Nothing more. Whatever you think I am involved in, I am not."

"Bullshit," 93 spat. "You people, your clade especially, are all involved in keeping us down. You've all got your fingers in everything: upload payments, the launches, the recession last decade … it's all happening here, and you Odists are in the middle of it!"

"Yes, some of my cocladists have been involved in political machinations," In All Ways admitted. "I am sure you have read the *History* and *Ode*. But that is not me. That is not what I do here. I have been a welcoming face here for centuries, and I have no plans to cease being true to myself.

"Not to mention, whatever grand conspiracy you are looking for … is not. There are politically active System residents, but they cannot *do* anything but offer suggestions. The System does not have ancient caves full of hidden money to swing around for the bribes you imagine us paying: the operational fund covers maintenance and the occasional upgrade, and I am sure that those like your collective watch it like hawks."

93 shook eir haid. "You must not be in on it, then. There's got to be something up here. There's people pulling the strings, twisting the Earth for their own power, Jonas and True Name–"

"–Sasha," In All Ways corrected. "She changed her name and retired from politics–"

"–and who knows who else?" 93 waved eir hands. "And I'll find them. You can't stop me. I'll blow this place wide open!"

"You already did," In All Ways said. "Hence your messaging restrictions. We will not have you trying again."

93 huffed. "You can't censor the truth forever!" ey declared.

In All Ways sighed. "If you truly want to chase ghosts and conspiracies, you can do that. No one here can prevent it, except by bouncing you from sims. But I am here to teach you the basics of the System so that you understand the means of daily living as you embark on your quests."

93 glared at the skunk. "Isn't there someone else who could do this?"

"There are other guides, yes," In All Ways said. "I know many who could teach you at least as well as I can. However, they wanted me to take these meetings. I do not know which of those who bowed out did so because they knew they would not be able to resist the urge to boot you out of this sim with no lessons and no rep."

"And you wouldn't do that?" 93 was skeptical. "Or find one last bit of virus to silence me with?"

"Fuck no!" In All Ways exclaimed, startled by the detailed accusation. "I have given centuries of my life—calendar-wise centuries, mind you, not instance-wise—to teaching newcomers. I want everyone to be comfortable with the System so they can have the long wonderful lives it was meant to give them! What the hell makes you think I want to *kill* anybody?"

"I, uh," 93 stammered, thrown off by the skunk's sudden vehemence. "It makes sense, that they'd send someone to get rid of a threat, yeah?"

In All Ways sighed and shook her head. "Right, conspiracy theory.

"Moving right along, yes, you *could* have me find another teacher. Or you could refuse the tutorial entirely. These are choices you can, once you have been informed of the consequences, make. However, they would be fucking stupid choices.

"I ask that you please try your best to set aside your paranoia about my clade for just a few minutes so that we may go over the initial lessons. Then, I will go away and you will never need to encounter me or my cocladists again."

93 considered this. Ey had not expected an Odist to come across as this blunt and earnest. Sure, it might be a ruse, but, "Well ... all the sources I can remember didn't really have much bad to say about you, I guess. Like, sure, you're the friendly face

the Ode puts up to get everyone acclimated to the powers behind the curtain, but I haven't seen any accusations of the tutorial itself being dangerous."

Ey braced emself for a chorus of objections and the sharp pings of down-reps from eir collective over eir willingness to go along with the enemy's games, but none came.

"That is because the tutorial is not, in fact, dangerous. And you are entirely free to ignore my entire clade once you leave here, if you are worried about our manipulations. Now, shall we begin?"

93 looked intently at the skunk, hoping to catch something amiss in her expression, but found nothing. "Alright, fine," ey conceded. "Let's do this."

The tutorial session proceeded like most others from there. Mx. Ninety-Three got the hang of projecting eir intentions, needing less time and setup, as ey went along, just like most arrivals to the System. Ey forked and merged down without issue or complaint—how could an extra copy of em be a danger to emself, ey reasoned. From there, ey moved on to other routine tasks like checking eir rep balance or sending a sensorium ping, relaxing as ey did so.

In All Ways similarly relaxed into the rhythm of the lessons. Although the person she was teaching had played a key role in organizing the logistics of the Century Attack, ey was still a person who needed an introduction to the System, just like everyone else she or her constructs had met on arrival.

"That covers the standard topics," In All Ways concluded. "Do you have additional questions?"

"How do I stop someone from listening in on me?" 93 asked. "I heard that's a thing here. Is that for everyone?"

"You set up a cone of silence," In All Ways said. "You may ping me with one just—Ow, fuck!" She accepted the forceful ping from her student right away and continued on unfazed. This would not be her first—or last—ultra-high-priority message from an over-eager new upload. "And there are other security settings. You may edit ACLs on sims you have sufficient permissions for, and you can sweep sims you have rights on to remove anyone who does not have permission to be there. This is useful if you think someone may have snuck in before you locked the sim down."

93 nodded. "Seems like it's pretty easy to keep the grand cabal hidden," ey said. "They've added all these ways to make sure no one's spying on them. No wonder you're not in on it ... if *they* really didn't want you to be and that wasn't just an act."

"That is an interpretation of history you could hold, yes," In All Ways replied. "Though not one that is widely shared or particularly in accord with the record."

"I'll figure something out," 93 said, less confident than before. Ey dropped the cone, as ey didn't want to be too obviously hiding something. "The world deserves to see who's pulling the strings. Why everything sucks. How *they* ruined my life by getting the plant closed! 'Redundancy.' Bullshit."

"Neither the System in general nor the Ode clade in particular control the tides and ravages of capitalism, let alone business decisions in ... Springfield, yes?," In All Ways replied. "I would recommend that you find a target for your anger more plausible than a secret council that has remained hidden for nearly three centuries."

"Whatever," 93 snorted, shaking eir head. "You'll see the truth as soon as we're done finding it."

"I will be quite surprised if you find what you are seeking," In All Ways said. "But we will gain nothing from this discussion, yes? Have you any other questions?"

"Yeah, so, ... about forking," 93 asked. "I can send my forks off to go do things and only merge down when they're done? Or once they're in a bad spot and have to bail out?"

"Yes. We usually call that being a tasker or a tracker, depending on how long your forks stick around and how often you fork. There is no precise line between those strategies, but they are useful labels nevertheless."

"And I can change my appearance?"

"Yes. Just intend the changes while you fork like you did before."

After 93 mumbled a few words, the tutorial Aethorbox held three again. In All Ways, 93#Tasker, and 93#PeopleWatching. #PeopleWatching had lost the moles on #Tasker's face, making em even more unremarkable. #PeopleWatching was momentarily surprised that ey had not gotten a boost on the Numbers Station's internal rep table for becoming more average ... but that table didn't exist here.

"So," #Tasker asked, "now what?"

"If you have no more questions, this concludes the tutorial. You have already received the rep boost for completing these lessons. From here, you can move home—you have been given a private sim pre-filled with one of the standard housing layouts, which has been locked down to you because of your role in the Attack. We did not wish for you to be swarmed by a mob after the end of the tutorial. Or, you may go to any number of public spaces. I will leave once you are gone."

"Where's a good place to see a bunch of people?" #PeopleWatching asked.

"Stone's#009446876," In All Ways suggested on autopilot. "They have good beer and solid, if unpolished, music, if that is of interest."

#PeopleWatching thought about moving to that place—ey noticed ey had no trouble remembering the numbers—but it didn't work. Ey tried announcing eir desire to go there, and even tried walking forward as if ey was about to step into that bar. No dice.

"It's not working," ey said. "Feels like the door's closed."

#Tasker flicked eir fingers as ey queried the perisystem architecture. "I checked their ACLs. Looks like we're banned. Whole clade, it says."

In All Ways' gaze flickered between the two people in front of her. "Banned? Already? But you ... right, Century Attack. Slipped my mind. Many sim owners and mods banned the lot of you as soon as the pre-upload header came through the Ansible."

#Tasker looked at #PeopleWatching. "They're definitely hiding something."

"Yep."

"Let me just …" #Tasker put together a ping for the listed owner of Stone's. Default priority, nothing urgent. "Hey," ey said, "I'm wrapping up the tutorial, and In All Ways recommended your place as a nice spot to go next, but it turns out I'm banned. What gives? I just got here!"

As ey waited for a response, #PeopleWatching took the time to start up eir own queries. Most of the popular, famous, or happening sims had banned eir clade. The old town square from near the System's founding had not put a ban in, but ey did not want to go in case that was an oversight and not an intentional choice to be welcoming. Many of the small parks and nature sims had not bothered keeping out the century attackers either, but there was not a lot of people-watching or spying to be had in them. Other tentative options were places like fringe clubs or meetings of folks so leftist that they were *definitely* Feds … none of which were right for getting the lay of the land.

"I can't find any really good spots," #PeopleWatching admitted. "We've been locked out."

As ey said this, the reply to #Tasker's ping came back. "Yeah, no, you set foot in here, someone'll start looking to bash you unconscious with the nearest bit of furniture. Might even be me. I don't want that sort of violence at my bar. Call me back in a few centuries, maybe."

#Tasker forwarded the message to #PeopleWatching.

"Yeah, plan's busted," #PeopleWatching said. "Let's go home and figure out what to do about those damn elites." Ey quit out.

"Yeah, screw it," 93 said, now merged back down again. "See you around?" she asked In All Ways.

The skunk shook her head. "I do not engage with conspiracy theorists, sorry," she said. "Welcome, again, to Lagrange, Mx.

Ninety-Three."

93 moved home.

The skunk quit out.

The Aetherbox reset behind her, ready for the next tutorial.

93 started at the field of not-filled-in-yet outside eir new window and thought about eir experiences. All ey had now, ey realized, was time.

§

Marybelle Lee had not given her name or her soul to a collective. She had given her brain. Knowledge flowed between her fellows, who called themselves the Climate Action Resource Collective, as freely as water. Difficult questions from any member of the collective were bounced between its members so that they might chance upon one whose mind could see the answer.

As a cell of the CARC turned their minds towards the System, that drain on resources and people that stood in the way of fixing things, she had become the best of them at understanding it. Once the project grew firmer, she pulled the work of virus-making tighter around herself, becoming the most responsible party. Now she was here on the System she had set out to destroy.

As soon as she noted the discontinuity in her perceptions, Marybelle Lee opened her eyes. The room she found herself in was a cube of large gray stone panels, just like she'd expected.

Identity query for the person standing behind me, if any, please, she thought at the world she had been uploaded to. That was, she knew, roughly how things worked.

Knowledge appeared in her thoughts, even more firmly than answers from her collective. *Then I Must In All Ways Be Earnest#d5781ff9.*

Of the Ode clade?

A sense of confirmation.

"I see they've sent the tutorial skunk," Belle commented, turning to look at In All Ways. "In person, even."

"Greetings–" In All Ways began. "—that would be me, yes. It was decided that you should not be greeted by a construct, under the circumstances, and I volunteered for the job."

Belle nodded. "Got it. So, clothes. Clothes can be a pure intent item, so if I understood right, I just have to ..." She pictured the look she wanted: shorts and a T-shirt she'd gotten from a climate restoration conference years ago. "... run." Everything appeared as expected, and her shirt had even lost the stains it had picked up over the years. Classic programmer look, and definitely better than prison orange.

"Note," she said, out of the long-standing habit of sending useful insights to her collective. She received no response. Not even the thud of a communications-blocked error she would have gotten back in prison phys-side. Nothing. She was alone.

Her realization about the state of her mind was interrupted. "May I turn around, Ms. Lee? Marybelle?"

"Belle, please, Ms. In All Ways. And you may."

In All Ways nodded. "I have updated your ID. You will be able to change it later by intending it like how you intended to create your clothes. If you want to set a clade ID, the process is similar."

"Thanks," Belle said. "I remember there being endpoints for that."

"Should I stick to the script?" In All Ways asked. "It appears you have done substantial research before being uploaded."

"I've gotten a good theoretical understanding of the place over the years, yeah. Me and the general knowledge base of the CARC."

"I imagine you have," In All Ways replied, frowning. "And now you are here. Welcome to Lagrange, Belle." The usual courtesies never hurt, yes?

"Now I'm here," Belle echoed. "Here with no one and nothing I can do to help save the world."

"There are those here who agitate for change," In All Ways noted. "Make suggestions."

"*Suggestions,*" Belle scoffed. "We've had three fucking centuries of suggestions. We need *action*! We've *needed* action! Sure, we're," she held out her hands to give exaggerated air quotes, " 'stabilizing', but we could be doing So. Much. More."

Her anger dipped into melancholy. "And now I'm up here, on the damm System, where I can do fuck all. You bastards. Should've just had me killed."

"The author of our destruction calls us bastards," In All Ways remarked to her nonexistent audience.

"Well, you fucking are. So many people take one look at how shit life on Earth is and fuck off to the party in the sky instead of trying to *do* anything about it." Belle strode towards the skunk as she ranted. "And hell, any of you uploads who think they'll care go flaking out or take their sweet time doing anything remotely useful! You've got *all you need*—you don't need to eat, you can't forget, you can *fork*—and you waste that instead of helping! We're *dying*, damn you! Dying under the weight of problems you ran from!"

In All Ways stood her ground against the advancing torrent of rage at the System.

Belle stopped in front of the skunk and stared her down. "And don't think you're off the hook here personally, Ms.–" It took a moment for Belle's memory of a few minutes ago to supply the entire name "—Then I Must In All Ways Be Earnest of the Ode clade! I've read your tutorial conversation tree. You could've pointed some people at those activists of yours or something else that might *maybe* help instead of just chucking them out to explore aimlessly if they don't have plans."

"I am no weaver of fates. I give tutorials. It would be improper, perhaps even a profanation, a sacrilege, for me to marshal those lives entrusted to me into some grand purpose, for me to do as you suggest. Even though some subtle nudging is accepted by the community of guides and mentors, I will not do it."

"*Improper*," Belle scoffed. "A sacrilege to lift a finger to help Earth. Like you're on some fucking holy quest to let the System spin around and do its thing until the Sun fries it or whatever."

"I care deeply about the System," In All Ways replied. "A good friend of mine died to create this place, this end of death, imperfect though it may be. I have set out to honor eir memory by ensuring those who emplace themselves here begin their lives with an understanding of the world and, maybe even a glimpse of its beauty. Your summary of my motivations is not incorrect, yes."

"And that damn 'it's better on the System, everyone should just come up' attitude—whether people admit to having it or not—is why we had to—why *I* had to destroy this place!" she ranted. "Once people can't just bury their heads in virtual sand instead of giving a fuck about their own planet, they'll start to care! It won't just be me and some friends being those weirdos who're still trying!" she roared, barely holding back tears now. "Would your 'friend' have wanted to see Earth limping along like it has been? Would ey think blowing off your own planet counts as trying to end death?"

That she *of all people would presume...!* "Pray tell me," In All Ways responded tensely, barely holding her anger down, "why I should give a single fuck about an Earth that left an easily-disarmed gun pointed at our heads for my entire life, that had ample forewarning of the wound you and yours tore open and did *nothing*. That left the fruits of eir sacrifice to rot! Pray tell me, Ms. Marybelle Lee, why I would ever owe more than reciprocation of phys-side's systemic abandonment of my home."

"Because you're human?! Well, not exactly, but a person! Because we need to work together to fix our world, even if all you can do here—all *I* can do, now—is flood people with mail on the off chance that works!"

In All Ways shook her head. "My world is the cylinder at Lagrange. Nowhere else."

"Fucking traitor!" Belle cried in anguished frustration. "Fucking selfish *asshole!*" She jabbed a finger into In All Ways's ribs. "Fuck you! Fuck you!"

In All Ways jabbed back. "Fuck you too, Belle! Fuck you!" she shouted, her anger boiling over at last. "Fuck you for Should We Forget! And In The Wind! And No Longer Myself! Fuck you for twenty-three billion people!"

Her voice grew calmer and sadder. "Fuck you for thinking your cause was worth that many deaths."

The silence grew tense between Belle and In All Ways. As Belle stood there, she realized that she could rant all she liked, but that she couldn't be usefully angry. There wasn't anything she could *do* about the troubles of the Earth. Not really. Not here. Not alone.

"Note," she mumbled glumly, hoping to … send her collective the realization that getting punitively uploaded was bad for the mission? As if they did not know, as if the rest of the collective was not back on Earth, many of them in prison, as the scrutiny she had brought on had brought the collective's other actions into the light.

She did not even feel the prison sim blocking her transmissions. They just were not possible from here. Her existence as Marybelle Lee of the Climate Action Resource Collective was over even more firmly now.

"Give me a moment?" she said to In All Ways. "I'm—well, my whole goal in life's fucked now, and I thought I'd accepted it, but …" Belle trailed off.

"We have time," In All Ways replied curtly. *I could use some as well.*

Belle started to slide towards despair, but she interrupted her spiraling thoughts by noticing that her face was a mess from her earlier tear-generating rant. She needed a tissue.

I think I can just intend those? She thought, uncertain. She held out a hand and pulled a tissue out of an imaginary box near her, thinking that there was one there.

To her surprise, it worked! She had something to wipe her face with! As she started cleaning up, she realized the object she had summoned was the general suggestion of a tissue, something that smeared together everything she had wiped her face with before. Not quite right.

"So, how do I ..." she said quietly. She knew, from lots of accounts and technical reports, that the System could do better than this. She had studied up on the functions for object creation, though she had not expected to be using them through their native interface.

She thought about assembling code for creating a more specific tissue in her head. It was not an entirely accurate metaphor, she knew, but it had served her well while she was plotting out the bomb. She assembled the request, piece by piece, her train of thought jumping to specific memories for textures, form, thickness, and added in the plan to have the new object appear in her other hand, right at exactly *these* coordinates.

She jabbed a finger of her occupied hand down towards the ground to hit an imaginary Enter key.

A much more defined tissue, a blend of those nicer pricey ones Belle had sometimes used, appeared in her hand. She finished cleaning off her face and then, concentrating on the two pieces of crumpled-up paper in her hands, said "Erase."

They vanished.

"Note!" Belle said automatically, too caught up in the excitement of having worked out this new fact about the world to remember where she was just then.

"You could also pull those off the market," In All Ways commented. "They are free or really close to it."

Belle remembered she was still standing in a tutorial. "Yeah, but it's cool that I can do it myself. It's ... nice that all the studying the System wasn't a *complete* waste, even though the project failed and now...well, yeah."

In All Ways, who had used the break to dispel most of her urge to snap at Belle again, was not sure how to respond to this shift in her charge. So, she hesitantly suggested, "Shall we continue with the tutorial?"

The question brought Belle further out of her own head. She

was on the System, in an Aetherbox, talking to In All Ways. She was here and ... right. *Fuck.* "Mind if I send a message home first?"

In All Ways nodded. "You may do so, though I will ask that we keep the lessons going once you have sent it, even if the approvals have not yet been granted."

"Fair enough," Belle said. *Right, that's a thing now. Ugh. I'd forgotten about that bit.*

Belle knew she did not have to use any particular form to write a message phys-side: a handwritten note or letters of fire traced in the air would work well enough. However, she felt more comfortable with typing her short missive out. It would be weird to do a text chat without some simulation of a keyboard.

So, she shot queries at the construct market, looking for the components of her simmed coding setup. It would be nice to get back to it after all these years, to find some small glimmer of pleasure in this effectively pointless existence.

Her chair, keyboard, and monitor, appeared off to one side of her, with the peripherals floating in midair. The keyboard/display combo was listed as already set up for chat without the need to pretend there was a computer around. Belle stepped over towards har partial setup, but didn't set down. She was still searching.

"No one's done my desk pattern yet?" she said, surprised. "Sure, it's an obscure one, but still." She turned to one side, so she would not disturb the objects she had already summoned, and arranged her memories of long days spent coding on the net, of plotting out actions with her collective, at that very desk. She worked to weave these impressions into the construct and then, with a finality, she pointed at the empty space where a desk was to appear.

"No, too chaotic," she commented, waving the desk away. She had most of the code in her head now, and she just needed to tweak a few points so that it would look right this time. The desk flickered into existence, then flickered out again. *Still not quite right.*

The space in front of Belle soon showed the hallmarks of construct artistry, of actual oneirotecture. Desks flickered in and out of existence, iteration upon iteration. The ghosts of particularly useful attempts hovered in the farther distance, serving as reference points for aspects of the final work that were cumbersome to describe or remember. Belle's work grew frantic as the final tweaks went into place—- she was right there, she *almost* had it, just one more try! The joy of creation burned away the worst of Belle's mood, as it always had.

"Note annnnnnnd publish!" Belle declared, satisfied, several minutes later. She had gotten faster at commanding the System, and so she easily cleared away all the debris of her creative rampage. She put the desk under her keyboard. "Levitation off," she casually said. Everything settled into a realistic place.

Belle sat down and typed out her message to her wife. "Made it up safe. Don't know if I'll be able to call. Love you! <3".

Belle pressed 'Send' and watched the screen. The panel of volunteers who would need to approve this note did not take much time at all to vote it through to phys-side. A tension she had not noticed until then came out of Belle's shoulders.

"At least that went through," she said.

In All Ways cleared her throat. "That was good work, especially for a first project. That being said, we should finish the tutorial, yes?"

Belle looked over at the skunk, pushed her chair back, and stood up. "Right, right, got distracted. What's next?"

"Forking," In All Ways said. "That is, creating-"

"So I just need to put together a call to the fork methods for that," Belle interrupted.

"Probably. That is not a method I teach, but if it will work for you, I have no objections. Please fork, Ms. Belle."

Belle assembled her first fork instruction in her mind. She left her appearance the same, nudged the spawn point to her left, where the desks used to be, and was about to run when she had an idea. *Maybe two inches taller, just to see how that'll look.* She made the change and sent the fork request off into the collective engineered dream that was the System.

An instant later, her new, slightly taller, fork appeared next to her. The Belles turned to look at each other. "Wow!" they said together. "That's ... nice! I wonder if ...?"

The tree of experiments in forking rippled out from there. Height, body shape, hair color, outfit, gender (most of these attempts quit out soon after instantiating), species (much more persistent)—the Belles radiated out in a wave of exploration and evaluation.

Someone raised an arm and lifted the messaging setup to the ceiling to free up floor space. Someone else put music on, an upbeat dance tune emanating from the physically impossible "like there's a stage not too far in front of you" for each fork independently. The Belles pulled each other into this impromptu dance party in the tutorial room, carried away by the sensation of dancing with ... themselves, but not. It was a strange thing, a beautiful thing, a wonder that she could not have even begun to imagine on Earth.

None of the Belles had diverged in personality—nor had they been meant to—so, when the realization hit, it hit all of them. "Fuck," they said in a raggedly stumble that gestured at unison, and merged down to their root. They killed the music during the merges.

Belle accepted every last merge and buckled under the hammer of many dozens of variations on the thought she herself had just had.

"Fuck. I ... fuck, I think I get it now. Why everyone's got such a hard time explaining what this place feels like. Why most people forget the Earth. How much life you can have up here, how *wonderful* it is. I got so angry at everyone for doing what I just did ... eighteen and a half minutes after being uploaded."

In All Ways tossed an invisible thing at Belle. "I have awarded your tutorial reputation grant for successfully forking and merging. It is larger than usual to account for your home being within a private sim." She was not in the mood for mending shattering worldviews right now—she was here to give Belle the tutorial and little more.

"Shall we move on to the remaining topics?" the skunk asked.

Belle had summoned another tissue. "Yeah, sure, let's ... let's wrap this up."

The remaining tutorial items were a quick affair. Belle's experimentation had left her familiar enough with how to pull the world's levers to make the skills everyone needed trivial.

"And that concludes the tutorial," In All Ways said. "Welcome, again, to Lagrange, Belle."

"So now I step home and then ... whatever I feel like doing next?" Belle asked.

"Exactly."

"There anyone you think I should talk to?" Belle asked. "I don't want to go moping in bed if I can find *something* I could be doing. Anything, really."

"There is no one I would introduce you to at this time," In All Ways said. "The advocates I know of want nothing to do with you right now. You would cause too much drama, yes? I have given you the tutorial and my obligations to you are thus discharged. Your path from here is your own. Try to avoid genocide this time."

The skunk quit out.

Belle stepped into her home.

The things she had created followed behind her, and Belle sat down at the desk she had made and looked around. She had nothing to belong to here. Nothing to do, to save her from anger turning to despair. No collective surrounding her and pulling her up.

But, despite her losses, she had time.

§

In All Ways set her champagne down as she twitched from the rush of merge requests that she had been ignoring. She took a moment to merge all her folks down, integrating the memories of greeting the plotters behind the Century Bombing in parallel and some several other new arrivals besides. She shook herself as all the recollections settled in.

"Ways, you OK?" Ini Robbins, the fennec sitting across from her, asked. Ey, and eir down-tree Elliah, had grown close to In All Ways in the two centuries since they had met during a memorably disastrous tutorial. *From panicked combat to brunch dates,* the skunk thought as her instances' experiences settled in. *Perhaps even they will grow... but not with me.*

"I am fine. I needed to merge down the tutorials I sent out before I came here. I still grow twitchy when too many memories pile up."

"That was the Century Attack folks, right? How'd it go?"

"Well enough. Some personal crises, but those are not unusual. The strangest tutorial was, surprisingly, a man I met personally only because it felt like I should. His brain took the idea of having an up-tree instance a *touch* too literally."

"And?"

"He pulled a Serene and forked into an actual tree, right there! I had to call a systech to talk him through that one."

"No way!"

"Shit happens. All those people uploading, something has to go wrong once in a while."

"True that."

And so, the conversation floated away to other topics, and life flowed onward in a stream of well-spent time.

§

Once the Century Attack was fading from news to history, consideration of the sentences imposed in its aftermath led to an amendment to the articles of the System's secession. Physside politicians, nudged along by starlight chats, realized the potential danger of forced uploading as a penalty, not to mention the possibility of stopping someone unwillingly uploaded writing back.

Therefore, the Accords were amended to provide that no one could be involuntarily uploaded except as a penalty for crimes against the System.

Phys-side, these changes passed with a sense of quiet relief. Sys-side, they passed with a shrug.

In practice, the sentence of involuntary upload became a piece of trivia and an incentive for clinic bombers to plead down. Even when it was imposed, phys-side governments were quite reluctant to seek imposition of a no-quitting order or communication restrictions, as those would bring the crimes to the System's attention through the need for bilateral approvals and juries. Without the extra process, the penalties were only blips in the perisystem feeds of interest to news junkies and academics. What they did not really see up there could not hurt them, after all ... right?

And so, life went on.

Afterword

Full Credits

Marsh Madison Rye Progress with contributions from Samantha Yule Fireheart

Interlude: "Feeds" (in order) Samantha Yule Fireheart, Madison Rye Progress, Madison Rye Progress, Andréa C. Mason, Caela Argent, JS Hawthorne, Andréa C. Mason

Interlude: "Nasturtiums" Madison Rye Progress

Interlude: "Columbines" Samantha Yule Fireheart

"Game Night" Michael Miele

"Home From the Game" Caela Argent

"A Well-Trained Eye" Andréa C. Mason

"Toward Eternity" Thomas "Faux" Steele

"Prophecies" Madison Rye Progress with contributions from Samantha Yule Fireheart

"Journal of Diago Pereira" Nat Mcardle-Mott-Merrifield and Sarah Bloden

"Millwright" Andréa C. Mason

"The Party at the End of the World" and "Sentences" Krzysztof "Tomash" Drewniak

Acknowledgments

Thanks, as always, to the polycule, who have been endlessly supportive, but most especially to The Lament, so many of whose words appear within this book. Thanks as well as to Tomash, Ellen, Andréa, and all the rest of the Post-Self community, who have helped build this lovely world.

Thanks also to my patrons:

$10+ Ammy; Andréa C. Mason; Donna Karr (thanks, mom); Erika Kovac; Fuzz Wolf; green; Kit Redgrave; Merry Cearley; Mx. Juniper System; Orrery; Rob; Sariya Meolody

$5 Some Egrets; ramshackle; Christi; Erica; Junkie Dawg; Lhexa; Lorxus, an actual fox on the internet; Norm Steadman; Petrov Neutrino; raxraxraxraxrax; Sasha Moore, Strawberry Daquiri; ubuntor; Zeta Syanthis

$1 Alicia Goranson; Ayla Ounce; Bel; BowieBarks; Katt, sky-guided vulpine friend; Kindar; Muruski; Peter Hayes; Ruari ORourke; Sethvir; Yana Winters

Thanks is due as well to all of the backers of the *Marsh* Kickstarter, without whom this would not be possible:

Krzysztof Drewniak, Nathan Merrifield, Andréa CERES Mason, Lhexa, *Strawberry, Amdusias, Saphire Lattice, Ash Holland, Michael Miele, Ashley Hale, Mimir, Vendryth, Petrov Neutrino, Alexandrea Christina Leal,* Kuviare, Nova, Vernon Jones, Andy Oxenreider, LadyLenalia, ramshackle heather, MisfitMephit, Some

Egrets, NightEyes DaySpring, critters-system, doctorlit, Rachel Dillon, Joel Kreissman, Kate Eckhart, Giantrobots42, raine, Ayla Ounce, Alicia E. Goranson, James Tatum, Saghiir, Ember Cloke, Payson R. Harris, Vulpis, lenientsy, Campbell Royales, Laura, AntarcticFox, ubuntor, Asha Jade Goodwin, Barac Baker Wiley, Me, Robert Armstrong, Sethvir, Richie